Sara-Ella Ozbek was born in America and raised in London. After receiving a BA honours in English Literature from the University of Exeter, she worked in fashion for several years before going on to study screenwriting in New York. Her first novel, *The High Moments*, was published by Simon & Schuster in 2020. Other work has appeared in the *Independent*, *Because*, *Suitcase*, *Tatler*, *Drugstore Culture*, *Voyage D'Etudes* and *Soho House Notes*. Additionally, she writes for film, television and theatre.

Also by Sara-Ella Ozbek

The High Moments

SARA-ELLA OZBEK

NOTHING I WOULDN'T DO

**SIMON &
SCHUSTER**

London · New York · Sydney · Toronto · New Delhi

First published in Great Britain by Simon & Schuster UK Ltd, 2021

1 3 5 7 9 10 8 6 4 2

Simon & Schuster UK Ltd
1st Floor
222 Gray's Inn Road
London WC1X 8HB

Simon & Schuster Australia, Sydney
Simon & Schuster India, New Delhi

www.simonandschuster.co.uk
www.simonandschuster.com.au
www.simonandschuster.co.in

A CIP catalogue record for this book is available from the British Library

Paperback ISBN: 978-1-4711-8799-5
eBook ISBN: 978-1-4711-8800-8
Audio ISBN: 978-1-3985-0160-7

Typeset in the UK by M Rules
Printed and bound in Great Britain by CPI Group (UK) Ltd, Croydon, CR0 4YY

For my parents.

PART I

OCTOBER 2018

CHAPTER 1

Being a 28-year-old woman is legitimately less fun than being a 27-year-old one because the people you meet at parties suddenly seem to fall into two categories: too sober to flirt, or too fucked to fuck.

I explained this to Clara in the form of an anecdote, lying in bed one morning, while she sipped a cup of English Breakfast tea and I wished that I drank English Breakfast tea instead of coffee bought only from very specific cafés. The anecdote was a capsulized – and perhaps dramatized – description of the birthday party I'd been at the night before, where two thirds of the room got up and left as soon as the cake had been cut. That's right, two thirds, and I'd only been in Club Twenty-Eight a month. The point of the story was that, in among the two thirds who flattened their hands over the rims of their wine glasses every time a refill was offered, was the shaggy-haired photographer whom I'd spent the better part of three months trying to casually run into, because we'd once had a really laughy conversation at a wedding about all the ways to sign off an email. ('Excuse the brevity and any errors. I'm on my period.') I took his departure as a sign that I should draw a line under thoughts of a potential *affaire de cœur*. You wouldn't leave a party if someone you were remotely into was there, would you?

3

I finished the story with an aghast statement: 'One guy was driving back to the country, after dinner!'

'And what did the rest of you do?' asked Clara, her voice both stilted and dulcet, as it has been since she was a child.

'Sat at the table drinking rum and water because no one could be bothered to go to the shop for mixers.' Together, our voices sounded like gravel being rolled through honey.

'I don't know which night sounds more depressing,' she said. Of course, we both knew which one she thought was more depressing. 'But at least you stayed away from the "too fucked to fuck" category.' She even made 'fuck' sound silky and sweet.

'That is true,' I said, knowing that she was referring to one individual in particular who had never been known to refuse a refill. 'I'm almost four months clean of him now,' I added, even though she hadn't asked, and even though I thought about Mr Too Fucked To Fuck almost every day and the only thing stopping me from picking up the phone to him between midnight and mid-morning was the fear that he wouldn't reply.

'I wish I could've come last night,' she said, which was a white lie, either for my benefit or that of our mutual friend whose birthday she'd missed, on account of too much to learn for Monday's audition.

'How're those lines going?' I asked, taking a swig of water from the plastic Evian bottle that I'd bought in a moment of rebellion, but which was now causing a cellophane-wrapped globe to weigh down on my chest.

Clara shrugged, lifting the mug to her lips, and her blonde fringe came tumbling forwards like tiny theatre curtains. When she realized it was empty, she glanced inside indignantly, like the tea had failed her. I wished that I could conjure more tea, right then and there. But, as I couldn't, I helpfully offered to go over lines with her.

'That would be heaven, if you're not too busy,' she said, setting the mug aside having rendered it useless.

There was a heap of laundry glowering at me from the corner of the room, empty toiletry bottles that needed replenishing, a birthday cheque from my tech-unsavvy mother that needed depositing, the latest Ottessa Moshfegh novel by my bed calling out to be devoured, hair in desperate need of a colour touch-up – who knew brunettes went grey in their twenties? – and I really did need to turn that idea for an article into a pitch – 'How To Dress Like A Man Booker-Nominated Author' – before the moment passed.

But it was rare to have Clara in London for the weekend and even rarer for her to be here without Ed. There was also the old chestnut of my constant striving to make sure that living with me was as joyous and fun an experience as possible, so that she wouldn't be tempted to shack up with him prematurely. And I did have a way of getting her to memorize lines like no one else. So, of course, I told her I'd be happy to help. I could probably even trick her into drinking a bottle of wine with me afterwards.

Once it was settled as a plan, Clara daintily removed herself from the cloud of my bed and I felt a twinge in my chest that would've made me call out, 'Don't go, please don't break this moment of hungover, girl-loving bliss!' had I no basic understanding of how crazy I'd sound. Instead, I brought up the issue of her birthday, the following week, reminding her that I needed her final guest list for the small do I was organizing. It wasn't a surprise party; it was just a party that Clara had no interest in organizing for herself, so I had taken on the task, as I had done for most of her birthdays. Every year, when she muttered words about not bothering to do anything, I'd jump in and say, 'I'll plan a party for you,' and she'd shrug like, 'Fine, suit yourself,' but she always had the best time. I was determined that this year would be no different, especially because we hadn't done one the previous year. Ed had taken her to Hong Kong instead.

'Oh, you do the list,' she said. 'You're better at these things than me.' With that, I watched her walk off in her matching silk pyjama set. I used to say that Clara was like a creation of F. Scott Fitzgerald's, with her breathy voice, doll-like appearance and slightly nervous disposition. But then, I hated the thought of her having been created by a borderline misogynistic white male, so I decided that she was a Jane Austen character. It suited, since she had a look and manner that made people instantly assume that she was stupid, which she'd tease for a while by staying silent throughout a heavy conversation, until suddenly piping up with something far more insightful and informative than anyone else had come near to. I lived for those moments.

I threw the duvet away from my own bare flesh. I liked to sleep naked, because when I woke up, for a split second, my brain would be tricked into thinking that I'd slept with someone and I'd get a small fraction of an adrenaline rush. It also made me feel thinner. I climbed out of bed, feeling dense, like my insides had all expanded within the frame of my body from the rum. I put on a pair of the Marks and Spencer cotton briefs that I'd bought in bulk the year before, when I'd finally learnt that I wasn't obliged to wear overpriced lacy thongs that cut a line from rectum to clitoris for my whole life, and wandered out into the flat.

Every morning, emerging into the homeliness of that place, I felt both grateful to be there and fearful of the day that I wouldn't. Though I'd only ever lived in a flat owned by Clara's family, for a token donation of rent money, I knew how much it cost to live in London and felt an anxious flutter whenever I thought of what I could afford in real-life circumstances. I dreaded the time I'd be holed up in a shoebox alongside the motorway.

A few rooms away, the loud and powerful rush of the shower began. Clara was starting the day like a responsible adult. Meanwhile, I meandered into the kitchen, where I found the ash of a mini pizza in the oven. I had a vague recollection of putting it in there when I'd arrived home, but, clearly, no recollection of taking it out. Sheepishly, I used an oven mitt to remove the tray and ran the singed circle under the cold tap. Then I reached for a small Moroccan glass on the shelf above, filling it with a sachet of Dioralyte and water from the Brita filter. I stirred until it turned murky pearl then downed the whole thing in one go. Honestly, I felt brighter within seconds.

Dioralyte is a fantastic creation.

I don't remember exactly when I met Clara, only that she became a reoccurring fixture of my life, in the way that you only accept when you're very young. We were six years old, according to the date that my mother began working for her mother.

It was a year after we'd moved over from Israel. My mother had just given birth to Ezra, my half-brother, whose father we had followed across the ocean just in case my mother had a chance with him. Turned out, she didn't, but thanks to the British passport that she had acquired when she was briefly

7

married to *my* father – I was the product of post-divorce copulation – we got to live in a one-bedroom flat in Earl's Court, and enjoy the pleasure of a London winter with no central heating, during which time I was forced to spend every Shabbat with my father and his ancient parents so that I wouldn't be forgotten in their will.

And then my mother met Bella Mortimer at a life-drawing class. When they recounted the story, they claimed to have instantly bonded over Clara and I – their daughters, exactly the same age – and a shared love of culture. What I had since gathered to be the truth was that my mother divulged her situation – two kids, two absent fathers, no money, no family in London – and Bella, a vulture of a rescuer, swooped in. She had just started a charity venture getting underprivileged children off the streets and into the arts. On the spot, she offered my mother a job – flippantly, I'd always imagined: 'Oh well, you must come work with me. What fun!'

From that day on, it's difficult to recall a childhood memory that did not, in some way, involve the Mortimers.

Bella was not an obvious match for my Jewish immigrant mother. She came from an eccentric, upper-class family, who believed in free love and forgetting to bath your children – 'Aristo-bohemia,' my mother called it, with a touch of derision. She was vibrant, provocative and vulgar, while my mother was something of a prude. Her husband, Derrick Mortimer, was a bald-headed New Yorker – 'bald man syndrome' my mother would say in reference to anything he did – and a world-renowned architect who spent most of his life travelling. He wore thick-rimmed spectacles and loved talking about his wine and art collections.

I don't remember the first occasion that Clara and I were

thrown together. I don't remember if there was any resistance, or if we fitted together like two pieces of a jagged-edged puzzle, or if we had, for survival purposes, decided to become best friends the very first time we'd met. I just remembered hours spent on top of a pink Wendy house and tents made out of sheets, draped over Clara's four-poster bed. I remembered the two of us sardined alongside Bella as she sat up in bed, with a glass of red wine on the bedside table and the bottle next to it, intermittently getting up to smoke out of the window. I remembered begging Clara's older brother Fabian to let us play with him and hiding from Ezra, whom I'd felt disconnected from since the day my mother gave birth to him and he commandeered all of her emotional resources. I remembered Bella tucking a napkin into my neckline because I was such a messy eater, while she could barely get Clara to eat anything at all. I remembered all these little things that had, over the years, stitched me into the fabric of their family.

My mother worked for Bella's venture for nearly seven years. She managed volunteers and liaised with the endless stream of freelancers that Bella brought on to avoid setting up anything that resembled a real company. My mother never dealt directly with the underprivileged kids – whom Bella often invited to camp out in the house when things got rough at home – because she said she didn't feel comfortable with them. She did attend the committee meetings made up of Bella's overprivileged friends, whom she couldn't admit she felt equally uncomfortable among. Bella must have paid her more generously than one would normally expect to earn at a charity because, suddenly, she no longer asked me to pocket loo roll from school when we'd run out. Suddenly, we were the kind of people who ate at the local Italian restaurant on multiple evenings and got bought new clothes when old ones became hole-ridden. Not only was I no longer forced to Shabbat, but my mother did everything she could to prevent me from going, to dig the knife in with my father, who was now the one begging for more time with me.

My mother didn't know how to cook, which I realized later in life was because she didn't eat. So, we spent most mealtimes at the Mortimers' in those years, though my mother always found a reason to opt out if Derrick was around. His moods were too unpredictable for her anxiety levels to cope with. Sometimes, he'd arrive at the table with a great smile on his face and tell a story that would have everyone doubled over in hysterics. Other times, he'd sit with heavy eyebrows, barely saying a word, unless it was a complaint about the food. Everyone would tiptoe around him on those occasions – everyone except Bella, who seemed to become even more vociferous than she usually was. We'd all chew through the tension, hoping he'd ignore her, like he sometimes did, rather than erupt and call her 'one hell of a cunt', as more often happened.

I was used to fractured marriages, but my own parents' understated, calculated animosity seemed so minor compared to Bella and Derrick's theatrical fights. I have an early memory of two male police officers in the entrance hall of the Mortimers' house, accusing Bella of the theft and vandalism of Derrick Mortimer's car and ordering her away from the property. Clara and I watched from the top of the stairs as Bella laughed and calmly stripped every piece of clothing from her body. She stood there stark naked, tall and spindly like a black widow spider, shouting, 'Come on, arrest me, boys!' at the blushing policemen. Fabian stayed in his room, as he always did when drama occurred, and Clara cried hysterically, while I squeezed my arms around her tiny shoulders. But, as terrifying as it was, even at the age of seven, I thought it was the most fantastic thing I'd ever seen a person do. I didn't know at the time that she needn't have done it, since the police would never have arrested her once they found out that she and Derrick were married. I just saw someone who was so unafraid.

Things changed for our extended family set-up thanks to the mammoth marital argument that happened when Clara and I were eleven. It occurred in the middle of the night and had culminated in Bella getting into her car and driving away. The next day, hours passed with no word from her. And then hours turned into days. My mother wanted to call the police, but Derrick refused to let her. After a week, Bella's sister arrived from the country with her own daughter to look after Clara and Fabian. And finally, after three weeks, Bella returned and whisked her traumatized children off to Disneyland Paris, as if nothing had happened. Where she went for those weeks, or why, I have never discovered, and Clara hasn't talked about it since.

My mother had been so furious with Bella that they didn't speak for a long time, even when working in the same small office. Soon after, my mother's job no longer existed. She returned to long days at home in the mustiness of a cluttered flat, caring for me and my brother, who was having a hard time learning and making friends. It also meant that she needed to return to her unhealthily entangled relationship with my father, from whom she'd been separated for twelve years, begging him to get her out of debt, promising him more time with me, though she didn't have the same agency over how I spent my Friday nights anymore, so Shabbat was out of the question.

Through all of it, however, I stayed closely enveloped in the

Mortimer fold. I continued to spend my evenings and weekends at their kitchen table and was invited on all the family holidays. Bella continued to treat me like one of her own children. Clara remained the closest thing in the world to me.

I'd always wondered if I would have grown up with a completely different personality and outlook on the world if my mother hadn't gone to life drawing that day. Maybe I would have started accompanying her to synagogue on Friday nights when that suddenly became a thing for her and embraced my many-blooded heritage. Maybe I would have learnt how to save money to do the things I'd always wanted to do and not just the things that I happened into. Maybe I'd have cultivated a relationship with my own brother, made more of an effort with my father and felt like I had strong roots of my own.

Maybe – but the truth is, we'll never know.

CHAPTER 2

You know that you're no longer in your mid-twenties when you go out on a Saturday night and your hangover is still a thing on Monday.

I worked at a magazine called *Close Up*. It was one of the few magazines that still made money, having been one of the first to jump on the bandwagon of *We're more than just a place you can read progressive yet highly elitist articles written by accomplished in-house editors and a handful of influential contributors; now you can shop the look, book your colonic, stream our product-placement-littered content and buy tickets for our Q&A with the CEO of Be-A-Better-Person.com*. It was one of the magazines that you dreamt of being able to say you worked for when you were an aspiring journalist, fresh out of university, in the midst of an economic crisis. So, when you were offered a job there, you didn't even care that the salary was the national minimum wage or that you would be working in a department that had nothing to do with editorial content. And seven years down the line, your job title would be Events & Special Projects Coordinator. Parenthesis, Not A Journalist.

I stared at my computer screen for most of the morning, flagging one email after the next. I did, however, manage to write to five different bakeries requesting a reasonable price for a multi-tiered birthday cake with the words 'We Love You

Clara' iced onto the surface. Then I went into the art department and lay down on the floor next to the printers until the team came back from their meeting. Even though they were my allies, they had no interest in my self-induced misery, so I trawled off to the beauty cupboard to see if there was anything in there that could save me from myself. I'd heard that medicinal mushrooms were the new thing.

The beauty cupboard was stacked full of masks, oils, creams, serums, acids, make-up, shampoos, funky nail polish, fragrance, health supplements, jade rollers, cryo balls, kegel eggs, teeth whiteners, state-of-the-art beauty tech and half of Korea's skincare stock. My favourite thing to do was show up to a girls' dinner with a bag of beauty cupboard cast-offs to hand out to appreciative friends. I peered into the cupboard and picked up some sort of neck and chin vibrator, fiddling around with it curiously, until the voice of Dymfy, our beauty editor – sorry, our beauty *director* – shot over my shoulder, making me jump.

'Whose naughty hands are those in there?' she said, all squeaky and Swedish.

I turned around to reveal myself, vibrating contraption in hand. Dymfy raised her eyebrows, not a crease in sight. Thanks to her healthy glow, I immediately felt ten times worse.

'I take it we're spick and span for Saturday, Miss Jax, since you have time to be in here?' she said, half schoolteacher, half nightclub hostess.

'Aren't we always?' I said, avoiding a smile, in case she judged my crow's feet.

When I first started working at the magazine, I – along with the rest of the staff – would ignore all of Dymfy's requests for an extra pair of hands at various summits she'd been asked to talk at and she quietly relished the fact that I could no longer do that. The beauty department used to be like the government's environmental department in the nineties. Something no one payed attention to. That is, until Dymfy got Insta-savvy and grew herself a following of 182.9K by posting make-up tutorial videos and bikini selfies, at which point our editor-in-chief started saying things like, 'Jax, do make sure you're giving Dymfy enough support,' like she was a patient in a psych ward. By now, Dymfy had her own blog, shares in *Close Up*'s wellness store, and I had to give up my Saturday to work at her first book launch.

I switched on the vibrating contraption and felt a charge travel through my arm. 'What's this for?'

'Turkey necks.'

'Didn't know we'd gone into poultry.'

Dymfy sighed. 'What are you doing in my cupboard, Jax? What do you need?'

How long have you got?

'Something for the bags under my eyes, please,' I said.

Dymfy made a W with her fingers to frame my eyes and blew a puff of air through her lips, which felt nice and cool on my tired lids. She shook her head. 'Dehydration. More water. Less alcohol.'

Ground-breaking advice. But, in my heart of hearts, I knew that Dymfy was right and that it really was that simple and that she had a two-book deal and I didn't, so I headed into the kitchen in search of something salty.

The fridge had been cleaned out over the weekend and all I could find in the cupboards were chicken stock cubes. It was a sign of how off-kilter I was feeling that I dissolved a whole cube in boiling water and downed it in one go, not least because I was a vegetarian. I just really needed that salt.

Within five minutes, my stomach started cramping up. It had been nearly three years since I'd had any meat substance, and anyway, you're probably not supposed to consume an entire stock cube in one go.

It came out in the loo in one gratifying explosion.

I went home to an empty flat that evening, since Clara was staying at Ed's place. Our cleaner, Derrinda – Clara's family's cleaner – had been in that day, and the place was spotless. I almost wished that it was a mess since that, at least, would have been a good excuse for getting straight into bed. When it was tidy and beautiful, as it was then, I felt like I had to make the most of it. But I had no energy to cook a complicated meal and drink red wine out of one of those very thin wine glasses or scroll through Netflix to find something that was worth committing a few hours to. And anyway, none of that was fun to do alone.

So, I made baked beans on toast, which I ate on the sofa while reading a Lenny Letter piece, announcing their shutdown. I had been meaning to pitch a story to them for years.

As usual, I had left it too late.

Come Thursday, I was itching to hit the pub after work. The only thing stopping me was Clara's birthday the following day. Since I'd organized it, I thought I should probably lead by example and be on cracking form. Particularly because Clara didn't get the part she'd auditioned for. I felt slightly responsible, though I knew that wasn't logical.

My last meeting that day was with some mixologist who'd been recommended to me by my *Evening Standard* counterpart, who said she always booked his service when she thought an event needed a touch of the *avant-garde*. My expectations weren't high given that she was the kind of person who wrote 'fuq' instead of 'fuck' in emails. The whole thing sounded a little like event sabotage, but I agreed to meet him anyway because I was always interested in meeting new people, in case they could be absorbed into my nexus.

As I waited for him outside the lift, I expected the doors to slide open to reveal a trilby-clad, bearded East Londoner scribbled in tattoos. So, I was surprised to be confronted with a baby face, curly hair and a weatherproof jacket.

'Are you Jax?' he asked uncertainly, probably because I was staring blankly at him, rather than introducing myself like a normal person.

'I am. You must be Ned?' I said, looking directly into ice-grey eyes, which had something so earnest about them. A hand appeared from underneath the rubberized sleeve of his jacket and met mine for a shake. 'Thanks for coming,' I said, leading him through to the sofa in the corridor alongside the fashion and beauty cupboards.

'This is a lovely office,' he said sincerely, taking a seat. He explained to me in wholehearted detail how he and his team worked to design bespoke cocktails that perfectly fitted the theme or mood of an event. They had recently introduced a creative service, whereby they could dress and decorate not only the bar area, but the whole venue. To say that Ned didn't fit the theme of Modern Cocktail Entrepreneur is to say the least. He seemed more like someone who should be talking about Egyptian ruins on the BBC. So, my guess was that he wasn't really an avant-garde mixologist, but a clever person who had found a gap in the market for avant-garde mixology and had built a lucrative business out of it. Why couldn't I think of something like that?

He pulled his iPad from a tote bag and started sliding through images. 'This is a wedding we did last month,' he said, showing me a cave with hundreds of candles that appeared to be levitating in a curved shape over the bar. Next was a long wooden bar with a romantic train set running the course. A Halloween pumpkin extravaganza. A cynosure bar mimicking a globe. And – wait for it – a trilby-clad, bearded barman scribbled in tattoos. Aside from the trilby man, each image was more impressive than the previous one.

By the end of the meeting, I had booked Ned and his bearded team for Dymfy's book launch, which was two days away. There wasn't really room in the budget for it, but something told me that I just needed this mixologist in my life, and that Dymfy would too.

Walking him to the lift, I asked, 'Any fun plans tonight?', and immediately freaked out that I sounded like I was angling for a date.

Ned, however, didn't look the least bit perturbed. He replied enthusiastically, 'I'm going to a light exhibition at the Tate and then checking out a pop-up cocktail bar on the Southbank.'

I really wanted to ask if I could come too, but thought that might be taking it a bit far for a first meeting, and a work one at that. *Calm down, Jax.*

After my new friend Ned departed the building, I booked an overpriced yoga class to stop myself from taking the pub-leading fork in the road. On the way to the studio, Clara texted to say that she was going to be in that night, after all, and was cooking me dinner. Immediately, I cancelled the class, seething at the robbery of a fifteen-pound cancellation fee. I speed-read *ES* magazine on the train back to Canonbury and picked up a bottle of red wine and a packet of Kettle Chips from Sainsbury's on the other side.

As soon as I walked into the flat, the luxuriousness of multiple scented candles embraced me. Clara was much more liberal with the candle-lighting than I was, so it always felt instantly more like a spa when she was around. When I moved in with Clara, it was the first time that I'd felt like I was living in a real home. Having gone to a London-based university, I had stayed at my mother's for far too long, particularly given that she was – in simple terms – a hoarder. She disguised her hoarding as collecting, so I hadn't fully comprehended it until I moved out and found myself spoilt for space, despite the fact that Clara's flat was smaller than my mother's. Until then, I hadn't realized that all the cultural norms of family life – such as a dining table or television – had been edged out of our home by her clutter.

I closed the door loudly to signal my arrival. Clara called out 'Hi!' from the kitchen, over the voice of a BBC news reporter that was playing on the speakers all around the flat. I walked in to find her prodding a large piece of seasoned tofu, as the reporter alerted us to Harry and Meghan's touchdown in Australia.

'What a wonderful wife you are,' I said, hugging her from behind. She wasn't even a vegetarian, which made the tofu all the more adorable.

'Aren't I, just?' she agreed, adding another pinch of salt. Neither of us cooked well, since I'd never had the opportunity to learn from my mother, who hated food, and Bella had a habit of not letting anyone into the kitchen because she often bought pre-prepared ingredients.

'I forgive you for having a two-year affair,' I said, plucking a piece of feta cheese from the Greek salad that was sitting on the counter and popping it into my mouth.

Clara gave my sticky fingers the side-eye. 'Well, you know,' she said. 'It's a passing thing.'

'Marital life.'

We both laughed.

For the first few years that we lived together, Clara and I had done everything as a pair, from grocery shopping and cooking, to partying and being hungover. We had the same self-defeating humour and laughed our way through our early twenties. But the three years that had followed her meeting Ed at a wine tasting were different: she was seldom hungover because she hardly went to parties; she spent little time at home and when she was there, he was usually there too, which meant that the laughter in the flat had diminished because she seemed to be wary of cracking jokes in front of him.

I took two wine glasses out of the cupboard. 'Glass of red?'

'Not for me,' she said, and a little note of disappointment chimed within me. Then she added, 'Saving myself for tomorrow night.'

'On a scale of one to ten, how excited are you?' I asked, pouring a glass for myself regardless.

'Ten and a half.'

'Only half as excited as me, then,' I said, holding out my glass to cheers. She clinked it with the end of her spatula. I went on, 'So, I've booked a table from seven-thirty.'

'Great, I'll come straight after dinner.'

Dinner?

'Where's dinner?' I asked, trying to quell any giveaway inflection of angst in my voice.

'I don't know. Ed's booked somewhere. Just an early one, we'll be done before nine.'

I wondered how long the dinner plan had been a thing for. I knew that it hadn't just arisen. It was so very Clara to hold back disappointing news until the last minute, and then flippantly kamikaze you with it, as if that would make it less disappointing. I knew that saying anything other than 'That will be lovely' would make me a very psychotic best friend, but I did secretly hope that Ed might wake up the next morning with chronic diarrhoea.

CHAPTER 3

I went straight to the pub after work on Friday. Since we were now at an age where everyone's jobs had become a whole lot more demanding than they had been a few years ago, I was there on my own for a good deal of time.

Omni was there, but she worked there, so she had a pretty good excuse. I didn't have an excuse, except for the fact that I'd organized so many of the same goddamn events that I could pretty much do my job on autopilot: reconfirm guest list, reconfirm press attendance, sign off on menu and send out ROS or 'run of show'. I could even boast a new avant-garde mixology team for this one. *There you go, Dymfy.* There was nothing more I could do, so I'd fabricated a Friday afternoon meeting to get me out of the office early. That's what we all used to do, back in the days of limited professional responsibility.

'I need to score action tonight,' said Omni, while the Friday-nighters elbowed their way towards getting served. 'I've got the horn,' she added, surreptitiously sliding me a glass of white wine. On the rare occasions that I went on dates, this was my pub of choice, so that *laissez-faire* Omni – with her edgy nose ring and punchy T-shirt saying, 'TIPS PLEASE' – could slip me free glasses of wine to make me look cool.

'Hey, tip lady,' said a tall man, who could not be called

anything but handsome, even though I hated him for calling her 'tip lady'. He hovered over my shoulder with his iPhone in one hand and a pint of beer in the other.

'You've already got a drink,' Omni pointed out, as some liquid sloshed out of his glass onto my shoulder. 'So, I'm guessing you want my number?'

What I absolutely loved was that I knew Omni was doing it for no other reason than to amuse me, which it did. She never cared whether or not she was embarrassing herself, which meant that she never would.

'Actually, I just wondered if you can charge my phone,' said the tall, handsome stranger.

Omni placed one hand on her hip and the other on the bar, leaning towards him like a 1950s pin-up girl, and everyone at the bar was suddenly staring at what a romance novelist would call her 'ample bosom'. Her tits. 'By my bed?' she asked, with a mischievous glint in her eye.

Again, I loved it, because it was for me.

'No, behind the bar,' said the man, whom I now took to be a total bore.

She gave a fleeting flash of her trademark warm smile – she was normally very unintimidating, really – before resuming The Coquette. 'What do I get if I charge your phone?'

'You get to hold my phone,' said the tall, handsome colossal bore.

'I'll come back to you,' said Omni, dropping the act entirely. At that, I collapsed over the bar in a fit of tittering laughter.

Omni was Clara's cousin, but you'd never know it because their personalities were opposite ends of the spectrum, and also, Omni's father was Indonesian, so they looked like nothing of the same genealogy. What I most adored about Omni was that she didn't work at the pub to support some creative venture like a singing career or CBD product line. She just really loved working there. It was all she wanted to do, and she excelled at it. I admired her for her absolute assuredness, while the rest of us all flailed around in a desperate panic to do more, be more and reach a very specific and ambitious point in our careers by the time we hit thirty. *Tick tock, tick tock.*

'So. What's new?' she said, leaning towards me, ignoring everyone who was now demanding service from her.

For some reason, I had an urge to tell her about the not-so-avant-garde mixologist, but that seemed like underwhelming news considering that all he'd done was come in for a meeting. Instead, I said, 'I'm in that space of mind where I don't know when I'm going to have sex, ever again, in my life.' I said it in a serious tone of voice because it was a serious matter. Since I'd been trying to steer clear of – while constantly thinking about – one particular person, I had lost the sense that the pursuit of intercourse with any other human being was an actual possibility.

'That happens to me, sometimes,' said Omni.

'When does that *ever* happen to you?'

It had never happened.

'Sometimes when there's a lull, it turns into a dry patch—'

'What's a dry patch for you? How long?'

She shrugged. 'A month.'

I gave her an *I rest my case* look. Then I glanced south and said, 'It's probably started moulding,' not miserably, but secretly quite miserable about it. 'Sometimes, I think I've had sex and then I realize I'm just thinking about a time I had a wank.'

Omni laughed in appreciation. 'Why don't you ask Dymfy to start a social media campaign? Hashtag resurrect Jax's rotting fanny.'

I would have laughed, but as she said it, my peripherals caught sight of Fabian, Clara's older brother, who had arrived just in time for an image of my corroding sex organs to be burned into his brain.

'Hello, trouble,' he said, with an accent and manner that would make you think he'd come right off an East London council estate.

I loved being called 'trouble'. It made me feel girlish and naughty. The feminist in me could not reconcile why I felt that was a good thing.

With me taken care of, Omni slipped off back to work, leaving us alone.

'Long time. Where've you been?' said Fabian, and my heart edged towards my stomach. I was irrationally worried that for every event that Ed was at instead of me, a piece of me would be chipped out of their minds, until they virtually forgot who I was, despite the twenty years they'd known me for.

I reached for my go-to armour: 'I've been chronically busy at work.'

Chronically?

'Boyfriend?' he asked, a twinkling smile in his eyes.

'Don't be ridiculous!' I said, and he laughed his open-mouthed, cheeky cackle. I joined in, mimicking the laugh almost exactly.

Then I saw Tim walk through the door and my body tightened anxiously. Fabian was going to find Tim wildly unacceptable, and I always felt the need to impress him, which was a pre-existing condition from childhood, when he had seemed so much older and worldlier than us.

'Evening,' said Tim, arriving next to us with his hands in the pockets of a city slicker suit, which was finished with a novelty beer pint emoji tie.

'Hi, Tim. Flying solo?' I asked, a winking reminder of the fact that he'd only been invited because he was Alice's boyfriend.

'Yeah, best way to be,' he said, looking at Fabian in the hope of basic masculine complicity. Tim still lived in tribute to his halcyon days of single lad life, though we all knew he was as firmly pressed under Alice's thumb as one could be. He added, 'Alice is outside, on a work call,' with a jeer in his voice on the words 'work call'.

Fabian held out his hand. 'Hello, mate, I'm Fabian.'

'Tim,' he said, offering a limp hand in return. That was as far as the exchange went. I was already panicking about whether or not everyone was having a good time.

'Did you watch the footie today?' asked Tim. Predictable though it was, at least it was something that Fabian could relate to, which eased my discomfort a little. But as they conversed animatedly about teams and players, I kept thinking, *Why doesn't he at least take off that tie?*

Eventually, Alice strode in – the only person I knew who could stride, not squeeze, her way through a crowded pub – brisk and tight-jawed.

'The longest five minutes known to man!' whined Tim.

'When did time-keeping become your forte?' said Alice, throwing every inch of her glossy hair behind her shoulder with a gentle toss off the head.

I wanted to say something along the lines of 'touché', though I couldn't think of anything less cliché that had the same effect, but it didn't matter because—

'Touché!' bellowed Tim.

Alice ignored him and leant over to brush my jaw with hers, which was her personal equivalent of a massive hug. She smelt like expensive figs.

26

'How are you?' I grabbed her cold hand and hung onto it, because an air kiss just wasn't enough for me sometimes.

'Not great,' she said, retrieving her hand to wave at Omni, indicating an intense need for a drink. 'Had my coil reinserted this morning.'

'Keep that to yourself, why don't you?' said Tim, thinking he was being funny, when actually, in my mind, there was nothing less attractive than men who couldn't talk about cervical implants or periods.

'Oh, I'm so sorry,' said Alice, balancing tall on her high-heeled leather boots. 'I forgot that you'd never had a metal claw shoved nine inches up your vagina so that some idiot can shoot his load off into your womb once a week. I'll keep it from your delicate ears next time.' She delivered the whole thing like she was in the middle of a business proposal.

'Someone woke up on the wrong side of their single bed today,' said Tim.

Alice stared at him like he was a halfwit (which he may well have been) and said, 'We woke up together.'

'Yeah, it's a joke,' he responded feebly.

'Take off your tie,' she snapped. *Thank God.*

I met Alice at the age of sixteen, when we were both waitressing at a corporate event. After spending two straight hours ferrying silver trays of champagne in and out of the kitchen for stockbrokers who were full of lewd jibes and exaggerated glances down our shirts, Alice turned to me with a full tray and said, 'Shall I do it?'

'Do what?' I had responded.

Without another word, she flipped the tray over, and every glass went crashing loudly to the floor, a tsunami of fizz exploding around our feet. Alice shrugged, turned around and walked straight off. I'd decided then and there to make her one of my closest friends. She invited me to her parents' house one night for crudités and cigarettes – which I found utterly chic – and I'd brought Clara and Omni along. Omni had made her laugh with tales of misbehaviour, while Clara had sat hunched at the end of the sofa, her shyness manifesting as rudeness, to the point where Alice had asked, 'What is the matter with your friend?' right in front of her. But, as tended to happen, Clara gradually bonded with Alice by delving deep into her soul late one night. It was the usual pattern: I found friends for us, caught them with a net, and Clara swallowed them whole. Soon, we were a tight-knit foursome.

In those days, Alice used to dress in head-to-toe high street that she somehow managed to make look like Chanel. Now she actually wore Chanel, thanks to the six-figure salary that she'd negotiated herself at a global political PR firm. She'd met Tim at a wedding. He was the good-looking best man who had vowed in his speech that he'd never settle down. Alice, ever competitive, saw a challenge and went for it. We still all wondered if she was attracted to anything more than that.

As more friends arrived at the pub for Clara's birthday, we moved onto the table that I'd reserved and ordered round after round of drinks. Nine o'clock came and went. So did nine-thirty and nine-forty-five. At ten o'clock, Clara finally walked in, holding Ed's hand. She had a look about her. It was a look that sat somewhere between excited and . . . Was it smug?

Before she had even reached the table, I knew.

My eyes darted towards her hand. She was holding it palm up, hiding what was sure to be a fuck-off diamond.

'Sorry, we're late,' she said, sweet and unobtrusive.

I smiled through the anxious pounding in my chest and

opened my arms to her. She hugged me with one arm, keeping the elusive overturned hand close to her side. I wished she would just come out and say it, but instead, she hugged Omni in exactly the same way, and then Alice, and then Fabian, and then everyone else. After she'd one-arm squeezed every last person, she sighed loudly, pulling her lips into the widest of smiles, her perfectly white top and bottom teeth gnashing together. Everyone waited, as if she were about to give a speech. I guessed that they were all thinking the same as me, though probably with a far less intense background dialogue.

'We have some news . . .' she finally said, her eyes glinting at Ed. He held his hands out in presentation of her and gave an awkward nod of the head.

Clara's forearm shot up, like she was a marionette whose string had just been yanked, and the eager audience were finally allowed to feast their eyes on a rock that seemed absurdly large for such a dainty hand. Like every actor's – or puppet's – dream, we were engaged, responsive and present. We made all the right sounds – squeals, gasps, 'Fuck off's!' – and the right gestures – clapping, flapping, groping.

In the middle of it all, Clara clasped my wrist and said, 'I didn't expect it at all.'

'I did,' I said.

I didn't.

'Really?' she said, turning to face me full on.

'I had a feeling.'

I hadn't.

Sternly, I told myself that I was nothing but happy for my best friend, who was literally glowing with joy, while a big red question mark over my home life and security started to flash away in my brain. And then, even though Clara had just hugged every single person there, she was doing the rounds again. While that was happening, I saw Alice polish off her signature vodka on the rocks – 'Chic!' I always said when she ordered it – in three long gulps. I wished that I, too, had a strong drink to hand.

Fabian gave Ed a distant pat on the back. They couldn't have been more different if they tried, and their evident lack of camaraderie made me feel a bit better about Ed having monopolized the role of Clara's other half. *You're no me, Edward.* Clara thrust the ring in front of Fabian's face pointedly. I assumed the gesture said, *Fuck you, now I'm the one leaving,* to her brother, who had always had a habit of running away from reality. Whether it was into his room, into a K hole, or off to New York – though he couldn't sustain himself there for long – Fabian had always been somewhere else when any of their many family dramas ensued.

Ed loitered behind them, with flushed cheeks. He had a slim scarf looped around his neck, hanging equal lengths on both sides. It reminded me of when he'd first asked Clara on a date, and she'd sent me a screenshot of his profile photo – in which he was sporting a similar look – that she'd captioned, 'Favours a scarf [laughing face emoji]'. Back then, I hadn't for one second thought that the date would ever progress into something serious. I'd started to suspect that she really liked him when she'd said, 'He lives in Wimbledon. It's actually very easy to get to.' Wimbledon may have been lovely, but it sure as hell was not easy to get to from Canonbury. Or anywhere.

'We need a celebratory round. Tequila shots, on me!' I declared. It was nearly the end of the month and I had no money, but that was what credit cards were for. Generosity emergencies. Ed may have bought a whopping great rock and a Michelin-star dinner, but he'd never buy a round of shots for the gang. I started doing a headcount, out loud.

'Just half a pint for me, please,' said Ed, in his trademark tone that resembled a middle-aged politician trying to avoid a tricky question from a member of the press.

'Oh yeah, me too,' said Fabian, mischievously. He caught my eye and we both laughed, conspiratorially teasing. Whenever Ed came out with Clara's friends, he was all, 'I'll have half a pint, I'm taking it easy these days.' But a night out with his pals from the Nottingham Uni hockey team and Clara's phone would be inundated with videos – from people with names like Swigger and El Legendo – of a half-naked Ed singing 'Jerusalem' or stealing phallic road traffic equipment to do God knows what with. ('So gauche,' Alice would always say, which Clara would always ignore.)

I felt a dip in my stomach as I paid for the shots that added an extra figure onto my already worrisome credit card debt. Then I handed them around with a smile. When I came to Clara, I saw Ed flickering his eyes between her and the little glass. She and I clinked our glasses together. I threw the shot back, feeling it burn through my throat and chest. When I slammed it down on the table, I noticed that Clara had only had a tiny sip of hers. There was a look on Ed's face that I could have sworn was triumphant.

On Ed's advice, Clara had become wary of drinking too much, because when she got drunk, she wasn't just drunk like the rest of us were. She was old-school, falling-off-chairs, skirt-over-her-head – or someone else's head – wasted. Those times were my absolute favourite. I remembered how she'd danced on the table at her mother's fiftieth birthday, surrounded by the Gipsy Kings singing 'Bamboleo'. I remembered how she'd fallen over laughing when one of the guests said, loudly, 'Blonde girls should not flamenco dance!' I remembered her lying on the floor outside a nightclub in Ibiza, insisting that she was already in bed. I remembered the time she fell in the Princess Diana Memorial.

All that was when we were 24-year old spring chickens. Before life was serious. Before life was Ed.

I had expected Clara to stay out late that night and bask in the congratulatory excitement, but neither of them could wait to get out of that pub and back to his flat, which was no longer as far away as Wimbledon. As anxious as her news had made me, it was heart-warming to see how much the two of them wanted nothing but to be alone in each other's company.

I walked them out to their Uber. While Ed fussed around trying to find the driver, Clara turned to me and touched her fingers to my elbow.

'You'll be my maid of honour,' she said. 'If that's OK?'

I almost smiled, but then shocked both of us when the smile turned into a whimper of sorts. Clara laughed and flung her arms around my neck. I rested my chin on her shoulder and my eyes prickled with tears, as the ring on her finger glistened under the streetlight. It wasn't simply that she had chosen me to be her maid of honour. The usual Clara thing to do would have been to forget to ask me every time we were together, and then drop it into a text message when she was sure we wouldn't see each other for a few days, to avoid getting too sentimental. Perhaps she was a little drunk, after all.

'You'll be a great maid of honour,' she said, releasing her grip on me.

'And you'll be such a perfect bride.'

The Uber arrived and a flustered Ed gave me a hasty double kiss goodbye, before sweeping Clara away. I stood with my hands grasping onto opposite elbows and watched the car get smaller and smaller until it disappeared around a corner.

I checked my phone for the first time all night. The mixologist had confirmed his arrival time for the book launch and informed me how excited he and the team were, punctuated with a grinning face emoji. I smiled to myself, amused, since I thought that all men hated emojis. That was a thing, right?

The door of the pub opened, and Alice emerged, bundled in a cream shearling coat, followed by Tim.

'Are you leaving?' I asked, hoping that she was coming out for a cigarette, or to put Tim into a car alone.

But she nodded. 'Coil drama,' she said, which I took to mean, *Tim drama*. She added a sincere, 'Sorry, Jax.'

'Don't apologise!' I said, receiving her air kiss.

'I'll call you tomorrow, to *discuss*,' she said, with raised eyebrows.

'Yes, we need to *discuss*.' I was relieved that I was not the only one who felt something other than pure excitement at Clara's news. Or maybe she meant that she wanted to discuss her coil drama. As they walked off, Tim reached out to put his arm around her and she shoved him off.

At least I still have Omni, I thought, until I went inside to find her sitting knee to knee with the tall, handsome out-of-battery-iPhone bore. They were about to have a fuck fest. I could always tell. And you know what? Truth be told, bore or no bore, I was a little jealous.

Fabian was still sitting at our table, buried deep in his iPhone, and I knew that he'd be off somewhere else. I also knew that that somewhere else would involve drugs, and I didn't want to take those. Regardless, I walked over to ask, 'What are you doing now then?'

'Finding a party,' he said, without looking up, or pronouncing the 'T' in party. 'You coming?'

'Depends whose party. And how old they are,' I said, because Fabian was somewhat known for being the oldest person at a party full of Gen Z's.

'Don't be ageist,' he said.

'Why not? Everyone else is.'

'I'm not. I'm always flexible.'

'Downwardly flexible,' I quipped.

He laughed, and said, 'As are you, I've heard,' clearly referring to something dirtier than age. Fabian was best friends with Too-Fucked-To-Fuck, whose real name was Leo. I'd met him a few years back, at a day rave that Fabian had organized with a DJ who went by the name of 'Matcha Latte Peng'.

Fabian's phone started ringing and he answered with, 'Yo.' I thought I might try answering my phone like that one day. He said the word 'Bruv' a few times as he extracted the address of a house party in West London that was sure to be crawling with his Gen Z friends. I knew that I'd regret my decision to go when I was on my way home in a 45-minute, 1.8 x surcharge Uber, with some child in a bucket hat and a diagonally slung bum bag. But all my pals were otherwise engaged, and I wasn't ready to go home to dwell on my troublesome abandonment issues alone.

'We'll see you there, me and Jax,' said Fabian, and I guessed that it had been decided for me. And then I heard him say the words, 'No, Leo's working tonight.'

I didn't look up, or in any way let on to the fact that

those three words had sent my mind straight down a mucky rabbit hole.

If Leo was working, it meant that if I were to – hypothetically – WhatsApp him, I wouldn't be disturbing him on a date, or at some epic party. There was so little chance of rejection when Leo was working. Unless, of course, he'd met someone at work. But the odds were low. Where exactly he did meet any of the 101 women he seemed to have had flings with, I had no idea, because he was virtually impossible to casually run into. And the bonus was that, when Leo was working, he probably wasn't too fucked to fuck.

'I'm actually going to call it,' I said, as Fabian tapped an address into the Uber app. 'As much as I'd love to rub shoulders with well-to-do ketamine addicts.'

'Suit yourself, Tinkerbell,' he said, chuckling and rubbing the top of my head with his knuckles, far less disappointed than I'd hoped. Tinkerbell was a nickname that his father had given me when we were children. I had always liked the nickname, thinking of myself as a tiny fairy with a huge personality, until I realized that it was a pop psychology term used to group all women of a certain size with a certain amount of ambition into one demeaning category.

Surreptitiously, I took out my phone and opened a message to Leo. The last messages between us had been four months before, after a night spent drinking tequilas at Slim Jim's, a grubby bar down the road from my flat where we knew that we wouldn't run into anyone (though our fling wasn't a secret, we didn't flaunt it openly in the realm of our everyday lives) and then had a sleepover after which I'd started to realize that my feelings for this casual fling had started to simmer into something that resembled . . . well, I couldn't stop thinking about him.

That was a problem considering I had always known Leo was not the person that I should be pursuing anything more than 'casual' with.

That was when my fuckless days began.

I held my thumbs over the mini keypad and rapidly resurrected the thread.

Me:
Hi lovey how are you? What you up to
tonight? X

My finger lingered over the send button.

I had been clean of him for four months and, every day, I thought of him a little less. Yes, there were times when I wanted to share an inside joke, or even a deeply personal revelation, since our casual fling was 50 per cent drunk sex, 50 per cent drunk therapy. And there were still certain triggers that made me want to call him, such as sex scenes in movies, or seeing myself naked in the mirror. But his actual physical presence would surely take me straight down a mud slide and land me back at square one of my emotional assault course. The alternative was returning home drunk – and therefore horny – to the flat that belonged to Clara, wondering how many weeks, or days, I had left to live with my best friend and how many rodents I'd have to share my next place with.

I hit send.

Then I pulled a third stool – or wheel – up to Omni's table, placing myself closer to her than was necessary and as far away from iPhone guy as was possible. Omni draped an arm over my shoulders. 'Jax, this is Will. He was just telling me about his favourite book,' she said, with a wink in her voice that said, *Wait for it.*

36

'Which book is that?' I asked, mimicking her tone.

'*The Magus*,' said iPhone guy, who disappointingly now had a name.

Beneath the table, Omni pinched my thigh and I grabbed hold of her finger. We had always joked that the reason we both refused to go on dating apps was that we didn't want to waste any of the precious nights of our twenties – or liver damage – in some concept cocktail bar with a pseudo-intellectual whose favourite book would no doubt be *The Magus*.

'Interesting choice,' I said. 'What do you like about it?'

'Well, it's about a young Oxford graduate with a powerful addiction to women—'

'I know what it's about,' I cut in. 'But why is it your favourite book?'

'Have you read it?' he asked doubtfully.

'Of course she's read it!' Omni jumped in defensively. 'She's got a bloody double first in English Lit. She's read more books than anyone I know.'

'Oh. Well done,' he said, suitably patronizing. 'It's the complex interplay and deconstruction of gender roles that fascinates me.' I was certain he'd lifted that right out of someone else's academic paper. 'And the way the author examines the validity of the novel.' As the plagiarism went on and on, I checked my phone, rereading the message I'd sent. I suddenly felt paranoid about the word 'lovey', which I had previously thought sounded lackadaisical-cool, but on a second read, sounded more like a senior citizen trying to strike up a chat on the bus.

'I really related to the main character in a lot of ways,' was how Mr iPhone – now Mr Magus – finished his review. He clearly had no idea it featured a nasty misogynist as its protagonist.

Omni smiled, then gave me a quick glance of, *Can you believe this guy?* I knew she'd still sleep with him though. That's why she was the only person I'd be able to tell if I ended up seeing Leo.

If I told Clara, she'd say, 'Why? Why are you doing it to yourself?'

Why?

Because I feel anxious and lonely and need someone to either fuck the shit out of me or give me a cuddle.

Suddenly, my phone lit up in my lap. It was him.

> Leo:
> I'm just finishing work. I think I'll be done in an hour so let me know what your plan is if you're out and about? X

Feeling a swell of satisfaction that ballooned over any reservations I'd had, I typed out a response. I wasn't in the mood to play it cool by waiting half an hour to reply. *Tick tock, tick tock.*

> Me:
> Ok cool. I'm out still but not sure how long I'll last. Let me know when you're heading back x

Not a bad idea to lay a bit of pressure on, I thought, given that the ball was creeping into my court: the kiss at the end of the message, the appeal to let him know what *I* was doing.

'I'm off,' I said, leaning over to kiss Omni on the cheek. I'd tell her about Leo in the morning, in case she did try to talk sense into me. I took a cigarette from her before I left and smoked it on the way home, walking to kill time. It was rare that I smoked alone these days, having given up cigarettes for a Juul, and subsequently having found 'Juul' too annoying a word to keep saying, therefore deciding to compromise at social smoking only.

By the time I arrived home, I was still short of a response to my message. A tremble of panic crept through me. What if he didn't actually come? Thinking you were going to have sex and then not having sex was the biggest aphrodisiac, which also made it a catalyst for slow-burn insanity. It would make for a troublesome end to the evening, given my already delicate mental state.

I decided to give him a nudge.

> Me:
> Home now and suddenly v awake

Translation: I'm on great form and up for fucking all night long. He understood me perfectly.

> Leo:
> I'm leaving now.
> You can come to mine if you like?

I couldn't go to his flat. He had no living room. It served to remind me that the type of man I was attracted to was the type of man who lived from kitchen to bedroom.

> Me:
> I'm home already and don't want to go out
> again but come here if you want

Leo:
Shall I ring the doorbell?
Don't wanna wake anyone

I understood that he was trying to figure out if Clara was home or not. Clara didn't like anyone to smoke inside when she was around, and Leo smoked far too much to keep going outside, especially in the winter. I clarified my state of aloneness in the flat.

Leo:
Ok cool I'm gonna come

There was no going back from this odd decision of mine now. Rallied by his compliance, I added a request.

Me:
Please bring ciggies 🙏

Leo:
Ok!

Feeling giddy with the prospect of actual real-life sex, even if it was with someone that I'd actively been trying not to have sex with, I poured myself a glass of red wine – the wine that I had bought for Clara and I – touched up my make-up, tweezed a few black hairs from around my nipples, set the living-room lights to the perfect brightness, lit one candle – any more would look creepy – and put on a Spotify playlist entitled 'Smooth Operators'. That was me, a smooth operator. I didn't change out of my jeans and fake Gucci T-shirt combo, because I liked the idea of appearing to have made no effort at all. That's what you did when you wanted to keep things *casual*, right? That's what you did when you didn't want to fall into a place of Can't Stop Thinking About Him.

By the time the doorbell rang, I'd already finished one glass of wine and quickly poured myself another before buzzing him in. I reset the playlist to the beginning so that he didn't miss Marvin Gaye, and stood at the door to the flat, waiting. Seconds later, Leo emerged from the darkness of the stairwell, a beacon of colour. Beneath his coat, I could see that he was wearing pink jeans and a floral shirt unbuttoned to mid-chest, looking just as delicious as he had the last time I'd seen him.

'Hello,' I said, smiling against the doorframe, like, *Oh God, can you believe we're back to this again?*

'Hey, darling,' he said, in his Transatlantic accent – part Argentinian, part American residing in London – swooping to kiss me on the cheek. With just that, I remembered why I loved seeing him so much. Even though we both knew it was never going to be anything but casual for an array of reasons – namely that he was a drug addict and a sex addict, who seemed to habitually Houdini, and that I had enough problems with emotional availability as it was – he was never afraid of the minor intimacies. He didn't worry that calling me 'darling', or cuddling through the night, or getting breakfast in the morning would make me think that we were about to get married.

'Here, I brought this for you,' he said, handing me a half empty bottle of wine.

'God, you spoil me!'

'Don't ever forget it,' he laughed, ducking to follow me into the flat. He was 6ft 4 and about an inch wide, with stubble that was usually overgrown. Omni called him The Bean. 'It smells of you in here,' he said, as I led him to the sofa, all smug about my living room.

'Because I live here,' I said, although I was actually stupidly flattered that he'd retained a sensual memory of my aroma. I added, 'Not for long, though.'

'Are you moving out?'

I turned to him with my thumbs tucked into my jean pockets. 'Clara got engaged.'

His face dropped and he quickly pulled me into a hug. I was touched that he not only knew me well enough to know that I was feeling on edge about losing my best friend and home all in one day, but that he cared enough for his face to display shock so automatically, as if he were feeling my pain for me. I pressed my face into the grizzle of hairs on his chest. He smelt lewd and filthy, like someone who'd been on too many benders in his life. His scent reminded me of the first time we'd met, at Fabian's Matcha Latte Peng day rave. When we'd first got chatting, Leo had told me that he was about to go for a tantric massage. He ended up sacking it off and staying at the rave to watch the Chemical Brothers with me. Something about being a better option than a tantric massage had turned me on. It didn't occur to me at the time that he may actually have stayed for the Chemical Brothers.

'Have you been working lots?' I asked.

'Almost every night.'

Leo had saved up enough money to start an app, then got excited by the popularity of Bitcoin, which he thought would make him a millionaire but had instead lost him his whole fund in one go. He'd never had the inclination to start again, and instead worked as a manager at a restaurant owned by a friend of Bella's and Derrick's.

'Did you bring ciggies?' I asked.

'Of course.' He pulled two packets from of his pocket: Marlboro Gold for me, Marlboro Reds for himself. Clara always knew when he'd been over because of the smell. ('How can anyone below the age of sixty-five still think it's a good idea to smoke reds?' she always asked with disdain.)

'Fabulous,' I said, pulling the plastic off the packet with my teeth while using my other hand to pour him a glass of wine. Dexterous, aren't I?

'You look well, darling,' he said.

Well.

'So do you. You look like you've been ...' I was going to say 'on holiday', then I realized that he was actually paler than usual.

'Stuck indoors?' he finished the sentence for me.

'No, you look like you've been working out.' I tried to save it, although he'd never worked out in his life. 'You look great.'

I handed him the glass and sat down on the sofa, casually, seemingly disinterested in whether he wanted to join me or not. Of course, that meant that he did join me and we immediately launched into a conversation about global warming, woke culture and our favourite pubs of the moment, like two best friends who hadn't seen each other for far too long. Eventually, he pierced into that friendly dynamic by rubbing the side of my thigh affectionately, back and forth, back and forth. My God, it felt a joy to be touched, even through the thick fabric of my jeans. That touch was all it took for the polite conversation to dissolve. Next thing, I was straddling him on the sofa, as our lips rolled over one another's and his hands went sightseeing beneath my T-shirt.

'How come you stopped calling?' he asked, not exactly sounding hurt by it, just curious. *Ego.*

'Why do you think?' I asked.

'You fell in love with someone else?'

'A likely story,' I rolled my eyes. 'I just didn't think what we were doing was healthy.'

'Mmm, well, you know I've never been into all this wellness crap,' he said, cupping my jaw with his palms.

I added, 'And anyway, you haven't exactly been calling me.'

'I've always left it to you.'

'Why?'

'You're in charge,' he said, and it made us both smile humorously. Suddenly, it felt like we were very in tune with one another.

'Are you dating anyone?' I asked, as nonchalantly as if he were a totally platonic friend.

He laughed. 'I'm not a dater.'

'Are you sleeping with anyone, is what I really mean.'

He responded with absolute conviction, 'Only you, darling.'

'Hardly!' I said with a snort of laughter.

'I've just been laying low, really,' he added, moving my hair across my clavicle and over my shoulder, one side and then the other. 'I've been working hard and haven't been going out that much.'

Whether I believed him or not, I liked the idea that when I'd been stressing over the thought of him in a playground of obliging women, he'd actually been sitting quietly in his kitchen or bedroom, thinking about the last time he'd had sex with me. Turned on by it, I went in for a long plunging kiss to put a full stop on the conversation. He hooked his long fingers underneath the crook of my bottom and stood up, taking me with him. I wrapped my legs around his slim hips, hitching one foot onto the other, so that I was fastened to him like a belt.

When we drew breath, he caught sight of himself in the mirror over my shoulder. 'God, you're right, I do look like I've been working out.' I glanced over my shoulder, curious to see what he was seeing, since I had totally fabricated the compliment. He reached one of his hands further beneath me, admiring his long, spindly forearm. 'Wow,' he said.

'What do you want to do?' I asked his reflection.

He shifted me higher up onto his hips, like a child, and looked at me square in the face. 'Shall we get you dressed?'

Of course, I'd always known that the jean and T-shirt combo wasn't going to cut it for Leo, which may have been why I decided to start the encounter in the outfit. Defiance, or the pretence of it, at least.

'Are you choosing, or am I?' I asked, trying to recall what kind of a state my wardrobe was in. We were back to our old ways faster than I could've imagined.

'I am.' He carried me through to the bedroom and placed me on the bed. I sat there with my legs outstretched in front of me as he drew the wardrobe open and peered inside. He shifted through the garments with precision and intrigue, like one of the fashion editors at work might do, until he found something he liked: a little black dress. For all his everyday eccentricity, his kinks sure were basic.

'OK,' I said, a jeer of complicity with myself in my voice. Playing dress-up for Leo amused more than it aroused me, which perhaps made me feel more in control of the situation, especially since it seemed to turn him on so inexplicably. He took the dress off the hanger and held it out. I removed my shoes, jeans and T-shirt. 'Nice bra,' he said, nodding at the lacy number that was just about ready for the bin with its slack elastic.

'This old thing?' I said, again a little joke to myself, but he also tittered at that one. I stepped into the well of the dress. Then I turned my back to him and reached to lift my hair out of the way. I had bought that dress specifically for work events that were on the smarter side, and it was also one that I used to measure whether I'd gained or lost weight by how tight it felt, an unhealthy trick I'd learnt from my mother. I noted that I'd lost a little weight as Leo pulled the zip up along the length of my spine.

'Knickers?' he asked.

'Top drawer.'

Discerningly, he rummaged through my underwear. Next thing I knew, he was holding up none other than a pair of white cotton briefs. My gym pants.

'Surely these are by no means sexy?' I said, taking them from him and holding them taught in front of me. They were the kind of pants that Clara would call 'illegal'.

'Trust me. They are,' he said.

OK, it's your fantasy. I pulled them right up to my waistline, beneath the dress. Leo handed me a pair of heels to step into. I spread my arms in proud display, *Ready!*

Who am I? I thought, at least in retrospect.

He looked me up and down with a light smile, impressed by his own work. 'Are you an art dealer?'

'Am I?'

'I think you are.'

I'd have preferred schoolgirl, given my sensitivity about edging towards the end of my twenties, but hey, art dealer it was.

'I gather you want to buy a painting today, sir?' I said, taking on the deep voice of a middle-aged cigar-smoking man. 'Let me show you our private collection.' The heels clicked along the wooden floor, as I walked out of the bedroom. In the living room, I proceeded to price up all of the mirrors, prints and light fixtures that had been bought by Clara's parents. I started with low prices – 'five pounds, twenty-four pence' – and then I could see that my humour was taking him out of the fantasy, so I went up to the thousands.

The dialogue was, as ever, predictable:

'Isn't there another way I can pay?'

'Yes, but it wouldn't be professional.'

'You don't look like someone who plays by the rules.'

'You think I'm badly behaved?'

'Are you?'

'I don't mix work and pleasure.'

'Come on, let me bend you over the table.'

'That's not an appropriate way to talk to your art dealer.'

'But it's turning you on, isn't it?'

'I'm married.'

And on and on it went. I knew that it was my job, in this situation, to resist and stave him off, but I also really just wanted to get into the sex part.

So, I finally gave in. The art dealer said: 'I'm bound by professionalism and my wedding vows. If you want me, you'd have to force me.' As soon as I said it, I felt guilty for sexualizing, and possibly even trivializing, every woman's deepest fear. But before I could dwell on it, I was up against the wall, pinned at all different body parts, my movement and breath constricted. I felt even more remorseful for enjoying it. But it wasn't my fault that I'd been brought up in a culture that had celebrated content – from acclaimed literature to pornography – which was based around demeaning my whole gender. I couldn't help the fact that social order placed me in a position of powerlessness. So, how could I help but find being soaked in control and authority anything but arousing? How could I help but crave an all-out patriarchal fuck?

The gym pants came off. I used my free hand to wriggle my fingers down into the warm space between Leo's legs, but apparently, he was less turned on than I was. 'Art dealer's not doing it for you?' I mumbled, my lips still beneath his.

He let out an irritated, throaty breath of air. 'It will come.'

'Don't worry, I'm a huge fan of half-mast,' I said lightly.

'Don't do that,' he said, releasing me from his grip, suddenly very serious.

'Do what?'

'Don't make a joke out of it. It makes it worse.'

'Sorry,' I said sincerely, eager to learn how to be empathetic to the pitfalls of manhood. 'Can I do anything to help?'

He cleared his throat and went to get his wallet from his coat pocket. I understood what it had come to. Like Omni, Leo always seemed to have several almost finished grams of illegal substances floating upon his person. Hospitality life.

'Do you want some of this?' he asked, shaking a little packet of numbness at me. I found it hard to believe it was going to make his erectile problem any better.

'Not yet,' I said, implying that I would of course join him in being wild and fun later, even though I didn't want to. If I was going to have sex for the first time in four months with a person whom I knew I shouldn't be having sex with, I wanted to at least feel it.

'Do you mind if I do?'

'Of course I don't mind.'

Art dealer persona firmly shaken, I stepped out of the high heels and walked to the kitchen to mix up a vodka lime soda while he filled himself with powdered optimism. When I returned, he was sitting on one of the dining chairs looking weathered, like he'd just been through something dramatic in the short time I was gone. Seeing him like that, I felt bad for him. He really was just a sweet guy with a shitload of issues so deeply embedded that no one would ever be able to make sense of them. I could relate to that.

I placed the glasses on the table and sunk down onto his lap, folding my arms around his shoulders. I rubbed his back comfortingly, perhaps maternally, and let my warm neck fall against his.

'I've missed you,' he said, wrapping his own arms around me and relaxing into the embrace.

'I've missed you too,' I said softly. 'I didn't think we were going to do this ever again.'

'Don't be silly. We'll go on doing this forever.'

'Do you think we'll still be sleeping with each other when we're both married to other people? Have an agreement that we're allowed to meet up once a year?'

'I love it when you give that chat,' he whispered, all lusty suddenly.

I don't know what exactly it was that aroused him so much about the hypothetical infidelity contract. Was it the wrongness of it, or was it the idea that my desire for him was so uncontrollable that he'd always come a little above whoever I eventually did fall in love with? If I ever did fall in love. Whatever it was, we were back in the game, with a real, old-fashioned pre-narcotic hard on. Leo was like a worm on my hook. I slid off his lap and waited, hands on hips, as he fumbled to undo his belt and trousers. And then, out it came, as if it was seeing the light for the first time. *Here I am, ready to conquer the world.* I quickly stifled the bright-eyed warrior, lest it should disappear again. Leo held onto my waist and squeezed his eyes shut, probably concentrating hard on keeping momentum going. I gripped his shoulders and looked up at the ceiling, trying to remember what it was about this that I always craved so much. Between us both, we really were shrinking the act of sex to its most primal purpose: two bodies seeking satisfaction from one another.

It had been so long since anything had been up there that it started to get painful pretty quickly. As much as I'd wanted it to start, I now wanted it to end. I knew he wasn't likely to finish. I couldn't remember if I'd ever known him to. So, I suggested we take a cigarette break from the job. He could never resist a cigarette after hearing the word spoken out loud.

I collapsed on the sofa, naked, and lit a Marlboro Gold, imagining Clara entering the next day, pinching her nose. Leo put on his boxers and joined me. We blathered and chain-smoked for almost an hour, breaking only to refill our glasses. As I got sleepier and sleepier, he got chattier and chattier. At some point, I shut my eyes and almost drifted off. When I opened them, Leo was standing up, pink trousers on, buttoning up the floral shirt.

'What are you doing?' I asked.

'I'm going to leave you to sleep,' he said. 'You're tired. And I'll just keep you up.'

That was not part of the deal. I was in it for the whole package: sex, pillow chat and waking up in the morning with my skin against the skin of another human being.

'I want you to stay,' I said. It was a command, not a request.
'I can't sleep, I'm still wired,' he said. 'It's better that I go.'

I reached for the throw at the end of the sofa and wrapped it around me, in the interest of preserving a touch of decency while he walked out on me. I arranged myself in a position that said, 'I am not happy about this', without having to actually say it: arms crossed over my stomach, knees firmly pressed together, chin tilted upwards, mouth a straight line and absolutely no eye contact. *Ice him out, Jax, that's sure to work!*

He had his coat on and was adjusting the collar. Then, finally, he crouched down in front of me, taking my shoulders in his hands. 'All good?' he said. I gave him one small shrug, with my eyes on the brass floor library lamp in the corner. Leo leaned in to kiss me and I offered my cheek. 'Don't be angry,' he said, and I gave him another shrug, but still no words. He sighed and took his phone from his pocket. I glanced down to see the Uber app. He really was going. I was about to be left alone, post-coitus, in the silence of the flat. I couldn't quite take it tonight.

'Can I have a line, please?' I said, finally looking him in eye. A small bit wouldn't hurt, I reasoned with myself.

'You want one?'

'Yes. I do.'

'OK.'

Like sex, drugs were something that I hadn't done for a long time, but unlike sex, they were something I did not miss. But as Leo sat down to organize a line, I felt, for now at least, that I had him back. So, I consumed the drugs to keep myself awake, and then I couldn't feel anything when the sex resumed, except for a tingle of victory that he was still there.

By the time I finally lured him to actual bed, it was getting light outside. He took a Xanax to help him wind down and soon fell asleep, while I lay there wired, too scared to take one in case my heart stopped. I nestled close to the snoring, skinny man beside me, taking advantage of the opportunity for skin-on-skin contact.

CHAPTER 4

Dymfy was close to having a mental breakdown when I arrived on Saturday. Cause of near breakdown: a dead hedge.

I found out while I was purchasing a £4 oat milk cappuccino from an artisan coffee stand, when she sent me a WhatsApp simply stating: 'THEY SENT A DEAD HEDGE!!!'

The hedge was a backdrop for press photographs, which I'd ordered from a reputable botanist. I very much doubted that it was dead. I responded to her message with a fallen leaf emoji, which I quickly realized was the response of someone who'd taken class As and had less than two hours sleep. I added that I'd be there soon. Then I opened the WhatsApp group chat made up of myself, Omni and Alice, entitled, 'No More Clara'. The joke was that Clara never replied to the group with the four of us on it, so Omni had started a new one to avoid bombarding her with our never-ending inanity. The group was sometimes used to talk about – or, admittedly, to moan about – Ed. I started typing as I waited for my coffee.

> Me:
> Is it wrong that I'm not 100% thrilled about
> the engagement?
> Am I jealous???

Omni:
Jealous?! Of Ed?

Me:
Lol

Omni:
Think she will outgrow him way quicker than
she thinks sadly
Everyone is sooo desp to get married

Me:
Societal fault

Omni:
Don't think anyone thinks about who they
gunna be stuck with
They just think, oh well at least I'll be
married! ✅

By the time I picked up my coffee and walked out, we were
twenty-five lines into reasons we didn't think the engagement
was right. Alice hadn't said anything, which worried me.
Two singletons with red-hot overdrafts slamming the concept of marriage sounded like bitterness. But when there was
a grown-up in a committed relationship involved, it carried
more gravitas. Luckily, I knew how to spark her interest.

Me:
Might have to steal that ring to buy a flat 💍

Within seconds of seeing the word 'ring', Alice was typing . . .

> Alice:
> It's not a diamond.
> Not that it matters. But Ed told Tim it was
> And it's not
> It's aquamarine
>
> Me:
> Morning
> How's Coil-gate?
>
> Alice:
> I think I gave birth to it.
>
> Me:
> Ouch! Are you OK???
>
> Alice:
> I'm fine
> Bathroom is a crime scene
>
> Omni:
> How's Tim taking that?
>
> Alice:
> I hate him.
>
> Me:
> 😂 😂 😂 😂 😂

Omni:
How do you spell chilli

Me:
As in chili 🌶️
Or chilly 😶
Or chile 🫓

Omni:
🌶️ that one. Thanks!

I wanted to tell them about Leo, but felt awkward divulging it in writing, so I put my phone away. I was feeling unexpectedly satisfied about the whole exchange – bar the unnecessary drug-taking – since we'd had morning sex and he'd kissed me outside Canonbury Station for a long time, showering me with compliments.

When I arrived at the event space, Dymfy and the hedge in question were having a standoff in the entrance. In fairness to her, it did look pretty dead. She glared at it with her hands on her hips, as if her eyes had the power to miraculously trigger photosynthesis. The hedge stood firm and stubborn.

I analysed it for a few seconds and then conceded, 'OK, I see what you mean.'

'I need to get the *Daily Mail*, Jax,' she snapped. 'I've invited Elizabeth Hurley, for God's sakes! The *Daily Mail* will not feature a picture of Elizabeth Hurley against a dead hedge!'

I had been known to have mental breakdowns over something as trivial as a hedge before, but that day, I was too hungover too care.

'It'll be fine,' I said. 'We can retouch the photos.'

'You're hungover,' she said accusatorily, turning to me.

'I am not hungover.'

'You have wine face!'

'Must be a backlog,' I said, and she huffed, unamused. 'Dymfy, how about we just don't use the hedge? I'll set up a new space for photos and we can return the hedge and get a refund. It'll look cooler anyway. A hedge is so last year's red carpet.'

An irritated gurgle came from the back of her throat. Clearly, she was annoyed that I'd come up with an easy solution when she'd just put all her energy into freaking the fuck out. 'I am not paying a penny for that hedge,' she spat, before whirling off, no doubt to administer some kind of pre-event enema.

I called the botanist and asked them to remove the structure. Meanwhile, I located a table and started to assemble Dymfy's books on top of it, like the leaning tower of Pisa.

The book was called *All About Ageing*. Topics covered were wrinkles, retinoids, vaginal rejuvenation, hormone rebalancing, injectables, glycation, non-surgical facelifts, surgical facelifts, micro-currents, water retention, the sun, bone density, bingo wings, swelling and scabbing, downtime, fat dispersal and other non-invasive and highly invasive procedures to 'heed off Mother Time'. Dymfy's face sparkled off the hardback cover, enticing neurotic Soul Cyclers at Planet Organic and time-weary travellers at Heathrow to part with £18.99: 'If you buy this book you can look as unnaturally gorgeous as me, with my big white teeth, glossy mane and gilded skin.' When the book first arrived at the office, I picked it up excitedly, exclaiming that I couldn't wait to read it, while internally swearing that I never would.

When I finished the book tower arrangement, I stepped back and took a picture on my iPhone. The photographer was not there yet, despite the fact that he was meant to arrive early to take stills, despite the fact that I'd told him the start time of the event was an hour earlier, given his propensity for lateness. I had to double check my emails to make sure that I'd definitely confirmed his services, doubting myself, rather than the 25-year-old Australian rave-lover who thought he was Mario Testino even though he made a living snapping B- to Z-listers clutching champagne flutes. I had, indeed, confirmed him. I fired off a message enquiring as to where the hell he was.

'Jax, we have a problem,' said Eliza, Dymfy's beauty assistant who was helping me on the door.

Another problem?

'That girl from *Made in Chelsea* who we had to turn down five times got herself on the list. Dymfy's going to freak!'

'She's not on the list, darling,' I said, trying so hard not to sound impatient. 'I did the list.'

'She's Orlov's plus-one!'

'Oh shit,' I said. Orlov was *Close Up*'s main investor. 'How do you know?'

'Inside information.'

I internally rolled my eyes. Eliza was the editor-in-chief's daughter and always had inside information.

'OK, well, nothing we can do about that,' I said, deciding that she could explain it to Dymfy, who seemed to have personal beef with said reality TV star.

'Can you believe she is so desperate to come that she had to go through our Russian investor?' Eliza cried, aghast. She loved the drama.

'Of course I can believe it. She's breasts-and-best-foot-forward socially aggressive,' I said, noting the fact that I was in – what one might call – *a stinking mood.*

'I wonder if anyone's ever described me that way,' a familiar voice rubbed at my eardrum.

I turned around and was caught off guard by those ice-grey eyes. 'Ah, thank goodness. My avant-garde mixologist!' I said, and then realized that it sounded very derisive.

'This is my team,' he said, suddenly businesslike, as a line of bearded men and one heavily tattooed woman trickled in carrying large boxes.

'Great, if you could set up at that table over there, that would be amazing,' I said, pointing him to the trestle at the end of the room.

'Thank you so much again for booking us,' he said, and my heart started to ache from the earnestness of it.

'Let me help you,' I said, following him to the trestle with a feeling that his energy may have the power to heal me on so many levels.

'Don't worry, you must have a lot to do.'

'Yes, but I don't want to do any of it,' I said, and he smiled with comprehension. Then, just in time to burst my sudden bubble, in walked the photographer, looking like he'd just rolled out of Fabric.

'You're late,' I said, even though he wasn't technically late for the *actual* start time.

'And you look Amish,' he retorted, evidently referring to the floor-length, pie-crust poplin dress that I had opted for to make up for the exposing positions I'd been in the night before.

'I don't give a fuck,' I snapped.

'You should. You should start giving a fuck about your life,' he said with mock concern.

'I give a fuck about my life, not about whether you think I look Amish or not. Thanks, Kris.' As far as I was concerned, anyone with a subsidiary K in their name was not to be trusted.

'Someone needs to get laid,' he jeered.

Both furious at the suggestion that lack of male penetration made women crabby, and embarrassed that Ned had overheard the insult, I had an urge to shout, 'I've been fucking all night!' Instead, I said, 'Just go and make Dymfy feel important, please,' attempting to get him on side by making a spiteful joke.

When I turned back to the trestle, I caught Ned's eye. He looked away quickly, and I sensed that he had just seen a side to me that he really did not like.

Eliza and I stood at the door with iPads, checking off guest's names as they entered. I imagined each person with a floating hashtag above their head: #BeautyEditor #BeautyInfluencer, #SkincareAddict, #MakeupJunkie, #Aesthetician, #SurgeonsOfInstagram, #AntiageingExpert, #TurnBackTime. And, of course, #PlusOneofRussianInvestor.

My hangover seemed to be getting progressively worse with each name that I ticked off, until my legs started to ache as much as they did midway through a high-impact cardio class. Eventually, I could barely stand up. With authority and purpose, I turned to the assistant and said, 'Hold the fort for a sec, my love. I have to check on things inside.' I had a very clear plan in my head. I picked up my refillable water bottle with the *Close Up* logo glaring off it and headed inside. I marched across the room, briskly, in an attempt to channel Alice. But despite my obvious sense of intention, #PlusOneofRussianInvestor stepped obstructively into my path.

'Hi, so great to see you!' she said in a high-pitched voice that was really more like a whine. 'It's been ages.'

I looked at her blankly for a few seconds, before forcing my lips into a smile. I was fairly certain that we'd never met. I presumed that she'd clocked my *Close Up* water bottle and decided that I was someone she should pretend to know, so that she wouldn't have to cozy up to a fifty-year-old perverted tycoon in order to get onto guest lists for the rest of her life.

'Where was it we met again?' I asked, rather meanly, but I was curious as to what she would invent. Also, I felt shit about my own life having nose-dived into a bag of poison and couldn't help but want to bring others down with me.

'We met when I had, like, twenty thousand followers,' she said.

That wasn't the question, I wanted to say, but knew it would be too rude. *I don't care how many followers you have.* Even ruder. I would've really loved to answer with, *I'm not on social media,* but that would have been a lie, although I only used it for research and stalking purposes, not to post anything myself. Instead, I asked, 'How many followers do you have now?'

'Seventy thousand!' she almost gasped, with so much joy that I felt bad for having mocked her in my hungover little brain. I guessed that she thought I was someone who measured people's worthiness of my attention by how many followers they had, and perhaps I should've been flattered that she cared for my approval, but I was more concerned by what that said about me.

'Wow!' I said, with forced awe. 'You're killing it!' Then I excused myself and beelined for the mixologist's trestle, which they really had transformed into a feast for the eyes, using crates of different sizes, fruit, flowers and hanging greenery.

Ned was pouring orange-brown liquid into an ice-filled amber glass lab beaker. If a Victorian chemist had seen it in a crystal ball, they'd think the future world had gone mad. I slipped behind the table and tapped the back of his hand with my logoed, eco-friendly water bottle. 'I need a favour. Can you pour a dirty martini into this?'

His eyes flickered towards me and even though his expression didn't change whatsoever, I had a feeling that he was judging me. 'We don't make dirty martinis, I'm afraid.'

'For me, though?' I said, pressing my hands together in prayer. 'I hired you. I'm your boss.' That time his expression did change – from unreadable to very unimpressed. I jumped in apologetically, 'OK, I'm not your boss. But I'm really thirsty and I can only drink a dirty martini right now.'

'You want me to put vodka into your bottle, so that you can pretend it's water?' he reiterated my request back to me in plain terms. Where was that earnest grey-eyed man I'd met the day before?

'I'm extremely hungover and hair of the dog is the only thing that's going to help right now. I can despair about the state of my life tomorrow, when I don't have to work.'

Without saying anything, Ned took out all the ingredients for a dirty martini. He didn't respond to my emphatic thank yous. He just made the drink, then disappeared underneath the trestle with my water bottle. Seconds later, he was up again, returning it to me full of crystal-clear liquid energy. I took one sip and just the taste made me feel better.

I knew I should go back to the door to help Eliza, but the martini had given me a sense of power, and I thought, *Fuck it!* I'd done door duty on my own more times than I could count. I was the senior one in the situation, even if she was the editor-in-chief's daughter, and I had decided that I was not going back to that door.

Instead, I would hang out with this confusing mixologist, who may or may not have disliked me at that point. I leaned against the wall behind him, sipping from the bottle, and took out my phone. Clara had sent a message to the WhatsApp group that she never used. It was a photo of her and Ed in front of the Eiffel Tower. I gathered that she wasn't going to be home that night to watch *Roma* with me, as we'd planned. It probably wasn't exactly the best hangover film, anyway.

How nice to be taken to Paris, on a whim.

The party was nearing its end and I was one martini down. One was all it took for me to dig my heels into the ground and refuse to be dragged home alone by my other self. I sent out a round of, 'Where are you?' and 'Plans tonight?' messages to all of my active WhatsApp groups and individual threads. I didn't want another big night. I just wanted to sit at the pub, basking in the reassurance of friendly company and go home feeling ready to pass out, rather than arrive home to stew with anxiety about the absence of Clara, the uncertainty of my living arrangement and whether or not sleep would be available to me.

Alice was the first to reply that she was 'working/recovering'. I imagined Tim – whom I assumed must have been a completely different person behind closed doors – bringing her a hot water bottle while she sat up in bed with her Celine spectacles on, typing furiously on her laptop like the adult she was. She'd ignore him, until he kissed her head and she'd suddenly look up and they'd share one of those moments of complete comfort in each other's presence that I occasionally caught flicker between them.

Omni hadn't even read my message and I suddenly wondered why she'd needed to spell chilli. Was she making a chilli con carne for some dinner party that I wasn't invited to? Even as the thought arose, I knew it was ridiculous, but I couldn't stop it from lingering. Who had she invited?

Everyone else was either out of town – in the country – or at some pre-planned diary engagement. Spontaneity was no longer a thing, apparently.

Go home and be alone, Jax. What's the worst that could happen? Oh, you know.

By the time the guests started leaving, Dymfy was tipsy on avant-garde cocktails, which made me want to become her best friend. There was something about drunk senior colleagues that I found magnetic. I wanted to squeeze into a corner with them, get equally drunk, share secrets and do anything that I could to please them. But Dymfy was with her real friends – which made me yearn for mine – and I still had work to do. For one thing, I had to sit with the world's most infuriating photographer and go over every single picture to name-check important faces and point out 'faceless fillers', who were the people invited to fill the room. Kris and I positioned ourselves just behind the bar, on folding chairs. I immediately wished that we hadn't chosen to do the job right behind Ned, who was busily serving the last guests, because I felt self-conscious about my flippant labelling of the faceless fillers as, 'No one cares' or, 'Perma-plus-one' or, 'The brief was fresh and trendy so let's not namecheck Dumbledore'.

By the time we reached shot 267, I was feeling hot and sweaty and a little nauseous. I picked up my martini-filled water bottle and slipped out the back door for a breath of fresh air in among the rubbish bins. I slumped against the cool brick wall, urging my stomach to settle. My phone buzzed in my hand. Omni had responded. She'd sent a picture of two toothbrushes next to one another, the bristles intimately touching.

> Omni:
> At the risk of sounding like an ageing
> bachelor with commitment issues, Mr Magus
> brought his toothbrush with him last night . . .
> From the pub 😞
> And left it here
> 😱
> ?????????????????????????

I laughed and felt my stomach draw tight at the same time. I was always fearful that Omni was the next one to be sucked into the abyss of domestic entanglement. I was selfish about my single status, in that I loved being single, as long as other people were too. I didn't want a relationship, though at times I did feel under pressure to want one. I wouldn't have given up my golden twenties and all that single life had given me – friendships grown and solidified under the luxury of time, full nights spent out with no one to answer to, impromptu weekends away, recounting amusing sexual encounters to colleagues the morning after, the innate understanding and camaraderie shared with other single people – for trips to IKEA and group couples' holidays in the Lake District. But the more people who dropped off, the more anxious I became about being left behind.

The door opened and Ned came out holding a rubbish bag, his grey optics glowing like the eyes of a wolf.

'Do you have a cigarette?' I asked, not because I really felt like one, but because I thought that if he was a smoker it would be something that we could bond over.

'I always told myself I'd quit when I was twenty-five,' he said ambiguously.

'So did I.'

'I did quit.'

'Did you quit drinking too?'

'No, that wouldn't be ideal for my business.'

'Want to go to the pub?' I threw out. It was clear to me, in that moment, that I couldn't have been attracted to him – strangely attractive though he was – as I would never have been so bold as to suggest a drink otherwise.

'You're my boss, so I have to say yes, right?' he said, possibly joking, but more likely demanding an apology.

'That was a hideous thing to say. I'm not always such an idiot,' I promised. 'My best friend got engaged to someone who's not right for her, and I'm feeling a little sensitive.' It wasn't exactly true that Ed wasn't right for her, more that he wasn't right for an old version of her that I wanted back, but I felt I had to give my bad mood some weight that didn't seem entirely selfish.

He didn't buy it. 'That's probably the hangover. Alcohol depletes natural levels of serotonin in—'

'Are you mansplaining hangovers to me?' I said, unable to stop myself from becoming prickly again. Comedowns really are an awful thing. 'I can assure you I've had enough in my life to understand them.'

'I'm not mansplaining, I just know more about the science of alcohol than most people do,' he shrugged, placing the rubbish bag in one of the plastic recycling bins. 'Just like you know more about who's cool enough to be at a party than most people do.'

Sting! But point taken.

'Take it you're not interested in going to the pub with me, then?' I asked imploringly.

'I'm going to a cocktail bar, which you're welcome to join me at. Market research.'

'Research on me?'

'Well, I guess you are my quintessential customer.'

Even though it was his own business he was talking about, I felt like it was a dig. I could just imagine the business plan: *Our quintessential customer is a female, middle-class millennial embedded in the London rat race, who wants something quirkier than your average cocktail, but isn't overly adventurous.* Little did he know that my drink orders were stuck in the nineties.

But, dig or no dig, I could be his guinea pig for the night. As long as I didn't have to go home.

The cocktail bar was as contrived as the ones that Omni and I joked about having to go to if we ever succumbed to a dating app. An urban millennial shelter where they served drinks called, 'Kiss and Don't Tell My Wife' out of vessels that had been repurposed so many times they barely served any function. I couldn't bring myself to opt for a CBD mojito or a Caipir-heal-ya, so I was drinking lavender vodka out of an iPhone case welded inside a small vase, having been denied a plain old martini ('And please don't ask me if we serve Pinot Grigio').

Two cocktails in and I was wistfully digging up old photos of Clara, as if she were an ex. 'This is how she used to dress,' I said, showing Ned a photo from a music festival three years back in which Clara was wearing a scruffy combination of clothing and smoking a rollie. 'Now she dresses like a trophy wife. And she would never smoke, now. She wouldn't even come to a festival.'

'Tragedy,' said Ned, staring at the picture.

He'd gone from endearingly earnest to annoyingly sardonic and I couldn't help but feel that there was something about me which brought that out in him.

'It is a tragedy, actually. When someone loses their sense of what they want to do in life to please the person they're with. That, I categorize as a generational tragedy.'

'How do you know this isn't the person she's always wanted to be?' he challenged. 'Maybe now that she's found someone who she can be her true self with, she's the happiest she's ever been.'

'It doesn't work like that. You don't figure out who you are when you meet someone else. You figure that out when you're on your own.'

'Have you got that figured out?'

'How do you know I'm on my own?' I slurred accusatorily, hovering the lavender-filled beaker between us.

'I didn't say you were on your own. I mean, I don't care if you are or not. I was just asking if you'd figured everything out.'

'No one's figured everything out!' I said, too defensive, and a bit of liquid sloshed onto my hand. *Stupid vase.* 'I am on my own. I mean I'm single. Never really on my own. But I don't have a problem with it.'

'That's good. Neither do I. But I don't think that being with someone else means that you can't grow as a person.'

'When you're someone like Clara, and you're with someone

like Ed, you can't,' I said with finality and took a sip of the potent concoction.

'Are you worried about her or yourself?' Ned asked.

I eyed him over the top of the mini vase and thought about whether to lie. 'Both,' I admitted, thinking that I might as well own it since he would never have believed me if I'd said anything else.

'What is it you're scared of?'

Scared?

'I'm irrationally scared of people who lie down at the front of group photos. And I don't really trust people who carry hand cream.'

He looked confused, and said, 'You'll be fine,' stirring his own whiskey cocktail with a disused pen.

'Where am I going to live?' I whined. I suddenly felt like I wanted this grey-eyed man to fix all of my problems in this absurd bar, which we'd entered through a fridge.

'You'll find somewhere, like everyone else manages to,' he said, which I guessed meant, *You don't deserve special treatment.*

'Where? How?' My tone was uncannily similar to the reality star I'd met earlier.

Ned raised both his shoulders and his eyebrows, like it was so obvious. 'Go onto Google and type in "London flat share for X budget".'

The words 'flat' and 'share' next to each other prompted an image to arise in my mind of strangers with appalling hygiene standards borrowing my toothbrush and my stomach stirred anxiously. Suddenly, I felt like we were on different planes because he could never understand how much his simple 'Go onto Google and type in "London flat share for X budget"' made me panic. He didn't understand that I had built a whole world in which my friends had become my family and I had relationships with them that were more intimate than even some romantic relationships could be. He didn't know that I had spent all the years of my twenties weaving an interconnected structure of people who made me feel safe, and just typing the words 'flat share' into Google would be like an axe to that feeling.

'Do you live in a flat share?' I asked.

'I do.'

I felt guilty for thinking everything I thought, when there was this hard-working and potentially very successful entrepreneur with such gorgeous eyes sitting in front of me, but I also couldn't help but imagine introducing him to Clara and Ed as my boyfriend. 'This is my boyfriend, Ned. We live with ten strangers in a flat share.'

I had no idea why I'd suddenly forced him into an imaginary relationship with me.

'I just really love living with my best friend,' I said, by way of explanation for my sulkiness. 'Clara and I get on so well. I'll never find anyone I can live with that easily.'

'I know,' said Ned gently, taking a sip of his frothy whiskey. 'But things change.'

I didn't want things to change. I never wanted anything to change, unless I was the one initiating it. Could you be a free spirit and a creature of habit at the same time?

'I'll also never be able to afford to take a pay cut now,' I said miserably. 'So I guess the journalist ship has sailed.'

'Well. At least you plan good parties,' he said with a humorous shrug.

'Thanks,' I responded glumly. I looked around at the Saturday night drinkers, ignoring the coldness of the night outside, cradled by the security of chemical connection. I couldn't help but wonder whether most people in the room were single.

We finished our drinks and asked for the bill. I offered my much overdrawn card, but Ned paid, insisting it was a business expense. I then became awkwardly too eager to please, having never been great at accepting generosity just for the hell of it. My sudden change in disposition made for a rather uncomfortable goodbye. It felt more like the end of a blind date than a friendly work drink, though it did culminate in my promising to book him for every event from there on.

When I opened Uber, I was informed that the surcharge was at 2.0. I stood there for a long few moments, deliberating whether to take the night bus home, stewing over the fact that it would land me at the end of the eerily quiet street with very few lights. In the end, I booked the Uber because I figured that being broke was better than being stabbed. When I was safe and warm in the car, I suddenly felt ridiculous for having not just got on the bus and berated myself for spending unnecessary money. I stared down at my screensaver in which tiny Clara and tiny me grinned out of the bathtub together. It was a snapshot of a moment of total innocence, a moment when we were both happy because we were together.

As I walked into the flat, I caught sight of myself in the living room mirror, the same one that Leo had admired his arms in the night before. I looked myself in the eye and shook my head, in a gesture of disapproval. For what, I wasn't entirely sure. I took a step closer and peered deep into the darkness of my eye sockets. The face sure as hell was not looking its finest. 'Wine face,' Dymfy called it. *Vodka face. Cigarette face. Cocaine face. Sad face.*

71

Desperate to see myself as something brighter than a weathered piece of physiognomy, I pulled every last piece of clothing from my person and stood in front of my naked reflection. 'An attractive body is like a business-class ticket to life,' my mother had always said, feeding me the dangerous message young and often enough for it to have to embedded itself into my psyche. My gaze dropped to the bloated midriff concealing what used to be a six-pack, and I could've sworn that my left tit – which had always been lower than the right – had dropped another centimetre.

Fully committed to the impromptu body analysis, I slipped off my knickers and cast my eyes over the part of myself that I never knew how to refer to, since I'd heard a tantric healer on a podcast say that 'vagina' was a misused word. My first thought was, *God, I need a wax.* Then I pinched each lip with my thumb and forefinger and peeled them apart, making a sudden small gasping sound. I wasn't sure I'd ever examined the inner layers before. Everything looked squelchy and rather odd to me. There were so many bits that I'd never known about, even though I'd had this thing my whole life. Instinctively, I turned around and hinged into a yogic forward bend, gazing at my reflection from in between my legs. *No chance of anyone getting in that way,* I thought. Proudly anally retentive.

I stood up to full height and took a step back, to see myself as a shape, not an orifice. Looking at each dip and curve made me want to pick up the phone to a certain someone. Logically, I knew that I probably shouldn't get in touch, but something kept drawing me to it. The darkness of it, perhaps. Eventually, I couldn't resist. Though I knew I was in danger of falling into Can't Stop Thinking Of Him again, I reopened WhatsApp and messaged, speedily.

Me:
Heading home, want to come hang
out again? X

I picked up my clothes from the floor and went into my bedroom to choose an outfit, in case he said yes. When my phone
pinged out aggressively, I jumped on it so fast that a pain shot
right into a temperamental disc in my spine.

Leo:
Having a night in darling I am quite hungover x

I winced, grabbing the side of my body as a hot spasm shot
through the left side of my back. I tried to urge my torso
upright, but it was gone. I was lopsided. It always happened at
moments of high stress. There would be no Legs, Bum or Tum
workouts for at least three weeks now. So much for a goddamn
business ticket. I had always thought that sex was a way to stay
connected to my body, but in doing so I had totally given up
ownership of it. It no longer felt interesting unless it was being
touched or looked at by a foreign entity.

I threw the phone onto the bed, irritated with Leo for being
too hungover, furious with myself for texting, and hobbled to
the bathroom, still clutching the side of my body. Suddenly, I
wished that Ned hadn't gone home. I wanted to sit in a dark
alcove with him and divulge my deepest insecurities over vodka,
crudités and cigarettes. I wanted to burn the candle of my soul
at both ends, until it was fully singed and then start over.

I wiped off my make-up and brushed my teeth. Then I slid
into bed, weighted beneath the heavy, crumpled duvet and
closed my eyes. Tomorrow would be a new day, but the same

really. God, the relentlessness of life. *At least you plan good parties*. I imagined my headstone – supposing I were to drop dead from bad ecstasy or a disco ball to the head – with the epitaph reading, 'Knew all the best venues.'

And then, in a moment of epiphany, I realized that Ned had a point. I'd always felt internally ashamed that my only service to the world was to plan a good bash, though, externally, it was my *thing*. Actually, planning parties was something that many people were completely befuddled by. The prospect of planning a hen party sent the most level-headed of bridesmaids into a crescendo of madness that led them to request their friends to block out entire weekends in their diaries, a year in advance, and wire large sums of money for middle-aged men to flash their ding-dongs. Personally, I'd always thought that I could plan a hen party at a moment's notice, with my eyes closed and my wrists Velcro-ed together. It occurred to me that I'd be the one planning Clara's.

And then I realized that Clara, of all people, was the least likely to be able to handle the responsibility of planning a wedding. She couldn't even host a birthday party.

But I could do it for her.

Two weeks later, I had come up with a new life plan: I was going to quit my job at *Close Up* in order to focus on becoming a freelance journalist, while financially supporting myself by acting as a freelance event planner.

This new trajectory was in part thanks to my cocktail with Ned, but was really solidified over a long, wine-soaked lunch with Clara and Bella. After only just intimating that I could help with Clara's wedding, they suddenly both got it into their heads that I was the only person in the world who could plan it. Bella even offered an initial down payment, so that I could start the creative research. She knew it was the only way I'd be able to pull the plug on *Close Up,* which she'd been trying to convince me to do for years.

The funny thing was that I had spent more time in my life fantasizing about Clara's wedding than I had fantasized about my own. Maybe it was the notion in the back of my mind that no one had the money to pay for my wedding, or my inherent disbelief that I'd ever get married, but it just wasn't something I'd thought about.

After that lunch, the thought of anything but resigning was out of the question. I was confident that I could draw in a few other clients to keep me ticking over, until the journalism career kicked off in the starry-eyed way that I thought it would. With my schedule in my own hands, I'd have the time to do all the reading and writing that I'd always wanted to and could pitch my ideas to an array of publications, not only *Close Up,* who tended to reject my more risqué, potentially career-defining pitches.

There was a café near the office, from which I bought overpriced cappuccinos whenever I felt the need to treat myself well after treating myself badly. It was full of green plants and had long communal tables punctuated by the freelance community, with everything but their television sets hooked up to the sockets along the floor. I had always envied their freedom to spend the days tapping away at creative projects, sipping silky coffees, no doubt living their best lives. I was sure that they didn't break all of their promises to go to the gym, because they could go whenever they wanted, without worrying about their stupid key card alerting an Orwellian boss to their late arrival. They could go on holiday whenever they wanted and work remotely, rather than submit a request form only to be told that, *Sorry, there are already too many staff members off that week, and no we don't care that you can only afford to go on holiday when you've been invited as a guest and that this is the only week you've been invited anywhere, because single people often complicate the bedroom situation on group trips.*

So, I requested a meeting with the editor-in-chief to hand in my notice. Unfortunately, when the day came, I was not in the buoyant mood I'd hoped to be because I'd run into a friend at Oxford Circus who'd told me that she'd run into Leo – when he was supposedly 'having a night in darling' – with a Gen Z he'd introduced as his girlfriend. I guessed she didn't know that I'd seen him recently and was hoping we could humorously trash him and said girlfriend, so she was understandably surprised when I suddenly went pale. It wasn't as much the surprise as it was the humiliation of being lied to while straddling someone on your sofa and the utter irritation with myself for having called him at all in the first place.

As I sat outside the editor-in-chief's office, waiting for her conference call to end, my thumbs wiggled in the air above the screen of my phone and I considered how best to play this. I decided to go with apparent ignorance to see if I could catch him in a trap, as I'd rather have the conversation face to face.

Me:
Morning. Having a night in tonight . . . want to come hang out?

One tick appeared and then the other. I archived the thread so that it wasn't the first thing I thought about every time I opened my WhatsApp.

Then the editor-in-chief summoned me. 'Jax, come in!' I entered to find her sitting behind her desk with an open box of beauty samples in front of her and a man standing behind her painting bleach into her hair and wrapping it up in foil. 'This is Alberto. I've just been on a call with the association of influencers. Did you know there was such a thing? A governing body whose sole purpose is to protect influencers. It's the most ridiculous thing I've ever heard – we're the ones who need protecting from *them*! Anyway, they're all in a tizz about click-to-buy editorials.' She a mass delegator, who tended to speak more than she listened, so I knew it would be a challenge getting in there with my resignation before she was arbitrarily roping me in to help with her next assignment because her own team were overwhelmed. I took a seat opposite her, wringing my hands while offering some helpful but not too helpful thoughts on influencers and affiliate sales. Before I'd even finished my sentence, she was emptying a handful of Dr Lancer beauty samples into my palms, saying, 'Here, these are great for Christmas stockings.'

I felt guilty for abandoning her ship when she was so generously offering up her stocking fillers. Suddenly, I wondered if I should really go through with it. I'd been prepping myself for what I thought would be her inevitable plight to change my mind, pep-talking myself to stand my ground, but now I would surely crumble at her first protestation thanks to the Lancer samples.

'How's life?' she asked. 'Dating anyone?'

'I'm not,' I said. 'But my best friend is getting married.' I was trying to steer the conversation in the right direction before she could start handing me more samples.

'Stop it!' she lifted out of her chair excitably. 'Shall we do a wedding feature?'

As she scrambled under the mound of papers on her desk and opened various drawers, I leapt in. 'That's actually what I wanted to talk to you about,' I said, hoping she wouldn't think that I was jumping on the feature idea. 'She's asked me to plan her wedding. It's quite a big job for me – good money – and also I really do want to start focusing on writing, and I don't feel that I have the time to do that here without slacking on special projects.' Finally, the editor-in-chief located her phone inside a full ring-binder. She snatched it up with a look of satisfaction for having found it all by herself. I wasn't sure if she'd heard what I said. Apologetically, I muttered, 'So, with huge sadness, I think I'm going to have to hand in my resignation.'

At that she finally glanced up at me with a look that could only be described as false disappointment. Alberto gave me a glint of a smile. 'Oh, darling,' she said with a sigh. 'I've been waiting for you to do this for years. Your brain's going to waste here. We'll miss you. But very best of luck!'

I felt my insides go still. I didn't know whether to be relieved or offended. No need to stand any ground after all.

After a very brief chat about the specifics of resigning and the helpful promise of an outstanding reference letter that I could use for all future employers to come, I left the editor-in-chief and Alberto in peace. When I stepped out of her office, I checked my phone immediately. There, waiting for me, was a response to my trap of a message.

> Leo:
> Would have loved that but have a
> friend's birthday
> How was rest of your weekend?

My blood started to curdle with anger and my good-time exterior solidified to ice. Instantly, I typed, without thought.

> Me:
> It was fun. Particularly when I was told
> that you have a girlfriend. That was a
> nice surprise.

No response to that one. None at all.

PART II

MAY 2019

CHAPTER 5

Being a 29-year-old woman is legitimately less fun than being a 28-year-old one because, no matter how much you love being single, the message you've been batting away – that your twenties are your Cinderella years, with a free pass to Happily Ever After, and that life turns into a pumpkin when you hit thirty – suddenly becomes a final warning.

'That was the most boring wedding I've ever been to.'

'The bit between the church and lunch was far too long.'

'The speeches were wank.'

'No one was dancing.'

'Because the music was shit.'

'That DJ was about a hundred years old.'

'Why would you have the dancefloor in a separate room?'

'Are we in Paris?' slurred Clara as we sat tightly packed in a taxicab, winding down an English country lane.

'I wish we were in Paris,' I said, squeezing her leg with one hand, while the other clutched the back of Alice's seat to ward off carsickness.

'Isn't it terrible, all the money people spend on weddings, then everyone is so rude about them?' said Omni from my other side.

'They won't be rude about my wedding!' said Clara, leaning into me. She was skirt-over-head hammered. 'Because, I have you,' she added, dropping the weight of her head onto my shoulder.

Indeed, I had spent six months thinking of little else than Clara's wedding. From the location-scouting trip to the Sicilian island of Pantelleria – where Bella, Clara and I had spent the weekend making mid-afternoon stops at seaside cocktail bars and drinking white wine on our hotel room balcony late into the night – to the endless meetings with florists, caterers and calligraphers, and, of course, the hen party spent crawling pubs in a canal boat, not a day had gone by that the event hadn't been at the forefront of my mind and on the tip of my tongue. Now it was only three weeks away, and in all honesty, I couldn't have been more excited for the very thing that I had thought would send me spinning with the fear of loss.

'Will you do my wedding when I get married?' asked Omni, winding down the window to let in the spring night air.

'Sure, we can have a joint one in the OAP home,' I remarked.

'I'll be joining you at this rate,' said Alice as she rejected the tenth call from Tim, whom she was midway through an argument with. They always had arguments when she did things without him.

Then, out of nowhere, Clara tapped me on the knee and said, 'You're such a good driver,' and the rest of us giggled. I'd always wanted to know what it would be like to live inside Drunk Clara's mind.

When we arrived back at the guesthouse, Omni reminded us all of the time that I'd locked myself out in the corridor of a similar guesthouse wearing nothing but a pair of knickers, having mistaken the bedroom door for the bathroom and gone downstairs, naked, to ask for a key. The memory sent Clara to the floor in a fit of hysterics. The story always tickled her, but she found it particularly hilarious in her current state.

'Luckily she wears shit knickers,' she rasped, clutching her stomach.

'The type of knickers hardly mattered at that point, given I was covering my tits with my forearm,' I said, reaching down to lift her off of the ground. I was a little concerned that her laughter might suddenly turn to tears, as sometimes happened. She rose to her bare feet, having lost her heels at some point in the night. I couldn't remember the last time I'd seen her so careless and free. Probably because I couldn't remember the last time that I'd seen her out without Ed. He hadn't been invited to the wedding we'd attended because it was an old friend who'd spent the past few years living in Australia and – like me – didn't believe in the tradition of plus-ones she'd never met. Even though we'd slated the wedding itself for having been badly organized, we had made a whole weekend of the trip to the country and I was loving every moment of it because it reminded me of old times.

'Come to our room for a nightcap,' Alice commanded. 'I have half a bottle of champagne left.'

'I need to get this one to bed,' I said, threading my arm through Clara's.

'It makes economic sense to finish the bottle,' said Alice, completely serious.

'Where's Ed?' Clara asked suddenly, in a languid sort of way.

'Ed's in London, love,' I reminded her. 'You're sleeping with me tonight.'

I would have loved nothing more than another glass of champagne, swathed in the laughter of my favourite people. It was so seldom that the four of us were alone together. But

I knew that Clara was one glass away from diving headfirst into the toilet, and I didn't want her to remember the night that way. So, I said goodnight to the others and led her back to our room, where I fed her crisps and water like she was a little puppy. Then I gave her a mini facial using products left over from life at *Close Up*, explaining each one in detail, like I used to do when we lived together.

'I miss living with you,' she said suddenly, looking up at me through droopy eyes from where she was sitting on the loo seat.

'I do too,' I said, smiling down at her sadly, as I dabbed an energizing serum beneath her eye socket.

I thought she was about to say something of great depth, but then she reached into my cosmetic bag and screeched, 'What is breast oil?', holding up the little apothecary bottle that I had spent £35 on because the shop assistant had convinced me that cultivating breast awareness would lead to the integration of my sexual and spiritual self.

'It's my bosom buddy,' I said breezily. At that, we were both off laughing again. It felt just like the pre-Ed days. Planning the wedding had given us so much more opportunity to spend time together, as Ed wasn't getting involved in the creative. I worried that it was going to make it that much harder when it was over, but I tried to avoid thinking too far into the future.

I helped her up from the loo seat and we went to bed in that giddy state. Every time we fell silent, the mattress would shake beneath us – 'Oh God, there she goes,' I'd say – and she'd erupt into hysterics again.

We went on like that, in the dark, for ages.

This is what happiness looks like.

*

I woke up on the day of the pre-wedding party with a burst of energy and reached for the glossy notebook that had 'FEMINIST' in block letters on the cover, to begin my morning pages. I'd read about morning pages in a book about creativity that I'd delved into, since I'd not been having the easiest time with writing. My creative juices just weren't flowing in that department. Every morning, I was supposed to free-write three pages without stopping or thinking about what I was writing. I was determined to stick to it, since I'd rarely stuck to anything I'd committed to. Every time I pledged to give up alcohol – even just for a week – I'd find an excuse to drink. Every time I made a promise that I'd work out every day, that damn disc in my spine would flare up after the first week and I'd have to stop all physical exertion for a month. Every time I threw my cigarettes in the bin, I'd see Alice smoking and think, *Fuck, she looks amazing, I want one.* But morning pages were my thing now.

When I got to the end of page three, I quickly flung the notebook aside and sprung out of bed. The sun was shining through my tall bedroom window and the trees outside were blooming pink. I stood there for a moment, smiling at the beauty of it. I was still in Clara's flat, though without Clara. She had, as I'd predicted, moved into Ed's swanky purpose-built pad, with the porter and gym, soon after they got engaged. Her own flat was on the market to sell, but thankfully, no interest had arisen – the one silver lining in the grey cloud of Brexit – so she'd let Omni move in with me until it did.

I dressed myself in leggings, a sports bra and tank top with the words 'Under Stand Me' across it in rainbow shades. Then I walked out into the spring day, looking like a poster girl for the middle class. I gazed up at the chimneys of the Georgian townhouses that you'd only find in London, against the perfect blue sky, and I thought, *God, I love life so much that I don't ever want to die.* Perhaps it was because I was still buzzing off my weekend in the country with my favourite people or perhaps it was because my period had just ended and I had that feeling that the sun had just come out after a storm, but whatever it was, I bounced my way to the gym thinking how lucky I was to live such a charmed and convenient city life.

I arrived five minutes before the start of the circuit class, like a weekly delivery. Although I was now a freelance person who could go to gym classes at my own leisure, my freelance status also meant that I could barely afford my ClassPass membership. But I did keep the cheaper package, namely because of that Friday morning circuit class, taught by Curtis, a six-foot-tall Jamaican who was quite literally my wet dream. I got problematically turned on when he yelled, 'Get down on your knees, ladies.'

When I entered the studio, Curtis was engrossed in a conversation with a woman much older than me. I hated it when older women were in the class because he flirted with them way more overtly than he flirted with me. I slipped my hands into the loops of a TRX strap and slid down into a back extension. I stretched my legs to their longest point and pushed my buttocks out, thinking that I must have looked vulnerable and submissive, two things that I had a problem being in real life. I was also trying to release tension from my shoulder joints. An acupuncturist who had been interviewed for *Close Up* once told me I held all of my emotions in those joints, which made my back problems worse. After a few seconds, I could tell that Curtis wasn't going to look, so I stood up and waited patiently like a grown-up until, finally, he came over.

'Morning,' I said, wearing the kind of inviting smile that I would never have given anyone in an outside-world scenario.

'Morning, treacle,' he said. 'How's the smoking?'

Curtis had picked up the smell of cigarettes on me one day and now asked whether I'd quit every time I saw him. I fabricated ebb and flow stories in which I had and then stories in which I'd fallen off the wagon to keep him hooked on the saga of my self-destructive habits.

'I'm two weeks clean,' I said, although I had smoked a few nights before. 'But tonight, I have a big party, so who knows?'

'Keep going, babe. You can do it,' he said, wrapping his fingers around the muscle of my bicep, sending a piteous thrill through me.

When I couldn't sleep, I had a failsafe method that involved me on one of Curtis' fitness retreats in some exotic country. I am, of course, a successful journalist by this point, which is how I can afford the retreat, or maybe I've been comped. Curtis and I end up alone together – sometimes it's a late-night swim, other times he comes to my four-poster bedroom to give me painkillers for my backache (turn on!) – and it always transitions into the same thing. We kiss and he undresses me, then silently makes love to me in a way that is entirely to drive my pleasure – as if! – until the real life me drifts off, for some God-known reason.

I couldn't tell whether the fantasy was totally bizarre or totally cliché, but either way, I knew it was definitely weird to use it as a lullaby.

Throughout class, Curtis seemed to be paying me more attention than usual, often manhandling me into the correct exercise position, and I thought, *Maybe he does fancy me more than the older women.* There's a good chance that I was imagining he was doing anything more than being a good circuit instructor, but who cares, because it sent a fire through me that I intended to keep alight for the party later. I needed it if I was going to run into Leo. There had been no more moonlight trysts since my last angry text message to him, but I'd heard on the grapevine that he had a 21-year-old girlfriend who could take more blow than him, which was a first. I hadn't told a single person that I'd privately gone through the emotions of someone who had found out that their boyfriend of ten years had been cheating on them. I still thought about him daily.

I wished that Leo could see me there in that circuit class, strong, fit, flirting with Curtis, holding a plank longer than anyone thought I could, and walking out to buy a green juice – he wouldn't know that I shouldn't have bought it because I couldn't afford such luxuries – like the self-nurturing adult that I was when I wasn't bending over some table for him. I wondered if his child lover worked out and took care of herself in between her coke benders. I wondered if they worked out together or did normal things like cook meals and watch *MasterChef* when they weren't snorting or fucking. I suddenly panicked that he might decide to bring her to the party. She wasn't invited – obviously – but it felt very Leo to disregard things such as formal invitations and just turn up, wanting to show her off, and also wanting to show off to her that he got invited to such fabulous parties.

I finished my green juice and headed over to the Mortimers' family home in Willesden, which was quite possibly my favourite place in the world. It had been the talk of the town – or at least their part of town – when they'd uprooted from their Kensington house to deep dark Willesden, which wasn't even at the point of gentrification. 'She thinks she's being cool. I'm surprised she hasn't bought up an ex-council block,' my mother had said, strangely snobby from her cluttered two bed. But she and everyone else had to swallow their small-minded words when they saw the place.

In among the rows of suburban-style north-west London houses was a large yard, and at the centre of the yard, a 4,000-square-foot structure which had once been a factory building. Derrick had taken the shell, stripped it back and redesigned it in his trademark mid-century style, full of floor-to-ceiling windows, unexpected curves and angular details. Bella's eccentric family heirlooms and rustic homeware brought a warm, cozy feel to the place. I loved nothing more than a whole weekend spent in that house, especially on a hangover, which I'd done many a time thanks to Bella's open-door policy.

When I arrived there that day, the first thing I saw was a van parked in the driveway with the avant-garde mixologist's company logo gleaming off the side. Ned's business had segued into something more like avant-garde set design, so I'd brought him on board to turn the house into a spoil for the senses. We'd developed a 'working' relationship over the past six months whereby we both suggested each other to our various business contacts, and if we were ever on a job together, we'd go for cocktails afterwards – market research.

I had requested that he make the cocktails extra lethal that night, at Bella's instruction. 'A party can't ever be a failure if people are too drunk to remember why they hate each other,' she had said. *Cynical but true.* Bella had insisted on the pre-wedding party because she and Derrick had only been able to invite a handful of their extensive friendship group to the Sicilian destination wedding. Clara and Ed wanted to keep it 'intimate' – 'In other words, crushingly dull,' Bella had said to me privately.

I walked around the van to find several workmen already busily moving furniture around the courtyard. Among them, Bella sat at the tarnished iron table in a white dressing gown. She was haphazardly flipping through a pile of papers while expertly balancing a cigarette between her long fingers. 'Hi, darling. Come look at this,' she said, waving me over. 'I've just joined the committee of Help Refugees. I'd love to brainstorm ideas with you. I don't want to sit at those committee meetings like a silly rich person with nothing to say and write out the odd cheque. Maybe we can come up with a creative idea for an event to work on together. A concert or something.'

'I would love to do that,' I said, walking towards her as I wondered whether it would be ethical to charge a charity for my services. We hugged and Bella, as ever, was all limb and bones. Her hair smelt evocatively of cigarettes and Chanel No.5. She handed me the Help Refugees committee member welcome pack, after which she was instantly up on her feet and onto the next topic. 'Now, for tonight, I thought we could set up a little cloakroom area in the shed.' She pre-empted my next thought by adding: 'Which will give Derrick a heart attack.'

For most of his life at home, Derrick inhabited the shed that he'd built at the end of their garden. Whenever guests came over, he would take them on a tour of the house – 'My absurdly American husband,' Bella would invariably say – which always ended in the shed. It seemed that 'Let me show you the shed' was Derrick's equivalent of 'Let me show you my dick.' Those were the only occasions that family members were permitted to enter the genius's workspace. The idea that we hijack his pride, joy and ego as a cloakroom made me feel on edge. The last thing we needed was World War Three.

'I'm not sure that's a good idea. Maybe we should use the guest room?' I offered.

'No, because then guests have to go upstairs and it's messy,' she said, flapping her hand about nonchalantly. 'Let's use the shed. Derrick can divorce me after the wedding. It'll be a fantastic excuse.'

I had to laugh at that. When I was young, I'd never understood why they didn't just get divorced like everyone else seemed to. They talked about it plenty, but for them, divorce was like something on a to-do list, something that you cared about in the moment when the problem was annoying you but that you lost interest in by the following morning. As I got older, I realized that their anger was full of fiery passion and guessed that they probably had life-changing sex whenever it got to crunch time.

'I'm so looking forward to seeing your mum tonight,' said Bella, suddenly high-pitched.

'Oh, yes. So is she,' I said as my stomach simultaneously took a jump, realizing that I hadn't heard from her in days and she had not mentioned the party for weeks. Before I had time to dwell on it, Ned appeared from the side of the house and crossed the courtyard to his van. He raised an arm to wave in my direction as a wide smile spread from ear to ear. I waved back with an equal amount of enthusiasm.

'He's quite cute,' said Bella, not in a whisper.

'Yeah, ish,' I mumbled. I'd gotten over my pseudo-crush on Ned in the months gone by, since we'd become what you could call 'work friends'.

'Ish,' Bella repeated with an eye roll. 'You children are far too picky.' She stood up, leaving the welcome pack that bore a devastating image of a refugee child, in front of me. 'I'm going to get dressed. And maybe shower, if you're lucky.' With her silk white dressing gown blowing in the gentle breeze, she disappeared into the house, resembling a ghost. I glanced down at my phone and tapped out a message to my mother.

> Me:
> Hi Mummy. Haven't spoken to you all week!
> Seeing you tonight, right? X

She started typing almost instantly, though the reply took a while to come, given that she typed with one pinkie finger.

> Mum:
> Don't know. Not feeling well.

I felt a flutter in my solar plexus at the thought of another ailment. How many could one person have throughout a lifetime and still be, essentially, healthy?

> Me:
> Need anything?

She started typing and then stopped while – I imagined – trying to pin down whatever it was she thought she had. Her eventual response was a terse 'No'.

I thought of my mother sitting in the small flat in the mansion block that had been frozen in time. She would be wearing her dressing gown with prints of the rainforest on it, hotel slippers and a full face of make-up. I envisioned boxes and boxes around her, and my heart rate picked up just thinking about them. *What are those?* I'd ask, if I were there. *Christmas decorations*, she'd say. *It's May*, I wouldn't say. I let my imagination travel to her freezer, packed tightly with foods that had never been thrown away and enough sandwich bags to make lunch for an army – or refugee camp.

I picked up the phone to call her, hoping to absolve myself of some of the guilt that I'd felt since the day I'd left home, which always became more prominent when I realized I'd become lazy about checking in on her. She answered with the low, grim voice of someone who wanted you to know they were ill.

'Are you alright?' I asked.

'Just a stomach thing,' she said in her anglicized Israeli accent. 'Do you think you'll have time to drop by today?'

'Probably not today, Mum. I've got so much to sort out for tonight. I'm already at the house.'

'God, I hope Bella's paying you enough for this,' she snorted.

'Of course she is,' I responded, curt and defensive.

'Have you got money?'

My stomach tightened. 'Yes.'

I don't.

'How much?'

Not enough.

'Enough.'

'Shall I write you a cheque?'

'No, I have money. I'm fine. Thank you.'

Since she had inherited money from her father, she had been eager to splurge generously. She even helped out my poor father, who was broke, living in an ashram in India. But I had seen it happen too many times. I had seen her buoyed by a full bank account and, soon after, desolate when she had rashly depleted it. When I received my first pay cheque from *Close Up*, I discovered that cutting financial ties loosened the clutches of that burly guilt. From then on, I promised myself I wouldn't take any money from her, but it was difficult when I always seemed to be getting into debt myself.

'Are you coming tonight?' I asked.

'I'm not feeling well, I just told you.'

'Can't you just come for a bit? To be polite.'

I couldn't tell her that I'd basically pushed for her invite to both the engagement party and the wedding because I thought that she would have got upset if she'd been left out.

'I wouldn't enjoy it, anyway,' she said. 'I don't have any interest in Bella's friends.'

She always claimed this, which I guessed was her way of saying that she was paranoid that Bella's friends hadn't much interest in her.

'How's the journalism going?' she asked.

'I don't have any time to write,' I said brusquely, which wasn't really true. I had plenty of time. But I couldn't bring myself to tell her that I'd sat in front of my laptop, tapping my fingernails lightly on the keys, hoping that words would start sprinkling from my fingers like hundreds and thousands, to no avail. Nor could I tell her that writing, as yet, showed no prospect of filling my bank account and that I was taking on jobs like curating guest DJs for a West End nightclub to make money.

'Don't let yourself become too preoccupied with this wedding of Clara's. You'll lose focus of what you really want to do,' she said unhelpfully.

'This wedding is the only thing paying me at the moment,' I sputtered. 'And anyway, it's over in a week.'

And then what will you do?

'Oh, let me help you a bit,' she said.

'You really don't have to,' I said, more feebly that time. 'Bella's joined the Help Refugee committee.' I eyed the heartbreaking image on the table in front of me and a pain rose in my throat.

'Of course she has,' she scoffed. She'd always regarded Bella's interest in humanitarianism as a perverse fascination with poor people. I think it infuriated her to think that she had once been the perceived poor person on the receiving end of Bella's often-conditional generosity.

'She might be able to get me some work for them,' I said.

'Maybe you could do some work for someone other than Bella.'

'That would be great, if jobs grew on trees,' I retorted, which I knew wasn't a particularly intelligent remark, certainly not for a budding journalist.

'Have you spoken to your father?' she asked.

'Not this week,' I said. My father and I usually spoke once a week, while my mother had seemingly become his pen pal and tended to know intricate details about his daily life that always surprised me.

'Give him a call, he's feeling down,' she said. Last time she'd told me that, my father had refused to admit to me that he felt anything other than on top of the world. I couldn't work out whether she was hearing what she wanted to from him, or if he was telling me what I wanted to hear.

'I'll call him tomorrow,' I promised.

In the background, Ezra called out to her. I imagined him emerging from the darkness of his room, illuminated only by the glow of a video game on the television screen. The image pulled at the cord of my heart that was responsible for chiming guilt, since I'd let him go from problematic child to socially inept adult – now twenty-five years old and living at home with no social life – without once trying to intervene. I wondered if he still had the rotten tooth that I'd noticed, but made no mention of, the last time I'd seen him. I heard him say the word 'Mum' several times. Even after all the years, it felt strange to me. We had a shared experience of the most intimate of all relationships and had been bound to the same woman by the flesh of an umbilical cord, yet that was the only thing connecting us. And the further I'd pulled away from them when I was a teenager, the more possessive she had become of him, to the point where I felt like I really had nothing to do with the world that the two of them inhabited. I'd once overheard Bella describe it as 'Munchausen by proxy'.

The two of them had a conversation that went on so long that I eventually excused myself and hung up the phone. I knew that she wouldn't come to the party, which was a slight relief but also made me sad. Something in me wanted my mother to see me in my element, swinging among people who loved me, or even people who just loved having me around, as if that proved that I had fully extricated myself from her antisocial mould. I looked up at the blue sky and tried to fish around for some of that joy I'd felt when I'd stepped out of the house. I tried to access the fire that had been ignited by Curtis's flirting, but it had been snuffed out by my emotionally triggering phone call.

I took a deep breath, allowing the polluted city air – which almost seemed fresh in that courtyard – to seep deep into my lungs, and I felt my chest release.

*

Ubers pulled up outside the crittall and wood gate, one after the other, and guests stepped out to cross over the threshold from a gritty London street into a scene from *The Great Gatsby*. The magnificent structure of the Mortimers' house looked particularly spectacular that night. A pathway of twinkling lanterns led the way through the courtyard, which was dotted with French wrought-iron table-and-chair combinations, where the smokers lingered in candlelight, the odd vaper among them.

Inside, the open-plan living-dining room was erupting with hydrangeas, Belles of Ireland, well-placed disco balls and a lavish cynosure dining table crowded in fruit, oysters on ice and a lobster centrepiece. Attached to the main room was a hexagonal-shaped conservatory that had recently been built as Bella's 'reading room', but had been converted into a circular bar for the night. It looked like something out of a fairy tale – or at least a Pinterest board – with long stems of flowers dangling from every inch of the ceiling. I'd like to say that its splendour was largely down to me, but actually, it was largely down to Ned.

Every room and hallway of the house was bursting with people, young and old. You could tell it was Clara's night, since none of Ed's road-equipment-thieving friends were there. It was a blended crowd of established art dealers, film producers, food critics, high-profile hoteliers, magazine editors and the odd holistic healer or environmental activist. Parents, looking nothing like parents behind expensive cosmetic surgery and new season designer clothing, and their children, pointedly understated in comparison. Everyone knew each other in a way that only privileged people do. The parents were friends, the children were friends, the children were friends with their parents' friends. You'd think that when you were at a party with so many people you knew, it'd get to a point where you'd just give up on greeting everyone, rather than spend the whole night administering double kisses and 'How are you's', which were responded to with incautious, pessimistic overshares like, 'I've just come out of a deep depression' or 'I don't know where I'd be without micro-dosing.' But everyone powered on.

'I honestly think I've slept with everyone at this party,' said Omni, standing between Alice and me at the tightly packed bar. 'Except him,' she said, glancing at Ned, who looked characteristically earnest in his mixology.

Alice pointed at a geriatric on the other side of the bar. 'What about him?'

'I think he's a relative,' said Omni. 'If not, I'm in!'

Alice leaned over Omni sharply to look at me. 'And you? Eye on anyone?'

I shook my head. 'Fort Knox, over here,' I said, arranging my arms into the shape of an X over my pubic bone. I hadn't noticed any of the men in the room because my brain was like a satellite in search of Leo, even though I knew he was unavailable to me. If this was what it was like to have an ex-boyfriend, count me out. Leo was the closest thing to an ex I'd ever had.

'What about over there, your two o'clock?' said Alice, barely moving her mouth, as if the two o'clock in question could lip-read. I turned to glance at a clean-cut European – I guessed – on the other side of the bar.

'Not my type,' I said immediately.

'Yeah, well, your type is someone who's fucking sweating ecstasy,' said Alice with an eye roll.

'Good observation,' Omni giggled. 'What's my type?'

'Breathing,' said Alice certainly, as we were presented with three deadly cocktails.

'To you,' I said, raising my glass in Alice's direction, in cele-bration of the mega promotion she'd just been granted at work.

'Thanks,' she said, glancing around shiftily. 'I haven't told Tim yet, so don't mention it.'

'How have you not told him?' I cried. 'I'd have told every-one by now.'

'Me too, babe,' said Omni. 'In fact, I have told everyone.'

'Tim's complicated,' said Alice, taking a large gulp of the cocktail.

'You mean he'll be jealous?' I asked. It was the first thing I'd thought about when I'd heard about the promotion, and I'd relished the thought of Tim receiving the news. Before Alice could answer, Ned slid over to us and cast his grey eyes on me.

'We need more ice,' he said. He was the only person who could look both calm and exasperated in the same instance.

'I'll get it,' I said, glad for a reason to march through every room of the house with purpose, in the hope of spotting Leo somewhere on the way.

I walked into the main room, where I saw Ed's parents, prim and conservative, sitting on a sofa with Bella. She was wearing a vintage Ossie Clarke jumpsuit, her hair quintes-sentially scraggly, and flailing large gesticulations in front of them. I could tell she was midway through one of her infamous stories. I'd always loved Bella's stories, though I'd realized as I got older that many were embellished, or just fabricated. Whenever she began telling one, Clara and Fabian would find an excuse to quietly leave the room, given that the tales often ended in an opium den or an orgy.

Clara had been nervous about Ed's parents coming to the party and had acted like she was preparing to host the Prime Minister, which Bella had found both irritating and amusing.

Clara had told us that they drank very little and certainly wouldn't be consuming Ned's death-trap concoctions. They knew nothing about wine, she made the mistake of saying, so Derrick refused to waste any of his good stuff. She thought they might drink champagne, but she'd never actually seen them pop a bottle open, so I ended up making a last-minute trip to Oddbins for a middle-market Merlot. It turned out they were happy with champagne.

I scoured the room for the scraggy, tall man. The last time I'd seen him was outside Canonbury, glowing after morning sex, as I tried to extract myself from his kisses and compliments because I was late for Dymfy's book launch. Sometimes, I wondered whether I would stoop to a threesome with his child lover in order to do that again. I'd never, in fact, had a three-some, but there was a first for everything. He was nowhere in sight, so I slipped into the kitchen for ice.

Clara was in there with her aunt Moll – Omni's mother – both of them leaning against the counter, huddled conspiratorially over their drinks. I felt like I was interrupting something as I approached them. 'All OK in here?' I asked brightly, putting a hand on each of their shoulders.

'We're hiding,' said Clara. I noticed that her glass was almost empty.

'I'm hiding, Clara's keeping me company,' said Moll, who had the same wafty Englishness as Bella, but was introverted and earthy, unlike her sister. Moll and Clara had always had a special bond, possibly because they were both adverse to the wildness of their family, possibly because everyone referred to them both as 'shy'. It was true that Clara was painfully shy as a child, though always very inquisitive. As an adult, her shyness became the thing that made her completely captivating. Perhaps it was because – even when she was skirt-over-head wasted – there was something unobtainable about her. It blew everyone's mind to see Clara acting on stage, seemingly completely at ease and unreserved, given how introverted she usually was.

The kitchen door opened and Derrick walked in, raising his glass towards us. 'This is where the party's at!' he said theatrically. He opened his palm to reveal a small plastic bag full of rainbow-coloured gummy bears. I assumed it was not an innocent selection of Haribo. 'Want one?'

'Dad, please!' said Clara, batting his hand away. Clara really hated it when her parents offered narcotics to her friends, though her glazed-over eyes did make me wonder if she wasn't a few gummies down, herself.

'Are you coming out?' I asked.

'I don't want to talk to anyone,' she said, hunching her shoulders and snaking her arms protectively across her belly.

'Have another drink,' I suggested. 'I'll make you one.' I opened the fridge which was full of liquor and mixed up a tequila lime and soda. Clara took it from me with a languid grin. I could tell she was well on her way to being drunk, which was fantastic news. She really did need to be drunk in order to socialize.

I pulled two big bags of ice from the freezer and blew a kiss in Clara's direction as I left the room. I headed back to the conservatory. That's when I spotted him, leaning over the bar. I didn't approach him, even though I'd been looking for him all night. I watched from a slight distance, as Leo ordered a drink from Ned. Something about seeing the two of them interact made me feel both uneasy and inexplicably turned on. I felt like Ned was looking directly – and so earnestly – into my deepest insecurities, and I kind of loved it. I slipped behind the bar to pass the ice to one of the bearded bar men, speaking to him in an instructional but friendly and flirtatious way, without looking at Leo or letting him know that I had seen him, even though I could feel him watching me.

When I stepped out from the behind the bar, he was there, arms outstretched, waiting to greet me like an old friend, not someone you'd shared your darkest fantasies with and then done a disappearing act on, with no explanation of the fact that you'd actually got a new girlfriend.

'Oh, hi,' I said casually.

'You look absolutely gorgeous,' he said. 'That dress!' He always made a point of talking about my clothing, even when he wasn't dressing me up like a doll.

'Thank you,' I said. I deliberately refrained from asking him a question, which was contrary to the way I usually gabbed on, always feeling responsible for keeping the conversation lively. I wanted to torture him with the notion that I could be angry at him. He couldn't handle the thought of not being liked by absolutely everyone.

'So, how are you, darling?' he asked.

'I'm fine,' I said curtly. My coldness was doing nothing but making the interaction painfully awkward.

'OK,' he said. 'You don't seem yourself? Are you alright?'

'Yes, just . . . having social anxiety,' I said, not because it was true, but because it seemed to be the trendy thing to say, since it had become a feature of the zeitgeist. People who really did suffer from social anxiety, like Clara, would never say it. Clara would be more likely to avoid attending a party altogether, whereas I'd never cancel the chance to be out among people on account of my alleged anxiety.

'You look great,' he said again. Then he pinched the fabric

of my dress between his fingers. 'Must be new. I don't remember it from the dressing-up box.' It was undoubtedly flirtatious, which initially made me angry, and then aroused, and then angry at myself for being aroused.

I laughed, a slightly confused laugh, and asked, 'Sorry, but aren't you in the throes of new love?' I crossed my arms to indicate a cold stance. However much I had hated Child Lover in my mind, I would not sleep with her boyfriend, or anyone's. It was a line of the sisterhood that I swore to myself that I'd never cross.

'The throes,' he repeated. 'No, not anymore. Not sure I ever was, actually.'

'That was short-lived,' I said, smug, mocking, as my secret prison of jealousy finally collapsed.

'Yeah, well, she was crazy,' he said.

And what a surprise to hear a man say so.

'That's your type, no?' I said.

'Crazy and mean.'

Even better.

'Sorry to hear that.'

Sorry, not sorry.

'Thank you, you're sweet,' he said, sliding his long arm over my shoulders. Then he dipped low, so that he was close enough for me to smell his Marlboro Red breath, and said, 'Shall I take you down to the dungeon?'

I exhaled a short laugh, as a yoyo sensation shot up and down from throat to sternum. It was caused by a tangle of arousal and total panic that I would fall back into the clutches of our destructive game of fuck tennis. 'I need to find Clara,' I said. With that, I walked away, a sense of power rising within me. How dare he assume I was so instantly up for it, after all this time? By walking away from that conversation, I was

105

walking away from the danger of suggestive smiles and intimations, which would lead to the danger of spiralling into a filthy encounter in the basement.

I walked into the corridor, where there was a queue for the bathroom. At the end of it, I noticed an unusual collection. Theodora, Clara's 85-year-old grandmother, with grey hair to her waist and a glazed-over look (that could be attributed to the hole that had been drilled into her skull by a shaman to release the spirit of her vitriolic late husband, whom she still insisted she was possessed by). Ed's mother, Emily, was standing against the wall with her hands pressed behind her back and her elbows flayed to the side, a look on her face that signalled confusion and attempted politeness. Moll and her husband, Budi, with his long hair and brightly coloured batik silk jacket. And Ed himself, at the front line.

I sidled over and pressed myself to Moll's side. She squeezed me into a one-armed embrace, a display of affection that I enjoyed in Ed's company. 'Mummy's telling her wedding story,' she said with a grimace of worry and wry amusement.

'One of my favourite stories,' I said enthusiastically. Theodora had married her second husband at an Ayahuasca ceremony in Peru, when Bella and Moll were small children. All they remembered was being woken up at midnight to dance naked under the full moon.

'Sounds like it was quite a lot of fun,' said Emily politely, her voice soft and honeyed, not unlike Clara's.

'Are you married?' Theodora asked in her deep croak, fixing her eyes intensely on Emily.

'Yes, yes. Thirty-two years,' Emily responded proudly.

'Thirty-two years!' Theodora scoffed with horror. 'You get less for murder, you know?'

Emily looked like she didn't know whether or not she was supposed to laugh. She glanced at Ed, who offered nothing more than a pursing of the lips. Moll and Budi were both disengaged, having suffered Theodora's scathing views on marriage for long enough. I laughed and shook my head at Emily, offering her some camaraderie because I felt sorry for her. She had appeared shell-shocked from the moment she entered the house, and Theodora was undoubtedly making that worse. She was terrifying.

'Ed, how's the house hunt going?' asked Moll. I nestled closer to her for protection. She rubbed her fingers up and down my shoulder in a motherly way.

'Slow,' said Ed. 'Not a huge amount on the market.'

'London's ridiculously expensive, isn't it?' said Moll, who lived in the countryside and grew her own vegetables. 'I stopped at the window of one of those estate agents, just for fun. I nearly had a heart attack.'

'Well, actually, we've been looking at houses in Gloucestershire,' said Ed.

'Gloucestershire?' I said, and immediately felt self-conscious about my confusion. It only took a second for me to realize that Clara and Ed were looking to buy a house outside of London and that Clara had deliberately held that information back from me. Every time I asked her what areas they'd been looking at, she would mutter that everything was just so expensive and they weren't sure yet. I felt embarrassed at being transparent enough that she could tell that her departure from London could just about unravel me.

'Clara and I went to see a few houses the other day,' said Emily, and my heart began to thump. 'There were a couple of nice ones.'

The bathroom door opened. Bella and Alice emerged, one after the other, their eyes wide and glistening. I felt a spasm within me that I recognized as FOMO. Even though I didn't want to take drugs, I wished that I had been in there with them, rather than out in the hallway talking about Gloucestershire. Alice consciously rubbed the heel of her hand against her nose before making a swift, shifty dash past us. Bella gave us all a wide-eyed, tight smile and waved with both hands. Then she pinched my chin between her thumb and forefinger and blew a kiss in my direction.

'Love you,' I said, returning the air kiss.

'Love you, darling girl,' she echoed. And then, 'Here.' She took my hand into hers and then swivelled it to close my fingers into a fist over a familiar form of plastic.

'Thanks,' I said, although I hadn't partaken in such things for months and had been hoping to turn months into years. As Bella disappeared, I slid the packet over my chest and stored it away inside my bra. Having seen Ed clock the whole exchange from the moment Bella and Alice walked out of the bathroom together, I avoided looking directly at him.

Gloucestershire.

By midnight, the tone of the party had descended from magazine-worthy aspirational elegance to that of a seedy underground rave.

Front and centre of that tenor was Leo. He was sprawled, all limbs, on a sofa beside the dancefloor, dopey-eyed and sweaty. He was talking to Marina, a friend of mine and Clara's who was sweet, marriable and annoyingly sex positive. Marina was most definitely not the kind of person you'd take down to the dungeon or mess around with. Meanwhile, on the dancefloor,

I was carrying out an interpretive dance to a Chaka Khan remix. With every twirl, I caught Leo in my field of vision, urging him to look at me, to witness how fun and performative I was. But he was deep in Marina and seemed unaware that I was even there. I knew that I shouldn't care, given that I was the one who had walked away from him earlier, not the other way around. But it hadn't quite granted me the freedom that I'd hoped it would. I didn't want to go down to the dungeon with him – *keep telling yourself that* – or fall back into dysfunctional entanglement. I just wanted him to notice me and – given the humiliating way things had ended – to feel like he was missing out on something. Because he was. *Wasn't he?*

Out of nowhere, Clara appeared, smiling, swaying and – much to my joy – 100 per cent wasted.

'Here she is!' I shouted over the music, holding out my arms. She fell into them instantly and naturally.

'Where's Ed?' Clara asked, her features melting down her face. I shrugged. Ed was nowhere in sight. She pointed at the ceiling and said, 'Need to pee.'

'I'll come with you.' I took her hand and led her upstairs to the big bathroom next to her old bedroom. A large freestanding bath was the main feature of the room. It was the same bath that we'd splashed around in as children and drunkenly slouched in at many a house party as teenagers.

'Are you having fun?' I asked, leaning against the door.

Clara reached under her skirt, feeling around for her knickers with difficulty. 'So much fun,' she slurred, and I beamed with pride. She continued on her search for the knickers. Realizing that she wasn't going to locate them any time soon, I guided her hand to help her and she wiggled them down her thighs.

'Thank God I have you to help me go to the loo when I'm drunk,' she said, plonking herself down on the loo seat.

'Thank God I'll be there on your wedding night to do it.'

'Hopefully I won't be this drunk on my wedding night.'

'I hope you will.'

She giggled languidly. Then she frowned and said, 'I can't pee,' looking so like a child, with her legs stretched out in front of her and her hands in her lap.

'Whistle. That helps,' I said, and started to whistle myself.

'How do you know that?'

'Festival trick. Try it.'

I continued whistling and Clara tried to join in but ended up simply blowing into the air. Nevertheless, the pee came streaming out in full force.

'Imagine if I'd never met Ed,' she said, out of the blue. I thought I saw her give a little shudder at the thought of it.

I paused, watching her close her eyes in relief at the emptying of her bladder. Then I asked, 'Are you moving to Gloucestershire?'

She shrugged slowly. 'Maybe. I don't know.'

'I heard Ed say that you were, and it made me feel very sad that I didn't know about it.'

'It's not definitely happening,' she said, glancing sideways at the bathtub.

'Please don't move to Gloucestershire,' I implored, fully aware that it was a wholly unfair request. Why shouldn't she live wherever she wanted to with the person she loved? By way of apology, I added, 'I'd miss you so much.'

'Aw. I'd miss you too.' She reached for loo roll and wiped. I held out my hand to help her up. 'You might move to Gloucestershire too, one day.'

'That's unlikely.'

'You might meet a man from Gloucestershire and then we can both live there.'

'I might never meet a man at all,' I said. I wasn't trying to guilt-trip her for leaving me. I was just trying to make her see that there was every possibility I might never meet anyone, so that she wouldn't forget how important it was that she remained in my life.

'Of course you will,' she said, draping her arms over my shoulders and dropping her head into the crook of my neck.

I lifted my arms to hug her. 'I don't know if I will.'

I really didn't know.

'Are you worried?' she asked.

'No, of course not,' I said, because I couldn't bear to be perceived as someone who could be worried about something as old-fashioned as romance. But I couldn't deny to myself that, deep down, there was something that resembled worry. I had been trying to keep it at bay because I didn't want to become a person who placed their whole life's happiness on becoming yoked to another human. I just wanted to go back to being twenty-five with less of an overwhelming pressure to carve out my future. Was that so much to ask?

When Clara pulled out of our hug, she made a quick decision to step into the bathtub. She sunk down and reclined against the ceramic slope of the tub, her head lolling back. 'I'm so drunk. I need to sober up.' She looked up at me through glassy eyes. 'Do you think we can find something to help?'

It took me a few seconds to work out what she meant, and when I did, I was surprised by the request. 'Oh, I actually have some,' I said, pulling the packet out of my bra and holding it up to be sure that it was in fact what she had meant. 'Someone just gave it to me.' *'Someone' being your mother.*

'Teeny, tiny bit,' she said, making a 'teeny, tiny' gesture with her thumb and forefinger.

'A micro-line?'

'Micro bump, maybe.'

I hadn't seen Clara take drugs for years. It's hard to say why I was suddenly so excited by the fact that she wanted to do so, then and there, with me, when I hadn't even planned on it myself. On the rare occasions I had taken them, I'd always enjoyed the ritual more than I enjoyed the effect. There was an intimacy to the shared need for escapism and the excitement of rebellion.

I got in the bathtub with Clara and tipped a tiny amount of cocaine onto my fist. As I held it up to Clara, I perversely felt that I was getting one up on Ed. Clara sniffled the lumpy powder off my hand like an inquisitive puppy and most of it ended up on her septum. I reached out to pinch it clean, like she was a messy child. Then, I took some myself, because I couldn't let her do it alone.

'Clara,' Ed's voice rang through the hallway, outside the bathroom door.

Clara winced, pulling her mouth down into an expression that was more humorous than scared. 'Put it away,' she whispered. Ed repeated her name as I fiddled to stuff the evidence back in my bra. She called out to let him know that we were in there. The door opened and Ed glanced in, looking apprehensive. His eyes settled on Clara in the bathtub. 'Edward,' she said, reaching out to him with a loving smile, but also looking a little guilty.

His eyes darted around the room as he asked, 'Everything alright?'

'Everything's great, my love,' said Clara, beckoning him over with swaying hand gestures.

Ed stood in the doorway, pale in the face, moving his eyes around his sockets in large circles.

'Are you OK, Ed?' I asked. He looked pale in the face and sketchy as hell.

'I feel quite weird,' he said, which was evident. 'I . . . Your father gave me a gummy bear.'

'Oh dear,' said Clara with a light smile.

'Why "Oh dear"?' said Ed, a look of panic crossing his face. 'What's wrong with them?'

'Nothing wrong with them, my love,' she said. 'You're completely fine.'

'Clara. What was in the gummy bear?' he demanded to know.

Clara shrugged light-heartedly. 'I don't know exactly. I think just . . . maybe some very strong cannabis.' She looked at me, as if urging me to confirm.

'I would assume so too,' I said.

'Are you serious?' Ed's terrified eyes leapt from me to Clara. 'Cannabis doesn't agree with me.'

'It's OK,' said Clara, reaching for his hand. She tugged him down into a squat next to the bathtub and held onto his face attentively. Clara wasn't nurturing by nature but had taught herself to be that way in her relationships. I supposed that she thought it was required to fit the description of 'wife material', whatever that was. She stroked Ed's temple and said, 'We'll look after you.'

Ed stared at her, then slowly ran his thumb along her nostril. He looked at the thumb, scrunching up his own nose, and wiped it on the side of the bathtub, getting rid of the white residue like it was something filthy. I suppose it was fair to think of it that way.

'Jax was just helping me sober up,' said Clara, suddenly

looking nervous, and I wasn't sure whether she was jumping to my defence or throwing me under the bus. Ed nodded, stood up and turned to walk away.

'Ed?' Clara called after him. But he was out in a flash. 'Ed!' She quickly clambered out of the tub and staggered after him. 'What's the matter?' I heard her say on the other side of the door, as I stood there with a clenched jaw, confused by what had just gone down.

'What's the matter?' he repeated incredulously. 'I feel sick and dizzy!'

'You're just stoned, darling.'

'I don't want to feel like this anymore!' His voice was full of alarm. For a second, I felt sorry for him. We'd all been there.

'It will pass,' said Clara gently.

'I didn't plan on being stoned at all, tonight. Or ever, for that matter!'

'Then why would you take a gummy bear from my dad?' she said, in a pitying sort of way. 'You really think my parents are going around offering out pick and mix?'

'I don't know, Clara! I didn't think about it, because my parents don't go around offering drugs to people!'

'Good for you!' she said, raising her voice suddenly. 'Mine do.'

I stepped out of the bathroom to join them in the corridor. 'Ed, let's go down and get you something to eat. That'll help.'

'I want to go home,' he said, talking directly to Clara. 'I don't want my parents to see me like this!'

'You look absolutely fine,' I said. 'You can't tell.'

'How would you know?' he spluttered. 'You're more out of it than me. Both of you are!'

'No, we're not, Ed,' said Clara, sounding completely appalled by the idea. 'Don't be so rude.'

'You can barely stand up, Clara!' he said, which admittedly she couldn't, but it was more to do with alcohol consumption than anything else. 'Clearly because you've been snorting drugs in the bathroom all night!'

'She has not been snorting all night!' I answered for her, suddenly angry on her behalf. 'God, you're sounding judgmental.'

'Do you really think this is normal behaviour?' he said, looking at Clara, ignoring me. I'd never seen him looking so out of control. 'I've been spiked by your father! Your mother is chatting my mother's ear off, not making a word of sense. Your grandmother is smoking a crack pipe.'

Crack pipe?

'Thanks for pointing all of that out! Guess how that makes me feel?' cried Clara, her voice splitting and her eyes filling with tears.

'Everyone downstairs is on another planet,' Ed continued, clearly oblivious to her pain. 'This is not my life, Clara. And I don't want it to be!'

'Ed, it's just a party. Can't you loosen up a bit?' I said, trying to be the pragmatic voice of reason in this completely bizarre situation.

Ed whirled around, looked me dead in the eye and said, 'Can you just fucking leave us alone?'

I took a step back, shocked. I'd never seen Ed show anything that resembled anger and had certainly never been on the receiving end of any kind of outburst.

'Ed!' shrieked Clara, equally shocked through her tears. 'Say sorry.'

I felt a warm glow of relief that she'd leapt to my protection so instinctively.

'No, I will not,' said Ed. I couldn't understand why the

gummies hadn't chilled him out. He continued in a high-pitched yawp, 'I'm sick of all these fake moral compasses.'

'What are you taking about?' I said, looking at him like he was completely mad.

'Is this how you want to live your life, Clara? A drugged-up mess?'

'She's not a drugged-up—'

'No!' Clara rasped, tears streaming down her face now. 'I just want to have fun once in a while!'

'This is how you have fun?' he barked.

'It used to be!' she said, wiping a line of snot from her nose with the back of her hand.

'Well, I'm sorry if I've stifled your true self,' he said unkindly. It was so out of character for him to be anything but respectful towards her. He sounded like he might be about to break down in tears as he added, 'I thought you were someone different.'

'I'm not talking to you when you're stoned!' she snapped cuttingly, and stormed into her old bedroom. Ed stood there, swaying, looking absolutely terrified. Without a second thought, I followed Clara. She was standing in the middle of her room, shaking, either with fear or anger, or possibly just with coke shakes. 'He'll never fucking understand,' she said slowly and quietly.

'Darling, he's just paranoid from the weed,' I said. 'He'll be fine tomorrow.'

'No, he won't!' she said. 'He'll hold this against me forever. That's what he's like. He thinks I'm a disgrace.'

'Clara, you're twenty-eight years old, not forty-eight,' I said. 'You're allowed to have fun if you want to.'

'But I can't just have fun,' she said, as the tears started again.

'I can't have fun normally! Every time I try, something ends up going wrong. Like this!'

'Let's have this conversation tomorrow. You're thinking irrationally,' I said, choosing my words carefully.

'I come from a family of addicts and lunatics!' she cried. 'I don't want to end up like that.'

'You won't!' I took her hands into mine and rubbed them soothingly. 'Stop being so hard on yourself.'

'I don't want to go back downstairs,' she yelped. 'Can you get Ed?'

'Of course.' I left her in her old room – the princess room – and darted out through the hallway. I hurtled down the stairs and pushed my way through the crowd, avoiding eye contact with any of the drugged-up messes, as Ed would have referred to them.

I couldn't see him anywhere. He wasn't in the main room. I registered Leo, still in the same place on the sofa by the dancefloor, but Marina was no longer with him. I spotted Omni standing next to the DJ, wearing his headphones. Alice and Tim were at the centre of the dancefloor, having what looked like a heated discussion, while people flung their bodies in shapes around them. And then I saw Ed, slinking towards the back door with his head down and a bag slung over his shoulder.

'Ed!' I called. He ignored me, though I knew he'd heard me. I broke into a frantic run towards the backdoor. When I opened it, I came face to face with Ned. He was smoking a cigarette. 'I thought you quit when you were twenty-five?' I said, more aggressively than I'd meant to.

'Sorry,' he said, looking taken aback.

Over his shoulder, I saw Ed striding away and I darted after him in a way that screamed 'unhinged'. When I caught up with him, I said, 'Ed, you cannot just leave, after that!'

'I can do whatever I want,' he said. 'It's nothing to do with you.'

'I know that. But she's my friend and she's upset.'

'Let her be upset, then! Stop getting involved. You seem to think you need to insert yourself into every aspect of Clara's life. But it's her life, not yours.' The words came out without thought. They were not calculated or meant to hurt me. They were simply the truth. Ed disappeared around the corner of the house. I stood still, painfully aware that Ned was behind me. After a few seconds, he was beside me, offering me his cigarette. I took a long drag, urging all the toxins deep into my body, feeling an overwhelming urge to lie down on the ground.

'Are you alright?' he asked, sincere but notably hesitant.

'Yeah, I'm fine,' I said, forcing a smile in his direction.

'It's not wrong to care about your friends, by the way,' he said softly.

'Oh, I know,' I said lightly, shrugging as if it were water off a duck's back and not a throbbing pain in my throat. 'He's just stoned.'

'Can I get you anything?' he asked kindly.

I felt touched by his concern, but also demeaned by it. I didn't want him, or anyone, to know how deeply Ed's words had hurt me. I didn't want to be that person. I wanted to be the person who was fully in control of the situation and could not be struck by a few measly words. To assume that role, I reached out to rub Ned's arm in a slightly patronizing way, and said, 'No, thanks. You just get on with the bar. I have to talk to Clara.' I instantly regretted my prickly armour, but it was too late to reverse it, so I just walked off.

Upstairs, I reclined sideways on the four-poster princess

bed, soothing an uncontrollably sobbing Clara by stroking her hair, as I had done so many times over the years. She dialled Ed's number, over and over, but he sent her to voicemail every time. When he finally answered, she rasped down the receiver with so much desperation that it scared me.

'I'm so sorry! This is not how I normally behave. You know that. Everyone was trying to talk to me, all of my parents' crazy fucking friends. It was overwhelming. I hate them all and I just drank and drank ... I don't know what happened. You know I can't control myself. Please come pick me up and take me away from here!'

Take me away from here. She really did sound like Cinderella, or some other pre-suffragette heroine of a fairy tale. *Come in on your fucking horse and take me out of this situation that I'm in, because I can't do that for myself.* If Ed had been in the room, I could have sworn that she would have got down on her knees to beg. It made me realize something that I had been denying since the day she met Ed. It made me realize that Clara did not feel that she could survive life without Ed.

Imagine if I'd never met Ed.

Of course, he gave in and agreed to come back for her. He understood his position too well. He was her saviour and, sooner or later, saviours have to save. When Clara had calmed down, I took her into the bathroom to wipe her face with a warm flannel, cleaning the smudged makeup from her red, tear-stained face. She sat there, slumped on the toilet seat, her lips swollen from crying, letting out a gasping sob every now and then. When her face was clean, she got up and reapplied make-up in front of the mirror, returning it to a state of perfection. I escorted her downstairs and smuggled her through the party that was still in full swing.

Theodora was at the centre of the dancefloor, arms raised to the disco ball, as The Joubert Singers wailed out of the speakers. Leo was exactly where he had been before, as if no time had passed, but Fabian was next to him now. On the floor, Bella lounged against Derrick, his legs either side of her and his arms across her chest, the two of them giggling like teenagers as they passed a rolled-up cigarette between them. Clara didn't even look at them, or at anyone. We slipped out of the back door and across the courtyard. On the other side of the gate, Ed was waiting to take her away from the madness. The madness that I adored, the madness that had ruined her.

I opened the Uber door and watched as she fell inside, into his arms. He held tightly onto her and, instantly, I could see that this was the place she needed to be. This was the place in which she felt safe and loved. As they drove off, I imagined Clara making unnecessary promises like the obedient wife she was about to vow to become, in order to stay in that place. I had a flashback of a much younger Clara, in a similar state of tears, promising her mother that she'd behave, after she'd left us in the car at the side of a country lane and marched off in a state of parental overwhelm. It had only been a few minutes, but given that she was a mother who'd left her children for three weeks without a word, no wonder it had sent Clara spiralling. The memory sent a chill through me. I turned around and headed back inside, with one specific target to reach.

I beelined for that sofa.

Compulsive behaviour dies hard.

Leo stared at me through whacked-out eyes. I bent over so that he could hear me. 'Can we go to the bathroom for a sec?' I knew it was a failsafe method for engaging his interest.

'Of course,' he said. He turned to Fabian. 'Are you coming?'

I shot Fabian a look that meant one thing and he appeared amused as he shook his head. Then I took Leo by the hand and led the way downstairs, to the dungeon. We shut ourselves in the small utility room, dowsed in harsh strip lighting, and took lines off the top of the washing machine. As usual, the promise I'd made to myself meant nothing. *Put that in your morning pages.*

As Leo wiped up the residue with the end of his long finger, I leant against the edge of the machine, hugging myself with one arm and scratching my nose. He licked the finger, which made me grimace, and then he was ready to head back to the party. I didn't move.

'You want something, don't you?' he said, making a slightly irritated laughing sound, which I guessed was because I'd so ambiguously walked away from him earlier. I shook my head, with what I imagined was a glum expression, and he let out another short nasal laugh. All I wanted was for him to ask if I was alright. Sure, I could've volunteered the information that I wasn't, but why did I have to do that? He stepped in front of me and pulled both of my hips towards his. Then he grabbed my breast and squeezed it several times, like he was trying to milk me. 'Am I allowed to kiss you?'

'Well, you're already touching my tit, so it would be weird not to,' I said, gripping the side of the appliance behind me.

He kept one hand on my breast and used his other to clasp my jaw, holding it steady as he brought his lips to mine. I exhaled into his mouth, a sigh of relief. *I've been through an imaginary break-up with you and told no one, but it's been killing me inside.*

When we parted for air, he said, 'Did I upset you last time?' *We're going to talk about that now, are we?*

I was quick on the defence. 'Upset is not the right word.'

'Fabian said that I upset you.'

'Did he?' I asked, surprised. I had never spoken to Fabian about Leo. I doubted that Clara would have, given that she didn't think Leo – whom she called my 'poison' – was worth any of our attention, and could barely stand it when the conversation turned to my liaison with him.

'Shall we talk about it?' he asked, sounding very much more grown up than he generally behaved.

'We don't have to,' I said hastily.

'I think we probably should,' he said. He loved talking about feelings when he was high, and only then. 'If things don't get spoken about, they stew and get worse,' he added, with the chemical wisdom of Gandhi in his voice.

'And if they get spoken about, you can't ignore them.' I said it humorously, but I totally meant it. I would rather bask in the façade that my lust was a real and poignant emotion than have him remind me that what went on between us was nothing to get upset over, just a bit of fun.

'I just didn't think you'd care if I was seeing other people?' he said, taking both of my hands into his. 'It's unlike you.'

'Look, I didn't want to cause an issue,' I said. 'It's just that you'd told me you weren't.'

I reminded him of that conversation, in acute detail, finishing with, 'I wouldn't have cared if you were, I was only asking.'

'God, your memory's good.'

'For a boozer, yes,' I said with a self-deprecating smile. 'I don't care what you do. But I don't like being lied to.'

'OK. Well here's the god's honest truth,' he said. 'I have missed you, a lot.' With that, he rolled his lips over mine, amazingly soft and tender considering the drugged-up state he was in.

'I've missed you too,' I whispered. I couldn't help it. He

slipped his hand beneath my dress, up the side of my hip, round my back to my bra, which he opened with a pinch of his fingers. 'What do you want me to do?' I panted, hot and frantic with a lusty desire to be commanded.

Soon after, I was supine on the cold stone floor and he was on top of me, his dry, musky Marlboro breath warm on my face. Our bodies merged and our flesh became indistinguishable. I held onto him tight, feeling like I'd returned to the womb. For a moment I felt completely safe. Suddenly, a sharp pain shot through me like a knife. I let out a gasp, which transitioned into a sob so abruptly that I couldn't stifle it.

'Shit, sorry,' said Leo, ejecting himself from me.

'It's OK,' I said quickly, holding onto his neck, urging him to stay with me. I hooked my chin over his shoulder so that he couldn't look at my face. So that he couldn't see me crying. There would be no two ways about it under such stark lighting. But my body was shaking, in any case, and I knew that he could feel it.

'I'm so sorry, darling,' he said, cradling the back of my head with his palm. There was something so warm and protective about the gesture that I leaned into it and allowed myself to openly cry.

'It's not you,' I said, all throaty, as I tried to locate the strength that was meant to come with vulnerability.

'It's not?' he said hopefully.

'No, not at all.' But was it him? I couldn't tell, because I couldn't identify where the emotion was rising from. I shook my legs as a way of asking him to give me some space and he sat halfway up. I folded my body into a spinal twist, pressing my head and hands onto the cold floor, hiding my face, while my pelvis was still pinned beneath him. Part of me couldn't bear for him to see me like this, but the other part was relieved that he was seeing me so uncharacteristically unguarded. I was harbouring some hope that it would force him to carry that head-cradling gesture out into the world and show me some care.

'Come here, darling,' he said, climbing off me and helping me sit up. I slumped against the washing machine and he shifted into the spot next to me, encircling me with his gangly arms. I let my head fall against him as my breath started to return to a normal pace. In a stretched-out silence, he stroked my hair and I gently pinched the skin of his forearm between my fingers, kneading him.

'I think I should go home,' I eventually said.

'Alright,' he said. 'I'll book you an Uber.'

'You don't have to do that,' I said with a smirk. I knew that he was only trying to do the right thing, but it wasn't enough.

'I want to.'

Stay with me. I wanted to say. *Come home with me and stay the night.*

But, of course, that seemed too much to ask.

I reached for my knickers, which were halfway down my legs, and pulled them up. He stood and returned his own trousers to his hips. It was only when we were both standing that I saw his droopy, glazed-over eyes and I remembered that he was completely out of it. This whole scene would be a blur to him in the morning. It would probably be a blur to me too, but one that clouded every other thought I had.

Before we left, Leo took hold of my face and kissed me lovingly, assuaging any lingering feelings – for both of us – that my unexpected tears could have been to do with him. He opened the door and allowed me to pass through first, ever chivalrous in his dungeon-fuck etiquette. When I stepped over the threshold, I found myself face to face with one of the bearded barmen. My first thought was that I hoped he wouldn't tell Ned that he'd seen me emerge from the laundry room, dishevelled and wrecked. But as I made to pass him, I heard the rattle of glass and turned to see Ned himself, loading empty bottles into a crate.

'Do you need any help?' I asked, trying to act like there was nothing untoward about the situation.

He looked up at me, gave Leo a fleeting glance and then shook his head. I felt like he was judging me, and it annoyed me after he'd seemed so genuine in his concern half an hour earlier. He cared about me when I was the damsel but had no understanding of the fact that even a damsel needs some form of coping mechanism, and this was mine. *So what?* I wanted to say to him. *So what if I fucked in the laundry room?* I wondered if he had another part of his life in which he got high and behaved recklessly. Probably not. He was too secure and in control of his life. He wouldn't be daring enough to discover cheap thrills. He wasn't the type to push his limits or take a moment out of reality to be a degenerate.

Good for him.

CHAPTER 6

When I left *Close Up*, Dymfy had given me a goodbye present of a complimentary two-night stay at a macrobiotic health retreat in Devon, which was obviously one of a hundred retreats she'd been gifted. I was planning on using it after the wedding, my own honeymoon for one, in the hope that I could finally get some writing done, with my mind clear of flower arrangements, seating plans, videographers, calligraphers and the irony that my life had become all about 'wedmin', even though I had no interest in marriage. But as I was feeling responsible for having been part of the incident that had most probably ruined Clara's night, I gifted it to her as a pre-wedding treat.

She wasted no time, booking herself in for Monday. 'It's such perfect timing,' she said brightly when she called to thank me, distracting me from the thought of Leo's hand cradling the back of my head the night before (in other words, I couldn't stop thinking about him). Indeed, it couldn't have been more perfect for a bride to be. It would see her up to Wednesday, when she'd return calm and glowing, having had her intestines flushed out with angel water – whatever that was – and her nostrils pumped with pure oxygen. She would fly to Pantelleria on Thursday, a personification of the wellness industry, while I would no doubt be pranging out about Leo's arrival.

'Thank you so much. You're literally the dream maid of honour,' she said lovingly.

I'd take the compliment, but in reality, I wished I were a maid of honour who had an endless stream of cash at my fingertips and could've said, 'You know what, I'm coming too!' Instead, I dared to ask, 'Everything OK with Ed?'

'Yes, absolutely fine,' she said, a tad curt. 'I just shouldn't drink that much. Ever.'

'Sometimes it's fun to though,' I added, as the thought of Leo clasping my jaw flashed behind my eyes.

'Better if I just live vicariously through you,' she said. The words took a sharp, quick dig into my gut and then retreated shyly. 'How are you feeling?'

'Fine. I mean, a bit hungover,' I said flatly. 'And a bit confused.'

'Why confused?'

'I think I'm in love with Leo.'

The sensation of our flesh merging and becoming one arrived in my memory and my whole body tingled.

'Oh God,' said Clara, her voice full of despair. 'Jax, I don't think you really love him. You should try and get over that thought.'

It wasn't exactly the response I'd been looking for – I don't know what exactly I'd been looking for – but I conceded that she was probably right.

Clara set off to Yeotown – The Home of Complete Wellbeing – on Monday morning. She sent a selfie to the WhatsApp group when she arrived to let us know that she was already off on a hike.

Omni:
Far too active!
Get that pipe up your bum and relax hunny

Clara:
Haha. Already scheduled that one in for
this evening 💀

Alice:
Bringing a whole new dimension to
pre-consummation prep

Clara:
He wishes!

Alice:
Ha

Me:
🖤 🖤 🖤
Enjoy my love

Alice:
Yes enjoy!

Omni:
See you Thursday 😩

As for me, the sexual health clinic it was.

I didn't know how long it was going to take – the number
of people waiting made me feel like I could've been there all

year – and I didn't want to ask, because I knew that it was a free medical service and that I was lucky to live in a country that offered such a thing. Everyone seemed to be sniffing their way through a summer cold, and I became totally paranoid about catching it. I couldn't afford to be sick for the wedding, but I also didn't want to get up and leave, because the truth was that I was there because I couldn't remember whether I'd had a tampon in when I'd slept with Leo. So, not only had I been feeling anxious about Clara's impending move to Gloucestershire and the fact that I may have ruined her pre-wedding party by instigating her fight with Ed, I'd also been lying in the bathtub sticking my fingers into my vagina, feeling around for a piece of landfill that may or may not have been there. Another reminder that drugs were not the one for me.

'This is why you should get a moon cup,' Omni had said, smoking a cigarette by the window.

'This is why I should absolutely not get a moon cup,' I corrected her. 'This would be happening every month.'

The receptionist called out a name that wasn't mine and I sighed irritably, to no one but myself. A hot pain throbbed away in my lower back, like a panic alarm. My mother had sent me an *Economist* article that morning explaining that back pain was to do with feelings of financial or emotional instability, which sounded annoyingly apt. My final instalment from Bella and Derrick wasn't due until after the wedding and my attention had become too preoccupied with it to hustle for other jobs. But I tried not to think about it because I couldn't afford to feel debilitated over the next week. I had to be strong and in control. I also couldn't afford to see an osteopath, since I'd lost the health insurance I'd had with *Close Up*.

Looking around the waiting room, I wondered if I could

actually be bothered to wait. How bad could a lost tampon be? But if I left then it would have all been a waste of time, and that was time I didn't have to waste. Thirty was looming towards me and I felt under pressure to spend every second of my day doing something useful, like progressing my career. I always felt that I was virtually drowning in personal admin that took away from the time that I could be writing. Part of me knew that was called procrastination, but the admin struggle was real. I also guessed that when you were close to thirty, you did not want to be a person who leaves a tampon to rot up there. That's an early twenties move.

My phone buzzed. A text from Bella, checking that we were still on for a brainstorm over dinner that night. I confirmed with a thumbs up and a little bit of apprehension, because I really didn't want to drink, ever again, given the way that I was feeling. Bella would be keen to share a bottle of wine – probably two, actually – and I didn't want to disappoint her, nor did I want to eventually become known as someone who was a bore to go out with. I didn't want to cancel the dinner because I was looking forward to time alone with her before the wedding to rant about the fact that Clara hadn't told me about Gloucestershire, and to psychoanalyze the fight at the party. It may have been unfair to Clara that I used her mother as a sounding board for my issues, but that was the relationship we'd always had. And anyway, if I was going to spend the whole day alone in the sexual health clinic, I might as well get drunk in a fancy restaurant instead of eat toast alone in bed.

I opened my email inbox which was top to bottom with a bombardment of promotional mailouts. What happened to all that crap about GDPR laws? There was an email from the caterers, confirming the full menu and a reminder from

Alitalia to check in for my flight. And then I felt a burst of excitement as my eyes latched onto an email from Natasha, the features editor of *Close Up*. The subject heading: 'Possible commission'. I opened it quickly.

Darling,

Am guest editing the Lit Review and been fucked over by fuckwit journalist. Need someone to interview poet Anthony Anaxagorou about decline of the male genius myth (yawn). This Wednesday at 4pm at his home. 600 words from his perspective. I can pay £150. Deadline Friday.

Let me know if you can do ASAP.

Miss you!

A surge of energy forced its way through my war-torn body. Not only was *The Literary Review* the first legitimate publication that I'd ever been asked to write for, but being paid to write at all was a new thing for me. Immediately, I googled *Anthony Anaxagorou*. A British-born poet and writer. Anaxagorou was the first young poet to win the London Mayor's Poetry Slam with his poem 'Anthropos' in 2002, according to Wikipedia. He was thirty-six years old. He looked virile and amorous, staring out at me several times over from the rows of Google images. Involuntarily, I saw an image of his long, tattooed arms wrapped around me. I quickly located him on Instagram and scrolled through his pictures, looking for some sign of a wife or girlfriend. I felt oddly thankful that I found none. Suddenly, I got excited by the thought that the interview was taking place at his house and started racking my brain for the perfect outfit. I also thought about how I could make my opening line of the interview – that I was ironically going to write from his perspective ... what a meta romance! – sufficiently flirtatious.

And then I thought, *Really, Jax*? My first interview for a real, respected publication and all I was thinking about was whether I could sleep with the talent. Even for someone who had a habit of spending long periods of time in forced celibacy, I knew that was not normal thinking.

'Jacqueline Levy?'

I sprung up from my seat without thinking and my back seized up cruelly. Clutching the side of my body, I followed the voice into the small surgery.

A rotund African nurse smiled at me warmly. 'So, I hear we're going searching for a tampon?'

'I've never felt more relaxed in my entire life,' Clara told me over the phone on Wednesday morning.

'Oh, I'm so pleased,' I said. It really did bring me joy to know that what I'd given her had shifted her into a state of total serenity, after I'd done exactly the opposite, nights before.

'I'm actually paying to stay on one extra night,' she said.

'Oh great,' I said, even though my gifting ability suddenly felt a little less extraordinary. 'So, will you go directly to the airport from there?'

'Yes. Actually, I wanted to ask if you had time to go to the flat and pick up a few bits for me?'

'Sure.'

'Really? I know it's annoying, but I don't want to ask Ed, as I'll end up spoiling surprises.'

'I'm very happy to do it, love,' I said. 'I can go today, before the *Lit Review* interview.'

'Thank you, thank you, you really are the best,' she said, and I sent a kiss through the phone in response. 'I'll tell the porter to let you in. I haven't actually spoken to Ed, but I'm guessing he's at work.'

'Great. I'll help myself to his cash stash on the way out.'

'Yes, do! Buy us some expensive champagne for the flight,' she joked. 'Good luck with the interview. I can't wait to see you!'

'Me too. I'm so excited!'

We told each other we loved each other and hung up.

I went back to my laptop, to continue prepping for the interview, more hurriedly now that I had to go via Pimlico. I dressed myself in a T-shirt bearing the slogan, 'What Do Women Want?', a long, pleated, geometric patterned skirt and trainers. I'd chosen the outfit carefully, trying several different combinations before settling on the one that I felt sent out the right message: hardworking journalist, provocative and full of integrity, looks after herself and has her shit together. A fun-loving feminist who also cared about style. Unfortunately, a giant sanitary towel was chafing away between my legs, since I couldn't be trusted with a tampon, after a shrivelled black one had been painfully extracted from me with metal pliers. A part of me desperately wanted to tell Leo that it had happened, so that it could be a shared experience, but I had been advised by every girlfriend I'd told – basically anyone who would listen – that I absolutely should not talk to him about it. Apparently, it was a turn-off.

Ed's flat was everything that an expensive new-build should be. Highly functional, gleamingly clean and entirely soulless. Being inside it was like being inside an iPod.

Clara had texted me a list of what she needed: 'Five or so pairs of knickers, pink Hunza swimsuit and like two or three dresses for daytime. Also in the wardrobe in the spare bedroom there's a black and pink box, please bring. Mum bringing the wedding dress and outfits for the other events and I have my passport with me so think that's everything, right?!'

In Clara and Ed's bedroom, I gathered the items that she'd asked for while trying to remember all the questions that I wanted to ask my British-born poet, so that I didn't have to continuously glance at my notes like an amateur. I was slightly worried about whether I had enough battery on my iPhone for the voice recorder to last an entire interview, but I was just hoping for the best.

The spare room had virtually never been slept in, since Ed wasn't keen on entertaining guests. I opened the cupboard to find the pink and black box, which – it turned out – was from Agent Provocateur. It surprised me, given that Clara and Ed weren't the most sexual of couples. She had told me this herself, and in all the years I'd lived in the room next to her, I had never – thankfully – heard so much as the creak of a bed spring. Of course, I couldn't help but pry. I lifted the lid and the sheet of tissue paper inside. Beneath it was a black, lacy lingerie ensemble. I sat down on the bed and lifted the bra up in front of me to have a proper look. Stiff panels of silk pointed sharply upwards in a triangular design. Gaps had been cut out to reveal a tantalizing amount of skin, and maybe even a nipple. The matching knickers were equally alluring, with suspender straps dangling from beneath. I felt around in the box again and, sure enough, pulled out a pair of hold-up tights to complete the package. I couldn't picture Clara in this risqué coordinate, and certainly couldn't picture Ed's reaction to it. What would the dialogue between them be like? Did he have a secret persona that he switched to when he was hard and aroused? Doubtful.

I closed the box and placed it into her small weekend bag with everything else. As I headed for the front door, something caught my eye on the mirrored console table. It was an envelope, propped up against a framed photo of Ed and Clara in Hong Kong. It had Clara's name on it. There was no stamp or address, so it must have been hand-delivered. The handwriting wasn't Bella's. I thought that perhaps it might have been from one of Ed's parents. Maybe it was a cheque for a deposit on their house in Gloucestershire. The thought made my heart flutter. How was I ever going to buy myself a home when no one was handing me cheques for deposits? I reached for the envelope and lifted it between my fingers. As I did so, the back flopped open. It wasn't sealed.

Thinking it harmless, or not thinking at all, I slipped my fingers inside the envelope and pulled out a piece of writing paper.

Dear Clara,

I gather you have not been yourself, or, as I suspect, that you were never the person I thought you were. Certainly, not the person I believed I'd fallen in love with.

With that in mind, I feel it's appropriate to cancel the wedding.

You can explain it to people however you want to. I won't interfere.

There is nothing to discuss.

Ed

CHAPTER 7

As soon as I read the letter, it felt as if a flock of bats had been released inside my chest. When had he written it? That morning, or straight after she'd left for Devon? Had he decided, on the night of the party, that he would bolt as soon as he was out of her sight? Or had the thought come to him once she had left, when he was alone in his flat, being reminded of his past independence? Either way, I had played a part in setting Clara's actions in motion. Without me, she may not have taken drugs, had the fight, or gone to Yeotown.

The alternative was that he had silently been plotting a clichéd, quarter-life-crisis, cold-feet escape for weeks and that the fight at the party was the perfect excuse. But as far as I was aware, there had been no signs before that night that their relationship was anywhere near the rocks.

Panicking, I looked around the flat. It was even cleaner than usual. Every single pillow on their cream sofa was perfectly puffed. Derrinda cleaned their flat on Mondays. I knew that because she had followed Clara when she moved. It was now Wednesday and there wasn't any sign that the flat had been used. I rushed over to the bathroom. The double toothbrush holder above the sink was empty and there wasn't a razor in sight.

Ed was gone. He'd written a note that could be read in

five seconds and then he'd left. *There is nothing to discuss.* No? How about Clara's whole world falling to pieces? How about all the promises that had been sent into the abyss? *Nothing to discuss?*

I shuddered at the thought that Clara may have returned home on her own, a few days before her wedding, to find this letter. Suddenly, I had a memory of her at the age of sixteen, right after her first serious boyfriend had dumped her. She'd stopped eating for days and then she'd swallowed twelve Nurofen to try to make her heartache disappear. Fabian heard the sound of vomiting and found her on the landing outside her bedroom. Their parents were in the Bahamas at the time, so he called me. My mother and I met them at the hospital, where Clara had her stomach pumped. We hadn't spoken about the incident since, and Clara behaved almost disapprovingly when she heard of other people's mental health issues.

I knew that Clara had evolved since then, but I also knew that whatever any of us thought of Ed, she loved him. And as well as loving him, she saw him as her lifeline.

Imagine if I'd never met Ed.

Whereas I had chosen, over the years, to lean into the dysfunction of my upbringing, Clara had always tried to distance herself from it. Her life with Ed represented a kind of stability that she'd never experienced before. She had nestled into the safety of a world without mayhem. And I knew that she would never forgive herself if she thought that she had ruined her chance of a secure and maybe even happy life by behaving too much like her family. Worse, she may never forgive me. I imagined taking the train down to Devon and sitting in one of Yeotown's wood cabins, watching her read the letter.

I thought of the bats that had erupted inside my chest when I had read it and imagined the same flock, only with knives as wings, inside of Clara's.

I couldn't bear to watch it happen.

I couldn't let her feel that pain.

I made a quick decision.

'No More Clara'

Me:
Where are you both?
I need to talk to you now
In person
Urgent 🆘

Alice:
Are you pregnant?

Me:
No!
Clara related
Where are you?

Alice:
Work
Obviously

Omni:
Shit what's happened?

Me:
Can we all meet at Alice's office ASAP?

Alice:
You're scaring me Jax

Omni:
Me too babe

Then I emailed Anthony Anaxagorou, copying in Natasha. A family emergency. I couldn't make the interview.

Being inside Alice's office stressed me out at the best of times, with its digital doorman, aggressively bright colour scheme and weird playground-office aesthetic designed to keep employees trapped. But it was particularly jarring that day.

Alice and Omni were already waiting on a bright yellow sofa in the atrium. Alice was wearing a sharply cut suit and high heels, her eyes glued to the screen of her iPhone. Omni was in a T-shirt and a bohemian skirt that she must have had since 2008 and looked as if she hadn't been to bed. She lifted her arm to wave at me.

'What the hell is going on?' Alice asked, throwing her arms out questioningly as I charged towards them.

That atrium was so damn long. I felt almost out of breath by the time I'd power-walked my way to the yellow couch. I took the letter out of my pocket and simply handed it to Alice. Within seconds, her fingers were pressed flat over her mouth, though she showed no other sign of a reaction. Omni shifted closer to her and craned her neck to read. Her reaction was more visible: a gasp, a furrowed brow and then her green eyes darted up towards me in what looked like terror. I felt relieved that I wasn't completely alone in my emotions.

'Is this real, babe?' Omni asked, and I could tell how badly she was hoping that it was a hoax.

'A hundred per cent real,' I said apologetically.

'Where did you find it?' asked Alice.

'In his flat. She sent me over to pick up some bits for Pantelleria,' I explained, thinking about the lingerie ensemble, now a futile weight at the bottom of the weekend bag. 'I didn't know what to do.'

Omni stood up, bringing her hands to her head in a gesture of distress. 'Fuck. Does Clara know?'

I shook my head slowly, biting my lip.

'How are we going to tell her?' cried Omni, now looking at Alice. Evidently, we were both hoping that she would pragmatically offer a simple solution, as she normally did. But she said nothing. I sunk down onto the sofa and shook my head, arms flailing helplessly out of my shoulder sockets. *I don't know.*

'I need a drink,' said Alice, all of a sudden. We both concurred and followed her to the glass modular unit that was floating above a line of pool tables with the word 'BAR' on the door. I felt like I was in a fish tank, but I didn't really care because there was every alcohol imaginable up for grabs in the perfectly organized, transparent fridge. Alice pulled out a bottle of Grey Goose and made herself a vodka on the rocks. God, I loved her for that. Omni opened a beer and I cracked into the tequila, to soothe both my hysteria over the letter and my anxiety about the fact that I may have killed my writing career.

'OK, we need to think about this logically,' said Alice,

standing on one side of the island bar, her long, manicured fingers tapping the rim of her glass. 'We can PR this situation. Make it look like a good thing.'

I took a long gulp of tequila. 'How could it possibly be a good thing?'

'Well, clearly she's dodged a lethal bullet, hasn't she?' she almost snapped back at me. 'When does she get back from Nazi-wellness camp?'

'She doesn't,' I said, pulling out a bar chair and hoisting myself onto it. 'She's going straight to the airport.'

'OK. So, we'll have to go down and tell her.'

'I can't bear it,' said Omni. 'She's going to think we're surprising her and get all excited.'

'Or she'll think someone's dead,' added Alice.

'Maybe we can tell her Ed's dead,' I said, not even as a joke. 'It'll probably hurt less.'

'Or we could kill him,' said Alice, and Omni half laughed while also burying her face in her palms and running the balls of her hands over her eyebrow line several times.

And then I had a thought. In that moment, it unequivocally seemed to be the most sensible thought yet and the only way to protect Clara. 'What if we don't tell her, at all?'

They both looked at me with twisted features of confusion.

'And what?' said Alice. 'You'll stand in for him at the altar?'

'What if . . . and just hear me out on this before you jump down my throat,' I said, suddenly more of a problem-fixer than Alice was. 'What if we spoke to Ed and managed to change his mind? Then she'd never have to know.'

'We can't do that,' said Alice instantly, without giving my suggestion a nibble.

'Why not?' I said.

'Because this is nothing to do with us,' she said firmly, evidently trying to drill that statement into my mind. 'We can't force him to marry her and then just act like this hasn't happened.'

'What do you mean "force him"? He's the one who fucking asked her! He proposed. She wasn't even thinking about marriage.'

'Of course she was,' said Alice, an incredulous sigh in her voice.

'She had never spoken about it before he asked her!' I insisted.

'Yes, she had, Jax. She spoke to me about it,' said Alice softly.

To me. I knew that she hadn't meant it to sound conceited, but regardless, the two words were like a blow to my chest. Clara had told Alice something that she hadn't told me. She had excluded me from ultimate trust. I knew why she wouldn't have told me that she wanted to get married. Because I would have snubbed the inclination. How ironic it was that I was now the only one trying to make it happen.

'OK, fine. She wanted to get married. What difference does it make to what we're discussing?' I said.

'It's not like she pressured him into it or anything?' said Omni, which sounded more like a question than a statement of certainty.

'No, no, I don't mean that,' said Alice. 'I'm just reiterating the fact that there is an issue between two people, neither of whom are in this room.'

'We need to talk to him,' I pressed. 'If it was either of you, I wouldn't be as worried. But I am not actually sure Clara will ever recover from this. Not without a proper explanation at least.'

'Of course she'll recover. She's a human,' said Alice. 'Humans are built resilient.'

'Some more than others,' I added, looking at Omni for support. 'Come on, you know Clara as well as I do.'

'I know, babe, but I don't know what we can do,' she said helplessly. 'We can't change his mind.'

'After seeing this piece of bullshit, I'm not sure we want to!' said Alice, shaking the letter in front of us. 'What kind of a person leaves their fiancée in a letter?'

'That's exactly the point, Alice,' I said, throwing my arms into the air dramatically. 'Imagine being left by someone you love, in this way. It's easy for us to say that he's an arsehole and she can do better, dodged a bullet, etcetera. But we're not the ones who are in love with Ed.'

'Thank God,' Alice quipped.

I continued, 'At the very least, we could get him to go tell her in person. Think about how you'd feel if you read this letter from someone you thought you were going to spend the rest of your life with. Imagine if it came from Tim. How would you feel?'

Alice sighed and took a sip of her vodka, not even flinching at the taste. 'I'd commit myself to getting over it as fast as I could.'

'Fine, well you're a bad example because you're built of iron,' I muttered.

'Don't be mean,' she said, glaring at me sternly.

'I'm not being mean. It's a compliment.'

'No, it's not. You might as well have used that hideous term "ball breaker".'

'I didn't mean that!'

Impatient now, Alice slid the letter across the counter to me.

'You need to get on a train right now and give her this letter. And whatever needs to be done to get her through, we'll manage.'

I looked at the old-fashioned handwriting, rather feminine in its execution. I looked at the words that were so simple, yet so powerful in their ability to destroy a person. *I gather you have not been yourself, or, as I suspect, that you were never the person I thought you were.* Without another thought, I ripped the letter into six pieces.

The other two looked at me in shock. It was like I'd committed a crime that there was no returning from. And then I had my own moment of shock as I realized that was exactly what I had done. There was no going back now. I had destroyed the evidence. And it didn't even belong to me in the first place. My heart clunked around in my chest. There was a good chance Clara might well kill me at the end of all this, but I had made a decision.

'I love her too much,' I said, by way of explaining myself. 'I can't let her go through it.'

'Then I hope you're prepared to call him yourself,' said Alice gravely. 'Because I'm not doing it.'

It was only after we had tried Ed's number from the office line that we realized he had blocked all of us. When calling from any of our iPhones, we were greeted by his voice mailbox, but when we called from the landline, it rang through. Of course, he didn't answer. I wondered whether he had blocked Clara too.

'Where is he?' I cried desperately, loose and theatrical from the tequila. 'He's not been at the flat for days.'

'Maybe he's at his parents' house?' Omni offered with a tense shrug of the shoulders.

'Do we know where they live?' asked Alice, scrolling through her phone contacts, presumably to see if she knew anyone who knew Ed.

'Gloucestershire,' I said quickly. I hadn't forgotten that one.

'That's quite a big place,' she said impatiently. 'Do we have an address, a phone number?'

'Bella might have their number,' I offered.

'Let's not involve Bella,' said Omni. 'We don't want the whole family and half of London to know before Clara does.'

'Why don't you call Harry?' Alice suggested. 'He'll have a phone number for Ed's parents, at least.'

I hesitated. Harry was Ed's childhood friend, his best man and an ex-fling of mine. 'What if he already knows what's going on?'

'Jax, I really don't think you have time for all these what ifs!' Alice barked at me. 'Call Harry. Now.'

'Why don't you ask to meet him?' Omni jumped in. 'For a friendly drink. Get him onside and maybe he can help. God, this is like CSI, isn't it?'

'That's a good idea,' said Alice, her voice suddenly softer. 'Call him now.'

'I can't call him. He'll freak out if he sees me calling him!'

'Very mature,' said Alice.

'Seriously, he'll probably think I'm trying to shag him again.'

'I was just going to say, call him, meet him, whatever, but don't shag him,' said Alice seriously.

I mumbled, 'I'll text him,' and opened WhatsApp. Reading the last message that had been sent, I couldn't help but roll my eyes.

Harry:
Hi sorry for taking so long to get back to you
but I've done this before with girls and sadly
someone always gets hurt and I really like
being friends with you and would hate for us
not to be able to do that x

I quickly scrolled up to read our prior exchange.

Me:
I want a cuddle. Should I ask the man at the
corner shop downstairs?

Harry:
Haha

Me:
Should I put a lid on the casual sex idea? I
don't mind I would just rather know so I can
stop asking.

Harry:
I just don't want to mess you around as
you're such a good fun girl

Me:
Sweet of you but really I can look
after myself
I'm very aware we aren't right for each other
At all
I just quite like hanging out

> I like having sex and I really like having
> sex with you
> Nothing more
> So if you aren't into it please just say. I
> won't be upset

I half covered my eyes with my fingers as I read the messages. By the time I reached the last one, my head was fully in my palm. 'I'm too embarrassed.'

Alice groaned in despair. 'Any other ideas?'

I tipped my head back and pressed my fingers into the front of my throat, which was aching, dully. I had no other ideas.

So, I pushed my ego to one side.

I did it for Clara.

147

CHAPTER 8

Harry suggested a pub in the city as a meeting place. It was already filling up with Wednesday drinkers, suited men flaunting their well-paid masculinity and fully made-up women drinking away thoughts of lesser salaries and period pains. It was the first real day of spring and there was a feeling of hope and optimism. Life was becoming enjoyable, for some.

I sat at a corner booth, several tequilas down, nervously nursing a glass of white wine.

I saw Harry through the window first, looking at his phone and then glancing around to see if I might be lingering outside for him. Harry was chocolate-box good-looking, like a Gillette ad man, and couldn't have been further from my type. Nonetheless, I'd fallen head over heels for him after date three, because I was seduced by the fact that I was having good sex – and a lot of it, since he wasn't a wreck head – and I was dating someone with a real job who could afford to pick up the bill and who always texted me the next day. Also, double dating with Clara was fun. When he'd decided that things were moving too fast and he didn't want a relationship, I'd attempted to cling on by offering myself up for casual sex, but apparently, that wasn't for him either. I hadn't told anyone that I'd felt close to heartbroken for months, though far fewer months than I had done over Leo.

But as he came towards me, his white shirt blotchy with sweat patches, his tie tightly wound around his neck, I thought, *How did I ever think that this city slicker was the one for me?* I held up a hand to signify my presence and he waved, making his way over. It had been over a year since I'd seen him. He was still good-looking, but appeared significantly older, with deeper smile lines than I remembered.

'Long time,' he said, looking unsure as to how I was going to react to him, even though I'd called this rendezvous.

I stood up to kiss him on the cheek and said, 'So great to see you, darling,' like he was some old and long-forgotten flame whom I had risen worlds above but had nostalgic affection for. 'Sorry for springing myself on you so suddenly.'

'It sounded urgent,' he said, referring to the message in which I'd demanded that we meet within the hour.

'It is.'

'Everything OK?'

'I need to ask you something. And I really need you to be honest with me.'

'OK. I'm quite scared.'

'Do you know where Ed is?'

'That's . . . not what I thought you were going to ask.'

As curious as I was to know what he had thought I was going to ask, I pressed myself to stay on track. 'Have you spoken to him this week?'

'Just texted. Why?'

I sighed and asked, 'Do you know his parents' address?' Then, realizing how crazy I sounded, I waved my hands in front of me, eyes closed, motioning that I needed to start again. 'This is top secret, because Clara doesn't even know. But Ed seems to have cold feet.'

'About the wedding? Are you sure?'

I nodded. 'Absolutely sure.'

'He might just be laying low.'

'No. He wants to call off the wedding.'

'How do you know that, if Clara doesn't?'

I reached into my bag and pulled out the shredded letter. My heart thumped with panic as the pieces reminded me of my rash actions. I laid out the pieces, though it was hard to make out what the words said. 'He left her a letter. She asked me to go collect some things from the flat. It was just there, laying out for anyone to see. I couldn't help but read it.'

His eyebrows rose high, and suddenly he burst out laughing. 'And you ripped it up?'

'I was furious with him, Harry. It's not funny.'

'I know it's not, but fuck! This is crazy,' he said, still laughing. 'Clara hasn't seen it?'

'No, and I don't want her to see it, not until I've spoken to Ed.'

'What are you going to say to him?' he asked incredulously, and then laughed again at the thought of it.

'At worst I'm going to tell him to get into a car and drive down to Devon to tell her in person.'

'That's fair. And at best?'

'At best, I change his mind.'

'Not sure this is the brightest idea you've ever had, Jax.'

'Bright? You're the one laughing like a hyena.'

He ignored the insult. 'Why do girls have to get so involved in each other's business?'

'Because we care about each other. More than men care about us, clearly,' I said, pulling the pieces of evidence back across the table.

'Look. I know you mean well, Jax. But I really think you should just tell Clara the truth.'

'Ed has blocked my number. And Alice's. And Omni's.'

'God, he's really committed to this.'

'Can you imagine if he's blocked Clara as well? Imagine if I tell her and then she can't even get hold of him to get some kind of explanation beyond "There is nothing to discuss". That's how the letter ends.'

'That is quite brutal,' he admitted. He paused for a moment. I pushed my glass of wine towards him, offering a sip. He shook his head and sighed. 'What do you need from me?'

I almost leapt across the table at him in appreciation. 'Could you find out if Ed is at his parents' house? And then maybe help me get there without him finding out that I'm coming.'

'I don't know if it's the best idea to launch yourself on him.'

I spread my arms out in a gesture of helplessness. 'He's the one running.'

Harry took out his phone as he mumbled, 'He's going to kill me when he finds out I've aided your mission.'

'Who are you calling?' I asked.

'His mum.' He glanced at me and evidently thought twice about letting me listen in. He stood up and went outside. I gulped down the last of my wine and shook out my blouse in an attempt to cool down. When Harry returned, he looked slightly hyper with satisfaction. 'OK. Emily knows the wedding is off.'

'It's not off,' I almost shouted. 'There is a wedding happening in three days' time! No one except Ed thinks that it's off!'

'Alright, well, I pretended that I did,' said Harry proudly, and I felt touched by his sudden investment in what he seemed to think was a game.

'And what did she say? Is he there?'

'No. He's at his godfather's place in Paris.'

'Paris?' I spat with disgust. The same Paris that he'd taken Clara to the day after he proposed, he was now using to hide from having to face her pain. I wanted to kill him. 'What else did she say?'

'She said she's waiting for the call from Clara's mother. She's terrified of her.'

'Good, so she should be,' I said, suddenly imagining Bella's reaction with some pride.

'She's worried they're going to ask them to pay for the wedding,' he added.

'Is that really all she's thinking about, when Clara is about to have her heart broken?' I cried.

'Don't get angry with me. I'm just the messenger,' he said, holding his hands up in mock defence.

'I'm not angry with you. I'm angry with Ed. And I'm disappointed in you for being friends with him.'

'If I wasn't friends with him, I'd never have met you.'

'Yeah, and that may have been for the best,' I said bleakly. 'What else did his mum say?'

'She didn't say much. Just that she's shocked. She hasn't seen Ed. He told her not to get involved and went off to Paris.'

'Charming.'

'She asked me to check up on him.'

'And did you?' I asked, holding my breath.

'I tried him. He didn't answer.'

I shook my head in disbelief. Was he avoiding the whole world? 'I actually can't believe he's done this.'

'I can't either, you know.'

I pressed my fingers into my eye sockets. We were all meant

to fly to Pantelleria the next day. The guests would be arriving the day after. The flights had been north of 600 pounds. *Leo would be arriving.* Would everyone go anyway? Would we have the party anyway? God knows enough of it had been paid for upfront. Would I have to call each guest individually to explain what had happened and tell them that they shouldn't contact Clara because it would just make things worse? I thought of Ed sheepishly hiding away in some high-ceilinged Parisian apartment, eating Brie and staring at the Eiffel fucking Tower, while everything fell to pieces. Without even having had a conversation with her. I wasn't ready to give up yet.

'I'm going to Paris.'

Harry looked like he was about to laugh again, but quickly caught himself, realizing that I was serious. 'Don't be ridiculous.'

I took out my iPhone to look up Eurostar times. There was a message from Alice, asking for an update and threatening to call Clara if she didn't hear back from me. I started to type out a response, but a circling timer appeared at the middle of my screen before it went black. 'Fuck!'

It was unsurprising. I couldn't remember the last time I'd had a fully charged iPhone.

'Can you look up Eurostar times?' I asked frantically.

'You have lost your mind, Jax!'

'Please,' I said as I got up and hurtled over to the bar. It was busy and there was only one server who looked about fifteen years old. I had to fight for his attention and then he looked annoyed when all I asked for was a phone charger – it made me think of Mr Magus the iPhone bore who had suddenly disappeared into thin air after leaving a total of five toothbrushes with Omni – but nonetheless, he took it away to charge.

I returned to the table. 'Any luck?'

'Tonight's Eurostars are all booked up. You'll have to go tomorrow.'

'No, tomorrow is too late! We're all meant to arrive tomorrow. Ed included. What about flights?'

He handed me his phone. British Airways was fully booked but for one £700 seat, and all the other flights were too soon for me to make. I swore over and over, scrunching my eyes shut, desperately appealing to my brain for a solution. And then, an idea lit up above my head. 'Do you still have a car?'

Harry's eyes widened when he understood what I was suggesting. 'No. No. Do not even think about it.'

'If you want to do one thing in my life for me, ever. Please do this!'

'Drive you to France in the middle of the night, to maul my friend?'

'Harry. I know Clara better than anyone does. Even Ed. I have seen her go through some real shit over the years. Ed is everything to her. All she wants is to be loved, and when that's taken away from her, it's even worse than when it's taken from someone else. Last time it happened, she ended up in the hospital having pills pumped out of her stomach.'

'You mean she tried to . . .'

'I don't know if it was on purpose. But it happened. All I can say is that I don't know if she'll ever recover from this one.' I felt a twinge of guilt over using such a personal story about Clara to manipulate him, but I told myself that I was doing it for her.

'Jesus . . .'

I pressed my hands together in a prayer position, urging him to help me. 'Please.'

'Jax, that's a very sad story. And you know, I really like Clara. But I don't want to get involved. Also, I've just started seeing someone and I'm meant to be meeting her parents tonight. I really don't want to cancel.'

You never asked to meet my parents when we'd just started seeing each other, I thought. But then I'd certainly never offered the occasion up. In any case, it was irrelevant in the current situation but for the fact that I recognized that he wasn't going to help me. I returned to the bar to ask if I could check my phone while it was charging. The bartender looked at me with histrionic disbelief.

'I'm in the middle of an emergency,' I snapped, or maybe slurred, since I was definitely a tad drunk. I needed to talk to Alice and Omni, to discuss the next step in our plan. When my iPhone finally loaded up, I had three missed calls from Ned. I swore out loud as I remembered that I was meant to meet him with the flower-pressed place cards, so that he could give them to his flat mate, the calligrapher. I had now missed the first stepping stone towards a writing career and possibly screwed up the chances of a back-up career collaborating with my entrepreneurial avant-garde mixologist. I picked up the phone to Ned.

He answered brightly. 'Hey. I'm here. Where are you?'

'I am in the middle of dealing with the biggest fucking disaster you can possibly imagine,' I said, a reoccurring pain starting to throb at the crown of my head.

'What could possibly be that bad?' he asked.

I knew that he thought I was going to tell him the band had cancelled or something even more trivial, so I took some satisfaction in saying, 'The arsehole groom wants to call off the wedding and I haven't told the bride.'

'OK, that's a legitimate disaster.'

'Do you have the van?' I asked.

'The van?' he repeated.

'Can you drive me to Paris?' I pleaded with desperation. I added, 'I'll pay for petrol. And everything else.'

'Drive you to Paris?' he said, trying to make sense of the words.

'Ed is in Paris. Hiding. I need to get there to speak to him and the Eurostar is booked up tonight.'

I prepared for him to tell me that I was crazy, like Harry had. I prepared to be called a hysterical woman. I was nails out, ready to fight. But he just said, 'If you really want me to.'

'You can't drive to Paris!' Alice screeched down the phone.

I was back at the flat, getting my passport, phone charger and a change of knickers. I couldn't think straight enough to pack anything else. 'It's only six hours.'

'You're drunk!' she said accusatorily.

'Ned is driving, not me.'

'Jax, this isn't one of your parties that the DJ hasn't turned up for. This is real life! Clara's life!'

'You sound like Harry.'

'Why are you doing this?'

'I'm just trying to be a good friend.'

'You've done enough. Clara doesn't need you to make decisions for her.'

'Come on, Alice. Clara's never even had a wax without one of us telling her how thick her landing strip should be.' It wasn't a complete embellishment. For about a year after Clara started getting bikini waxes, she'd ask me to come into the room with her because she found it too awkward conversing with the beauty therapist about the aesthetic of her vagina. Now, she went alone, but still asked me to check it every now and again.

'This isn't a bikini wax!' Alice despaired. 'We need to tell her.'

'You didn't know her all those years ago, when it happened,' I said, referring to the incident that was becoming my go-to bolster. Alice was told the story by Omni and me on one of the nights we'd spent drinking wine at the kitchen table until the early hours, putting the world to rights.

'That was years ago!' she cried. 'You can't wrap her in cotton wool for the rest of her fucking life.'

Suddenly, Omni's voice piped up in the distance. 'I don't know if marrying someone who's not in love with her is the answer.'

'Of course it's not the answer,' Alice confirmed.

'But at least we could get him to speak to her,' I said. Then, desperately, I added, 'I feel like you're both against me.'

At that, Alice's softened her tone. 'We're not. We're just trying to be realistic.'

'Please just let me go to Paris and talk to Ed. If I don't find him, or he won't change his mind, I'll tell Clara. And I'll take the blame for all of this. I won't even tell her that you knew.'

'It's not about that, babe,' said Omni, sounding like she was close to tears.

'I know, but you know what I mean,' I said.

'Well, are you going to be alright alone with Ned?' Alice snapped, and even though it was a snap, I knew it was full of kindness. 'Should one of us come with you?'

'I'll be fine. I do have a lot of wedmin I might need help with though,' I said. 'In case the wedding does go ahead.'

'Send it over. I'm on it,' said Alice. I couldn't have thought of a more *on it* person to pass the baton to.

We exchanged words of love before I hung up the phone. My stomach dropped when I saw a message from Clara with the word 'Ed' in it. My eyes readjusted through the blur, and I read the whole thing.

> Clara:
> Do you know what flight Ed is on?
> Can't get through to him

My heart started racing as I realized that Ed had stooped as low as I'd feared he would. He had blocked Clara. For all he knew, she had read the letter by now and was calling to talk about it. Didn't she, at least, deserve the chance to tell him that she hated him? But she wouldn't have told him that. She would have begged him not to do it. And with a wedding set in two days' time, could anyone blame her for that?

I typed out as casual a reply as I could manage.

> Me:
> Same one as us I think love, but I'll
> double check.
> Get a good night's sleep!
>
> Clara:
> I will
> Thanks Mum
>
> Me:
> 😔

158

Clara:
By the way thank you so much for this and
everything you've done. I feel very lucky to
have a best friend like you. Love you a lot x

My stomach wove itself into a tight knot as I read her last message, thinking about all the ways that the following day could unfold. But Clara was happy in that moment and that was something, even if she was totally in the dark about her life and future. And I knew exactly where Ed was, since I had retained his godfathers' address from when I sent a congratulatory bottle of champagne to the flat, after they got engaged. There was hope that the situation wouldn't end in total disaster. I could find him and, fingers crossed, get him on a plane to Pantelleria. Clara would likely be crushed at some point, but even if I could work out a way to take away a millimetre of her pain, it would be worth it.

CHAPTER 9

The last train through the Channel Tunnel was at midnight. It would take two hours to drive there, so we made a plan to leave Ned's house at 9:30 p.m. for the half-hour leeway. I took an Uber down to Peckham, as public transport was too long and risky at a time like that. It was a terraced house on a very civilized residential street. It was not the kind of street that had come to my mind when he had mentioned the words 'flat share'.

A girl in a large knit jumper over a floral dress opened the door for me. 'Hi, come on in,' she said with a friendly smile. I followed her into the living room, immediately struck by the comfortable, homey atmosphere. *Love Island* played on the television and the smell of cooking wafted through from the adjoining kitchen, which the girl pointed me towards.

'Ned's in there,' she said sweetly, and fell into a dent in the sofa, fixing her eyes on the contestant who was talking about 'fanny flutters'. I walked through to find Ned hanging washing on a clothes horse, while a tall girl stood by the stove, stirring a pot.

'Jax, this is my house mate, Camilla,' said Ned.

'And I'm Beth,' the other girl called from the sofa. 'Sorry, I didn't even introduce myself. How rude of me!'

'Nice to meet you both,' I said. And then, remembering that I'd been conversing with Camilla the calligrapher by email, my voice suddenly turned high-pitched and professional. 'So sorry for the delay with the place cards. I have them here.' I handed her a Gail's carrier bag filled with pieces of textured card that Moll had hand-pressed flowers into, as if there was no doubt that we'd be laying them out on the wedding party tables in a few days' time.

'Wow, these are very fancy,' said Camilla, glancing into the bag. 'I'll have them done by the time you guys get back from Paris.'

'Amazing. Thank you so much,' I said, glancing at Ned. I wondered if he had relayed the situation to his flatmates, and whether they'd offered any opinions on my crazy plan. They made no mention of it, so I guessed it didn't really matter.

Camilla asked Beth and Ned if they wanted any of her vegetables, but they'd both eaten already. As they bantered away about their mealtime habits and odd food tastes, I caught sight of a chalk board on the wall, which assigned various house duties to the three of them on rotation. There was also a piece of paper on the fridge, listing house expenses and IOU's. It fascinated me because I'd never had charts or tables with Clara or Omni. We'd always picked up house essentials as and when they were needed, trusting that it would all even out at some point. Truthfully, I sometimes resented the fact that I always seemed to be the one buying loo roll – Omni could happily go a week without it in the house – but wouldn't dare mention it, as I knew it would be perceived as petty.

'Did you know each other before you moved in?' I asked curiously, leaning against the kitchen table.

'Nope,' said Camilla. 'I was the first to move in, with two guys. Then one of them left and Ned came. And then Beth's the most recent.'

It intrigued me that a revolving door of strangers had, between them, created an atmosphere so much more hospitable and operative than I'd ever managed, even though I had only ever lived with my best friends. The arrangement was marked with clear boundaries, something that I'd always believed to be a barrier to warmth and closeness. I was sure that they never jumped into bed together, or chatted while one was in the bath, or informed one another exactly when they'd be home, or when their period was due. I couldn't imagine they did any of the things that I felt were so important to fostering an intimate friendship, but they shared house tasks and bills in a way that created a sense of harmonious order and respect that I felt oddly envious of.

'Ready to go?' said Ned, stuffing a jumper into his backpack.

I was stunned that he hadn't yet changed his mind. In fact, his willingness to help me, without question, had thrown me off guard and I suddenly felt a panicked guilt that I'd asked such a huge favour of him. 'Are you sure you don't mind doing this?' I said, giving him one last chance to get out of it.

'It's a bit of an odd one. But I'm happy to do it, if there's no other way.'

'Thank you,' I said, truly grateful, since I didn't have a plan C at this stage.

We said goodbye to his housemates, who showed no sign that they were aware of why we were going to Paris. I climbed into the passenger seat of the small van that had Ned's company logo pasted across the side, and he tapped the address of the Channel Tunnel into the sat-nav. 'Eleven thirty-five arrival,' he announced.

'Great,' I said, though the shortness of the 25-minute window was troubling me. Ned turned the key in the ignition, shifted the gear stick with ease and pulled out into the narrow South London street. I'd always found that there was something attractive about men when they were driving, which may have been a problematic response. I reached into the Tesco bag full of snacks that I'd bought on the way over, in an attempt to make the journey as enjoyable as possible for him, and pulled out a large packet of salt and vinegar crisps. 'Have one of these,' I demanded, ripping the packet open. 'They won a crisp competition.'

'I absolutely love that you know that fact,' he said, so genuine in his enthusiasm for what he obviously perceived as niche knowledge. I smiled, thinking of the way I'd told Leo the same fact, and his response was, 'Don't tell me you've succumbed to the bourgeois crisp obsession?'

'Shall we play a game?' I asked, with a sudden realization that we were going to be spending the next five hours together. We'd only ever known each other in a professional context, and though we had become friends in a sense, I wondered whether we had enough material to fill the journey.

'We could just chat for now and save the games for when the trip gets really dire and we feel like we're hallucinating.'

'Good idea,' I said. I dove into my brain, filing through at a frantic speed, and then I came out with, 'Would you rather own a casino or a spa?'

He glanced over at me with a confused smile. 'Um ... spa I guess.'

'Really? The sound of water features would make me constantly need the loo.'

'Better than living under strip lighting and interacting with gamblers 24/7,' he said.

'I'd choose a casino, so I could dress up like Sharon Stone in the movie and drink martinis every day.' I conjured the image in my head – imagining that Ned was doing the same – of a me that was so far from any version of myself that had ever existed.

'Of course, you do love your martinis,' he said. 'Do you have brothers and sisters?' he asked, clearly thinking that it was his turn to ask a first-date-type question, even though we'd known each other for more than six months.

'A half-brother,' I said, licking the tart granules of salt from the ends of my fingers. 'We're very different though and not that close. Do you?'

'Two brothers,' he said. It surprised me that he came from such a boy-oriented background given his gentle nature and the absence of any signs of machismo. 'We're all very similar and very close.'

'Similar how?' I asked, intrigued at the thought of three Neds in any one room.

'Stubborn.'

'You are not stubborn,' I insisted, as if I knew him better than he knew himself.

'I am.'

I smiled and asked, 'Are your parents still together?', thinking that there must have been some fissure in the story-book set-up.

'Still very much together,' he said. *Very much*. Not even a separate-bedroom scenario. I wondered if I could ever truly connect to someone who came from such a perfect family. There were so many things that Clara and I naturally understood about each other, without having to pick them apart in detail, because of our similarly turbulent upbring-ings. Like the fact that Christmas was not something to get excited about, but to dread. Or the idea that boundaries were something that you tried to teach yourself to understand, rather than a given.

'Conventional families blow my mind,' I said, shifting to give my aching back a little relief. 'They're so far from what I understand. Clara wants to create one for herself, which is why she chose Ed.'

'Or they just fell in love?' he suggested. He quickly added, 'But, I guess you wouldn't do this to someone you loved.'

'No. You wouldn't.'

'Why do you think he decided to run?' he asked. Ned had been so polite and respectful about the situation that we hadn't even spoken of the issue. He'd just accepted it and put his foot on the pedal.

I shrugged and smirked at the same time. 'I don't know. Too much under-the-radar bum sex at boarding school?'

Ned almost swerved the car at that. 'I'm sorry?'

'I just mean that these men who were ripped away from their mothers and shipped off to some British boarding school before they've even stopped wetting the bed get turned into wrecks. There are generations and generations of bodies left behind by the stupid tradition. We're the only country that still thinks it's OK to send children away from home. How have we not learnt?' I got hotter at the neck and shorter of breath with every word. You'd think I was the one who had been sent to boarding school, given the level of anger I reached.

'Do you relate to him?' Ned asked softly, glancing over at me with such sensitivity that it took me a few moments to understand what he was implying with the question.

'To being an emotionally stifled wreck?'

'I just mean ... don't you have a problem with emotional confrontation yourself?' he asked, slowly and carefully.

'I . . . give me an example.' I didn't disagree, I was just surprised that he had the intuition to notice it, when I gave the outward impression of being incredibly open and free.

'Maybe I'm wrong. It's just the impression I got. I don't really know you well enough to say. Sorry, I didn't mean to offend you.'

Silence shrouded us as we joined the A2. I stared out at the three lanes, empty but for a set of headlights in the far distance, wondering what was ahead for me, for Clara. What exactly was I going to say to Ed? And would it make any difference? How badly would Clara's heart actually be broken? A Ferrari came speeding past us, loud, obnoxious, and it startled me back into high alert. I checked the clock and refreshed Google Maps. We were still set for an 11.35 arrival. I imagined what it would have been like if Leo were the one driving me. We'd have probably missed ten turns, stopped to buy cigarettes and I'd have been distracted wondering whether or not to reach for his hand. Still, I wished I were on a road trip with him.

I lifted one of my legs up onto the seat with me and cradled my knee in a self-soothing way. 'How's your love life?' I asked, assuming a light, conversational manner.

He remained serious and checked his wing mirrors and blind spots diligently as he moved lanes to overtake a horse box. 'There was a girl on my course who I dated for a little while.'

'What course?'

'I've been taking this course on gender politics and feminist studies at SOAS for the past couple of months.'

Swoon. 'That's my dream,' I said, which may have been slightly hyperbolic but not far from the truth. If only I had the time, money, resources and ability to commit to something as regular as a course. 'What was the girl like?' I imagined an attractive, quirky European with a short fringe wearing Doc Martins.

'She was much too clever for me, sadly,' he said.

'I doubt that's true,' I said.

'Honestly, she was like a walking trivia card that I could never keep up with.'

'Did it make you feel insecure?' I prodded.

'Very,' he said, surprising me with his readiness to admit it. 'No wonder she ghosted me.'

I laughed affectionately. 'Poor Ned.' I reached into the Tesco bag for a packet of chocolate Twirls, to help him alleviate the memory. 'What was her name?'

'Vicky.'

'Vicky-pedia.'

He laughed emphatically, scrunching up his nose like a rabbit and leaning over the wheel, which he gripped for support. I laughed too, more at his amusement than at my own joke. Then he asked, 'How's it going with the man from the party?'

I winced a little, reminded of the state that he had witnessed me in. 'He's sort of like an addiction,' I explained. 'A toxic one. I've known since the very beginning that I couldn't be with him. He's too unreliable. But I went back again and again. And now I'm stuck. Clever me.'

'Stuck, how?'

'I can't give him up.'

'Can't or don't want to?'

I lifted my shoulders to my ears. 'I love seeing him. I love being with him. Then as soon as I'm not with him, I hate him but miss him at the same time. It's all quite fucked up really.'

Something stopped me from telling him that I thought I might be in love with the creature he'd seen in the dungeon.

'Nothing wrong with fucked up.'

'Actually, there is. I wouldn't recommend it,' I said, like a worldly, damaged older woman talking to her young lover. He had no answer to that, so we sat in quietness for the next few minutes. Then, suddenly, I said, 'Quite odd that we're on a road trip together.'

He scrunched up his nose again to laugh. 'Yeah. Shall we listen to something?'

'That's a great idea.' I browsed through 'New & Noteworthy' podcasts and eventually settled on a tongue-in-cheek anti-feminist sketch show, which I hoped he would find as amusing as I did. But as we listened, every crude joke made me feel uncomfortable in a way that it hadn't before, and I felt oddly responsible each time Ned failed to laugh at a punchline. I was relieved when the twenty-five minutes were over and I could switch to a serious show about the corruption of power. We were barely halfway to the Channel Tunnel when I caught Ned sneak a gasping yawn.

'Sorry I don't have a driver's licence, otherwise I'd offer to take over,' I said, feeling ashamed about my lack of resourcefulness. *Pushing thirty and can't even drive.*

'Don't worry, I'm the only one insured on the van, anyway,' he said, which I interpreted as a sentiment that he wouldn't trust me to drive it even if I had a licence and was insured. No one trusted me to do grown-up things. Organize parties, fine, but God forbid I navigate a vehicle or hold a baby.

'And I've been drinking,' I added, feeding the narrative, by way of defence.

'Martinis?'

'Tequila and white wine. Not quite as chic, I'm afraid.'

We pulled into a service station for petrol, which Ned kindly assured me wouldn't take more than five minutes. He must have noticed my body tensing anxiously as I fixed one eye on the clock. I winced sensitively as I unfurled my legs from the car. The throbbing disc was now shooting pains down my left thigh. When my feet hit the pavement, I closed my eyes and waited for it to pass. Everything had to pass at some point.

'What's up?' Ned asked as he walked around the car to pop the fuel filler.

'Back pain,' I said. 'It'll go.' I took a deep breath that caught in my chest and swayed from side to side with my hands on my tailbone. 'I always get it when I'm stressed.'

'Have you been to a doctor?' he asked, reaching for the pump.

'I went to a chiropractor a while ago. But it was expensive, and he didn't really do anything, so I haven't been back,' I said, my tone becoming pre-emptively self-justifying.

'Can't you get it on the NHS?' he asked, frowning at me, so perplexed by my deficit in pragmatism. He inserted the pump into the hole and pulled the trigger. I found the whole thing oddly arousing.

'I'd have to wait three months to see a physio. And then they would only be able to do specific times, which wouldn't be possible if I had to work. So, I'd probably end up cancelling it in the end anyway.' It made so much sense in my head. But I could see by the way that Ned fixed his eyes silently on the gurgling pump that he read it as a glaring neon sign of childish self-destruction.

I tried to pay for the petrol, but Ned refused, insisting that he could write it off as a business expense, perhaps hoping that I'd put the sixty quid – *cost of fuel!* – into some personal healthcare savings account. Instead, I bought two coffees with extra shots for our dwindling energy levels and two packets of cigarettes, because if ever there was a time to smoke. We settled back into the van and I refreshed Google Maps again. We were about an hour away from the port and were still set to arrive with twenty minutes' leeway. *Look at us go.*

As we set off down the dark, empty motorway, Ned asked, 'Have you thought about what you're going to say to Ed when we get there?'

I took a sip of my coffee, feeling comforted by the simplicity of the bitter liquid. The truth was that I had been avoiding thinking about my eventual confrontation with Ed and being questioned about it sent my stomach undulating.

'Well. First of all' – I shut my eyes as I considered the horror of the imagined conversation – 'I'm going to tell him that their fight at the party was entirely my fault and that he shouldn't take it out on her.'

'Surely you can't take responsibility for a fight that was theirs?'

'It wasn't entirely my fault, but I can make him think it was,' I said. 'And I'll remind him of all the reasons he loves her.'

'Which are?'

'Oh, you know. Her nasal laugh. The way she never talks about wanting to make you feel better but will do something so caring like bring you breakfast in bed when you're feeling sad. The way she'll make it her mission to find something you've lost at a party and always finds it. The way she always takes down your Uber driver's licence number, just in case.' As I reeled off the list that sounded like the climax of a rom com taking place in the rain, I realized that I was actually stating the reasons that *I* loved Clara and I had no idea if they were the same as Ed's. I gathered from the fleeting glance that Ned gave me that he was thinking exactly the same. I added, 'And if that fails, then I'll tell him what a shitty person everyone will think he is when they hear what he's done to poor Clara.'

'You're very protective of her,' he mused with evident intrigue.

'She's easy to hurt,' I said quietly, though, in reality, she wasn't as feeble as I was making her out to be. How could she be a product of that family and not have built up resilience? The truth was that I was overly protective of Clara because I didn't want her to stop needing me. If she stopped needing me, she might presume that I'd stopped needing her, which I most definitely had not. And if neither of us needed one another, my fear was that we'd drift along side by side for a little longer, before eventually floating in different directions until we ended up on opposite sides of the same ocean.

The van rattled along the motorway for a while longer before Ned frowned and lifted his hands from the wheel. 'Can you feel that?'

'Feel what?' I said, as an anxious flutter rose in my chest.

He lifted his hands again. Then, with a knowing look of concern, he opened the window. There was a rhythmic thumping that sounded like a metal chain being dragged along the ground. Ned held his breath. 'Shit.'

The front left tyre of the van sagged to the ground like a sad balloon, half deflated the morning after a big party. I stood there, on the side of the M20, in a situation that couldn't have been a more perfect plot point for my journey – were I the heroine of a road trip movie – if it tried, and I couldn't help but wonder why my life always had to feel like one big cliché.

'Do you think it will carry us for one more hour?' I asked, even though I knew it was a futile – and downright stupid – question. Ned looked up at me curiously, from where he was down on one knee by the tyre. Clearly, he couldn't believe I was capable of asking such a thing. Immediately, I catapulted myself into crisis mode. 'Fuck, fuck, fuck. OK. What do we do?' I looked around as if for some magical solution that didn't involve the lengthy process of changing a tyre.

'We just need to change it,' he said calmly, pushing himself up to full height. 'It's alright.' He travelled to the back of the van and popped the boot.

'Do you know how to do it?' I asked frenetically.

'Yes.'

Even though I had no reason to doubt Ned, who was one of the most capable human beings I'd ever met, I googled, 'How to change a tyre'. I started reading the instructions out loud, with no idea of who'd written them. 'Turn on the hazard lights, apply the hand brake, apply wheel wedges—'

'I've got it,' he said tersely, lifting the wedge contraption from the toolkit. And then, politely, he added, 'Thank you, though.'

'Do you think you can do it quick enough?'

'Let's hope so. We don't really have any other choice.'

'What can I do to help?' I asked, just like I'd accommodatingly asked Leo what I could do to help with his non-existent boner.

'Nothing yet.'

I watched as he used a metal tool to remove each bolt from the wheel carefully, silently urging him to hurry the fuck up. Minutes seemed to be passing even faster than usual. It was the opposite of watching paint dry. The silver wheel plate fell to the ground. Then he put some contraption beneath the car and twisted it until the vehicle virtually levitated. In that moment, I wanted to marry him.

It didn't seem like there was much I could do to help – I sure as hell could not lift a car from the ground – so I lit a cigarette. Situations involving DIY tended to be the only occasions that I could resign myself to the kind of female passivity and deference that seemed to be so attractive to men. Perhaps if I ever wanted a boyfriend – 'if' being the optimum word – I should just continuously break things and call various men over to fix them for me until I found the one. In other words, marry a Task Rabbit. Not a bad idea.

It took half an hour to change the tyre. We scrambled back into the car with greasy hands and I begged Ned to ignore all speed limits, promising to pay for any penalties he received. He put his foot on the pedal and shot down the dark motorway.

Google Maps had us pulling into the port at 11:58 p.m. I watched my iPhone clock the entire time.

11:35 p.m . . . to 11:36 p.m . . . 11:50 p.m . . .

How fucking short could minutes be?

Finally, at 11:51 p.m., I saw a sign for the Terminal Service Ring Road. 'There!' I almost shouted. But Ned was already indicating. He pulled the van to the left and we were on our way to the terminal. I sat forwards, nervous and tense, following the moving map with my finger, my legs crossed tight against one another and an unnerving excited tingle in my groin.

We were going to make it. By the blink of an eye, we would be on that train, and then we could relax. Hopefully, we'd even get some sleep.

The robotic voice told us to keep left. We did so, following the road around a large curve, which felt like a fairground ride given the speed we were travelling at. And then suddenly, we emerged into an industrial lorry park. Ned slowed the van and we both peered out the front window, confused.

'This isn't right,' I said.

'No,' he said, and quickly put the van back into motion. As we followed the ring road out of the site, I pressed my legs tight together, holding my breath, or perhaps even quietly hyperventilating.

11:59 p.m.

We sped around a bend in the opposite direction. A signpost for the Channel Tunnel came into view. I visualized the van pulling up, the last vehicle to arrive up the ramp, before the shoot shut tightly behind us. I imagined exhaling the recycled air that was caught in my chest from taking such short sharp breaths.

00:00 a.m.

I covered my mouth with my palms, starting to feel dizzy. 'It's midnight,' I breathed, squeezing my eyes shut.

When I opened my eyes, it was 00:01 a.m.

I started telling myself that there could have been a delay. Trains seldom left on time in this day and age. But when we pulled up to the station, all I saw beneath the large 'PASSPORT AND SECURITY' sign were two empty glass booths and a white and red beam. There was no train in sight, no other cars, not even a human.

I pressed my hands up against the dashboard and hung my head between my elbows with a chanting chorus of 'Fuck' in my head. I felt the tension leave my muscles as my breath slowly returned to a normal pace.

'I'm sorry,' said Ned, and he truly sounded mortified.

'It's not your fault,' I muttered into my lap. 'I'm sorry for making you do this.'

'What do you want to do?' he asked.

I was amazed that he was still giving me the agency to make the decisions. 'I can't turn back now,' I said, sitting up suddenly and looking at him through the strands of hair that had strewn themselves over my face. 'There must be an early morning train. We could sleep in the van until then.' Ned turned his grey eyes on me and I could tell that he wasn't sold on the idea. But I wasn't ready to admit failure. I had to turn around this curdled disaster – which I was starting to suspect that I'd made worse – or at least find a way of watering it down. I returned to Google and, on discovering that the next train was at 6 a.m., I handed the phone to Ned.

He looked at the information, and then looked at me, pressing his lips together. 'Do you mind if I ask why you're doing this? I mean . . . is it really just about Clara?'

'What else could it be about?'

'I don't know. But maybe it's more about . . . you?' He was hesitant with his words, like someone who knew that they had a responsibility to bring up something that they'd rather leave buried.

'How could it be about me?' I asked, shifting uncomfortably in the seat.

'Just a stab in the dark . . . Maybe it's something to do with . . . abandonment issues? And, I don't know, maybe you've jumped into rescue mode in the way you'd want someone to do for you?'

'Just a casual stab in the dark?' I asked sceptically.

'Sorry . . . I don't . . . I know that's quite a personally

invasive thing to say. I just want to make sure you know what you're doing.'

'I appreciate it. And as much as I love a pop-psychology analysis, this is about my best friend and her mental health.'

'Got it,' he said immediately. You couldn't argue with mental health. He sighed. 'Six o'clock train it is, then.'

I gave a grateful nod. Then, suddenly, I dove across the gear stick and flung my arms around his neck. Seemingly surprised by the gesture – I wasn't sure if we'd ever hugged before – Ned lifted one arm to squeeze me. He adjusted himself into another position so that he could slide his other arm around, returning the impulsive hug fully. I inhaled his clean scent and the heat of his body. That hug felt like it was forming a protective shell around me, keeping me safe from harm's way, even if he had just come out with the most exposing thing anyone had ever said to me.

'Thank you so much,' I whispered. 'I'm going to buy you the biggest glass of champagne when we get there.'

'Don't know if I'll be in the mood at breakfast, but thanks.'

'Lavender test tube vodka, then?' I said, suddenly in a brighter mood, post hug.

He smiled. 'If you can find one in Paris, I'll give you shares in the company.'

'Uh . . . deal!'

Ned looked at his digital wristwatch, then glanced into the back of the van. 'I don't really want to sleep in the van. It has the company name on it and it's not the best look for the brand if we get a penalty.'

'OK. What do you want to do instead?' I asked, envisioning the two of us in a brightly lit diner at a service station all night long. I was suddenly so charged up with adrenaline that the idea of sleep seemed a faraway concept, but I knew I'd need to force myself into it if I didn't want to arrive for my battle a touchy, emotional detonator.

'Let's find a nearby hotel,' he suggested, reaching for his own iPhone.

'Sure,' I said lightly, though the thought of leaving the station with so little turnaround time gave me an anxious feeling. But given that I'd already put his business at risk by forcing him to drive at illegal speeds, I concluded that I needed to compromise somewhere. And it might as well be on a hotel.

The nearest hotel was a corporate chain for £69 a night. Checking in with Ned was a surreal moment in my life. If I'd had a premonition about it when I'd first met him at the *Close Up* office, back in October, I'd have been utterly confused about the direction my life was heading. To be fair, I was still utterly confused about it.

The receptionist didn't ask us any questions. She didn't even ask how many rooms we wanted, or the type of sleeping arrangement required. She just handed us one room card without looking either of us in the eye. Given the time of night, our non-existent luggage and the fact that I looked like I'd been pulled off the side of the road, I gathered that she took our check-in to be some kind of clandestine, sordid exchange. I wondered if she was used to seeing such things and had an urge to tell her that she should look into the eyes of the women hauled into her reception in the middle of the night, in case they were silently screaming for help. Thankfully, I wasn't.

Ned and I entered the room without raising any comment to the strangeness of the situation, or to the double bed that we'd have to share. Instead I said, 'Fifty shades of purple,' although there was actually only one unnerving shade of the garish colour in the room – but still an unnecessary amount. I'd once heard that suicide was a psychological property of the colour purple and had avoided it like the plague ever since. But that room was making up for all the purple I'd managed to keep out of my life until then. It did not bode well that it happened to be on the most dramatic and unusual night of my life to date. A shiver tickled its way down my spine as I took it all in.

'Do you need the bathroom?' he asked.

'You go first.'

There was something unsettlingly domestic about sharing a hotel room with a man I knew so little about, or with any man at all, for that matter.

The toilet flushed on the other side of the wall and Ned re-emerged. Our eyes met for a millisecond before we looked away from each other and I busied myself locating a plug socket to charge my phone. Then I slipped into the bathroom, closed the door softly and tried to go to the loo. I was dying to wee, but all I could think about was Ned being able to hear everything, given that his own urination had left nothing to the imagination. My pelvic floor had stubbornly locked up the gates and stood there with its arms crossed. *No way, babes.* Thank God I didn't have a boyfriend, since I couldn't even stomach an en suite. I decided to give up and try again once he was asleep. I splashed my face with water from the sink. A freshly used toothbrush was lying on its side on the stark white basin. I hadn't brought anything as sensible as a toothbrush in my panic pack, and I didn't really think I was there with Ned yet. So I squeezed a bit of his travel-sized toothpaste onto my finger and rubbed at my front teeth, making tiny squeaking sounds. I thought of Clara, brushing her own teeth in the luxury cabin at Yeotown, full of excitement for the weekend ahead. *You have to make this work, Jax.*

When I returned to the bedroom, Ned was already under the bed covers, scrolling on his iPhone. I noticed his black jeans, neatly folded on the purple armchair. 'Setting an alarm for four forty-five,' he said, without looking up.

'Perfect.' I stepped out of my trainers and slipped my skirt down my legs, wondering if he'd glance at me half undressed, perhaps even willing him to, or at least to catch me in his periphery, but he showed no signs of acknowledgement. I sidled into the space between the duvet and the rock-hard mattress, then removed my bra through the armhole of my T-shirt, like a pro. I glanced down at the T-shirt as I did so. *What Do Women Want?* Equality. Independence. Affection. A saviour?

Ned set his phone aside and switched off the lights. In the darkness, I was acutely aware of his breathing, subtle though it was. How would I know when he was asleep? It had been so long since I had shared a bed with any male species except Leo. The space between our two bodies felt both thick and magnetic. I thought of the way he'd hugged me in the car and that fleeting sense of safety that I'd felt. Something in me felt desperate to return to that place. I rolled over, towards him, half expecting some force to stop me from nestling into the side of his body, but it didn't.

Ned lifted his arm and let me lie in the crook of it, his hand resting lightly on my shoulder. The gesture was hospitable and generous, a contrast to the usual dead-weight limbs I had strewn over me. He cupped the sharp bone of my shoulder in his palm, in a way that assured me that he was fully present in that gentle embrace. His calm stillness was tactful and unassuming, accepting the moment of warmth for exactly what it was.

Then, as suddenly as the impulse to roll into him had come about, a cold fear washed over me. It was something like recognition of reality, of the possibility that I may have crossed a line. Was I being suggestive? It would take so little from there. A small thrust, a gentle stroke, an untoward grasp. A feeling of guilt littered with specks of panic started to weave an intricate web through me. I didn't want to lose that feeling of warmth that we'd cultivated in that embrace, but the truth was that I'd already lost it thanks to my rattling thoughts. And the next day was going to be stressful enough without a post-coital elephant following us around. I made a noise that implied I could have been asleep as I disentangled myself from him and rolled over. I hooked my fingers onto the edge of the mattress, clamping myself in place.

Again.

I did it for Clara.

CHAPTER 10

Luckily, Ned and I could both claim exhaustion and the absence of coffee for our lack of fluid conversation the next morning. But in reality, our laid-back dynamic had inevitably shifted after the wordless physical contact in our shared bed. Additionally, I couldn't quite shake his unnervingly astute observation – *Maybe it's more about . . . you?* – from my mind.

I went downstairs before he did, so that I could pay for the hotel room like the feminist I was, hoping that it would surprise the presumptuous receptionist of the night before, but she had gone off duty. Ned bought coffees on the train and we both buried into our iPhones. Clearly, I was not going to make it onto my planned flight to Italy that day. I didn't exactly know how I was going to explain that to Clara but was silently hoping that by the time we got to it, I'd have totally changed Ed's mind and all would be fine. *Cross that bridge when you come to it.*

Alice and Omni wouldn't be up yet, but I had a barrage of messages from the night before, when I'd simply told them I was staying in a hotel until the first train left, before switching my phone to airplane mode.

> Omni:
> Stop!!!!!
> 🙈

Alice:
There seem to be a lot of barriers to
execution going on here.

Omni:
It's literally like a movie

Alice:
Let's have a call in the morning. I say we
give it to midday and then we call Clara.

Omni:
Ned must be like . . . 😕

Alice:
Have you got enough money for this trip?

I ignored the chit chat and sent them a status update, informing
them that I was soaring through the Channel Tunnel, and that
someone should redesign the hotel chain in question. When I
closed WhatsApp, I automatically opened every other app on my
phone – BBC Weather, The Pattern, Hormonology, Instagram,
Twitter, Facebook – even though there was nothing specific I
wanted to look at. I closed all the apps fully by sliding them
up the screen and then for some reason reopened half of them
again. I landed on Facebook, which I hardly ever used. Jittering
with nerves, I began to scroll, staring at it with the concentra-
tion of someone trying to understand something confusing and
important. Apparently, it was some girl's birthday, but I didn't
recognize her name, probably because she'd got married and
expunged her identity to anyone who knew her back in the day.

Nothing I Wouldn't Do

As I was scrolling, a status update caught my eye: 'JOURNALIST FRIENDS – please send pitches for articles on female friendship asap!' It was Natasha's status. The features editor whose bridge I'd set fire to only hours before by letting her down at the last minute. But I hardly ever scrolled through Facebook, and it felt serendipitous that I'd chosen to do so. That status – and that topic – was calling out to me, giving me an almost instinctive urge to write. It was an urge that I hadn't felt so strongly since I'd left *Close Up*, and I was suddenly more awake and alive than I had been five minutes before. With Ned's voice in my head – *'Maybe you've jumped into rescue mode in the way you'd want someone to do for you?* – I opened the Notes application on my iPhone and began:

23 May 2019 at 06:52

So many of us find it hard to give what is required to make a romantic relationship work perfectly, but to our female friends, we give it our all. The article I am proposing is based around the notion that we, as women, give everything to our girlfriends in order to create the fantasy relationship that we know we may never have. But in giving all that we do, the truth is that we are not doing it for them. We are doing it for ourselves. What we give, we expect back. We take on the traumas of our closest friends, like a safety blanket, in anticipation of our own hypothetical, existential and actual future traumas. Because when they happen, guess what we will expect from our girlfriends? Everything.

The words came cascading from brain to thumb like water jets, suddenly appearing on the screen of my phone as if by

183

magic. It felt intoxicating. If I could have locked myself in a silent room for a whole day with nothing but a laptop and my thoughts, I would have. When I reached the end of the pitch, I returned to see what I'd written and I felt as if the three succinct paragraphs had been written by someone else, someone far more intelligent and experienced than myself. I changed a few words and cleaned up the typos, before scrolling up to title the pitch: 'The emotional intimacy of female friendships: Why we give everything we have and more.'

I copied and pasted the text into an email and sent it to Natasha with an opening line of 'Trying my luck . . .' I didn't expect her to respond, but I had nothing to lose by sending it.

It was 10 a.m. when Ned and I finally found ourselves in the metropolis of love.

I had one goal: to get Ed on a plane to Pantelleria that same day, come hell or high water.

Ed's refuge was a flat in the Marais. I remembered elements of it from the photos Clara had sent us when she was high with excitement over the engagement. I felt entirely crushed by the thought that she might never get to be there again. My stomach gurgled with nausea when Google Maps announced that we had reached our final destination. This was it. This was the climactic moment of the movie. And who knew how it would end?

'Do you want me to come in with you?' Ned asked apprehensively.

'Yes, please.'

He nodded and said brightly, 'I'm sure we can get a better coffee here than the Eurotunnel's finest.'

The address I had was above a bakery with baguettes hanging

decoratively in the front window. As we got closer, it became clear that the baguettes were intricately shaped as penises. They had been baked in a range of sizes, speckled and clean, ribbed and smooth, all tied up with neat, coloured ribbons.

'He's hiding in a dick bread shop?' I said derisively, and Ned laughed. I wondered why Clara hadn't sent us a picture of the penis bread, instead of endless espresso cups and champagne glasses. Surely the bakery she was staying above would have been a far more interesting contribution to the group chat?

I hadn't eaten anything except crisps and chocolates for almost twenty-four hours and seeing the bread made me realize how starving I was. I wanted to charge inside and commit carbicide, but I thought that chewing the head off a penis baguette in front of Ned was a step too far in the current circumstances. I lifted my finger to ring the doorbell but paused. 'I'm nervous.' The whole plan had made sense with three tequilas, a glass of wine and thoughts of heroism pumping through me. In the cold light of day, however, I could sympathize with the argument that I had officially lost my mind.

'Do you know what you're going to say?' Ned asked.

I shrugged, thinking that I really should have written my thoughts down first. 'He's going to be so shocked to see me.'

'I don't know if he will, you know. He has to expect there'll be some upshot to just disappearing days before his wedding.'

Being reminded of what Ed had done gave me the push that I needed. I quickly pressed my finger over the doorbell of Apt 3. Seconds later, there was a buzzing sound and the door latch released with a click. We exchanged a confused glance as I pushed it open. Had Ed seen us from a window? Were we at the right place at all?

I stepped into a very narrow carpeted entrance hall,

beckoning Ned to follow. There was an old-fashioned lift with a sliding cage door and a rickety wooden staircase. Not quite the marble extravaganza I'd always pictured. I was sure that the lift would break down, given how the journey had gone so far – perhaps that was even Ed's plan, in letting us up – so I insisted that we take the staircase. When we got to the third floor, the door of Apt 3 stood ominously ajar. I lifted my knuckles to it, shrugging at Ned, and knocked three times.

'Hi,' a voice called from inside.

'You go first,' I whispered. 'He'll be less freaked out.'

'And more confused,' said Ned, but stepped inside neverthe-less. I followed a few steps behind, into another small entrance hall, with mustard yellow walls and a tall distressed mirror. I stood still as Ned rounded a corner. Then, from somewhere out of my sight, I heard him stutter awkwardly, 'Oh hi. I'm really sorry. We thought Ed was here . . .'

'Not a problem,' a soft American voice said.

Suddenly, Ned retreated back into the entrance hall, look-ing somewhat shell-shocked. I threw a questioning glare in his direction. Before he had time to explain anything, a vast structure of a man appeared from around the corner, wearing nothing but a muslin cloth, which he was still fixing into place around his waist. Poor Ned must have walked in to find the man entirely naked, which made me wonder why he had so willingly buzzed us in without a word. Perhaps he had been waiting for someone else.

'Hi, welcome,' said the structure in a soft accent that I deduced was more likely to have been French Canadian than American. He had long frizzy blond hair pulled back into a ponytail and wore a beaded necklace and several bracelets. I couldn't imagine a person less aesthetically likely to have been a godfather of Ed's. I had been expecting some stiff, uptight retiree.

'I'm sorry to bother you,' I said, sounding more British than ever, having been thrown by the whole thing. My heart had been thumping all the way from London with the anticipation of seeing Ed and I suddenly felt as if someone had pulled the rug from beneath me. 'I'm a friend of Ed's . . . sort of. A friend of Clara's, actually.'

'I see,' said the structure, stretching his mouth over to one side of his face, nodding pensively, like he was trying to suss me out.

'Would you mind if we came in?' I asked.

'Well, I've always said four's a crowd but three's a threesome, so come on in,' said the structure, as he turned to amble back around that corner.

I threw Ned a glance that was slightly amused, slightly apologetic and altogether confused, and we followed the man into one big, high-ceiled room. There was a bohemian feel to the place with its slightly worn furniture, artistic clutter, antique appliances and far too many plants. A large shelving unit against the wall was inexplicably filled with old television sets and VHS players. Even more out of place was the family-sized trampoline covered in splats of paint that had also made their way onto the parquet floor, with a canvas dangling from the ceiling above. Sunlight poured through the full-length windows and half of the space overhead was taken up by a mezzanine that appeared to be a bedroom, framed by an art-deco railing.

The man went straight to the kitchen and turned to face us with his hands on his hips. 'You want a glass of milk?'

'No, thank you,' said Ned politely as I shook my head slowly. *Milk?*

'Have a seat, please, make yourselves comfortable,' said the man blithely, gesturing at a kitchen table. It was covered in newspapers, with a conspicuous loaf of penis bread playing centrepiece on a large chopping board. One of the testicles had been sliced in half and the doughy innards were visible. 'What were your names again?' asked the structure, as Ned and I gingerly placed ourselves on two of his mismatched chairs.

'I'm Ned.'

'I'm Jax.'

'Jax,' he repeated. 'Huh. I'm Patrick.'

'This flat is amazing,' I said, suddenly imagining Bella arriving and throwing her long arms in the air in exultation, booming, *My God, this is just fabulous!*

'Thank you. I've had it for a long time,' he said, opening the fridge and taking out a bottle of milk.

'And we loved the bakery downstairs,' I added, in a feeble attempt to demonstrate our position as open-minded, liberal millennials, who would perfectly fit into bohemian Paris, as opposed to the sort of uptight Brits you might expect Ed to know. Or was I the only one who placed Ed in that category?

'It's great, isn't it?' said Patrick, as he fussed around with mugs in the sink.

I glanced up at the mezzanine. The double bed was unmade, an ethnic throw bundled at the foot of it. There were no visible signs of Ed in the flat, or any guest. The sofa did not appear to have been slept on and there was not a suitcase in sight.

'So, what brings you to Paris?' asked Patrick, pouring milk into a ceramic mug.

I pressed my hands between my thighs, suddenly feeling that I was in a situation way too confrontational for me. Rich, given that I was the one who had crossed the Channel in the name of confrontation.

'We thought Ed might be here?' said Ned, when he realized I wasn't going to say anything.

'Uh-huh,' said Patrick, placing a hand on Ned's shoulder. 'Gosh, you're very tense.' He dug his thumb above Ned's shoulder bone and started rubbing into it. 'Can I offer you a massage?'

'That's very kind,' said Ned, his neck rising in colour. 'But not necessary.'

'You sure? Aromatherapy massage? The way it ends, it ends.'

Ned shook his head speechlessly, and I laughed, hoping that would break the ice. Patrick smiled, patted Ned on the back and took a seat at the head of the table. He pulled the board of penis bread towards him and began cutting it into neat slices. 'Did you come all the way from the UK to look for Ed?'

'Yes,' said Ned pointedly, looking at me, which I took to mean, *You had better start talking.*

I piped up. 'Just to be totally transparent, I'm Clara's maid of honour. And she doesn't know that Ed wants to call off the wedding.'

'Right,' said Patrick, not looking the least bit perturbed. 'So, you're here to ...'

'To talk to Ed,' I said. 'Is he here?'

'Do you see him?' he responded, which could have been construed as rude, but in his dulcet voice was nothing but charming.

'Listen, I know that you're Ed's godfather and that you don't know me at all,' I began. 'But I have to tell you that Ed is meant to be getting on a plane to Italy today. Clara thinks he's flying with her, as planned, and that they're getting married on Saturday.'

'Why does she think that?' he said, with an incredulity that was clearly meant to patronize me.

'Because I've hidden it from her,' I admitted. 'It's not fair that she should find out in a note and then not be able to confront him. It isn't right.'

'You don't think so?' he said, eyebrows raised.

I was totally thrown off by his response. 'Do *you* think so?'

Patrick sighed and stood up, adjusting his muslin loincloth. 'I don't know,' he said, like he was sick and tired of hearing about the situation already. 'I'm afraid you've caught me at a slightly hectic point in time. I'm preparing for an exhibition.' With that, he headed off across the room towards the trampoline.

'Are you an artist?' asked Ned, with a level of interest that could only have been touching to Patrick, given that he was, as usual, the definition of earnest. I felt a glow form around my heart as I looked at him and felt so thankful that he was there with me. God knows how Harry would have behaved, had he succumbed.

'Uh-huh,' said Patrick, retrieving a selection of paintbrushes and a palette of colour from a side table. Then he hoisted one leg onto the trampoline and indelicately clambered up, taking us by total surprise. I looked at Ned, who was watching with genuine intrigue as Patrick positioned himself in front of the suspended canvas. The next second the whole structure of Patrick was bouncing up and down on that trampoline, taking a stroke at the canvas each time he was suspended in the air, the loincloth threatening to disengage with every jump.

My confusion was clouded with annoyance and frustration, which left no room for amusement, even given what was going on. I was outright offended. He was doing it to fuck with me.

'Do you always paint on a trampoline?' I muttered, trying to keep any hostility out of my voice, though I knew that it had crept in.

'Always,' he said, with no further explanation.

'That's very niche,' I added.

'It is,' he agreed.

I sighed, stood up and walked over to the trampoline, keeping my eyes firmly fixed on his bouncing ponytail. 'Can you please tell me where Ed is, Patrick?'

'Look, if you've tried to call him, you'll know that his phone's not working,' he said, closing one eye and holding his arm out, paintbrush upright, to measure perspective. I highly doubted that he had enough control in his ridiculous technique to deal with composition. 'So, I can't get a hold of him any better than you can.'

'But he is here?' I pressed.

'Sure. He's here,' he said lightly.

'Do you know when he'll be back?' asked Ned from the kitchen table.

'I thought that was him arriving just now, but it was you lovely people,' he said, and I couldn't tell if he was being sardonic. 'I don't know exactly when he'll be back. It's a stressful time for him.'

'It's a stressful time for me too, as you can see,' I said snappishly. 'I made poor Ned drive me all the way from London.'

'Why didn't you get the Eurostar? It's so easy.'

No shit.

'Have you seen my collectibles?' asked Patrick, pointing his brush in the direction of the old TV and VHS sets.

It was then that I lost my patience, realizing that he was going to go on fucking with me for as long as it took to get rid of me. 'You know what? This may be amusing to you, but this is Clara's life that is about to fall apart. Your godson made a promise to her and he has walked away from it, with no explanation. She is about to have her heart broken and she will spend the rest of her life wondering what she did wrong. You really should stop treating this like a joke!'

Patrick's bouncing slowed and then stopped altogether. 'I don't think it's a joke. I just know the story from a different perspective,' he said cryptically.

'What perspective?' I cried. 'Enlighten me! So that, at least, I can enlighten her.'

'Look, why don't you guys take an hour. Walk around, see Paris, there's a fantastic restaurant on the Rue du Temple. Leave your number and I'll have Ed call you when he's back.'

'We don't have time, Patrick!' I said, exasperated, but softer, feeling like I may have got through to him just an inch further than before. There was hope of getting this strange man in loincloth on side. 'Please, Patrick. I realize that what I've done is completely unreasonable and meddling. But if I don't speak to Ed, I've just made this situation a hundred times worse. I'm panicking, big time. I feel kind of sick.' I was imploring him to put himself in my position, in the current situation, since Clara's perspective didn't seem to be of interest. It was entirely true that I was becoming more and more terrified of the consequences of my puerile actions.

'More than anything,' Ned piped up from behind me, 'it's better for Ed if he gets all these conversations out of the way now. Things will only get worse, and I assume he's not planning on hiding out in Paris forever. He should have his say, tell his side of the story, kill all the rumours.'

I threw an affronted glare in Ned's direction at the

suggestion that Ed was anything but a villain in this story. But I had to bite my tongue when I saw Patrick's face. He was nodding thoughtfully, seemingly in agreement. I was sure that it was more to do with the fact of Ned's gender than his sentiment, though I wasn't about to raise that point when we just seemed to be getting somewhere. But then, Patrick shook his head – apologetically I have to admit – and said, 'Sorry, kiddo.'

I crouched down on the tiny ledge of the penis bakery, with my head hanging between my knees and a cigarette burning down between two fingers. The position of helplessness was killing me. I wanted to grab onto someone – anyone – shake them and scream, *Just let me fix this!*

'What am I going to do?' I mumbled at my crotch.

'Jax, I think it's time to tell Clara what's going on,' said Ned softly.

The thought of delivering the news to Clara down the phone was cryogenically freezing my blood cells. But it was too late for me to descend on Yeotown and cradle her in my arms. She would be preparing to leave for the airport, fresh, flushed and full of eagerness. What if she was taking one last walk by the ravine and tripped over from the shock of the news, cracking her head open and tumbling in to drown? Yes, I was catastrophizing, but with good reason. The situation was, by definition, a catastrophe. And one that I had whipped up, no less.

'I need to call Alice,' I said, like a charged felon grasping for one last opportunity for legal support. 'I can't tell Clara while she's all alone.'

'Are you ever going to tell her?' Ned asked uncertainly.

It was a good question. When the moment came, would I

be able to? I pressed my lips around the end of the cigarette and inhaled forcefully, thinking about the 5,000 cells in my body that were being killed off by that one drag (thanks to Dymfy for that delightful fact). I looked down at the screen of my phone and the two grinning eight-year-olds trapped behind that shield of glass. I wished that I could smash it open, dive in to scoop them up and nurture them as children should be nurtured. I wanted to climb into the bathtub to tell eight-year-old Clara that she was full of capacity to look after herself and tell my eight-year-old self that I was as loveable as anyone else. That I was *enough*.

But it was too late for any of that, so instead, I dialled Alice, hoping to God that she had a plan that resembled a solution. She answered with a brief, 'Tell me.' Alice tended to open conversations with a command.

Suddenly, Ned closed his hand around my wrist. It was the first physical contact we'd had since the night before and the memory of the same hand cupping my shoulder surfaced for a brief second. Then I realized that he was alerting me to the front door opening behind us. Patrick emerged, dressed in linen trousers with a matching shirt.

'I'll call you back,' I muttered into the phone and hung up. I looked up at Patrick, hopeful and pleading.

'Let's go talk to young Ed.'

Patrick gave us the lowdown on his arrondissement like we were visitors on a walking tour as we weaved our way through the streets. It amazed me that he thought I could really think of anything that moment except for what I was going to say to Ed, but then the tour was probably for Ned's benefit.

We crossed over the road to a busy street corner, on which

stood a quirky purple building – I did wonder what was with all the purple that was suddenly cropping up in my life – with tables scattered out onto the pavement. It was packed full of vibrant Parisians enjoying a morning coffee. Without saying anything, Patrick slipped inside, beckoning us to follow. We squeezed into the packed-out interior, rickety and as unusual as the outside. The row of bar stools and a few tables were equally crammed with young people, adorned in nose rings, bandanas and tattoos.

'Ed's in here?' I asked dubiously.

'I thought he might be,' said Patrick with no further explanation. He lifted his arm and waved at someone behind the breakfast counter. A bald-headed man with a long moustache, wearing a tank top to show off pumped-up arms, returned the wave and blew a kiss in his direction. He slipped out from behind the counter and walked towards us with a friendly smile on his face. He and Patrick hugged for a long time, while conversing in French. After a brief exchange and an emphatic laugh, Patrick turned to us and introduced us. '*Les amis d'Edward de Londres.*'

'Ah!' the man opened his arms. He planted a kiss on both of my cheeks then moved onto Ned. Once again, Patrick spoke to the man in French, and I heard the word 'Edward' in the sentence. The man answered in his clipped French voice, 'Épicerie.'

'Épicerie?'

'*Oui.*'

'*D'accord, cherie.*' We said goodbye to the mystery man and Patrick led us out, explaining, 'He's gone to the grocer.'

'To the grocer?' I asked, somewhat perplexed. I wondered how Ed could have been on close enough terms with someone who worked at a beatnik Parisian coffee shop to have told him about the mundanities of the rest of his day.

'Probably to pick up bits for lunch,' said Patrick, which answered none of my unspoken questions.

Nonetheless, my heart started to race as I caught sight of the greengrocer on the other side of the street. I was one step away from having to execute my own crazy plan.

'Ah, see,' said Patrick, pointing over the road. 'There he is.'

CHAPTER 11

I felt none of the emotions that I'd expected to as I watched
Ed from a distance. I had anticipated a hailstorm of fury to
start whipping around inside me and laser beams of hatred to
jet out of my eyes. I had prepared myself to exercise all of the
self-control within me not to dive right at his throat. But as I
watched him carefully picking vegetables, treating each one
tenderly as he placed it into the basket on his arm, I felt none
of those reactions. There was something different about him.
He wasn't standing erect and puffing his chest out as he usually
did or holding a barrier of *Don't Come Too Close* around him.
He looked peaceful and content in his solitude.

'Let me go first,' said Patrick. I conceded with a nod and
kept my eyes on Ed as he approached him. Patrick placed a
hand on his godson's shoulder. Ed turned to him and smiled,
before pointing out something on the vegetable stand.
Suddenly, I felt utterly remorseful that we were here, that we
were about to ambush his peaceful withdrawal. I watched as
Patrick leaned in close to talk to him, still holding onto his
shoulder. Ed's eyes drifted towards us, and the nest of anxiety
that had woven itself into me began to quiver with dread. I
could barely move.

I wished that Ned would take hold of my hand or put his
arm around me, but that would have been strange. The two

of them talked for longer, with nothing but a few passing cars between us and them. I was happy to be watching it all on mute. That's what I did when I was watching a nerve-racking film on my own. Pressed the mute button when it got too much, and watched the plot unfold in the safety of silence.

They turned towards us. Patrick guided Ed across the road with a gentle hand on his back, as my heart thumped at my chest aggressively. *Pipe down, it's only Ed.*

Ed didn't look me in the eye, but at the top of my head.

'Hello, Jax.'

'I suppose you're here to lambaste me,' said Ed, once we were all squeezed onto an outdoor table at the purple café that Patrick managed to negotiate for us by way of hugs and kisses. *Lambaste?*

'Actually, I'm here to try to stop you from doing this,' I said seriously. 'And even I know that lambasting you would not be the best way to go about that.'

'Well then, even you should know that this really is nothing to do with you,' Ed pointed out.

'Do you think you're the first person who's said that to me in the past twelve hours?' I said wryly.

'Then why are you here?' he asked, not exactly unkindly, glancing at Ned briefly.

'Who doesn't love a trip to Paris?' Patrick interjected cheerfully, and somewhat unhelpfully.

'Ed, how can you do this to her?' I breathed desperately. 'How?'

'You know so little about the situation,' he muttered, as a gangly waitress – who looked something like I'd imagined Vicky-pedia to – arrived with a tray of coffees. She leaned across the table to hand them out, which awkwardly broke the flow of the conversation.

'I know enough,' I said, irritably ducking underneath the waitress's arm. 'I saw what happened on Friday night.'

'Friday night has nothing to do with it,' he said, to my surprise. 'And what exactly did you "see" happen?'

'Well. I watched you gaslight her to within an inch of her life!' I blurted. I knew it was provocative, but in that moment, I couldn't help it.

'Oh please,' Ed scoffed, looking around from left to right, as if he were about to get up and leave.

'You know how insecure she feels about her family, and you twisted the knife into her wound. You made her feel like a crazy drunk and then you left her with a few sentences in a letter. Do you understand that Clara will feel responsible for this, for the rest of her life, because of that night?'

'It's nothing to do with that night or that fight. And Clara knows that.'

'How could she possibly know that, from your ambiguous letter?' I spat angrily.

'Trust me. She knows,' he said, with a darkness in his voice that was utterly cryptic.

I squinted, trying to decipher what, exactly, he meant. I glanced at Patrick who was nodding along, like, *I told you so*. I thought back to what he had said earlier – 'I just know the story from a different perspective' – and suddenly it clicked in my mind that there was a piece of the puzzle that I was missing. Feeling helpless, I looked at Ned, quietly begging for support.

Leaning on the table, he lifted himself out of his elbows to speak, 'It's probably worth saying now that Clara doesn't know about the letter.' He watched me nervously through every word, perhaps even in fear, wondering if he'd overstepped the mark. I shrugged. It was going to have to come out at some point.

'What do you mean?' Ed asked, anxious frown lines forming across his forehead.

Everyone at the table was now looking at me. 'I found the letter in your flat before Clara did and I ripped it up and came here without telling her,' I admitted with a sigh. I felt like a naughty child who had just been caught.

Ed's expression changed from anxious to completely dismayed. 'Jesus, Jax! She's meant to be flying today.'

'So are you! So are we all,' I reminded him, as if he didn't know. 'Why do you say that Clara will know why you've done this? If it isn't to do with the other night?' I asked, uncertain of whether I wanted to hear the answer or not.

'Let's just say that there's a side to Clara that no one seems to be aware of,' he said, stirring his cappuccino with a tiny silver spoon, turning the chocolate-dusted froth into a brown swirl.

'I know every side of her,' I said firmly.

'No, you don't,' he said, with so much certainty that it sent a chill through me.

'What don't I know about her?' I spat, insulted by the implication. 'Tell me.'

'Well, I take it you don't know that she's been cheating on me?' He threw it out, like an unexpected hand in a poker game.

I didn't even give the words a second of consideration before spluttering with disbelief, 'Don't be ridiculous!'

'That's exactly the reaction I expected from you,' he said. 'And I'm the gaslighter?'

'Where the hell did you get that from?' I cried, aghast at his conviction over something so absurd.

'I don't have to share that with you,' he said with superiority, like it was classified information that I didn't have a high enough level of clearance to be privy to. 'I know that it's true. And Clara knows it too.'

'I don't believe you,' I said, crossing my arms over my chest and exaggeratedly shaking my head from side to side.

'No, of course you don't. Because you don't know Clara as well as I do,' he whipped.

That's when the hailstorm of fury that I'd been expecting earlier came rising up from within me. 'I've known Clara for twenty years. I know her better than anyone.'

'You're her friend. Not her lover,' he said in an oddly gentle manner. 'You do not know everything about her.'

The anger morphed into an anxious sadness as I realized that he was right. A friendship could never be the same as a relationship. There were facets of Clara that I would never know as well as Ed did. An image of the Agent Provocateur lingerie made a brief appearance in my mind, before I pushed it away and replaced it with an image of Clara sitting on the loo seat at her parents' house, saying, 'Imagine if I'd never met Ed?'

The issue at hand was not whether Ed or I knew Clara more intimately, because anyone who knew Clara would know that what he was saying made no sense. It was a basic fact of her nature that a secret love affair would cause her too much anxiety to face. Certainly, she wouldn't have been able to do it without leaning on someone – on me – for support throughout the whole thing. If what Ed was saying was true, she would have known that I wouldn't judge her for it because – I was ashamed to admit – I would have been excited by the mischievousness of it. Clara would have known that about me.

'I don't know what you've heard,' I said, twisting my dirty

hair into a knot at the base of my skull and holding it there with my finger, 'but it's not true. You need to see her face to face, so that she can tell you that.'

'Why would I want to see her, so that she can lie to my face?' he said, spreading his hands out questioningly.

'Where did you hear this story?' I asked, raising my voice a little. 'Who told you?'

'I'm not talking semantics,' he said. 'You really should tell Clara about the letter.'

'It's too late,' I said. 'I ripped the letter into pieces. And Clara is on her way to the airport. So are the whole family. And tomorrow, all of your friends will be too.' I was pushing him into a corner because the thought of arriving in Pantelleria without him, given this new information that I had no clarity on, was too much to bear. I knew that one way to get him onto the plane – if only to face her – was to remind him how awkward the situation was for everyone else.

'And you want me to get married, so that we don't ruin your party?' he said.

'It's not my party! It's your wedding!' I said, as hot sweat came seeping out of my armpits.

'Really?' he cried. 'Because you've spent the past eight months acting like it's nothing to do with me. *Now* it's convenient for you to see it as my wedding, when it's not even mine anymore!'

'You know what, Ed? Even if she did cheat on you, the fact that you won't look her in the eye and confront her about it is pathetic,' I hissed. 'More pathetic than the fact that I "over-insert myself in her life" as you so kindly told me the other night.'

'I didn't mean to upset you, Jax—'

'You didn't,' I said, far too quickly. 'I don't feel bad for wanting to be a good friend.' I met eyes with Ned for a second, having paraphrased his words to me. He smiled and I felt like my point was validated.

'I'm not saying you should feel bad. But if you don't think that this trip of yours proves my point, well, then, it wouldn't be the first time we've failed to see eye to eye.'

I sighed. I did see his point. 'I know that I acted rashly,' I said, 'but regardless of whether you agree with what I've done or not, you need to do the right thing. The grown-up thing.'

There was a long silence. Then, suddenly, my phone started ringing. It was on the table face down, the baby blue cover with illustrations of different shapes of breasts glaring up at us. Gravely, I turned it over to confirm my fear. Clara was calling. Her smiling face flashed up at us ominously. When Ed noticed, his face dropped. He rested his brow line against his fingertips and closed his eyes.

'What do you want me to say?' I asked softly. 'Please think carefully.'

He let out a large sigh of stress and suddenly stood up. I thought he was going to storm out, but he just stood there, breathing heavily through his nostrils. He looked at Patrick helplessly.

Patrick squeezed his arm and spoke softly. 'Go on, kiddo. You gotta face the music.'

I threw Patrick a grateful look as I moved my finger towards the green phone icon, preparing to answer.

'Fine,' Ed rasped. 'Tell her I'll be there tonight.'

CHAPTER 12

'It's my fault. I fucked up the flights,' I lied down the phone to Clara. She was at Heathrow Airport, waiting to board the plane with her whole family, except for Omni, who was texting me from the disabled toilet, where she was flat on the floor dying of a hangover and pranging out about every lie she had told that day. I was sitting outside a café opposite Patrick's flat with Ned, while Ed packed, quietly panicking about whether Omni would have remembered to bring everything I asked for, given her current state.

'So, when will you arrive?' Clara asked, oblivious to the whole clusterfuck I'd made of her orbit.

'On the next flight,' I said, which wasn't completely a lie. Ed and I were to travel through Rome, just like they were doing, only we were coming from Paris and would only just scrape onto the internal flight. I was praying that there were no delays, or I'd be shacking up in an airport hotel with Ed, guarding his room like a jailer.

'I haven't spoken to him for days,' said Clara, sounding a little uncomfortable.

'His phone's not working,' I said quickly. Another lie that she'd know was a lie as soon as she heard what had been going on.

'Tell him to check his emails if his phone's not working,' she muttered. 'Will you make it to dinner?'

'Just,' I said tensely. It was the first time in our friendship that I hadn't looked forward to seeing Clara. My stomach turned over every time I imagined her excitement at our arrival, only to have her night – and possibly life – bulldozed apart. There was a part of me that was hoping that Ed would arrive, remember how much he loved her, witness her happiness, and be unable to go through with it. I knew that it was wrong of me to will them both into a marriage that may not have been right, but I couldn't bear to think of the fallout.

'Text me when you land' was the last thing she said before we said goodbye. I took a sip of my Campari soda. The taste was both bitter and sweet and somewhat unpleasant – not quite the Martini I would have liked – but apparently it was a 'light' drink. Ned had ordered a San Pellegrino, since he had a drive back to London ahead of him. He needed to take the van home, pack up everything for the wedding, if it did happen, and join us in Pantelleria the next day. Or not.

'You can go if you like,' I said, checking the time on my phone. I felt guilty thinking about his long drive back alone, worrying that he'd start to like me less with every hour that passed. But I was also relieved on his behalf, that he was free of this absurd situation. I added, 'You have a long drive ahead of you.'

'I'll wait until you've left,' he said, totally unfazed. Something about it made me feel so supported in my madness.

The door opposite us opened and Ed stepped out, wheeling a large suitcase behind him. He really had packed for a long-term stay. I stood up and Ned followed suit.

'Good luck,' he said. 'Keep me posted.'

I reached my arms towards him and flung them around his neck. I wanted to display gratitude, large amounts of it, but I didn't know how to do that other than clinging to him for dear life, similar to the way that I'd clung onto Leo on the floor of the Mortimers' utility room.

Leo.

I released Ned and gave a weary smile. 'Drive safely.'

Before I got into a taxi with Ed, I took a photo of the penis bakery, mainly because I knew it was the kind of thing Leo would find amusing, but I couldn't exactly send it to him without explaining why I was in Paris.

Ed and I barely talked on the way to the airport. By the time we arrived, we were being polite to one another, both of us happy to pretend that the circumstances were different in order to make the journey bearable. Once we were through security, we parted ways, feigning various errands that had to be done.

I inhaled a Camembert baguette from Paul, then slipped into the Relay newsagent to kill time. I flipped through various magazines, trying to envision my name on the pages in order to manifest my dream career. One day it was sure to work. *Time* magazine had an article about 'Single Women Literature'. Apparently, there was a whole subgenre of that title, spearheaded by *Bridget Jones' Diary* and *Sex and the City*. In my mind, it didn't exactly do what it said on the tin. Bridget Jones and Carrie Bradshaw weren't on quests to settle happily into singledom. Their calendars were crowded with tumultuous dates, kinky weekend getaways, lover's punch-ups, Mr Rights, Mr Wrongs and Mr Bigs – far more action than the average single woman encounters in a lifetime. They did nothing but actively look for love. If you're going to create a subgenre that compartmentalizes society so crassly, at least get it right and call it 'conscious coupling literature for women'. I felt unnecessarily irritated by the whole thing. I was certain that *Any Human Heart* and *Less Than Zero* did not fall under the category of 'Single Men Literature'.

I replaced the flimsy *Time* magazine to its pompous position on the shelf. Then I purchased the overpriced *Vanity Fair* magazine, to look cultured yet fashionable – an insider, perhaps – a Diet Coke and a packet of ready salted crisps. The French didn't seem to be into salt and vinegar. I joined Ed at the gate, where he was waiting like an obedient prisoner.

As we were boarding the plane, I opened my emails. To my surprise, there was a brand-new message sitting in my inbox, from Natasha. It was like magic. My creative visualization had actually worked. Finally.

Nervously, I opened the message.

Darling. Very bold to pitch to me so soon after you must have guessed that I'd called you a cunt several times over. BUT . . .

This topic was made for you

I like your writing a lot

This angle is fucking genius

Even when you're a cunt I FUCKING LOVE YOU!!!!

Deadline 1 week. 600 words. Standard Close Up main feature contributors' rate – you know the drill. DON'T LET ME DOWN THIS TIME!!!!!

A thrilling ripple shot up and down the front of my body, jolting me alive. I had had articles published in *Close Up* before, but those were small 250-word pieces for columns like 'Travel

Hacks' and 'Party Diaries'. To have a full-length main feature was golden. In addition to the fact that I would make £600, *Close Up* was known for pioneering new writing talent. Other publications often looked to it for the next big thing in journalism. That could be me. The next big thing. Baller.

DON'T LET ME DOWN THIS TIME!!!!!

A bit of pressure was never a bad thing.

Last chance not to fuck up your life, Jax.

I had always known that Clara wanted a destination wedding, but because it was Clara, I knew that it couldn't just be anywhere. So, I'd called up the travel editor of *Close Up* to ask her for the most exceptional place she'd ever been to. Without hesitation, she said, 'Pantelleria, darling, the black pearl of the Mediterranean' – which I imagined she'd lifted straight from an article. When I'd mentioned it to Bella, she was exuberant. She'd been dying to go there ever since she'd seen Giorgio Armani's house on the island, in an interior design magazine. Immediately, she booked our recce trip.

All three of us had fallen in love with the rugged Sicilian island within half an hour of landing among the formation of volcanic rocks and wild greenery. It may have been the best weekend I'd had all year. Without anyone but me there to judge – which she knew I wouldn't – Clara was back to her 'old' self. She wasn't putting on any airs and graces, which meant that she was automatically funnier. She wasn't watching her drinking, or Bella's, and even had the odd cigarette. By the end of the trip, we'd settled on the wedding venue. It was a vast estate with a view of the sea and land that went on for miles. Up at the main house was a pool and courtyard, perfect for a large event, and a magical stone-walled garden, which we had decided to use for photographs. The land was dotted with small domed-roof habitations made of lava rock, called *dammusi*. Bella announced on the spot that she was going to book them all out for guests to stay in. Clara kept on pointing out that it would take the cost way over the budget that her father had given her.

'Oh, please. Just tell him to sell a painting,' Bella dismissed the concern with an unphased wave of the hand in between the lines of broken Italian she was throwing at the puzzled booking manager.

'I wonder if it might be a bit rustic for Ed,' muttered Clara half-heartedly a few times. But eventually, she let it go, because to admit that Ed would not be enthralled with an island that we had fast become obsessed with was to admit a distinct lack of compatibility between them. I had envisioned Ed arriving with a turned-up nose that we'd all be forced to ignore. But as I sat next to him in a local taxi, swerving down the narrow road lined with cacti and bougainvillea, he stared out the window and said, 'This place is beautiful.'

'Not too rustic?' I said quietly. I didn't even mean it to be a dig, but it came out that way and he didn't justify it with a response. Instead, he quietly watched the sun go down in the pink-blue sky. I filled the silence with a fact: 'It's actually closer to Tunisia than Italy, so that's why it looks more North African.'

'Who will be there when we arrive?' he asked glumly in response.

'All the family. Clara, Bella, Derrick, Fabian. Moll and Budi and Omni. Theodora.' The last name I added with an eye roll, trying to inject some humour into the situation.

'And they'll be having dinner?'

'I guess so. Or maybe they've waited for us. Since you are the groom and all.'

He shifted uncomfortably and let his head drop against the window. I thought of how different the night could have been had we all arrived at the same time, awe-stricken by the beauty of the island and full of nothing but joy. But I was seriously idealizing what could have been. In reality, there were too many unpredictable characters and too much long-standing tension in the Mortimer family to be able to rely on the beauty of a place to make for a harmonious, serene weekend.

The taxi turned into the long gravel drive of the estate. Ed craned his neck to look up at the house. 'Is this it?' he asked with a troubled look on his face that made him seem like a child. Suddenly, that feeling I'd had upon spotting him at the grocer returned. I felt sorry for Ed.

'Yes. It is,' I said softly.

'Nice place for a wedding,' he said, with no hint of irony in his voice.

'Yes. It is,' I repeated.

The car skidded to a halt and the rattle of a rising handbrake marked the end of our journey. I had succeeded in my absurd plan. Ed was at the house. But the question of what came next was lingering over me, making me feel claustrophobic in my own body.

Ed took a deep breath in. 'Do you want to go in first, to explain the situation?'

'No, Ed. I really don't.'

'No. OK.'

We climbed out of the taxi and unloaded our bags. Ed took the driver's card, making it obvious that he was expecting to leave the house that night. Where he was planning to go, I had no idea, since there were no flights out until the following day, but I didn't want to make it my responsibility. We ascended the gentle gradient stone staircase towards the illuminated house at the top. As we got closer, the sound of music playing and the muffle of chattering voices came into earshot, then Bella's laugh, loud over everything else.

'Sounds like quite the party,' Ed mumbled.

He remained one step behind me as I followed the voices. We passed by a long table underneath a pergola that had been set for dinner. I took us around the corner of the house and just like that, we had jumped onto the whirling carousel of a Mortimer family gathering. Familiar figures were lounging on the white and wood outdoor furniture, irradiated by the light of flames coming from a large rust bowl firepit. Bella was strewn languorously across a throne-like chair, her legs dangling over one arm and her bare feet crossed at the ankles. I quickly scanned the configuration of luxuriating humans for Clara, but I couldn't see her.

'Here are the kids,' Derrick announced, being the first to notice us. He raised his hand in an exaggerated wave. He was wearing a Latin shirt, which was unbuttoned to cut a deep open V down his chest.

Bella dismounted her royal seat and advanced towards us, her arms spread wide like an eagle with a cigarette burning bright at the end of its wing. She hugged Ed first, which I supposed was fair enough considering that she still took him for the groom-to-be, but I was put out by not being her first port of call. 'Welcome, darling,' she said, holding onto Ed longer than I imagined he would be comfortable with, smoke rising above them. 'I'm sorry your parents aren't here with us.'

Ed had long before convinced his parents that there was

211

no need to arrive until Friday, in order to avoid another Mortimer–Montgomery mismatch. 'Yes, they're sorry too,' he said in a heavy tone of voice, and I couldn't work out whether he was playing a part or euphemizing. It made me wonder whether his parents were actually sorry that there wasn't going to be a wedding. Remembering the bewildered look on his mother's face at the party, I guessed they were more likely to have been relieved.

'You must be dying for a drink, both of you,' said Bella, wrapping her long arms around my neck and kissing the side of my head.

'Dying,' I confirmed into her bony clavicle.

'What can I get you? Champagne, wine, tequila?' Each drink she reeled off gave me a greater sense of urgency about needing to ingest it.

'Wine would be nice,' said Ed, to my surprise. I'd expected, *Water, please,* but I supposed that even the controlled needed something to take the edge off when circumstances were extreme.

'I'd love a tequila. But I'll do it, you sit down,' I said, though I hadn't even put my bag down yet. Bella started hollering out in her bad Italian and, seconds later, various staff members materialized out of nowhere to take drink orders and luggage.

Then nearly the whole family were on their feet, greeting us with a level of enthusiasm that I could see was overwhelming to Ed. Theodora stayed seated by the fire, a bowl of shelled pistachios in her lap and a glum look on her face. Omni also remained were she was, sprawled on a Persian rug, aiming a baffled look in my direction. I gave her the tiniest shrug to indicate that I had no answers for her, as Fabian worked his arms around my back. 'Welcome, trouble,' he said, placing a kiss snugly on the skin of my cheek. 'We've just been talking about you.'

'All good I hope?' I said, in a mockingly refined voice to excuse the cliché. But I really did hope that good things had been said.

'Of course. Mum's been a human Tinder for you all night.'

'I haven't!' said Bella, her voice all high-pitched and a look on her face that said, *Don't tell her that, you idiot!* I guessed it hadn't been all good after all.

'Any spare drug addicts or unemployed basket cases going, send them my way,' I joked, which brought on a collective laugh, though I caught Fabian and Bella share a knowing glance. Obviously, they'd already unpacked my terrible taste in men. I just hoped that it hadn't been with pity. I added, 'Extra points if they've got a criminal record.' Everyone laughed again, more emphatically, sending a beam of warm light shining through me, even as I wondered what reasons they'd come up with for my constant unexplained avoidance of romance. I couldn't help but imagine Fabian relaying my self-deprecating joke to Leo.

And then, Clara emerged from the house, resembling an angel in a blue and white dress with bell-sleeves and a floating skirt that swept along the ground. My heart sank as I thought of the pain that was about to pierce through her beautifully polished exterior. Her body language seemed tentative, I noticed, except for the small smile that her lips were curled into. She immediately took a seat on the end of a wide cushioned bench, crossing her arms and hunching her shoulders protectively to fully assume the position of an introvert. Hellos and goodbyes made her feel socially awkward no matter who they were with. I headed straight over and placed myself next to her, pulling her into a heartfelt hug.

'Hi,' she said. As I held onto her, she made an 'Aw' sound, clearly taking my emotion to be over her impending nuptials. If only she knew what the past twenty-four hours had entailed. If only I could warn her what was ahead without wreaking havoc. When I released her, she kept her eyes fixed on Ed. She must have known that something was wrong given that they hadn't spoken for days, but did she know the extent? It seemed that she was waiting for him to come to her, but he was avoiding looking in her direction altogether. The situation could not have been any more uncomfortable to watch for those of us who knew what was going on. Omni and I stole a quick glance at each other. That's when I noticed Moll's eyes skipping between Clara and Ed. I wondered if Omni had let her in on the secret. If so, how many other people knew? Did Clara know?

'Ed,' I called out, shifting away from Clara slightly, to make room for him to enter her breathing space.

Ed turned to us, his skin almost grey and that same endearing troubled look on his face. There went that pang of sympathy inside me again. He slipped his thumbs into his pockets – a stance I'd never seen him take – and took a few nervous steps towards us. Between the two of them, they looked like a pair who'd had a one-night stand before finding out that they were related, not two people who were about to make a life commitment to one another. Clara kept one arm folded over her abdomen, and with the other she flipped her palm open, resembling a street beggar. I was taken by surprise when Ed hooked his middle finger over hers.

'How was your flight?' she asked quietly, swaying his hand lightly.

'Fine,' he said uncertainly. Then he added, 'I had a calzone at Rome Airport.'

She let out a tiny mock gasp. 'Oh no, you might come out in hives for the wedding.' She smiled. He smiled. Their middle fingers remained entwined. I was so torn by their interactions. All of a sudden, they looked like two people who could have no destiny that did not include one another. Quite a far throw from the accidental incest scenario I'd created for them seconds before.

Closely, I watched Ed, who was hardly breathing. I was waiting for him to say, 'Clara, we need to talk' in that middle-aged-politician-dealing-with-difficult-press voice. But he didn't say anything.

'Shall we have dinner? Everyone's starving,' Bella's voice came booming over the others. 'Everyone except Mummy, who seems to have eaten the entire bowl of pistachios, shells and all.' She grabbed the bowl off her mother's lap and held it up like show and tell. 'Look!' It was nearly empty.

'You're meant to eat the shells, Arabella,' Theodora said defensively.

'In which obscure culture?' Bella threw back at her.

'They come out in the loo,' Theodora added grimly through the curtains of wiry grey hair flanking her face.

'Oh, too much information, Mummy!' Bella groaned.

'Bells,' Moll spoke up quietly but firmly, shaking her head. Bella retreated with an eye-roll, whirling off to lead the way to dinner. I watched Budi put his arm around Moll, and she met his hand with hers, up on her shoulder. I wondered how two women could come from the same parents and upbringing, having been so close in age, and be so different. But then I supposed Ezra and I weren't exactly cut from the same cloth.

Clara tightened her hand around Ed's, using it to pull herself into a standing position. She looked up at him, craning out of her neck, begging for a kiss, and he leant down to grant it to her. I wondered how he could possibly kiss her when he was so adamant in his belief that she'd betrayed him? Was it just a story he'd spun to get me off his chest? Or was he so English that he was going through the motions to save himself, and everyone else, from an awkward situation? Somehow, I thought the latter was more likely, given his earlier conviction.

He must have caught me gaping at him in disbelief because almost immediately after the kiss, he came out with a mumbled, 'Can we talk in private?' He spoke the words so quickly, I wasn't sure he'd actually said it.

'Sure,' said Clara. She turned to me. 'Can you just get everyone to start without us?'

'Of course,' I said, my eyes flickering between them, resting on Ed for longer. I hated my complicity in the situation. I hated the fact that she would imminently become aware that I'd known what was about to happen, all this time. I hated that she'd learn that I'd lied about everything from the flight confusion to Ed's broken phone and so much else. Why the hell had I done it?

As Clara and Ed disappeared into the house, Omni grabbed my wrist. 'I can't handle this, babe, it's too much.'

'You have no idea,' I said through clenched teeth. 'I need to fill you in – later.' As we reached the table, I announced that we should start eating without Clara and Ed, trying to hit the perfect combination of brightness and despondency to keep everyone's attention off the tension that would inevitably permeate, but also so that they wouldn't think my tone was inappropriate when they learnt the truth.

'Have they gone for a quickie?' asked Derrick, denoting that he was in performance mode, which usually led to inappropriate behaviour and, therefore, drama.

'Don't be revolting, Derrick,' said Bella, although it sounded like something she would've said.

'What? We had a quickie earlier,' he said, arms outstretched innocently.

'Urgh, don't remind me,' she groaned. Then, to everyone else: 'You know, when I married him, he had a full head of hair. I married Mick Jagger and ended up with a blanched almond.'

'And I ended up with Tarzan, King of the Jungle,' said Derrick, fluffing his own straggly, knotted hair with his fingers.

Bella cackled, but I was nervous that the playful teasing was on the cusp of shifting into full-blown abuse. It was absolutely not the time for one of their screaming matches. I gathered from the way the rest of the family silently looked at their empty plates that they were equally nervous about an impending eruption. 'The food looks so delicious,' I tried to deflect, glancing into a bowl of scarlet soup drizzled with thick olive oil.

Bella continued by tugging on the material of Derrick's Latin shirt. 'And this, Derrick? You look like an old ballet dancer.'

'Derrick, tell us about the wine,' I interjected, before he could retaliate. Wine was Derrick's favourite topic and it was the one thing that didn't bother Bella, since she loved drinking it. Moll gave me a small congratulatory smile as Derrick went off on a tangent about the Tuscan Tignanello. Thankfully, the soup – which turned out to be chilled watermelon gazpacho – also became a deflector, as we joined heads to figure out the ingredients. Heirloom tomato. Watermelon. Garlic. Red wine vinegar. Almonds.

Our empty bowls were cleared to make way for the main

course: squid ink linguine with crunchy breadcrumbs and clams. Bella asked whether she should call Ed and Clara down, but I told her to leave them. I finished my drink quickly and stopped myself from having another. I needed to be clear-headed enough to pick up the pieces when they fell into a heap on the ground. I needed to be there for Clara, and not just physically, but 100 per cent emotionally present. When the main course was over, Budi asked if I thought that Ed and Clara were alright. I didn't answer.

'Darling, come talk to me, over here,' demanded Bella from the other end of the table. 'Bring a chair. And some more wine.'

With a combination of reluctance and relief, I picked up a bottle of wine and the floppy canvas chair I was sitting on. I planted it down between Bella and Moll, falling into it with a dramatic sigh.

'I can tell that something's going on,' said Bella, leaning in close to me. 'What is it?' She looked more excited than concerned.

'Wait for them to finish. Clara can tell you herself,' I muttered awkwardly. Having already hidden so much from Clara, the last thing I wanted to do was reveal the entire thing to her family before she'd even had time to digest it.

Bella stood up rapidly. 'I'm going to get them.'

'No, no,' I almost shrieked, jumping up to grab her arm more forcefully than I had meant to. She gave me a strange look and I felt that I had, for the first time, crossed a bound-ary with the woman who had no understanding of the word. I looked over at Omni desperately, urging her to support me, but she was flirting with a bearded waiter and was a million miles away from what was happening. Part of the family after all. I squeezed Bella's hand, trying to be affectionate rather than overassertive, and begged, 'Please, don't.'

'Well then tell me what's going on,' she pushed. 'You can't expect me to sit here quietly waiting, if you're not going to tell me anything.'

'Ed's having second thoughts,' I blurted out under my breath.

'Ed is?' she said, too loudly. 'Surely not?'

'I wish it were Clara,' I said. 'But it's Ed.'

'Clara's always having second thoughts. She doesn't know what she wants,' said Bella flippantly as she resumed her seat at the table. 'She's just one big mess of half-formed thoughts, to be honest.'

'That doesn't mean it won't hurt her,' I said, almost tearful in my defence of her. I so often sided with Bella, not openly, but subtly, because I was nervous of getting into an argument with her. But this was one time that I couldn't. This was serious for Clara, and I needed her mother to understand that.

'But it's a good thing that they figure it out before they get married, isn't it?' said Moll. 'I mean, thank goodness he's here to discuss it.' Her pointed remark informed me that she did, in fact, know what had been going on. I checked Bella's expression to see if she showed any signs of recognition over Moll's comment, but she was absentmindedly pulling a cigarette from a packet on the table.

Fabian leaned across the table, opening his hand for the cigarettes. 'What are you conspiring about?'

'Ed wants to do a dirty on us,' said Bella glibly.

'Bella!' I cried, dropping my face into my palms as a furious ripple of anxiety ran through my body.

'Fuck him,' said Fabian, with seemingly little understanding of – or interest in – the gravity of the situation. There was no point trying to make him see any side of the situation that wasn't Bella's. He idolized his mother, whom he had more of a best-friend relationship with than a parental one. I wondered if it was why he was never able to keep a girlfriend for long.

'Let's open another bottle,' Bella said impatiently, gathering the empty wine bottles from the table and taking them inside. I was worried that she would just put them down and march upstairs. It would be so like her. But she reappeared with two fresh bottles, barking, 'Derrick, you're not doing very well with the wine tonight.'

A platter of pastries filled with sweet, creamy ricotta came and went. Omni disappeared, as did one specific waiter. A large amount of wine per person was consumed. Bella, Fabian and I smoked the entire packet of cigarettes as the tale of Ed's attempted escape made its way around the table, until not one member of the family was in the dark, which made my stomach swirl in a sickly way. By the time Ed emerged timidly from the house, he was nothing more than a character in a soap opera. His audience looked at him not with hatred or anger, but high anticipation. No one said anything.

Ed looked directly at me, which was a rarity, as he said, 'Can you go up to Clara?'

Crisis mode activated, I jumped up and shot inside, ready to console. I caught a glimpse of Ed, taking a seat at the table with the family. I wondered how exactly that was going to play out and was relieved that I wasn't there to see it.

The house was cavernous, with many routes to different locations. It took me a while to find the winding staircase that would lead me up to the shell grotto that Clara was staying in. 'Clara?' I called as I ascended.

A brief silence. And then a steady voice, 'Yes?'

I entered the grotto to find Clara framed in the structure of the four-poster bed that was almost identical to her childhood one. Her legs were tucked behind her and her skirt spread out, making her look irresistibly like a mermaid. She had red cheeks and puffy eyes, but she was not crying. Her mouth was slightly open, in an aghast sort of way.

'Are you alright?' I asked tensely.

'How could you do this to me?'

CHAPTER 13

When we were little – maybe eight years old – Clara and I had accompanied Bella on a work trip to New York that must have fallen during half term or Easter. We stayed at The Plaza, which Bella thought would be fun because we loved the *Eloise* storybooks. Whenever she was off meeting patrons of her charity, Bella would drop us at her in-laws' Upper East Side apartment to play with Clara's cousin, Hazel.

Hazel was four years older than us, which seems like a whole generation when you're as young as we were. She was – what we called in those days – 'a tomboy', who always had grazes on her knees and was constantly being told off by adults. Playdates with Hazel made Clara uneasy because, in both childhood and adulthood, Clara hated getting into trouble. Even the slightest suggestion of a ticking off from a figure of supposed authority and she'd get a blotchy neck and retreat like a snail into its shell.

I was somewhere between the two sides, in that I had a voice in my head that always told me to behave, yet I loved the idea of kicking that voice to the curb and doing whatever the hell I wanted. For that reason, Hazel's anarchic ways and total indifference to being caught beguiled me. In most situations, Clara was the one whom other children clawed for attention from. She was the Queen Bee of the playground, though a quiet one. Whoever claimed that children are void of prejudice had never been one, or, more likely, had been so traumatized by the experience that they had blocked out the memory of it. Naturally, little girls gravitate towards the one among them who is the prettiest, the smartest and – this is true – whose family is the richest. Clara was all of those things.

But when we were with Hazel, all of a sudden, I was the one being pincered. From one side, Hazel tugged at me, urging me to rebel, and from the other, Clara yanked me firmly back into place. One of Hazel's favourite games was 'Knock, knock, Ginger'. She'd knock on the door of one of the other apartments and then dart into the lift or down the fire escape as one of the residents called 'Hello?' down the corridor. Clara was reluctant to get involved, but I promised her that it would be fine – we were faster than the old people who lived in the block. But when the moment came, Clara stood frozen on the spot in front of a weary neighbour, as Hazel and I hurtled down the fire escape. Of course, Clara then took the brunt for every round of the game that Hazel had ever played and had never been caught for.

We waited on the fire escape, but Clara never came. She wasn't in the apartment either. When we took the lift downstairs, we found her sitting on the bench in the foyer, right near the front door. She had a particular look on her face. It was something that sat between defiance and outrage. Through that look, her tiny eight-year-old voice said, 'I don't want you to be my friend anymore.'

Eight-year-olds have a habit of making big sweeping statements like that and forgetting them an hour later, unaware of the concept of integrity. But that wasn't the case for Clara. When Clara had a feeling, she committed to it. I did everything I could think of to make her like me again. Gave her my favourite Barbie doll – problematically Baywatch Barbie – let her sit at the window seat on the plane, ate macaroni cheese off her plate so that she wouldn't be forced to (food made her anxious). Eventually, she came back around, though had we not been forced to spend so many hours together by our mothers, I don't know to this day if she would have.

I never quite got over the fear of losing her. When the two of us went to New York again, as teenagers, the feelings from that trip came flooding back into me as if they were really happening. By that point Hazel was wilder than wild. Though I still found her irresistibly persuasive, I always made sure that I was outwardly aligning myself with Clara. I was careful not to take a shot of tequila or any substance that Hazel might have been offering if Clara wasn't.

In my early twenties, *Close Up* sent me to New York to help with their Met Gala afterparty. On my last night, I met up with Hazel and got so drunk that I missed my flight the following morning. I ended up staying with her for three more days. I never told Clara about that extension to my trip. Weeks later, at a Mortimer Sunday lunch back in London, Bella flippantly said, 'What fun that you stayed with Hazel in New York. What's her new flat like?'

Nervously, I told her that the flat was lovely, and that I'd missed my flight due to a mix-up with the cars, so Hazel had kindly helped me out. My gaze drifted to the other end of the table, where Clara was sitting. She had that look on her face, the look that I remembered so clearly from all those years ago. Like emotional muscle memory, the feelings came flooding back. She didn't say, 'I don't want you to be my friend anymore', but, regardless, I did everything I could to make her happy – asked her a million questions about drama school; showed her pictures of herself, marvelling at how beautiful she was; sent her a package of goods from the beauty cupboard.

All because of that look.

And there she was, nearly thirty years old, with the exact same look on her face. A look that made my stomach churn in a dizzying way.

How could you do this to me?

'I'm sorry I didn't tell you,' I began calmly.

'Have you lost your mind?' she almost hissed with disbelief.

'I was trying to protect you,' I said, stepping closer to the bed and gripping onto one of the wooden posts.

Clara closed her eyes and opened them again, hot air steaming through her nostrils. 'What makes you think that you need to make decisions for me? Do you think that I can't make them on my own?'

'Of course I don't think that, Clara—'

'Do you think I'm an idiot?' she challenged.

'Clara . . .'

'Or a child?' she added, sounding even more aghast at the idea. But there was something childlike about the way she was holding herself. She was glaring up at me with something resembling defiance that could have also been construed as hatred.

'I don't think any of those things.'

'I'm a grown woman, Jax. I'm a hell of a lot more grown up than you are,' she threw out cuttingly. 'I don't need you, or anyone, to look after me.'

'Did he tell you that he tried to leave you in a letter?' I blurted, quickly feeling like I was under siege.

'Yes. He did.'

'The week before your wedding?' I pressed. 'And then switched off his phone and made himself unavailable? Did he tell you that?'

'He was angry,' she said, sounding far too understanding.

I paused, considering what she meant by this. *He was angry.* I placed my hands on my lower back, rubbing into the burning pain and frowned at her. 'Did you cheat on him, Clara?'

'Yes,' she said, defiantly looking me in the eye, like a teenager forcing a parent to take her rebellion seriously.

'When?' I asked doubtfully.

'It doesn't matter.'

I swung myself down onto the bed, leaning against the post, and twisted my face into an expression of dubious disbelief. 'It just seems strange that you never told me.'

'I don't have to tell you everything,' she said, slicing me in half like a kitchen knife.

'I tell you everything,' I said sadly.

'No, you don't,' she said, as if I should know what she meant. True, there were some things I left out of conversation, and white lies that I told, but I would never leave her out of a big story in my life.

'You really did cheat on him?' I said, urging her to tell me the truth.

'Why would I lie about that? It doesn't exactly reflect well on me.'

'OK, well, I didn't know that. So, when I saw the letter, which was virtually three lines ... I'm sorry, but it broke my heart. It broke my heart to read it because I was imagining your heart breaking. I didn't want you left hanging in limbo with that fucking three-liner.'

'You shouldn't have gotten involved,' she said adamantly, with no acknowledgment of the fact that I'd done everything I'd done to stop her from getting hurt. I'd lost my mind for her.

'So, what's happening now?' I asked, straightening my spine out against the post to ease the pain. 'You're not getting married?'

'I am. We've worked things out.' At that, she didn't look at me, but at her own shiny nails.

'Right. So, in theory, it's a good thing that I brought him here?'

She spread her arms into a helpless shrug of *Do you really want me to answer that?*

'You don't have to marry him, Clara,' I said.

'Stop telling me what to do!' she exploded, her voice breaking and tears surfacing in her eyes.

'I'm not telling you what to do,' I said, leaning forward to touch her foot, hoping to calm her down. She pulled it away from me and scrambled backwards like a crab until she flopped against the pillow. I continued in an equable tone, 'I'm just saying that you don't have to.'

'Yes, I do!' she shrieked. 'This is all I've ever wanted. Of course I have to.'

'You're the one who always told me never to settle,' I reminded her softly.

'I'm not settling! I'm marrying the best person I could ever find. I love Ed, he loves me. And that's all!'

'And he's forgiven you for cheating on him?' I asked with raised eyebrows. 'Just like that?'

'Yes,' she said, triumphant, with finality. 'I'm going downstairs to have dinner. With Ed. I think it's best that you and I give each other a little bit of space, for now.'

'What, you don't want me to come to your wedding?' I said, a panicky flutter in my chest.

'I didn't say that. I just said I need a little space. It's not a big ask, considering the night I've had.'

You sound so like your mother was the cruel thing I wanted to say to her but didn't. She did sound more like Bella than I'd ever heard her before. I pulled one of my knees up into my chest, cradling it. 'You know I didn't do this to hurt you?'

'Yes, I know that,' she said tersely as she got up off the bed.

'Then why are you so angry with me?' I asked, resting my cheek on my knee. I watched her check herself in the mirror and wipe the stray mascara from beneath her eyes. A loaded silence followed.

Clara turned to look at me. I thought she was about to shake her head and say that she'd overreacted. But instead, she said, 'Because you didn't really do this for me.'

It was my turn to well up with tears. I pressed my lips together as I blinked them away. 'I swear I did.'

'Get some sleep, Jax,' said Clara. And with that, she left me there alone.

I lay down on the bed and stared up at the spiral pattern on the ceiling. *Because you didn't really do this for me.* Was she right? That had, of course, been Ned's analysis of the situation. But all I'd been thinking about from beginning to end of this farcical scheme was Clara. How *she* would feel and how *her* life would be ruined. All I'd wanted was for her to have the conversation and closure she deserved. Had it been nothing more than the perfect distraction from my own life? It was true that, just for the short amount of time that I was the knight in shining armour looking for the princess's lost prince, I hadn't been thinking about what I looked like naked, or whether I'd ever be given a mortgage, or if I'd screwed up my future by making the wrong choices in my twenties.

I sat up quickly and blood rushed to my head. I glanced up at the ceiling and forced a breath deep into my belly to wipe away the repetitive star pattern that had formed in front of my eyes. Then I looked around the room. The weekend bag that I'd packed for Clara at Ed's flat – which Omni had brought for her – was in the corner, half unpacked. I could see the pink and black Agent Provocateur box inside. Perhaps there was indeed a side to Clara that I had never – and would never – know. Perhaps we can only know so much about our friends, and that's why we need lovers in our life. To understand our shadowy selves. Thinking about it in that sense, Clara had been right when she said I didn't tell her everything about me. She didn't know my darkest desires and most lewd fantasies. Sure, I shared stories of art dealer role-play scenarios over a glass of wine to make her laugh, but I didn't divulge the things that really turned me on.

Suddenly, a memory came to me. It began with a sound that is evocative for virtually anyone who grew up in the nineties: the sound of dial-up internet. The phantom keys being punched in, the flat ring establishing connection to another planet, the alarming siren followed by an apocalyptic crackle, like the final strive for glory. And then, silence, welcoming you into a new world.

Clara and I must have been nine years old when the Mortimers had dial-up installed in their townhouse. There was a single Microsoft computer, which sat in the first-floor television room. Clara and I constantly argued with Fabian for its use, captivated by the miracle of being able to access unique and scintillating information about all of our favourite films, books and toys. Somehow, in those Yahoo searches, we found our way into the world of the chat room. Those rooms, virtual though they were, seemed nothing short of entirely mesmerizing. Hundreds of strangers connecting to each other from across the globe in a whole new language. We soon learnt that 'ASL' meant 'Age, Sex, Location' and 'BRB' was 'Be Right Back'. We started using the abbreviations casually, feeling grown up and knowledgeable for doing so. We were part of a new wave. We understood it better than our parents did. We were out there in the world.

And then came the day that we typed 'S-E-X' into that search engine. I don't remember if we did so spontaneously or if we'd been told to by an anonymous screenname in a chat-room. Nor do I remember exactly how much we already knew about sex. Most probably, all we knew was that it was a thing that adults did. Something we would do one day, perhaps.

Typing 'SEX' into a search engine in today's world takes you to hundreds of pages of informative pieces in *Cosmopolitan* or *Psychology Today* or the NHS sexual health guide. But back in those days, it was a one-stop ticket to the platform of porn. Willies dripping in milky liquids and boobies that looked like large rubber toys.

When my mother came in to call us down for lunch, Clara and I froze like two baby rabbits in front of glaring headlights. She walked around to look at the screen as Clara fumbled to close the many windows that we'd opened.

'Get off!' my mother barked immediately. 'Sit there,' she snapped her finger towards the sofa. Clara and I quickly darted over and sat deep in the folds of the cushions, wishing that we could be sucked into a magical world of protection by that piece of furniture. 'This is disgusting. Absolutely disgusting,' my mother shrieked, as she grabbed a throw from one of the chairs and threw it over the screen. 'No more internet! I'm shocked.' She left to get Bella. We waited, very quietly, in disgrace, I remember, with a sticky, sickly layer of guilt spreading through my stomach.

When Bella came in, she glanced at the computer and calmly removed the throw and closed the browser. My mother hung back in the doorway looking fraught. Though normally the louder and scarier one, Bella spoke quietly, as adults did when they had a difficult situation to address. She did not look at me, but took Clara's hand and said, 'Come, darling.'

My mother addressed me from the doorway, 'Let's go home.' When we got into the car, she said, 'It's not your fault. It's the internet.' She didn't look at me when she said it, or for the entire drive home. We never spoke directly about the incident again, but that sticky layer sat there in my stomach. Often, I'd hear her relaying the story to friends, or even acquaintances, warning them of the dangers of the web. Every time she repeated it, that stickiness would harden until it crystallized into shame.

I suppose it was because of that long-solidified, brittle layer of shame that I never told anyone when I started having my first sexual urges at the age of twelve. Especially not Clara, who covered her eyes and squealed during sex – or even kissing – scenes in movies. It felt strange when she lost her virginity before me, to her sixth-form boyfriend. I waited and waited for someone special to come along, because that was the thing to do, but time and time again, they failed to make an appearance. I felt distinctively inferior to all my friends who were doing away with their V plates, left, right and centre. I hated not being able to get involved in the discussions about bladder infections and morning-after pills.

And I hated the fact that, although our first foray into the concept of sex had been the same, Clara seemed to be fine with it and I was the one with issues. But sitting there in the shell grotto, turning over information that was so confusing, so out of character, I wondered if our problems were more similar than I'd realized.

When I went downstairs, Ed and Clara were eating the dinner they'd missed, while Bella and Derrick chatted to them, drinking wine. Clara had her back slightly turned away from her parents, I noticed, a familiar stance of hers. Bella was resting her chin on her hand, her eyes glazed over from the wine. When she saw me, she smiled and croaked, 'Coffee, darling?', and I felt comforted by her warmth and inclusion. I declined the coffee nonetheless, respecting Clara's request that I keep my distance. It felt strange to see them sitting there in apparent normality, when the situation felt so abnormal from where I was standing. After saying goodnight, I headed off down the estate to the little lava-built *dammusa* that I was sharing with Omni. The light was on, and I desperately hoped that she might be in there, but all I found was my wheely suitcase, standing upright in the middle of the room. I guessed that Omni had found more exciting affairs elsewhere that night, and that I could look forward to wallowing in solitude.

I sat down on the edge of the single bed, my legs stretched out in front of me and slumped at the spine. I took the wedding itinerary out of my bag and looked at it, slightly crumpled and limp in my hand. There was a scheduled wedmin meeting in the morning, the rehearsal in the afternoon and drinks for all guests down at a low-key seaside bar, which had been my find. I wondered whether Clara would be talking to me through any of it.

My phone lit up on the bed and I tilted it towards me to read the WhatsApp message.

Harry:
Should I claim my travel insurance yet???

The text in the white bubble a few lines above that message jumped out at me and hopped around tauntingly: *'So if you aren't into it please just say. I won't be upset'.* Why wouldn't I have been upset that someone who had allegedly liked me enough to take me out to dinner sober on more than one occasion no longer wanted to fuck me like an empty vessel? Why shouldn't my feelings have been hurt, like any other person's would have?

I closed WhatsApp immediately, hiding away all the bad decisions of my past and present. And then I opened it again, homing in on the worst decision of all. I tapped out a message to Leo, fast, without thought or reservation, and clicked send before reason had the chance to get a look-in.

Me:
Think I might miss you a little . . . x

The message was, at best, cryptic, but for me it was the most emotionally forward thing that I'd ever said. It was certainly a step up from 'You out tonight?' or 'Hang later?' He was due to arrive for the wedding the next day. I felt an urge to tell him everything that had happened and for him to hold my hand and tell me that he knew I'd done it all out of love and loyalty, nothing else. He'd embrace me with his long arms and then probably fuck me with half an erection and maybe let me cry into his shoulder again.

There was no air conditioning in the *dammusa*, a detail that I'd previously shrugged off as rustic charm. But it felt less charming when I was actually lying there with a beating heart trying to get to sleep. During the night, I woke up frequently and sat up to check if Omni was there. I felt a tangled mix of irritation and dread every time I saw the empty bed. Should I be going out to check on her? Yes, she was a grown-up who could look after herself, but what if something bad had happened to her? What if she had been date-raped and there I was, a sweaty mess, tossing and turning in bed. Would I ever forgive myself? Would Clara ever forgive me? For anything?

Just go to sleep, Jax, because things are always clearer in the morning. You would say that.

CHAPTER 14

There were a few seconds after I woke up, before I'd opened my eyes, when I'd forgotten that anything out of the ordinary was going on and I felt as happy to be waking up as I had done on the morning of the pre-wedding party, when I'd felt so grateful just to be living. But as soon as my eyelids peeled themselves away from the gloss of my eyeballs, I saw the bright sunlight creeping through the grates of the blue shutters, and I remembered where I was. I remembered that I'd lied to Clara, dragged Ned all the way to Paris, texted Leo and slept badly. I pulled the sheet over my head, although I was boiling hot, and closed my eyes again. I wanted to return to the cocoon of sleep, the only place where nothing had to be dealt with.

But I was awake and could barely turn from side to side thanks to the pain in my back that was even worse than it had been the day before. I couldn't fall back to sleep, so I wriggled my hand out to do the first thing that I did every morning: I checked my phone. No response from Leo. A message from Alice – 'Update?' – and one from the bank: 'You are about to go over your agreed limit on account ending 378 today, 24 MAY. To prevent fees being charged, please pay in cleared funds before 3:30 p.m.'

Talk about adding insult to injury. Where had I been when everyone was sneakily siphoning money into these elusive savings accounts, while complaining that they were 'so broke' at the end of every month? Not being able to go out for dinner when you're sitting on forty grand in savings does not classify as 'broke' in my opinion. Dropping cash on martinis whenever you wanted to, even if it took you into your overdraft, was closer to it.

I felt a tug of yearning for my days of employment. The commute alongside other swashbuckling members of the rat race reading *City AM*, my first coffee of the day occasionally from the overpriced deli, the morning debrief about the night before with my colleagues, reading crap on my computer screen and not feeling guilty because I was still being paid, free food in the fridge, free beauty products, being given tasks to complete and completing them, asking for advice. I missed the excitement of being in a museum after hours, prepping for a big event and staying late with the team to namecheck the photographs, getting progressively drunker on leftover champagne, then deciding to go out. I missed getting paid. I missed the editor, and the sub-editor, and the interns. I even missed Dymfy. Her book had become a bestseller. I had texted her to say that I was proud of her and that I was available for freelance assistance on social media. She responded with the emoji of two raised hands and movement lines. I guessed that was emoji language for #blessed.

I had no way of clearing my debt, short of asking Bella and Derrick for my final wedding planning payment, which I couldn't bring myself to do. I hated asking for money, even when it was owed to me, and I certainly wouldn't do so on a day that was already bound to be uncomfortable. My mother was arriving soon and I was going to have to swallow my independence and ask her to help me out. She'd jump at the opportunity of ensnarement, regardless of whether she had money to spare or not.

I texted her, asking if she wanted to meet for lunch. Then I heaved myself out of bed, where I involuntarily came face to face with a floor-length mirror. I locked eyes with myself and shook my head disdainfully. My face looked like it had been padded out with pin cushions, which could have been thanks to the flight, dehydration and the stuffy bedroom, but more likely the non-stop alcohol consumption of the past week.

Stop judging yourself, my logical voice said. In the bathroom, I cleansed my puffy face, applied hyaluronic acid and used my rose quartz Gua Sha to drain all the excess fluid that was causing it to look like a beach ball. I moisturized, massaging the skin like a facialist would do, and applied SPF 50. Dymfy would have been proud.

After downing three large glasses of water and throwing on a kaftan that I'd bought specially for the trip, I felt like a grown-up. I took out my phone and assumed the role, composing a mature adult message to Leo.

> Me:
> Good morning. Are you free to meet me for
> a quick coffee when you arrive later? Would
> be nice to make friends x

The mature adult persona did it to take control of the situation, but the truth was that I really just wanted to see him.

I picked up my phone and my plastic folder full of wedding shit, put on my sunglasses and left the room. On the way up, I spotted a familiar body curled up on a sun lounger with her eyes closed. I placed myself on the lounger next to the sleeping

Omni and took out my itinerary. At the rustle of paper, one of her eyes snapped open, while the other remained tightly shut. She cleared her throat and closed the eye again.

'Morning,' I said, which she replied to with an incoherent mumble. 'Where did you end up last night?'

'Oh. Some hut where they keep all the towels,' she croaked.

'Only the best for us, right?' I quipped softly.

She giggled a little, still half asleep. 'I couldn't remember which one was our room, so I slept on the couch. Then I got too hot.'

I felt a little better about my night of anxiously checking her empty bed, knowing that she too had been sleeping alone, after presumably no more than a fumble in the towel shack with a flirtatious waiter. 'Clara's so angry at me,' I said, starting a doodle of arrows on the side of the itinerary.

'She'll get over it,' Omni yawned. 'I'm pretty confused by why this wedding is still happening, to be honest.'

'You don't know the half of it, my love,' I said. That woke her up. She pushed herself into a seated position and listened as I told her everything that Ed had told me, concluding the story with the bombshell that Clara had confirmed it. And then I started to panic that I'd done exactly what Clara wouldn't have wanted me to do. I'd spread the story, even if it was only to Omni.

'I won't say a word, I promise,' said Omni, after I begged her not to tell anyone. 'But who the hell has she been cheating on him with?'

'I have *no* idea,' I said.

'Do you think that she just found the thought of cancelling a whole wedding, when everyone's about to arrive, too much?'

I dropped my head in between by knees. 'Maybe. I'm such

an idiot. I should have just told her when I found the letter and let her make the decision then.'

'Yeah, but, babe, all the reasons that you didn't do that still stand. At least you got him in front of her. That's major!' she said, like I'd just received a huge career accolade.

I smiled sadly. *Sweet Omni.* I felt my phone vibrate beneath my leg. It was Leo, sending the fastest response to any message in the history of his text messaging life.

Leo:
Aren't we friends already? X

I sighed and flopped back against the sun lounger. 'In other news, what am I going to do about this Leo situation?'

'Well, I don't think you're in love with him, to be honest, babe,' she said, squinting at me in the sunlight.

I felt a jump in my stomach as she said the words. I didn't remember telling her that I was in love with him. Nor could I bring myself to tell her that I'd curled up to Ned in bed just to feel less alone. *We share everything with our female friends, except the things that make us feel truly vulnerable.*

Omni continued, 'You're too good for that shit. But if you think you are, then maybe you just have to tell him?'

I gnawed on the side of my lip as I considered what that conversation would look like.

I think I'm in love with you.
Oh darling, you're so sweet.
No, really, I am.
That turns me on.
Are you in love with me?
Sure, if you want me to be.

What shall we do?

Well, I know you're not into anal, but I'd love to try it one day if you don't mind, since you're in love with me and all.

'I just told him I want to be his friend,' I said, handing my phone over to display the messages.

'What a turn-on,' she said. '"Aren't we friends already?" Sorry, but how many friends do you know who fuck each other over and over and don't speak in between? Idiot.'

I smiled dejectedly and held out my hand in request for my phone. Then I used her observation to type out a reply.

> Me:
> Don't think friends treat each other
> like we do.
> Not a conversation we have to have but may
> be useful x

The last I added to keep face: *I'm practical not emotional. I'm not a Hysterical Woman demanding commitment and emotional support, because, in truth, I'm not sure I can offer it in return.*

Leo started typing immediately, which almost sent me rolling off my sun lounger in shock. Had I been missing a trick all these years with the straightforward honesty thing? Was it, in fact, the biggest turn-on of all, contrary to all the women's magazine psychology we'd grown up with? He stopped typing and started again, several times. I waited with bated breath for the moment that I found out whether the man I'd fantastically turned into the love of my life cared about me one iota.

> Leo:
> That sounds like a great idea. I value your
> friendship and you deserve better treatment
> from me. Flight gets in around 2. Let's try
> and meet before the drinks party tonight?

I handed the phone to Omni, with a confused sigh. What had I been expecting, really? *I treat you like I do because I am so in love with you that I don't know what else to do.*

'OK. That's nice,' said Omni with a note of surprised positivity in her voice.

'What do I say?' I asked helplessly, feeling totally out of my element.

'Say you'll go for a drink with him, babe,' she coaxed. 'And then figure out if it feels right to tell him how you feel. But you know, you have to be prepared that you might not get the answer you want.'

'I don't know what answer I want, anyway.' It was true. I could tell him that I might have been in love with him, despite the fact that I wasn't sure. But even if I was, I didn't exactly know what to do with that supposed love. I didn't want Leo to be my boyfriend, so what did I really want to get out of the revelation? Perhaps all I wanted was for him to understand how I felt, possibly tell me that he felt the same way, and then I'd feel less alone with these mystifying feelings that were a means to no end. Perhaps, we could continue our 'casual' relationship in a more caring and loving way. And perhaps, eventually, I'd be less clouded with thoughts of him and be able to at least consider someone else.

I rattled out a reply as Omni positioned herself into a downward dog beside me, in an attempt to release the toxins of the night before.

Me:
Thank you, me too. And sure, I'm free
after the rehearsal. But really only if
you're feeling it – please don't do it just to
placate me x

I couldn't help but feel the need to chuck the ball firmly over into his court by absolving myself of responsibility for this alleged drink plan. I didn't really believe that it would go ahead. It all seemed far too straightforward for an enigma like Leo, whom I had learnt not to expect much from.

'Who told you I was in love with him?' I asked, suddenly remembering that I definitely hadn't told Omni about that.

'Clara.'

Clara and Ed didn't come down for breakfast. Bella was hungover and not a morning person at the best of times, so she sat silently drinking a strong coffee and reading an Italian newspaper, which I was sure she couldn't understand. Derrick read out various bits from the *New York Times* – Assange is indicted, Weinstein tries to settle, the Saudis are still bombing Yemen, and the Cannes Film Festival is in full swing – on his iPad. Moll and Budi traversed a map of the island with their fingers, planning a day trip. Fabian and Omni discussed how they were going to source drugs for the 'party'. No one mentioned anything to do with the night before, probably for fear of setting Bella off.

One thing I was certain about was that there was a huge question mark, in everyone's minds, over whether this wedding should be happening. I couldn't help but feel that if I had just kept my oar out, there wouldn't be. And, contrary to how

I had felt when I read that fateful letter, I was now convinced that it would've been a good thing.

By the time Clara and Ed came down for our scheduled wedmin meeting, Bella had come back to life. Moll and Budi were off for a swim in a cave and Omni and Fabian were sunbathing by the pool. Clara didn't look at me as I laid out all the itineraries and seating plans. Nor did Ed. Bella was watching Clara with an amused smirk as I went over all the details for the following day. Uplighting, twilight trees, party favours, brass bands. *Wedmin.*

'That lovely cocktail man is arriving today, isn't he?' said Bella, with no idea that that lovely cocktail man had driven to Paris and back to facilitate my impulsive madness. I confirmed that Ned was, indeed, arriving today and we went on to talk about photography, flowers, hair and make-up. I made a joke about the fact that the local hairdresser had no hair, and Clara laughed, before remembering that she was angry with me and retreating again. Then we went on to talk about music. Fabian had arranged for Matcha Latte Peng to grace us with his presence.

'We'll turn the music off at two a.m.,' Clara tossed out at random. No timeframes past the first dance had ever been discussed before.

'Two a.m.?' Bella almost shrieked. 'Are you mad?'

'That'll be a first for a Mortimer party,' said Derrick. 'I don't remember a single one that ended before five.'

'Two a.m.,' Clara repeated with finality.

'Oh, Clara!' Bella despaired.

'It's not your wedding! It's mine,' Clara reminded her.

'I'm not trying to hijack your wedding, for God's sakes! I just think it's rude to ask all your friends to pay six hundred pounds to come here for you and then kick them out.'

'That's what most people do,' Clara challenged. *Normal people.* 'Two a.m. is a normal time to finish a wedding. In fact, it's quite late!'

Bella looked at me like, *Can you believe this shit?* and I looked down at my nails, only just realizing that I hadn't had time to get the manicure I'd planned.

'People are welcome to stay,' said Ed, suddenly the voice of liberal reason. 'We might not last past two, but that doesn't mean everyone has to leave.'

'I'd rather not wake up the morning after my wedding to drug addicts who haven't slept,' Clara sputtered. Something told me that she was speaking directly to me, about me, even though she too had been that person way back in our early twenties and even though that wasn't me anymore. It was an ironic time for her to turn pious when she knew that I knew she'd been engaging in some mystery act of infidelity.

'Alright, well, we're going to have to arrange something in another location for these poor guests who are being turfed out,' said Bella, turning to me.

'Oh, Mum, please!' snapped Clara.

'What about that bar that makes the delicious margaritas?' Bella continued. 'Can we call them?'

'Bella,' said Derrick warningly. 'Stop.'

'We should get going, Clara,' said Ed, tapping her on the forearm.

'Where are you off to?' I asked.

'I'm taking Ed to the mud lake,' said Clara, barely glancing at me. Her voice was still littered with anger – either at me or her mother, or both.

'Alright, you go off to the mud lake and enjoy yourselves,' Bella erupted sardonically. 'We'll be here sorting out your

244

fucking wedding, which I'm still not convinced either of you really want to have!'

'Bella!' Derrick interjected, roughly closing his freckled hand around her skinny wrist. But Clara was already up and inside the house, swerving the argument that was about to escalate. I wondered what had happened after I'd gone to bed the night before. Had Bella discussed the situation with Clara? Begged her not to go through with it? Or had she simply festered internally, waiting for a moment just like this one to have her outburst. Somehow, the latter felt the most plausible.

Ed remained seated, his cheeks flushed red and his eyes darting nervously along the wooden table.

'Go enjoy the lake, Ed. It's magical,' I said, remembering the day the three of us had spent basking in the hot magnesium mud pool.

'Great, looking forward to it,' said Ed, with forced cheerfulness. He stood up, politely asking if he could get anything for anyone while he was out.

'There are no shops at the lake,' snapped Bella, lighting a cigarette.

'Thanks for offering, Ed,' Derrick added pointedly, throwing Bella a look.

Ed was barely inside the house when Bella started again. 'I don't know why you're so keen to defend him. You do realize that he was about to leave your daughter at the altar? If Jax hadn't brought him here, we'd all be swimming in her tears and paying the cancellation bills.'

If Jax hadn't brought him here.

'Which would have been cheaper than a whole wedding she doesn't even want,' muttered Derrick.

Bella rolled her eyes and looked at me. 'What are you doing today, darling? Shall we go for a drive?'

'I said I'd meet my mum for lunch,' I said, feeling a stab of guilt about turning Bella down, especially when she was paying me to be there.

'Oh, invite her here, for a drink,' she said brightly.

'I'll ask her,' I mumbled. But, in all honesty, I could think of few things more stressful than watching my mother and Bella grow progressively drunker throughout the day, possibly ending up in an argument.

I had sent my mother a collection of affordable bed and breakfasts in Pantelleria town, but in the end, she found a hotel on her own. I wasn't convinced that it was within her means, but who was I to judge anyone's spending habits? Particularly when I was about to ask her for a loan that I might never be able to pay back.

When I arrived, she was sitting at a table in front of the hotel, wearing a white silk wrap dress with long curls of dark hair cascading from beneath a wide-brimmed straw hat. It reminded me how fabulous she could look when she made the effort to leave the chaos of her tiny flat. She lifted her hand and waved at me. 'Hello, sweetheart,' she said, her accent sounding more Israeli than usual. I bent down to hug her, nestling into the smell of motherliness, the ultimate safety, even if just for a moment. 'You look well,' she said.

'Really?' I asked, taking off my sunglasses and placing them on my head to show her what I really looked like.

'You look skinny,' she added.

And skinny was everything.

'Stress,' I said curtly.

Ignoring my cry for concern, she beckoned over a waiter, whom she'd already made friends with. 'Do you want any food? I've already eaten.'

No, you haven't.

'I'm fine, thanks. Just a cappuccino please.' I wasn't about to start enquiring about the availability of alternative milks because I knew it would drive her crazy. Even though she ate next to nothing, she found modern dietary requirements very irritating. Probably because she was suspended in a different era and refused to face the fact that the world had moved on in any way.

She ordered an espresso, sexing the waiter with her eyes before he departed. Then she asked, 'Is Clara enjoying the celebrations?'

'Not so much,' I said ominously.

A sparkle appeared in her dark eyes. She leaned towards me with her elbows on the table. 'Oh dear. Why?'

I told her everything. From the letter, to my senseless decision to rip it up and drive to Paris, to the elusive cheating revelation and, eventually, Clara's fury at me. My mother shook her head slowly and tutted her tongue. When I'd finished, she said, 'It doesn't surprise me that she's being mentally abusive.'

'Mentally abusive?' I repeated. 'To who?'

'To that poor man,' she said, and a noise came sputtering unattractively from my throat. She always took the man's side, no matter what the situation. Then she added, 'And to you, sweetheart.'

'She's not being mentally abusive. She's just annoyed with me. She'll get over it,' I said, perhaps trying to soothe myself into that belief.

My mother started massaging her own slim, elegant hands

as she continued: 'She's actually so similar to Bella, beneath all that well-behaved sweetness. That's exactly how Bella would have reacted to me if I'd tried to help her.'

I resented her comparison of Clara and Bella because it naturally became a comparison of myself and her. And plus, my mother didn't have a natural instinct to help others, despite her Jewish blood, so the scenario was beyond hypothetical. When I'd first started going to parties as a young teenager, I'd tended to spend the night holding back the hair of some girl who'd had one too many alcopops, rather than scouring the place for boys to kiss. Whenever I'd recount tales of my heroism to my mother, she would angrily scoff that she hoped I wouldn't become 'The Florence Nightingale of parties'. I eventually told her that nothing made me happier than helping my friends, to which her dark response was, 'How sad that is.' I didn't stop playing Florence because it truly was my safe spot in those days, given that the alternative was trying to stand out among a group of competitive, scantily clad 13-year-old girls elbowing one another for pre-pubescent male attention. But I did feel like a sad person for doing it.

'Please be nice when you see Bella later,' I implored.

'Of course I'll be nice,' she said, in a way that was not exactly convincing. 'Bella and I are fine.' They'd run into each other over the years at various birthday parties I'd had, or talks that I'd organized for *Close Up*, and Bella always acted thrilled to see her, as if nothing had happened between them, whereas my mother had settled into a place of frosty politeness. 'Have you got enough money?' she asked, beating me to the chase.

I wished that I'd got there first. Now it would be difficult to own the situation. Awkwardly, I muttered, 'Actually, I wanted to ask if I could borrow a little.'

'I thought you would be low,' she said.

'Just until I'm fully paid up for the wedding,' I insisted.

From her large straw bag, which I could see was full of unnecessary crap, she fished out her cheque book. She was the only person I knew who still owned one, let alone carried it around daily. She rummaged further for the turquoise Tiffany pen that my father had given her before I was born. 'You know this might be it for you and Clara, don't you?' she said, as she scribbled the cheque in long artistic lines. 'I don't want to upset you. I'm just saying that you shouldn't be disappointed if things don't go back to the way they were before.'

'Why would you ever say something like that to me?' I said, my throat rough with emotion.

'It's not a big deal. Friends fall out.'

'I don't fall out with my friends,' I said firmly. Truthfully, I had never fallen out with anyone.

'Well, you should be prepared for it, my sweetie. It's part of life. When you have a relationship, and absolutely when you have children, you'll understand that your friendships fall to the bottom of the pile. So, don't put so much into them now. It's not worth it.'

I felt like she was hammering a nail into my heart. What could I tell her? That the closeness of my friendships was critical to my survival of life? That I'd been hibernating in a microclimate of support and nurturing to replace what neither she nor my father had managed to give me? That my friends were all I had in the world? That they didn't diminish or manipulate me, nor did they spread my legs and fuck me into a false sense of security and then disappear?

'How's Omni?' she asked suddenly, with a smile. She'd always got on well with Omni.

249

'She's good. Looking forward to seeing you,' I said, though Omni hadn't mentioned her.

'Does she have eyes for every man on the island?' she said with a small, chesty laugh.

'I don't know,' I said, not wanting to engage in the conversation. And then, with a sudden wave of guilt because she was giving me money, I checked in and added, 'She did end up with one of the waiters at the house last night though.'

'*Sharlila*, they'd say in Israel.'

'What does that mean?' I asked apprehensively.

'Let's say it means "slut".'

I emitted a loud and dramatic wince. 'Please don't use that word, Mum.'

'Why not?' she said, pulling her lip up as if I'd said something very unreasonable.

'Because it's a degrading term that the patriarchy invented to shame women for behaving too much like men,' I said indignantly, feeling the anger whipping itself up inside me. I really wished that I could keep that anger at bay. It so often stopped me from being articulate, especially with my mother.

'Oh, don't get into a millennial huff,' she said, more amused than irritated.

'Would you want people saying that about me?' I challenged. 'Because I'm sure they do.' I was twisting the knife into her because she had always told me that promiscuous behaviour was a sign of insecurity, which – as far as I was concerned – was an old-fashioned, simplistic view to take. We hadn't been brought up in the same society and culture that she had, which told a woman to hold off and keep herself for her husband. The message we'd been fed about sex was different. We'd come into the world in the nineties, with Samantha Jones, Brit-Pop and

Girl Power urging us to drink, talk and fuck like a man – like the kind of man we'd never want to hang out with – to put a stamp on our liberated status. Within that, some of us had forgotten to find a place to squeeze in our emotional needs.

My mother ignored my question and handed me the little slip of paper she'd been writing out. 'Is that enough to see you through? I can give you cash for the weekend.'

I'll use whatever vocabulary I choose to, as long as you're financially dependent on me.

'That's plenty, Mum. Thank you so much.'

CHAPTER 15

I couldn't have been any happier to see Ned standing outside the church when I arrived for the rehearsal. Out of context, against the stark whiteness of the Chiesa di Madonna delle Grazie, he looked like a different person. He was wearing round tortoiseshell sunglasses and seemed to be glowing golden. He shone a bright smile my way as I took lethargic steps up towards the church. When we shared an affectionate hug, a mental montage of all the hugs he'd ever given me rattled through my head on high speed. I wanted nothing more than to emotionally colonize him.

'I can't believe this is actually happening, after all that,' he said, sounding truly astonished.

I stepped back and shook my head. 'I've got mixed emotions about it.'

'Don't tell me you're regretting it?' he said, a worried and perhaps even alarmed expression crossing his face at the prospect that I was about to embark on some sort of sabotage mission. I don't think anyone would have put it past me at that point.

Before I could answer, a car pulled up at the bottom of the steps obnoxiously honking its horn. Derrick's bald head shone out from the driver's seat and, next to him, Bella waved energetically. A larger car pulled up behind them, and out stepped

Omni, Clara, Ed and his distinctly uncomfortable-looking parents. Under normal circumstances, I would have charged down the steps to hug everyone and drag Clara up by the hand. But as it was, I stayed close to Ned, feeling less alone in his company. My lips were smiling, but my eyes were dead behind the dark shield of my sunglasses.

'Hi, Ned,' said Clara politely, as she ascended towards us. 'Thanks for being here.'

Ed raised an awkward hand. It must have been strange for both him and Ned to think that they'd been sitting at a table in Paris not so long ago, while Ed revealed personal and incriminating details about the woman he was now about to marry. I didn't think it was a wise time to mention it to Clara and, thankfully, neither did they.

In the distance, I could see Moll and Budi ambling down the road, sharing an ice cream between them. Then a third car pulled up outside the church, at dangerous speed, manoeuvered by Fabian, with Harry in the passenger seat. It was an odd pairing. I wondered how much of a repartee they had managed on the journey, or if Fabian had blared techno music the whole way. Harry bounded up the steps like a large excitable dog. 'Not bad, Levy,' he said – the only person who referred to me by my surname – holding out his hand for a low high five. For a second, I just looked at it, reluctant to display any celebratory gestures. But then I felt bad for leaving him hanging in front everyone, so I gave his fingers a gentle tap.

'Best man,' I informed Ned, as Harry moved on, and Moll and Budi arrived at the church.

'Has anything else happened since we've been gone?' Moll asked quietly, handing the last bit of the ice cream cone to Budi.

'Not that I know of, but I might not be the best person to

ask at the moment,' I admitted. Moll gave me a supportive smile and stroked my arm quickly.

'My my, this is all quite strange, isn't it?' Budi added to her gesture. I could do nothing but shrug.

We all made our way into the church, chatting in civilized fashion. I always felt immediately more Jewish than usual when I entered a church.

The one and only condition that Ed imposed on the wedding was that the ceremony take place in a Catholic church. Luckily, all three churches on the island fit the bill, so we went with the most visually in line with the rustic wedding. The interior was small and simple. White walls, stone floors, wooden pews and a dome-shaped archway over the altar.

The priest spoke English about as well as Bella spoke Italian, so we all struggled to understand what he was saying. It took a brief game of charades to decipher that he wanted us to walk through the motions of the ceremony. We marked the route down the aisle. Bridesmaids first – Omni, followed by Alice and Hazel, who had not yet arrived. Then me, the maid of honour. Then *here comes the bride*. I was instructed to stand to one side as the read-through of the ceremony took place. Fabian rehearsed his verse from the Bible, which sounded comical in his faux East London accent and set Clara's family off laughing. Budi recited a poem he'd written for his own wedding about the meaning of love. There were prayers, the mention of hymns. And, eventually, it was time to practice the vows.

The priest began, in his heavy accent, 'Edward John Montgomery and Clara ... *Sunrise* Mortimer, 'ave you come 'eere to enter into marriage wid-out coercion, freely and 'oleheartedly?'

Awkwardness permeated the entire room. Clara and Ed both nodded, muttering an out-of-sync, 'I have.'

The priest continued: 'Are you pree-pared, as you follow di path of marriage, to love and h-onour each other for as long as you both shall leeve?'

I wanted to take out a metaphorical megaphone and bellow, *As long as you both shall live* repeatedly until they understood it. But, again, they muttered, 'We are.'

'Are you pree-pared to accept children lovingly from God and to bring them up according to dee law of Christ and 'is church?'

'We are.'

'Edward Percival Montgomery, do you take Clara *Sunrise* Mortimer for your obedient wife?'

Obedient wife. Omni caught my eye and we exchanged a mutually knowing smile. *Vomit!*

'To 'ave and to 'old, from dis day forward, for better, for worse, for ree-cher, for poorer, in see-ckness and in 'ealth, until death do you part?'

Ed swept the back of his hand across his brow line. It could have been due to the temperature, but I was sure that he was sweating nerves. I had a sense that Clara was giving me uncomfortable glances from the back of her head as he said: 'I do.'

I stepped closer towards the altar so that I could see the side of Clara's face as they went through the whole rigmarole again for her. I was searching for signs of regret. But when it came to crunch time – or the practice round of crunch time – I was distracted by the vibrating of my handbag. Quietly, I unzipped it to check my phone. An excited ripple travelled through me when I saw Leo's name on the screen.

Leo:
I think it's a great idea. Let me know when
and where darling x

I felt almost nauseous from the intensely reactive combination of exhilaration, nervousness and remorse amalgamating
within me at the thought of seeing him one-on-one in such
a quixotic setting.

'Okay, da reengs,' the priest called out.

Harry stepped forward, gleeful with responsibility, to clum-
sily hand over the wedding bands. The priest explained some
of the logistics that were hard to make out. Then, he ended
with, 'And then I pronounce you 'usband and wife and we
all go to drink.' Both families laughed heartily at the univer-
sally understandable joke, breaking the ice of the vows. And
that was that.

We walked out in the formation of pairs. Harry offered his
arm, which I took with an eye-roll. When we reached the
doors, everyone peeled off down the stairs, immediately gab-
bing away. I shook Harry off my arm and leaned against the
wall, mentally plotting how I was going to make my getaway
without anyone discovering the reason.

Harry planted himself right in front of me. 'Bet you're feeling pleased with yourself.'

'Not really,' I said, eyeing the width of his chest. I'd forgotten how wide it was.

'Oh, cheer up,' he said, placing a friendly hand on my shoulder. 'There's always divorce.'

'Why did you break up with me?' I asked him, out
of the blue.

He looked taken aback – so taken aback that he was unsure

whether to remove his hand. 'Gosh, um . . . this is awkward,' he laughed, and then repeated the word 'awkward' in a comically awkward tone of voice.

'It's just a question,' I said, soft and serious. 'It would be helpful for me to understand.'

'God, it was a long time ago, Jax,' he said, retrieving his hand and sliding it into his pocket along with the other. 'I can't really remember.'

'Try to remember?' I pressed.

'I just wasn't ready for anything serious,' he said. The words ejected themselves from his throat unconvincingly as he rocked back and forth on his feet.

'OK. With anyone? Or with me?'

'Um . . .'

'Be honest, please,' I implored.

'I just never really thought you were that into it,' he said quietly, looking embarrassed by what he was saying. 'I didn't think you cared about anything but the sex.'

I shifted my eyes up towards the blue sky as I turned the words over in my head. 'But we were getting to know each other,' I said, trying to work out what he meant. 'It wasn't just about sex. We went out for dinner. Multiple times.'

'But you always seemed like you just wanted to get home and have sex,' he said. Then he loutishly added, 'Which I'm not complaining about! Fine by me.'

I opened my mouth to object or even to complain that he was accusing me of being some kind of sex junkie, but the words got stuck on the way out. Perhaps that was because I understood that there was some truth to what he was saying, or at least to how he had perceived it. Sex, and the pillow talk that followed, had been the only way that I'd known how to relate to Harry, whom I really had so little in common with. I had never considered the notion that I was treating him as an object, a plaything, or the fact that he may have picked up on it. Had I, without realizing it, been the one in that situation who owed the apology? Suddenly, I wondered whether I had continued the pursuit of Harry in order to stay close to Clara in her new relationship with his best friend.

'Now this really is awkward,' said Harry in his jocular manner, responding to my pensive silence.

Before I could say anything else, Ned stepped out of the church. 'Was just having a look around. I don't think it needs much, it's so clean and simple. Maybe we keep the flowers really minimal?'

Harry tapped me on the arm and made a hasty escape. I smiled at Ned. 'Good idea.'

'Shall we have a drink somewhere and talk over everything?' he said. 'I feel like a debrief is needed.'

'I have to meet someone,' I said apologetically, hoping that he wouldn't ask who, but feeling that he may have already guessed. 'Let's chat at the party tonight?'

'Alright, whatever you like,' he said, so accommodating in his very nature. 'Do you need a lift?'

I watched as everyone below piled into their various cars. Bella called up to me, as she was half in, half out, asking whether I wanted to ride back to the house with them. I shook my head and gestured that I'd be there later. Then I turned to Ned, 'A lift would be great, thanks.'

I was almost disappointed when Ned dropped me off. I could've stayed in that car with him all weekend and felt content. On the way, I'd had to admit that I was meeting up with 'my addiction' but assured him that it was for nothing more than a reconciliatory conversation in order to avoid awkwardness over the weekend. He showed complete understanding and wished me luck as I got out of the car. I felt instantly ashamed for no easily explained reason.

I walked into the small bar wedged into the nook of a boat harbour, which Clara, Bella and I had gone to for sundown margaritas on our recce trip. It had all of the components perfect for new love: seaside setting, soft afternoon light, sultry Cuban music and deliciously lethal cocktails. I even had those flutters in my stomach that you get on a second or third date, despite the fact that ours was a beaten-down, bedraggled sort of love – if it could be called love at all – and that the feelings evoked by the setting were nothing more than the kind of fantasy we would have played out in the dark hours of the night. Leo was already there, positioned at a table on the corner of the wooden decking. He was wearing a white shirt, white jeans and aviator sunglasses that were sliding down the bridge of his nose. My God, he looked irresistibly gorgeous. As I approached, he smiled, lifted his long arm to wave, and I felt an awakening of sensation in my pelvis while my chest simultaneously closed up.

I reached the table, also smiling, and said, 'This makes a nice change to Slim Jim's.'

'Quite a different scene, indeed,' he said, standing up to kiss me on the cheek, prickling me with his overgrown stubble. 'You look beautiful, as always, darling.'

'Don't lie,' I said, full of self-deprecating humour, as I took the seat opposite him. There was a packet of Marlboro Reds on the table between us and nothing else. Leo immediately got up to order drinks from the bar, even though there was table service. I guessed that he didn't want to sit any longer without a glass of liquid confidence, and, to be honest, neither did I. When he returned with two margaritas, I gave a tight smile and sucked in a line of air, feeling like there was an uncomfortable shortage of words in my conversational well. Leo started talking about how much he hated flying budget airlines – 'Why so much orange? If you're going to run a shitty service, at least disguise it with better colouring!' – and then he informed me that the world would end by the middle of the following year, either by natural disaster or nuclear war.

'I guess we might as well enjoy the time we have here, then?' I offered in response.

'That or we just kill ourselves, so we don't have to see the fallout,' he said, pinching a cigarette from the packet, as if to bring himself one breath closer to death.

'Cheerful,' I said, ironically upbeat. 'That feels like an avoidant thing to do.'

'We are avoidants,' he said, giving me a flash of a smile, his tongue poking out from between two rows of teeth.

Half smiling, I rested my chin on my fist. 'You and me?'

'Love avoidants.'

'Maybe we need to go to therapy.'

'I would love to go to therapy with you,' he said, raising his margarita to cheers. 'Couples therapy.'

My heart started to pound, but I automatically said, 'That would be weird.' I lifted my glass to tap against his briefly, before taking a sip. It was my first drink of the day and even just that one sip gave me energy.

'It would be a little weird,' he agreed, lighting his cigarette.

'We could try therapy right now though,' I said, licking a few stray grains of salt from my lips. 'If you're up for it.'

'Great idea. You start.'

'OK. I asked you to meet me because I wanted to apologize for treating you like shit, from time to time.' I didn't know whether I would have said it were it not for my unexpected tête-à-tête with Harry, but since then, it felt like the right thing to say.

'You never treat me like shit, darling. You're always so sweet,' he said in a way that I read as patronizing more than complimentary.

Let me have this, I thought. *Let me take responsibility for my part in this, even if you don't want to take yours.*

'I know that I do,' I said steadily, taking off my sunglasses and placing them on the table, thinking that eye contact might force some interconnectedness between us in the way that I'd always relied on sex to do. I continued, 'And I thought that maybe you could apologize for treating me like shit. And then we could move on and be friends.'

'Apologize?' he said curiously, taking off his own glasses, flattering me by way of emulation.

'I know that I probably never seemed like I gave a shit,' I continued, that conversation with Harry still ticking away at me. 'But I did. And I still do.'

'What do you give a shit about?'

Far too much.

'About you, I guess?' I said. It was a question more than it was a comment. *Tell me how I feel because I have no clue.*

'I'm glad to hear that, darling,' he said, laughing a little, evidently perplexed. 'I give a shit about you too.'

'Really?' I asked, sceptical yet serious. 'Because sometimes, it doesn't seem like you do.'

'My love.' He looked at me intensely. 'Of course I do,' he

said, rolling the brown part of the cigarette back and forth between his finger pads. 'I just never knew that you wanted me to show it.' I heard what he was saying. I had invited his flightiness and impassivity. Once again, I had brought dismissal on myself.

'That's a defence, on my part.'

'Defence against what?' he probed, like he really was my therapist.

I took a breath that was meant to be deep, but really only went as far as my chest. I looked out to sea as I spoke. 'I never wanted us to be boyfriend and girlfriend. And I still don't exactly want that. But I can't help but feel ...' I released the trapped breath and fanned myself down with my hands. 'Sorry. It's quite hard for me to talk openly like this.'

'It's OK,' he said quickly, reaching across the table to grab my hand. He squeezed my fingers tightly. *I've got you.*

I continued with a now-intense pelvic charge and a tightly constricted chest. 'The thing is. Us in a relationship would be a total disaster. We're both as emotionally unavailable as each other, so there wouldn't be one person to pull the other out of that place. We're both lost in our careers. We'd probably be drunk 24/7. But the thing is ... I do ... even though I know it's not the right thing to feel ... I think I might be in love ... with you.' I kept my eyes on the gentle undulation of the ocean. Had I just tried to talk him out of a relationship and confessed my love to him in the same breath?

Nervously, I returned my gaze to the man sitting opposite me at the table. He had a sympathetic, and perhaps even satisfied, look on his face. 'Darling,' he said softly. He stood up halfway and leaned across the table to kiss me on the cheek for a few long seconds. I cupped my hand around his jawline with a strange feeling that I never wanted to let go. The perversity of surrendering my own emotional liability had left me feeling more desperate for his love than ever. As he returned to his seat, he said, 'We should have talked about our feelings before,' still holding onto my hand.

Before what? I thought. 'We did have conversations about feelings sometimes,' I said. 'But it was always at five in the morning, when we were drunk or high.'

'And naked,' he added, rubbing at my crotch with his very words.

'Yes ...' The image of both of us naked on Clara's sofa, our tongues clicking away with intensity, sent my whole body into a state of arousal. 'And naked,' I repeated. I let out a tiny involuntary noise of frustration and bit my lip. It must have looked sensual, even though I hadn't planned it that way. Leo mimicked the noise and the lip bite. *Fuck.*

We continued holding hands, or, rather, clutching onto each other. But he didn't say anything. He didn't say, *I love you too.* He didn't say, *I wish there was a way we could be together.* He didn't say, *Darling, maybe we'll just have to go on loving each other without consequence.* And still, I wanted him more than I ever had. But rather than telling him, I quickly said, 'Well, those days are over.'

'Don't say that,' he said, rubbing my fingers between his, doing exactly what I'd hoped he would do. 'What about our *arrangement?*'

'One day,' I said sadly. Perhaps I'd never been anything more than an arrangement to him, and if that was the case, I'd most probably been the one to instigate that dynamic. He stubbed out his cigarette and placed his nicotine-smelling hand over the two of ours that were still locked together. We exchanged smiles of humiliation and I felt that there was a mutual shame in our lack of attachment. Leo wasn't a bad person. It wasn't his fault that culture had taught him that women were there to be pioneered. And it certainly wasn't his fault that he wasn't in love with me.

'Well, if you are around later after the party,' he said, swinging my hand back and forth. 'Let me know.'

The intimation was clear. I shook my head. 'I really don't think I should.'

'I'm not going to tell you what you should or shouldn't do.'
Please tell me what to do and I'll do it.

'But the offer is there,' he finished, in the manner of someone who was laying a business deal out on the table. Then he asked brightly, 'How's all the wedding planning going?'

I felt a small sinking feeling as I realized that the conversation was over and that my revelation had led to nothing. I told him the wedding plans were all fine. I didn't tell him about the drama going down with Clara, as I'd fantasized about doing. I had exposed myself enough for one evening, and finally understood that my needs were not going to be met by this person, even though I'd told him that I loved him. Plus, I could hardly bear to recount the story again.

We chatted lightly until the final sip of our margaritas and then took a taxi back up to the estate, where Leo was also staying in a *dammusa*. As we made to part ways, he wrapped his arms around me, cradling the back of my head with his hand. He planted a kiss right on my hairline, hard and loud, like a parent might do to a child that they just love so much. It was utterly seductive.

Those days are over, remember, Jax.

'Let me know if you do want to hang out later,' he said

pointedly. His eagerness gave me a sense of exhilaration that I was angry at myself for feeling.

Of course, I knew that I should have answered with a clear-cut *No*. I should have set a boundary and backed myself all the way. But I didn't.

'Let me think about it,' I said ambiguously, turning towards the main house. I walked up the steps, feeling oddly upbeat all of a sudden, buoyed by the knowledge that I'd finally been honest with Leo about how I felt. I hoped that it meant that I was now ready to let go of him and move on. But I couldn't push away the truth. The temptation to spend the night with him was there and it was real. Part of me didn't believe in my own willpower not to. The other part of me knew that I definitely had bigger fish to fry.

As I arrived at the main house, something small and red went flying over my head. It landed in a splat on the ground. I looked down at the smashed cherry, its guts spilling out onto the stone floor. 'It's a popped cherry,' a voice came from above. I looked up, shielding my eyes from the sun. Omni and Alice were sitting on the edge of the roof, glasses of wine in hand. My heart went warm at the sight of their silhouettes against the soft blue sky, shrouded in the comfortable pleasure of Girl Talk.

'Wait there. I'm coming up.'

'About time,' Alice called down. 'We want to know where you've been by the way . . .' Her voice trailed off as I made my way around the house to the staircase that led to the roof. It was a flat surface with several smooth domes that popped up at random. I approached one of the domes and sunk down between my friends, arms around both of their shoulders, feeling like I'd entered the safety of my very own microclimate. The nail that my mother had pierced into my heart with her words began to loosen. I felt it virtually pop out when Alice hugged me, even though she hated physical contact, because she could sense that I needed it. I couldn't have been more grateful to her.

'How was the flight?' I asked, clinging on for dear life.

'Fine, apart from Tim being on it,' she responded dryly, which made me laugh, even though it was more worrying than funny.

'Where is he now?' I asked in a hushed tone.

'Napping. Thank God,' she said, offering me her wine glass.

'I filled her in on all the news,' Omni informed me, reclining sideways against the dome.

'It's a disaster,' I said miserably, lifting the glass to my lips. 'This whole wedding is a fucking disaster.'

'It could be worse,' said Alice. 'A girl in my office was telling me about a bride who called off her wedding because she walked in on her thirty-year-old fiancée being breastfed by his mother, the night before.'

'That cannot be true!' I shrieked.

'One hundred per cent true. Attachment parenting gone too far,' she said, dead seriously. A torrent of laughter cut through the middle of my stomach and I knew there was a good chance it would turn into tears if I didn't watch it.

Omni was equally hysterical. 'The conviction that you tell that story with is fantastic,' she said.

Our laughter was cut through by the sound of a deep voice below, saying, 'Ciao.' We all glanced over the edge of the roof to see the bearded waiter that Omni had disappeared into a towel shack with. He was holding a tray of dirty glasses that I guessed he'd picked up from the poolside. He raised a hand, fixing his dark Italian eyes on Omni with a lingering smile.

'Ciao, babe,' she said briefly. She rolled towards us, getting stuck in an awkward position on the dome in order to remove herself from his line of vision. 'Is he gone?' she mouthed. I peered over the side of the roof and confirmed that said waiter was nowhere in sight. Relieved, Omni sat up in a cross-legged position and said, 'Oh, I wish I hadn't slept with him.'

'Really, why?' I asked. 'He's very cute.'

'I know, but now we're stuck here all weekend together,' she moaned. 'And he was chatting away to Dad at the pool, which really cringed me out. And Mum kept on whispering in my ear, being like, "Do you like him?" I can't handle it.'

'Was it good sex at least?' Alice asked, a note of hopeful envy in her voice.

'Yeah, it was. That's the problem. Now I just want it again,' said Omni, tipping her head backwards in frustration. 'I've got the horn.'

'We need to get you a vibrator,' said Alice in a matter-of-fact way.

'No! God, no!' cried Omni.

'Why not?' I asked, helping myself to a sip of wine.

'I wouldn't be able to take it seriously,' she said. 'Honestly, I think I'd laugh at myself in the mirror while I was using it.'

'Why would you be looking in the mirror?' asked Alice.

'I don't know!' Omni gave a shudder of her hands. I'd always loved her for her zero-fucks-given fucks, but after so many years, she had become totally disassociated from her body. It made me wonder if I'd been wrong for encouraging her.

'I use my vibrator every morning,' said Alice nonchalantly. 'Just before my ten o'clock team meeting.'

'Shut up!' said Omni, clearly as staggered as I was by the revelation.

We both half expected Alice to admit that she was joking, but she remained deadpan as she said, 'You can get pocket-sized designs to fit in your handbag and use them in the loo when you need to.' At that, Omni and I erupted with laughter again. Alice blinked, looking a little confused, and then she smiled, though I could tell that she didn't appreciate our amusement. She continued, 'Being a sex pest is not chic. Keeping on top of my own needs makes it easier to withhold sex from Tim, as and when I need to.' At that, the laughter died down and nothing but the sound of the crickets sat between us. Alice seemed to read our minds in that space. 'I know you both think I should dump him, by the way.'

'Do *you* think that?' I asked gently, scraping her knee with the end of my fingernail.

For the first time ever, Alice looked lost for words. She threw her hands out in a helpless gesture of, *I really have no idea.* Then she said, 'I still haven't told him about the promotion,' so fast that I barely heard it.

'That's a problem, babe,' said Omni. 'You obviously don't believe that he'll be proud of you. And he bloody well should be. I am.'

'So am I,' I said.

Alice scratched the nape of her long neck roughly and looked out at the sun preparing to set. 'What if I never find anyone again?'

'Then you'll be just like us,' Omni responded in a whimsical tone of voice.

'Don't scare her,' I added, and we all laughed.

Suddenly, Omni sat up straight and asked, with genuine intrigue, 'Do you think I could ever have a boyfriend?'

There was a pause in conversation. I looked at Alice,

deferring to her, because I didn't feel qualified to answer the question. She resumed her usual disposition and said, 'If you stop treating first dates like a Karma Sutra workshop, then yes.'

Omni sputtered with amusement. 'Thanks, babe. I'll keep that in mind.'

'Seriously though,' said Alice. 'Less sex, less immediately, and you'll be beating them off with a stick.'

'Like me?' I piped up.

'Bad example,' said Alice, which made us laugh again.

'We should get ready for the party,' I said apprehensively, dreading the whole evening to come. It was strange to be having such a tender, familiar moment with my closest friends without Clara and to be feeling so anxious at the thought of seeing her again.

'I'll get my things and get dressed in your room,' said Alice.

I smiled, a warm glow emanating from inside me. I knew that it was partly to get away from Tim, but I also had a feeling that she suggested it because she understood the happiness that the three of us in one room – getting dressed up for a party like university students – would bring me. She also knew that I was thinking of nothing but Leo when she adamantly refused to let me wear the swampy, shapeless maxi dress I'd been planning to, insisting instead that I armour myself in a figure-hugging slip dress and wash my goddamn hair. And when we all assembled in the driveway to meet the minibus, she knew that I required safety in numbers, and granted me that solidarity by sticking close by my side, gently letting Clara know that we were in this together.

For that, I loved her.

CHAPTER 16

The Friday night drinks were taking place in Pantelleria's version of a dive bar, which wasn't really a dive since it had a wraparound porch with a postcard-worthy view and trays of tiny canapés. The dive bar had been another one of my ideas: keep it low key on the first night, to counteract the lavishness of the main event. It was another one of the ideas that Clara had loved at the time but had grown increasingly concerned about as the day drew closer, no doubt driven by what Ed and his parents would think. By the time it actually came around, she all but pinched her nose between her fingers as we walked in.

The wooden bar, usually topped with pints of Estrella, was now lined with rows of London's finest avant-garde mixology. Ned was putting the finishing touches on the cocktails that he'd suggested to compliment the local beer selection. He caught my eye and gave me a small, supportive smile. Immediately, I picked up two of the fancy spiced rum concoctions and started handing them out. *Please just get drunk, everyone.*

When I approached Ed's mother with the cold glass in my hand, she looked at it with an amalgamation of fear and guilt. 'Oh. Thank you. Um. I might just give it a few minutes. Could I . . . Would you happen to know where the ladies' room is?'

'The loo's in a different building, Emily,' Clara jumped in with an apologetic eye-roll. I so badly wanted to remind her

270

that we had thought it a good thing that the bathroom was in a shabby outhouse a short walk away, because it meant that the party wouldn't be broken up by guests hanging out in the cubicles all night. It wasn't the moment for that conversation, however, so instead I told Emily that I'd walk her there with pleasure. I offered Clara the cocktail that was still in my hand. She gave a terse shake of the head and turned away. Emily, who must have noticed my struggle in suppressing a reaction, smiled kindly at me. I led her out of the bar and up the gentle slope to the outhouse.

'Thank you ever so much. So kind,' she said as we reached it. Then, she hurriedly asked, 'Are you alright?'

The question took me by surprise. Automatically, I smiled to cover up the fact that I definitely was not alright. 'Yes. Are you?' I said, taking a sip of the rum cocktail that no one else had wanted.

'Oh yes. I'm a little confused but, of course, if they're happy, I'm happy.'

Was she trying to open a conversation about her son and Clara? I wondered how much she knew. 'Do you think they are happy?' I asked.

She wrung her hands as she spoke, 'Um. Well. You know. Ed doesn't talk to me a lot. So I'm not the best person to ask.' She interlaced her fingers, clasping herself for support. Then she opened her mouth and I waited eagerly for what she was about to say. Eventually, she spoke in a high-pitched voice, 'But, my gosh, what a spectacular place this is. You've really done such a wonderful job at organizing everything. Wow.'

I smiled, disappointed but not surprised that our potential moment of bonding had been a flash in the pan. 'Would you like me to wait for you?' I asked.

'Oh gosh, no. I'll be fine. Go enjoy yourself now, you deserve a break.'

I didn't think that enjoying myself was exactly on the cards for the evening, but I thanked her anyway and returned to the bar.

The first guest had arrived. It was my mother. I felt a twinge of anxiety, but also an odd sense of security as Bella handed her a cocktail, saying, 'You'll like this one, it's strong,' as a nod to their halcyon days of friendship. I approached them and my mother opened her free arm to me. She kissed my temple. I felt like collapsing into her arms and begging her to take me home.

Clara came over to greet her with reserved politeness, and my mother wished her *mazel tov*. The four of us stood there, chatting away, just like the old days. It felt so familiar. My mother and Bella, despite not having spoken for years by default, knew each other inside out, just like Clara and I did. I felt a prickle of wistfulness for the unity of our families. Behind us, Fabian and Omni were talking about music. She mentioned a band that she hated, and Fabian said, 'Don't say that in front of Leo,' bringing my ears out of the conversation I was having and into theirs, but there seemed to be nothing more to hear. I silently willed Omni to ask where Leo was, but she was already onto another topic.

From then, the guests started to arrive in waves, since there were only a certain number of taxis on the island. Clara returned to Ed and his parents, vividly staking her loyalty. My mood lifted more and more as people arrived, not only because the family was dispersed, but because everyone greeted me with so much enthusiasm and love. It was a helpful reminder that not all of my friends disliked me as much as Clara did at that moment. They all congratulated me on planning such a fantastic event, but as it turned out, everyone had seen Pantelleria in some Luca Guadagnino film that I was clearly too uncultured to know about. So, rather than having found an undiscovered rock, I looked like a film tourist. Somehow, that seemed like the least of my worries.

I heard Leo's voice – a drunken slur – before I saw him. He trundled up the steps in the same white outfit I'd seen him in earlier, with his long arm draped across Marina's shoulders. In an instant, a gauze of jealousy wrapped itself around me. I watched as Clara clocked him, then abruptly turned away with the slightest of eye rolls, evidently embarrassed by his presence. I glanced around for Alice, but Tim had arrived, meaning that she had her own problems to deal with. Quickly, I whirled in the opposite direction and came face to face with Fabian.

He grabbed my shoulder and leaned in close so that the husk of his voice rubbed my ear. 'Come to the bathroom with me, trouble.' I shook my head. He tutted with disappointment and said, 'You're not fun anymore.'

I could have killed him. Why was it that everyone else was allowed to have a million bad days, and when I had one, people pointed out what a bore I was being, instead of checking that I was alright? Why did it have to be left to Ed's mother, who barely knew me, to ask? Why did everyone expect me to be The Fun One every second of the day? At times, I was so aware of having to be The Fun One that I ended up having the least fun of everyone. Perhaps that was the answer to my question: it was my reputation, because I had created it that way.

Watching Leo from across the porch, I remembered the blatant honesty I'd displayed earlier. Perhaps playing it cool was not the way to go tonight. Perhaps playing it *adult* was the one. I pinned my shoulders back and started to strut towards him with purpose. But in my staunch determination, I walked right into a waiter, whose canapés went cascading to the floor in what seemed like slow motion, ending with the loud crash of the tray hitting the floor.

'Oh my God, I'm so sorry,' I gasped, immediately sinking to the ground in an attempt to gather all of the lost canapés into one place, but mostly, to hide. 'Just wanted some attention,' I quipped to all of the people who were looking down at me with mingled concern and amusement, my mother included. Next thing, a pair of beige heeled sandals with multiple straps wrapped around a thin ankle and pedicured toes came into view. 'Get off the floor,' the sharp, brash voice came from the top of the beige tower. 'You have pastrami stuck to your leg. I'd remove it, but I'm a vegan.'

'Oh, thanks, Hazel,' I said, peeling the limp pastrami from my calf. As I returned to full height, I caught a glimpse of Leo watching me with something like affectionate ridicule from a few feet away.

'Good to see you too,' she shot at me indignantly.

I was still in a fluster, so a proper greeting seemed impossible, but also, I barely recognized her. The last time I'd seen Hazel, she'd been stark naked on the fire escape of her Brooklyn apartment, serenading her neighbour with an X-rated rendition of 'I Touch Myself'. Now, she had a teardrop diamond locked to her left ring finger, an Upper East Side hairdo and a toddler attached to the side of her body.

'You got thin,' she said, looking me up and down with a nod of approval.

'Oh. Yeah, stress,' I said, wondering when she'd ever thought of me as non-thin.

'I like your dress,' I said, curiously taking in the pious,

high-collared, frilled and puff-sleeved creation that was such a stark contrast to the band tees and denim shorts that I remembered her in.

'Thanks, it's 1920s Victorian,' she said didactically.

'Nineteenth century?' I offered.

'No,' she said with impenetrable finality. She plucked an anchovy bruschetta from a passing tray, which I thought was odd considering she'd made a point of telling me she was vegan, rather than removing a goddamn piece of pastrami from my leg. 'This is Camille,' she said, shifting the toddler higher up onto her hip. 'My husband arrives tomorrow. Then, thank God, I can start jogging and sleeping again. I don't feel myself.'

Jogging and sleeping? I wondered when Hazel became preoccupied by things that you apparently didn't know were luxuries until you had a tiny being chewing your nipples off. Oh, how I'd have loved someone to be chewing my nipples that night.

'Oh hey, my husband has a brother in London who you should totally meet,' said Hazel, with her usual pushiness. 'He's rich. And single.' *From drug pushing to wedding pushing.* 'You're still single, right?'

'Yeah,' I said. 'I'm not really looking for anyone though.'

'I wasn't either. I just got lucky,' she said with a self-satisfied smile. 'It'll happen for you too.'

'Thanks,' I said. In reality, I had heard from Clara that – far from 'getting lucky', whatever that meant – Hazel had panicked when her gynaecologist referred to her thirty-second birthday as 'the party of the withering womb', called up a Wall Street banker who had been trying to date her for years and had 'accidentally' fallen pregnant a month into the relationship. Perhaps that would happen for me too. Perhaps that was the generational destiny for people like Hazel and me.

275

Party as hard as you can, panic and get yourself knocked up by the first person you can think of. I couldn't begrudge her for her smugness. After all, I played up the invigorated, career-striving, free-spirited party girl with superiority when I was in the presence of married homeowners and mothers-to-be. We all played up for the society that had set us against each other, even if we didn't recognize it.

'You seem different,' Hazel said sharply, the anchovy toast disappearing into the cave of her mouth.

'Different how?' I asked, a note of dread in my voice. I would put money on predicting that she was not about to hand me a compliment.

'There's something heavy,' she said, using her free hand to form a gesture that I guessed meant, *Energy.*

Stuck for an answer, I saw Alice passing by and lurched out to grab hold of her skinny bicep. She tripped towards me and stared at me with glassy eyes. She was drunk. 'Al, you remember Hazel?' I asked.

'Not really,' she said flatly. More than drunk. She was way gone.

'Clara's cousin,' I clarified. When no one said anything, I awkwardly added, 'Hazel is a pescatarian.'

'Vegan, actually,' she corrected me, picking a piece of anchovy bone from between her teeth.

'But you're eating fish,' I said.

'Yeah, I eat fish. No meat and no dairy.'

I looked at Alice, but her eyes were drifting around, completely glazed over. 'So, you're not a vegan?' I pressed.

'I would never eat the product of a mammal, basically,' said Hazel irritably.

And then, out of nowhere, Alice looked her direct in the

eye and said, 'Do you suck cock?' I turned to her sharply, with raised eyebrows. She looked at me, as if she was unaware that she'd said anything out of the ordinary, and shrugged. 'It's meat.'

I imagined the fisherman in the boats below watching the bar from a distance, twinkling lustrously among the darkness of the volcanic rocks, mimicking the stars overhead. They'd have no idea that their local haunt had been taken over by the English and turned into a melting pot of liquor-littered dynamics.

I leant against the porch fence with Omni, feeling agitated because Leo and I had barely spoken all evening, but for a hasty 'hello'. I thought the least he could've done after I'd been so honest with him was to have behaved like the friend he claimed he was. His interaction with every other woman he came into contact with – whether it was Hazel bouncing her daughter around, Marina cock-teasing him sweetly, or Theodora all but humping his leg – was just one big flirt. And even though I wasn't exactly proud of our dysfunctional attachment, I wanted the people around us to witness a glimpse of it. I wanted them to imagine us in those moments of inter-connection that came straight after sex, when you feel like you know a person so intimately. I needed my friends – and my mother – to know that the details of sex and romance were within my orbit.

Suddenly, Hazel's kid was at my feet, wrapping both arms around my left calf. I looked down into the bright blue eyes of the toddler. She quickly released my leg and stepped back, gazing up at me with both intrigue and apprehension. I bent at the knees and lifted her into my arms, feeling my back throb with pain as I did so, which made me think that I was too debilitated to ever be a mother. I bounced her on my hip a few times, as I'd watched Hazel do, and said, 'Hi.' What else could you say to a toddler? And then, as if by magic, Leo was at my side. Was that all I had to do to reel them in? Push out a child and wear it as an accessory?

'Looks good on you, honey,' he teased, his eyebrows twitching suggestively.

'Great. Let's make one,' I responded with a dark cynicism in my voice, as my head began to spin.

He laughed at my jibe as Hazel swept in to take the child away from me. 'Sorry! She's totally confused at the moment 'cause her dad's not here,' she said, going into a baby voice at the end.

'And I look like her dad?' I asked. I suddenly realized that I hadn't eaten anything since breakfast.

Hazel let out a snorting laugh. 'I'm taking her to bed. But tomorrow, Dad's on duty,' she said with a wink in her voice that told me she was getting ready to let loose. The thought both terrified and excited me.

As she walked off, for some reason I felt the need to say, 'I'm not into kids.'

'Of course you're not,' said Leo in an unnervingly filthy way.

Why 'of course'? I wanted to ask. My not being into kids was not a total lie because I didn't exactly have a natural way with children. Something about the idea of being totally responsible for them freaked the hell out of me. But I did desperately want my own. It was the one and only thing in my life that I'd always been certain of but could never admit to out loud. In fact, I always felt the need to claim the opposite, since it was so out of line with all my other desires in life. I had a feeling that my wanting children so badly was more to do with my own fear of growing old alone than it was wanting to nurture a tiny human being.

'You look so cute and drunk,' he said, taking a step towards me.

'Thanks,' I said. I didn't know how those two words fit together, but I certainly couldn't argue with that fact that I was drunk.

'Like a mole,' he added.

'Do moles get drunk?' I asked, and I think he laughed. My stomach churned. It started a slow ascent to my chest. 'I'm . . . bathroom,' I said briefly. I hurtled away from him, internally speaking to myself: *You're absolutely fine, just get to the bathroom.*

I wasn't absolutely fine. But I didn't want to pierce a hole in anyone's fun. I had held back many handfuls of hair while friends vomited their way through parties, but like hell would I ask anyone to hold mine back. I suddenly wished that the bathroom wasn't in another building as I wobbled out of the bar and up the sloped road. I didn't quite make it all the way up. In fact, I barely managed to tuck myself behind the main building before a surge of vomit ejected itself from my stomach. I pressed one palm flat against the stone wall and used the other to hold back my own hair, with a feeling that my body armour was falling away with every lurch.

At least I was truly fulfilling my literary stereotype: a haphazard, calorie-counting, chain-smoking, boozing single gal. But I wasn't a literary heroine of a subgenre. I wasn't a victim of bourgeois suburban dissatisfaction, or a nice girl who just kept picking the wrong guy. I was a genuine real-life fuck-up, incapable of emotionally supporting myself – or anyone else for that matter – who engaged in self-destructive, self-serving and vulgar sex, without apology. I was, what the critics would call, 'Hard to swallow.'

I finished the purge with a wail of sorts and dropped my forehead onto the wall. Seconds later, Ned appeared from around the corner. 'Are you alright?'

Though I knew he meant well – and though I'd longed for someone other than Ed's mother to ask me if I was alright – his concern felt like an annoying encroachment on my privacy. Had he followed me up there? 'Don't know what's happened to me,' I said, embarrassed by my sudden weak constitution. 'I never get sick from drinking.' It was true. It never happened to me.

'Do you need water?'

'I'll get some, in a minute,' I said brusquely.

'Wait there,' he said and quickly disappeared from sight.

I stayed exactly where I was, breathing in and out of my mouth, urging my stomach to settle. Then a figure emerged from the half-gloom, quiet and graceful. It was Clara. Noticing me, she stopped in her tracks. 'Everything OK?' she asked. I glanced at her briefly, surprised at the gentle twinge of concern in her voice, and also so grateful that she had been the one to walk around that corner. She was the only person that I wanted to see me in such a vulnerable state. She eyed the puddle of waste at my feet. 'You're never sick,' she mused.

I shrugged. 'Emotional vomiting.' As I said it, I realized that it was probably true. How else could I get rid of all my feelings other than violently expelling them from my gut?

'Oh, Jax,' she said, her voice full of pity and sadness. Not for us, but for me. 'Come here.'

'You hate the smell of vomit,' I said, holding out my hand to stop her from coming too close.

'Well, I don't think anyone loves it,' she said, a very Clara joke. I forced a small smile. She held her arms open, in a gesture that could have been a shrug as much as a welcome into a hug.

But I stepped towards her and fell into her embrace. She smelled of sea air and Chanel No.5 – not dissimilar to her mother. 'I'm so sorry, Clara,' I whispered into strands of silky hair. 'I lost my mind. I'm sorry.'

'It's OK,' she said quietly.

'It's not OK,' I said, and I meant it. I realized that what I had done was not only stupid, it was a betrayal. Best friends were supposed to believe in one another, and I had not believed in her. I had doubted her power of survival and had infantilized her. I had personified the patriarchy in deciding that this poor woman would never survive without this man. I had taken away her autonomy and control. How could I have expected her to have been anything but furious with me?

'I love you so much,' I said, sliding my arms further around her, holding on a fraction tighter.

'Jax, I love you as well. I really do. But in future, I need you to love me a little bit less, OK?'

I pulled back and looked at her. She had a very serious expression on her face, like she was trying to drill something into me. I understood what she was saying. I was the sad, single best friend who couldn't let go. My friendship was suffocating her and my love for her was verging on creepy.

Ned reappeared, holding a glass of water in both hands. Clara squeezed my hand. 'Come get ready with me in the morning, OK?' With that she released me and continued up to the bathroom. I took the water from Ned, silently wishing that he'd never arrived with it, but also feeling guilty that he'd gone to the effort and thanked him repeatedly. Tiny sips turned into larger ones, until the glass was half empty.

'I'll drive you back to the house,' he said.

I wagged my finger from side to side, making an 'mm-mm' noise as I gulped down the last of the water. 'I don't need to leave right now. I'll be fine.'

'OK,' he said uncertainly. He cautiously added, 'I think it's better that you do?'

'In a bit,' I said stubbornly, and made my way unsteadily back down to the bar. Returning to the throng of people, I couldn't spot Leo anywhere. Perhaps he'd taken my momentary absence to whisk Marina back to his stone cabin. Then again, he probably would have done so regardless of whether I'd been there to see it or not. I couldn't scope out Fabian either, so an idea fixed itself in my mind that he and Leo had gone back to the estate to drink tequila and smoke cigarettes on his porch, beneath the stars, swathed in the velvety night air. Despite having just been sick, I wanted nothing more than to join them in that romantic fantasy of mine. I just wanted, more than anything, to laugh.

It wasn't long before Clara and Ed left in a taxi with Moll and Budi. Ed was staying in Harry's *dammusa* that night. I wondered whether Clara would be happy to go to bed alone, for one last night, or if she would wish that I was there with her, as we'd always planned. I didn't think there was much reason for me to stay after their departure, since I could barely engage in conversation. So, I pushed my way into the small cavernous interior part of the bar, in search of Ned.

Just inside the doorway, Alice was pressed against the wall with one arm locked across her rib cage and the other clutching a tumbler of vodka on the rocks. Tim stood with his hand on the wall above her shoulder, a stance of attempted control. She deliberately looked away from him, with pursed lips, as he spoke to her in a vehement manner. 'You already care about work more than you care about us!' was all I heard as I passed. For a moment, I thought it best that I didn't get involved, but then I realized that if it was me, I'd have wanted the support of my friends. I turned to Alice as she closed her lips around the straw – one of the paper ones that Ned had brought from London. Tim reached over to snatch the glass away from her. 'Stop drinking! Stop.'

I put my hand on her forearm, raised my eyebrows and mouthed, 'OK?' She offered a quick nod and I could have sworn that I saw tears in her eyes. I wasn't sure I'd ever seen Alice cry. I said, 'Proud of you,' quietly, before slipping off towards the bar, where Ned was packing up his glasses. 'I think I will leave now,' I said, finally admitting defeat. 'You don't have to drive me though, if it's not on your way.'

'I've driven you to Paris. I think a ten-minute detour up the hill should be fine,' he said with a smile. I half laughed but was also mortified to be reminded of the different levels of madness that I'd passed through in the past few days.

The roads felt different in the dark. The narrow swerves seemed treacherous and there was something foreboding about the remoteness. Though it seemed wrong to do so next to Ned, I took out my phone and typed out a message to a certain someone: 'Fancy a nightcap?' I don't know whether I was still hanging onto the fantasy of a starlit ramble with him and Fabian, or if that was just me kidding myself. I didn't put the phone away as I normally would have done, but stared at the screen, waiting for him to read it and start typing.

'I don't know him at all,' said Ned suddenly. 'But I do know that you're better than that.'

I didn't look up from the screen as I said, 'Did they not teach you in your feminist workshop that women really don't need any more shame or blame heaped onto them?'

'I'm not shaming or blaming,' he said calmly. 'I'm telling you, as a friend. It really has nothing to do with feminism.'

But, of course, it had everything to do with feminism. I loved Ned for having enough interest to pay his hard-earned money to read bell hooks and learn all the right words to use. But his reading would never be the same as mine. He would never truly know what it was like to be a woman. He would never know what it feels like for your beliefs to be so inconsistent with your feelings. He would never have to live with the guilt of wanting to be body positive and simultaneously caring so desperately whether or not you looked good naked. He would never sit with the confusion of wanting to be respected, but also wanting to be objectified. He would never know that having your choices judged by someone you admired was the ultimate shame.

Instead of explaining all of that to him, in a calm and rational way, I irritably muttered, 'You wouldn't understand.'

'I'm not saying that I understand how you're feeling right now. But I do know that you will not feel any better if you wake up with White Trousers tomorrow.'

I laughed a little at the nickname and muttered a repetition, 'White Trousers.'

'Have you ever had a relationship?' he asked, seemingly out of the blue.

'That's a very personal question, Ned,' I said, suddenly businesslike, reminding him that I was his client, not his friend.

'Is it?' he asked, glancing sideways at me with raised eyebrows.

I paused. I guessed it wouldn't really be that personal a

question if I'd had a straightforward answer. 'I've had flings,' I said curtly. 'What's your point?'

'There's no point. I was just asking.'

'You mean judging.'

'No, I mean asking. Why would I judge that?'

'Because I don't exactly think that you know – from over there with your successful business and your perfect family – what it's like to be me.'

'Why don't you explain it to me then?' he said, flipping the indicator and turning down the road to the house.

'It's boring. You probably don't really care anyway,' I said with childish belligerence, in order to avoid having to talk about myself.

'Of course I care,' he said with an aghast breath, as if the idea that he didn't was truly horrifying.

'Why?'

'Because I like you, Jax. I really, really like you.'

A dramatic pause followed, just like it would have in a movie. The confession didn't exactly come as the surprise of the century considering how kind and giving Ned had always been towards me. But it still made me prickle with embarrassment. I wasn't used to people talking straight and meaning what they said. Immediately, I dove in with a cynical response: 'You mean you want to fuck me?'

'No, I don't mean that,' he said with evident frustration as the car rolled over the gravel driveway and the illuminated house came into view above.

'Oh, so you don't want to fuck me?' I said accusatorily. 'Thanks.'

'Can you stop saying that word?'

'*Fuck*? So, you like me, but not the way I speak? Because

that's a word I use a lot.' I had no idea where the aggression was coming from, but I couldn't seem to stop it.

'OK. I shouldn't have said anything. Maybe we can talk tomorrow,' said Ned, with so much rationality that it forced me to regain some of my own.

I pressed the balls of my hands into my eye sockets. 'I'm sorry, Ned.' I wanted him to say, *It's OK, I get it, I get you.* But he didn't say anything. He didn't excuse my behaviour or allow me to justify it. He left me sitting there beside him, drowning in my own indignity. To break the silence, I added, 'I can't really cope with conversations like this at the moment.'

'Conversations like what?' he said, bringing the car to a gentle break. He turned to face me, making me feel far too exposed.

'You know.'

'Did you understand what I was trying to tell you?' he probed, still so cool and composed in a way that I couldn't relate to.

'Can we just get through tomorrow first, please?' I begged.

'So, we're going to pretend that I never said it? Or that you don't remember, I guess?'

I sighed. 'I'll see you tomorrow.' I opened the door and got out of the car without another word. Feeling weary and shaken, I staggered off, not towards my own habitation, but in the other direction.

Leo hadn't responded to my text, but, conveniently, I knew exactly where everyone at that wedding was staying. It was one of the furthest *dammusa* from the main house, a good ten minutes' walk through the trees. I'd done that on purpose, to prove to Clara that I wasn't planning on being anywhere near him at her wedding. Walking through the velvety night air with tightly crossed arms, I hung onto the idea that he and Fabian would be sitting on his porch, smoking cigarettes and putting the world to rights. I was still convincing myself that I was a grown-up – of sorts – looking for nothing more than a nightcap, and perhaps a hug.

But no one was on the porch when I arrived. The shutters were closed. I'd come on a futile mission.

I was about to turn around, but a sharp sliver of light in one of the windows caught my eye. A shutter was ajar. A light was on. Leo was awake.

I took slow, stealthy steps towards the *dammusa*, like a cat moving towards its prey. As I got closer, I heard the sound of music playing. *Oh God,* I thought. *Oh, good God.* He was with a girl. I don't know how I knew – it's perfectly normal to play music on one's own – but I just knew. I whirled around and headed for the trees. But then a perverse curiosity got the better of me and I spun back again. I stood outside the front door, straining my ears to hear something over the music. That ajar shutter was tantalizing me. But what if he saw?

Carefully, I stepped closer to the window, sticking close to the wall. All I could see was the floor.

I moved an inch. There was something on the floor.

My chest split in two.

CHAPTER 17

It was the triangular wiring that was unmistakable. I'd never seen a bra like it until two days before. And there it was, wickedly strewn across the tiled floor.

I froze in stillness, flat against the wall of volcanic rock. There was a pause in the music as the song switched over. I heard a honeyed laugh that could only have belonged to one person.

Confusion was clouding anything that resembled an emotion. A bottle of red wine and two half-empty glasses sat on the small porch table. I took in the sight of the items, trying to make sense of what was happening. Had Clara come all the way down for nothing more than an innocent nightcap, which led to an unprecedented escalation of events? But why would she want to have a drink with Leo, the night before her wedding? Though they'd known each other a long time, she had no regard for him. She had nicknamed him 'poison', for God's sakes. Perhaps weighed down by stress, she had lost her mind in a drunken moment, as I had done many a time. But the bra on the floor said otherwise. Clara had walked to the furthest point of the land in her honeymoon lingerie.

Well, I take it you don't know that she's been cheating on me? Ed's words rang out in my head on repeat. There were so many questions that I needed answered. But what was I going to do?

Charge in there like I was his fucking wife, catching them in the act? Smash the wine bottle in half and run at them like Glenn Close in *Fatal Attraction*? Close my eyes and hope that the hallucination would disappear?

I walked over to the table and picked up one of the wine glasses, helping myself to a sip. I ducked underneath the table, hoping to find a stray Marlboro Red to ease my racing mind. But, of course, Leo must have taken every last one inside with him, seeing as he was partial to a mid-sex cigarette. Not with Clara, surely? She hated the smell of Marlboro Reds.

I slumped down into one of the chairs, where I finished both glasses of wine and what was left of the bottle. I could hear nothing but the music. Then, after God knows how long, the door opened. The music got louder for a second. Clara emerged into the stillness of the night, wearing the same dress she'd worn to the party, with her high heels in one hand and the triangular number wedged underneath her arm. Furtively, she closed the door behind her, muffling the music.

I let out a throaty cough and she jumped backwards with a gasp. 'Oh my God, you scared me,' she said breathily. For a split second, she looked truly terrified. Then she covered it with a small nervous laugh. 'Sorry, I was just getting something for Fabian.'

'Getting what?'

'His weed,' she said, rolling her eyes affectedly. 'He gave it to Leo earlier and forgot to get it back.'

'You came all the way down here, the night before your wedding, to pick up drugs for Fabian?' I asked slowly, my words dripping with scepticism.

'No, not for Fabian,' she said, and I could already see the first blotch appearing on her neck. 'I just thought that it might

289

help me sleep.' She was desperately scraping the barrel for a believable story.

'Can I have some?' I asked. Clara looked stunned by that request. She glanced at the front door behind her, perhaps wondering if she could continue the tale. Rather than allowing her to waste time with another concoction, I put her out of her misery. 'What the fuck, Clara?' Within a split second, she had started a brisk walk away from me. I got up and followed. 'How … When … How did this start? You barely even know him.'

'I've known him for years,' she reminded me, without stopping or turning to look at me. 'You met him through me.'

'But you never actually *knew* him,' I said, catching up to her.

She took ginger but urgent steps along the pebbly path with her bare feet. 'I do know him,' she said seriously.

'What, in a biblical sense?'

'In all senses,' she said, surprisingly calm. 'This had already started when I introduced you to him.'

When I introduced you.

'You were already sleeping with him?' I asked incredulously.

'No, not sleeping with him. The … connection … had already started.'

'Connection? Leo doesn't have a connection with anyone!' I shrieked. She made no response to that. Exasperated, I continued, 'And the sex? When did that start?'

'I don't feel comfortable talking to you about this,' she said, stopping to pick a dry pine needle from her toe.

'No shit, Clara!' I cried. 'Did you feel comfortable when I told you I was in love with him?'

'You're not in love with him, Jax,' she said dismissively.

'How do you think you know that?'

'You only want him because you can't have him.' She sounded like she was sick and tired of having to force me to see sense, over and over again. 'Unrequited love is really never about the other person. It's about yourself.'

'Are you really going to lecture me on the meaning of love, right now?' I was close to shouting, but I wasn't there yet. Shouting at Clara was not something that came easily to me, not even then.

'I'm not lecturing you. I'm trying to comfort you,' she said, sounding even more frustrated. 'I know you're upset, but don't make this into more than it is. You don't love Leo. He's just someone you've slept with a few times.'

The implication was clear. I had no ownership over him. I had no right to feel as heartbroken as I did. Technically, it was true that Leo was someone with whom I occasionally had sex. But that didn't take away from the fact that, internally, I had been through the rollercoaster emotions of relationship, break-up and reconciliation a hundred times over.

'How ... Why is this wedding happening?' I asked with incredulity.

At that, her lip started to tremble. *Oh dear.* Had I just made Clara cry? It was strange that, even given the situation, I felt terrible about it. 'Because I promised Ed that it was over,' she said with a shaking voice. 'That it had been a long mistake and I'd never do it again. Tonight was ... not meant to happen.'

'Sorry, but I'm more confused than anything else. Does Ed know that it was Leo you've been cheating with?'

'Yes.'

'And he knows that it's been an ongoing thing?'

She nodded. 'He forgave me when I explained. Because he sort of understood why I was doing it.'

'Why *were* you doing it?' I asked.

'It's private,' she whispered, as if the trees were listening to us.

I furrowed my brow in confusion. 'How is Ed still happy for him to be at the wedding?'

'We thought it would look strange to uninvite him. It would make everyone wonder. You especially.'

Me especially. So, they had spoken about me. I wondered if Clara had begged Ed not to make a fuss over Leo for my sake. And if so, I wondered if it really had been for my sake or her own.

When Clara spoke again, she sounded tired and oddly sensible. 'I don't think we should have this conversation now. We've both been drinking.'

I threw my arms up with an air of, *Does it really matter now?* Clara veered away, down one of the dimly lit paths. I let her go. I swerved through the trees, in darkness, the damn pine needles slipping into my sandals and pricking my skin. When I emerged, I was by the walled garden. I charged in, feeling like someone who was spiralling towards insanity and possibly had the potential to become violent. Confined between four walls, I let out a long-held gasping sob and doubled over, clutching my stomach dramatically.

'Hi,' a voice said, and I yelped in fright. I whirled around to see a figure sitting on a bench, almost invisible, with nothing but the almost full moon to illuminate him. 'Where have you come from?' said Ed.

I paused for a few seconds, pressing my hand to my forehead. I could tell him everything. I could reveal that whatever promises she'd made to him in that shell grotto the night before meant nothing. The crickets buzzed frantically, like they were trying to alert us to danger. Slowly, I opened my mouth to speak. 'I was just taking a walk. Can't sleep yet.'

'Me neither.'

I took a seat next to him. 'How did you find out?'

He turned to look at me with a surprised raise of his eyebrow. 'You know?'

'Yes. I know.'

'I see,' he said, with a touch of humiliation. For the first time, I felt that we were chiming the same note. Ed sighed. 'A modern cliché.' I looked at him questionably. He added, 'Text messages on our shared iPad.'

I took a deep breath, trying to imagine what those text messages might have said, before letting out a long sigh. 'Why are you marrying her?'

'I believe she'll stop when we're married,' he said, as if trying to convince himself of it. Then he added, in a feeble voice, 'And we both have our faults.'

'That wasn't what you said yesterday morning,' I reminded him.

Ed said nothing for a long time. We both stared at the moon, with its missing slice of light. Then, finally, he spoke. 'We had an adult conversation about it. Things always make more sense when you look at them logically, instead of emotionally.'

'You find that easy to do?' I asked, shifting my glance sideways to look at his profile. He gave a gentle shrug of the shoulders. I smirked. 'This whole thing is really fucked up.'

'Are you upset?'

'What do you think?' I threw the words out with more hostility than I meant to.

'That's why I didn't want to tell you.'

Something about his subtle expression of concern for my

feelings touched me. I welled up with emotion. 'I wish you had,' I croaked. 'I would've left you in Paris.'

'You wouldn't have believed me.'

I've known Clara for twenty years. I know her better than anyone.

Ed was right. I wouldn't have believed him. I wouldn't have believed anyone, had I not seen it – or at least a fragment of it – with my own eyes. My thoughts meandered to that Agent Provocateur piece, discarded on the floor. It would forever be burned onto the lobe of my brain, reminding me of the unpredictable and uncontrollable multiplicity of human behaviour.

The lingerie alone had seemed too salacious for Clara, but *Leo*? The thought that she would go anywhere near him seemed too absurd for words. But perhaps it was no surprise that there was a part of Clara that needed a shady side of her life in order to go on living the other. For all her attempts to mould herself into an archetype of normality – whatever that was – she had never really healed her wounds of her past. She had simply covered them in so many plasters that they must have been burning and itching for attention. With all those lacerations caused by living in a storm of fury, pain and confusing reconciliation, and, of course, by nearly being abandoned by her mother, how could she not still have a dissolute undercurrent?

I wondered how she behaved when she was alone with him. Did she ask what he wanted her to do, like I did? Did she dress up in a basic black dress and high heels and pretend to be his art dealer? No. Clara wouldn't have done any of that. She would have been prim and untouchable; Leo would have gone in carefully. And what was really getting to me was that I knew he would have found her even more alluring for it. He wouldn't have seen her resistance as prude, or boring. He would have tied a knot in his twitching cock and been careful with her. They probably had better sex than he and I did. After all, I'd never truly yielded to the neediness of intercourse.

Ed wished me goodnight and left me sitting there on the bench. I guessed that he didn't want to give me an inch to tell him anything more than I already had, preferring to swim in the gloomy bliss of ignorance.

I returned to my empty *dammusa*. I gathered that Omni wouldn't be back tonight. Alice was somewhere else on the island, in a bed with Tim, her own world crumbling around her. I couldn't call my mother because I didn't want to admit the truth of what I had discovered. It would be all she needed to pick our years of friendship to pieces, and a part of me still wanted to defend it.

I sat on the edge of my bed and rocked back and forth along my spine. In one quick movement, I lifted my laptop from the floor, laid back against the pillow and placed it open on my stomach. There I typed out 600 words of an article. As I wrote, my mind flew back to October, when I had turned to Leo with my thumbs tucked into my jeans pockets and said, 'Clara got engaged.' I had been touched by his rapid reaction, thinking that he knew me so well that he could feel my pain for me. But, actually, his reaction was to do with his own feelings about her engagement. Not mine.

I read my article once through. I copied the text and pasted it into an email.

I clicked send.

CHAPTER 18

A small part of me thought that Clara might have come to find me that morning. But she never came. And why should that surprise me? How many times had I seen her cryogenically shut herself off to even the smallest of confrontations? She'd learnt, through years of witnessing fights that were so charged that they sometimes became physical, that the easiest way to move through life was to build an igloo and hibernate until any storm – however big or small – had died down. Why should I be an exception to her?

I lay in bed for a long time, letting several alarms go off. As predicted, Omni was nowhere to be seen. Memories from the night before flashed up on the screen of my mind in no particular order. The bottle of wine on the porch table. The honeyed laugh through the wall. My strange chat with Ed, to the sound of crickets clacking. *You're not in love with him, Jax.* Vomiting behind the dive bar. My inner child throwing an outward tantrum at Ned, as we swerved down a dark road. *You only want him because you can't have him.* Hazel and her wifely blow-dry. The canapes crashing to the floor. My mother – did she notice how drunk I was? *I like you, Jax. I really, really like you.*

Eventually, I heaved myself out of bed, with a dense headache and a searing pain all down my back that felt like it could end me.

It was Clara's wedding day. The day that we'd both – oddly – been dreaming about since we were little girls. The day that I'd spent the past eight months working towards. And I had no idea how I was even going to look at her. I certainly couldn't push any kind of discussion or confrontation. However hurt I felt that she had crossed the one line that I knew I would never cross with a friend, she still deserved to have her day.

I didn't spend time draining my face with crystals or laying green teabags over my eyes. I didn't even bother to wash my hair. I just threw on a bathrobe and walked slowly towards the main house, my entire body lopsided. Hair and make-up would already be underway. I imagined that Bella was pouring a glass of champagne while Clara protested that it was too early. Moll would walk in with a plate of fruit, reminding everyone to line their stomachs. Omni may or may not have been there, lying flat on the bed with a cold towel over her head. And then, in I'd waltz, pretending that everything was fine.

The worst part was, I wouldn't be able to tell anyone what I'd discovered. I'd have to carry it around like a secret stash of SSRIs in my pocket. Everyone would undoubtedly think that my cold stance with Clara was to do with my being jealous that she was getting married and I wasn't. Because no one really believed me when I said that I didn't care if I ever got married or not. They assumed it was some defence mechanism that I'd decided to install in case I never did. Was it a defence? Was I fooling no one but myself?

Up at the house, Moll and Budi were eating breakfast under the pergola. They greeted me with cheerful '*Good morning*'s, as if nothing were wrong. I picked up the Bialetti coffee pot and tipped it over a blue and white china cup. One gravelly brown drop hit the bottom and my heart sank.

297

'The girls took a fresh pot up,' said Budi. 'They're all in Clara's room.'

'Eat breakfast though, darling. Your stomach needs lining,' said Moll, as I'd predicted. How well I knew that family.

'I will,' I said, though I wasn't hungry at all. I lifted a small tangerine from the table. 'What's the atmosphere like?'

'Too much for us,' said Moll.

'Yes, much too much for us shrinking violets,' Budi added, reaching for her hand. I smiled, but also felt an ache in my chest, witnessing what I knew was true love. Perhaps I should have seen it as hope, but at that moment, hope seemed like a faraway concept.

I ambled through the house, jamming my finger into the top of the tangerine to break the skin. I tore off small pieces, collecting them in the palm of my hand. There was a woman at the bottom of the spiral staircase, hopping nervously from one foot to the other, a large camera swinging from her neck. The photographer.

'Hello,' I said wearily, feeling very much over wedmin. 'I'm Jax.'

'Oh, Jax! So glad you're here,' she said excitably, without even introducing herself. To my surprise, she was English. 'The lovely bride is getting done up and I'd love to get some shots. But she said she's not quite ready for me. But, really, this is the time I need with her. Before and afters are ones that she'll treasure!'

'OK, I'll see what's going on. But if she's not ready, she's not ready,' I said, as I started my ascent of the staircase.

'I'm gagging to get my teeth into some of those visuals, you see!' the woman almost yelped.

'Why don't you take a seat outside and help yourself to

coffee. I'll come and get you when Clara is ready,' I said, quickening my steps. As I neared the top, I heard Bella's voice coming out in indecipherable snaps. Then, thankfully, an interjection from Alice followed by Omni's infectious giggle. I emerged from the depths of below, entering the grotto.

'Morning, darling,' said Bella brightly, though her voice was somewhat croaky from a hangover. 'You had a nice long sleep.'

'I did,' I confirmed. My eyes landed on Clara. Her hair was being tugged by the local hairdresser whose shiny bald head reminded me of Derrick's. Omni knelt on the floor next to her, painting her nails. Clara glanced at me, trying to read my mood. I gave away nothing, so she said nothing. I was the one to break the wordlessness between us. 'Morning, Clara.'

'I steamed your dress,' she responded quickly, nodding at the vintage floral garment hanging on the bathroom door. I wondered if she was trying to guilt-trip me by letting me know that she'd spent the morning of her wedding running steam up and down the dress that I was to walk down the aisle in.

'Shouldn't I be steaming yours?' I asked despondently.

'Least I can do,' she said in a clipped voice.

Was it her clumsy way of apologizing? I couldn't tell. Nevertheless, I muttered a simple, 'Thank you.' I spotted a coffee pot, identical to the one downstairs, on a low table. Gratefully, I poured myself a cup of fresh coffee. The silky dark liquid swirled around for a moment, steam emanating from its surface. I added a drop of milk, just the right amount. Taking the first sip, I wished that I could dive into the cup and reside in the millisecond of pure joy that the familiar ritual of my morning coffee unfailingly brought me.

'My daughter has decided to have her hair scraped up,' said Bella, cutting the glory short. There was something overbearingly possessive about the way she said, *My daughter*. She added, 'Though it's totally wrong for the dress and the setting.'

'Well, it's my choice,' said Clara curtly.

'You're not getting married at the Ritz, darling,' said Bella acerbically, as if the idea were completely ridiculous and out of reach, though the Ritz would probably have been cheaper than the Sicilian extravaganza that they had spent so much money on, trying to make it look like they'd spent nothing at all. 'Don't you think it looks better down, Jax?' Bella asked, walking around Clara, inspecting the start of her updo from all angles.

I shrugged, disinterested, despite the fact that I'd spent hours of days creating hair and make-up mood boards full of tousled styles. I sat down next to Alice on a cream loveseat.

'Morning,' she said in a low voice. 'What's up?'

I shook my head, ripping out one small tangerine segment before offering the rest to her.

'Nothing,' I said.

'Please!' she scoffed sceptically, taking the fruit and setting it aside. Bella was talking to the hairdresser in 'Italian' as Clara flinched repeatedly. I took a sip of coffee, closing my eyes, and willing it not to let me down. Alice respected this by refraining from interrupting me. When I opened my eyes, she gently said, 'Tell me later.' And then, lowering her voice even further, she added, 'Take Tim off the seating plan.'

'Why?' I asked, without thinking, tapping my finger against the thin rim of the cup.

'We've broken up.' My head jerked out of my neck as I spun to look at Alice. She gave me a tiny, tight smile and a nod of, *it's done*. 'He's flying back today,' she added. Her expression

300

instantly returned to its usual deadpan steadiness, but her eyes were darting around in their sockets.

'Are you alright?' My hand automatically went to her thigh, though that was unlikely to be comforting to someone who hated physical contact.

'No, not really. But I'm sure I will be.'

I set down my coffee and wrapped my arms around her shoulders, feeling her body tense in my grip. 'You will be,' I confirmed, with firm belief in my words. Alice would be fine. If only I could tell myself that with the same conviction. I felt her arms rise to lightly rest across my aching back, returning the hug in her way. She had just broken up with her boyfriend of three years, yet she still noticed that my mood had edged even further down the slope since the day before.

When we parted, there was a second in which I thought that I might finally see her break, but she quickly pulled it together and said, 'Made of iron.'

'Ball breaker,' I added, followed by an ironic laugh that she echoed.

Then she let out a sad sigh. 'It's fine,' she said hastily. 'He had a penis like an engorged clitoris.'

Coffee came spurting out of my mouth like it was a temperamental tap and landed all over Alice's face as a sputter of uncontrollable, shocked laughter emerged. She closed her eyes and reached for a napkin to wipe her face. Soon, both of us were close to tears; happy or sad, I wasn't quite sure.

'What's going on over there?' Bella called out, eager to get in on the fun.

'Nothing. Alice is just making me laugh.' I took a deep breath to calm myself but was once again overtaken by giggles. It was a real relief.

When the hairdresser had completed his work, Clara's golden strands were tightly pulled against her skull, the ends twisted into an elegant bun on the crown of her head. Then the make-up artist, a friend of Bella's, began on her already perfect face, gossiping away as she did so.

Soon, Hazel and child joined the soiree. Hazel informed us, by way of a whole room address, that her husband had touched down on the island. *Thank God for that.* Next, Moll appeared in a dark green velvet dress, asking if there was anything she could do to help. Immediately, she was pulled into the conversation with the make-up artist. Bella subsequently got entirely naked, in order to try on several dresses, asking everyone in the room for their opinion. Clara barely said a word, but I could see from the stiff way she was holding herself that she was becoming more and more agitated by all the activity going on around her. It was when Hazel's child let out a high-pitched scream that she closed her eyes and sucked in a breath. I knew what that meant. She couldn't take it anymore.

I stood up from the loveseat. 'Why don't we give Clara some space to get her dress on?' I suggested.

'We can do it now,' said Bella, roughly pulling the wedding dress from its hanger. Expectantly, she held it open in front of her. 'Come, poppet,' she beckoned.

I stayed close by as Clara peered down into the well of the dress. I recalled the day in the bridal shop, when she had pretended not to care what she wore, while I'd been close to tears at how beautiful she looked in the Venetian lace creation. But when she stepped into that dress, on the day of her wedding, I felt like the castle of our friendship was crumbling to pieces. Yet still, I wanted to be the one to lace it up. The atelier had instructed me on the very particular method for bringing the dress to a close around Clara's body. I was the only one in that room who could do it properly. I even made a point of walking her to the bathroom to get away from all the fussing family members and closed the door behind us. Then I laced the dress to perfection, listening to the sound of Clara's dry breathing.

'Don't forget to drink water,' I said.

'I won't.'

As I secured the laces in a knot, I suddenly couldn't help but think into the future, beyond the one day of her wedding. Would things ever be the same again for Clara and me? Strangely, the thought wasn't littered with panic, as I would have expected, but something more like curiosity. For once, I didn't want or expect anything from her, perhaps because I knew that I couldn't and that I never really had been able to. I buttoned the soft fabric of the dress in a straight line to cover the laces. 'There you go.'

She caught my eye in the mirror. 'Thank you,' she said. I felt like it was loaded, but by that point, who fucking knows?

With Clara fully adorned, I went into a separate room to change into my dress and apply a clumsy slap of make-up to my worn-out face. When I returned to the grotto, the number of people seemed to have doubled.

The too-ambitious photographer had found her way in and was standing on the bed, looking like she was treading water. She bellowed frantic instructions that all began with, 'Lovely bride.' Moll made a show of despairing over Theodora's dress, which had marijuana plants printed all over it in a repeat pattern. Theodora responded with elderly outrage that it was a spiritual healing plant. Hazel sang, 'Row, row, row your boat' on a loop to her intermittently crying child. Derrick and Budi playfully argued over an Indian jacket that they both wanted to wear.

Alice stood behind Omni, forcibly brushing her hair. A champagne bottle popped open. An iPhone bleeped. Fabian cackled loudly. Bella finished one of her stories, punctuating it with the word 'cunt' as she poured golden bubbling liquid into glasses.

Clara looked at me through all the commotion of dysfunctional festivity and I thought she was saying, *Get me out of this, please. Stop this from happening.*

'Can we all go downstairs for photos, please?' I yelled over the chattering voices. When no one moved, I grabbed onto Alice for help. 'Please can you get everyone out of here?'

'On it,' she said. In expert fashion, she persuaded everyone down the spiral staircase one by one, like the high-rolling PR that she was. *Fuck you, Tim,* I thought, as I watched her with pride. Inevitably, the ambitious photographer made an attempt to hang back, but Alice proceeded to manhandle her out.

Then I was alone with Clara. She stood still in one spot, with a surprised look on her face, or perhaps her hair had just been pulled back too tightly. Her face had drained itself of blood, leaving her usually glowing skin almost as white as her dress. She looked like the image of Cathy's ghost that I conjured in my head every time I read *Wuthering Heights* or heard the wails of the song. I half expected her to reach for a pillow and tear it to shreds in a fit of delirium. But instead, she said, 'This hair doesn't work with the dress, does it?' rather irritably.

'You look beautiful,' I responded, even though the Grace Kelly updo wasn't exactly right for the whimsical style of the dress, which is why I'd spent all that time on the mood boards. Clara bit down her lip before remembering that she had lipstick on. I took a cautious step towards her, afraid that she might bolt if I got too close. 'You still can get out of this, you know.'

'No, I can't,' she said calmly.

'Why not?'

'Because. There are a hundred people sitting in a church waiting for me to appear in a white dress looking like the cover of *Tatler* magazine.'

'You are *Vogue*, if anything,' I said in mock-alarm. She smiled and, for a moment, I forgot about everything. For a moment, I was ready to bundle her into the Pantelleria equivalent of a FedEx truck and transport her to safety. I added, 'Those hundred people don't have to be married to Ed until death do they part.'

She shook her head. 'I've made a promise to him. I'm not letting him down.'

'Is that really why you're doing it?'

Clara pressed her lips together and looked away from me. I thought she was going to speak, but she abruptly bundled her dress up into her arms and walked past me. I heard the clomp of her shoes carrying her down the spiral staircase. I waited a few seconds, allowing her the moment of privacy that I knew she needed, and then followed. We headed into the walled garden for photographs.

The photographer had arranged everyone into a traditional family photo formation. Unsurprisingly, Bella was pushing against any implication of convention by lighting a cigarette in the middle of a shot. The keen photographer squealed with excitement when Clara arrived, the last piece of the puzzle. Without saying anything, I stood back, out of shot. I wondered whether Clara would look at the picture, in years to come, and think, *Where's Jax in this one?*

The family formation disassembled naturally, much to our photographer's chagrin, and we all started ambling towards the driveway, where cars awaited us. Alice fell into stride beside

305

me on the path and pulled two Marlboro Lights from the depths of her Prada clutch bag.

'She doesn't want to do it,' I said quietly, receiving one of the cigarettes in my palm.

'I know,' said Alice. 'But we've meddled enough for one wedding.'

'You mean *I've* meddled enough?'

'No. All of us.'

'So, what now?' I asked with a weary sigh.

Alice turned towards me with a lighter and the shield of her gel-manicured hand. She lit both of our cigarettes then turned her face towards the sun and squinted as she blew out a steady line of smoke. 'Clara gets married,' she said. 'And we'll all be there to support her through her divorce.'

Would I be there for that? Did I *want* to be? Those were the things I wondered as I watched Clara, several metres ahead of me, clutching onto her father's arm. It was an absurd thought that we were already planning for the divorce of a couple whose marriage we hadn't even celebrated yet, but somehow, it was also an unavoidable one.

We arrived at the gravel driveway and I couldn't help but think of my graceless stumble away from Ned the night before. My heart started pounding at the thought of seeing him at the church. He had predicted that I would pretend I didn't remember the conversation. I so wanted to prove him wrong, to avoid the cliched version of myself that had manifested itself in his brain, but honestly, I couldn't think of any other way to avoid the crippling awkwardness that I so dreaded.

I rode to the church tightly packed into a car with the three other bridesmaids, plus the toddler who seemed to have become part of the wedding retinue. The vintage dress, which had seemed like a charming idea when I tried it on in Brick Lane, was suddenly just vintage sweat.

Hazel had only just been made privy to the whole story and therefore had a million questions, to which I repeatedly shrugged. Eventually, Alice told her to let it go and Hazel snapped, which conjured a cold mist of tension that we really did not need. Omni deflected by quick firing questions at the toddler. The child stared at her curiously, entirely silent for once, offering no answers. Omni huffed, 'Your chat's shit, Camille!', which even made Hazel laugh, successfully shattering the icicles.

When we arrived at the church, Ned was at the top of the steps with a clipboard, standing in as wedding planner, since wedding planner was doubling up as maid of honour. The horror of the night before landed in my mind and I tried to shoo away the memory, but it kept swooping about tauntingly. *You shouldn't act like you.*

I expected him to avoid me, but he leant over the wall and looked me in the eye to give me the information that Clara should wait a few moments. I passed the message on and herded the rest of the family up. Bella lingered at the bottom to smoke one last cigarette before the ceremony. Alice and I also hung back.

None of us spoke for a moment. A moment of serenity. A moment that was so perfectly broken by Bella, who looked at Clara and said, 'You do know it's not going to last, don't you?', nonchalantly taking a puff of her cigarette.

Clara's eye darted around. She held her lips firmly in a pout to stop them from trembling. Watching her, I really did forget everything that had happened over the past few days. I could deeply and viscerally feel the pain that she felt, hearing such words come out of her mother's mouth, moments before she walked down the aisle. In that moment, I truly hated Bella. Hated her for being so spiteful, so unmotherly, not only then, but always. A surge of shame washed through me as I thought of how often I'd made myself her ally.

'So what?' I said. Both Bella and Clara looked at me sharply. I went on. 'As long as he treats her well, and loves her – which I know he does – so what?'

An uncomfortable silence shrouded the group. All we could hear was the sound Alice's clutch bag popping open, followed by a rustle. From the bag, she pulled a minibar-sized bottle of vodka and handed it to Clara, with a quick warning of, 'Mind your lipstick.'

I wondered how many she had in there. One for me?

To my surprise, Clara unscrewed the cap and poured the vodka into her mouth.

Great, now the bride smells like a distillery, thought the part of me that still wanted the wedding to be perfect.

Fabian called out from the top of the steps, 'Mum, time to go in.'

Bella chucked her cigarette to the ground and stamped it out with her foot. She left it lying there, despite all the hours she spent sitting on committees of various Extinction Rebellion fundraisers. Then she reached out to hug Clara with a cheerful, 'Good luck, my darling,' despite having just hurled a grenade of a comment at her. Then she trotted up the steps and took Fabian's arm to walk into the church.

Clara's eyes skipped from me to Alice, and it was undeniable that she was on the verge of tears. I wanted to say, *It's not too late*, but I was afraid that, in fact, it *was* too late.

'It's OK,' said Alice, brushing Clara's arm with the tips of her fingers. 'Let's go.'

Clara hitched up the front of her dress and I bent over to pick up the train. I held it in my hands as we ascended the staircase towards Derrick, Ned, Omni and Hazel, like we were on the way to heaven. Ned did not ignore me when we reached the top, as I would have expected him to, but instead he stepped close to me and muttered a civil, 'Hey.' I returned it with a desperate look of, *You can't even imagine how bad things are.*

Inside the church, the organ started to whine. Ned gestured at Omni to let her know that she was up. She began the procession, entering the church with comically large steps. I felt my stomach gurgle with nerves. Alice followed her in, perfectly poised, and then Hazel holding Camille's hand.

I looked at Clara, hoping for some moment to pass between us. She did not return my gaze.

It was Ned who gave me a supportive squeeze of the elbow. It made me want to yell out, *Why don't you hate me?* Perhaps I'd feel less guilty about my behaviour towards him if he did.

I stepped inside the Chiesa di Madonna delle Grazie and a hundred faces turned to look at me. Had I not ventured down to Leo's *dammusa* the night before, I'd probably have been walking down the aisle wondering whether he was looking at me, or through my dress with imaginary X-ray goggles. But all I could wonder then was how he felt about watching Clara marry someone else. It probably turned him on. All his chat about our infidelity contract when we were both married to other people was only ever a fantasy. With Clara it was real. It was a dirty secret kept between them. She was fulfilling that fantasy in a way that I never could. I wondered if he had heard my argument with Clara unfold outside his bedroom. I hated the idea that he'd think himself some kind of Eros, ripping the solidness of a beloved female friendship in two.

As I reached the altar, my eyes brushed over Ed. He had that look on his face, the one that I seemed unable to remain emotionless about. It wasn't just anxiety. It was fear.

Clara appeared at the back of the church, clutching Derrick's upper arm. She sailed towards us like an apparition. When she reached the altar, she and Ed smiled at one another but did not join hands.

The priest said all the same words that he had the day before. The whole same shitty recitation. But that time, they went right over my head. Everything seemed a blur.

CHAPTER 19

I felt like a tuning fork in a world of high vibrations at the wedding reception. The tale of Ed's disappearance and my mission to get him to the altar had spread like a calamitous wildfire. Everyone and their mother felt the need to offload their thoughts and feelings about the story onto me, not knowing that I had possibly come out of it the most emotionally skewed of all parties. I emitted one note, which wasn't even mine. *If they're happy, I'm happy.*

It's a beautiful wedding, at least.

It was truly magnificent.

The newlyweds took their first dance under the full moon radiating against a perfectly cobalt blue sky. I watched from a distance, sitting at the end of one of the long banquet tables with my mother, both of us content in the other's silence.

My mother wore a printed silk kimono dress and a turban on her head. She looked cultured and stylish. Not someone you would imagine to be a social recluse who had food in her freezer from 2009. 'What are your plans when you get back?' she asked, daintily picking a piece of table foliage apart.

'I don't know, Mum,' I said, quick and impatient. 'Please stop asking me.'

She raised her eyebrows, startled by my reaction. 'That's the first time I've asked.'

There was some truth to that. She hadn't asked about my plans for a while. I supposed it was a normal question for anyone to ask, but when she said it, I heard, *When are you going to start building foundations for yourself?* and immediately became angry that she hadn't put any blocks in place to get me started.

'My plans are my business,' I responded.

Don't bring up the money.

'I just—'

'Don't bring up the money.'

'I just want you to be alright. Is what I was going to say.'

Then make everything alright. Please.

My throat went tight and I could feel emotion rise in my chest. I pressed my middle fingers into my tear ducts to try to suppress anything from escaping. My mother reached out and wrapped her fingers around my wrist. From there she forced her hand up to meet mine and our fingers interlaced. I collapsed onto her shoulder. My friendships were breakable, after all. I could do everything in my power to keep them intact, but at the end of the day, other people's actions were out of my control. But my mother would always be there. She was my family unit. And Ezra, even if we were disconnected in many ways – we were both hers.

We both stared out at the swimming pool. It was perfectly turquoise and luminescent. Eventually, my mother sighed and kissed my temple. 'Do you think it's rude if I leave?' she whispered into the warm space between us.

'Not at all,' I said. 'I'll walk you down.'

We stood up and made our way around the pool hand in hand. As I strode along the edge of the water, I imagined what it would be like to dive in and reside at the bottom in my vintage dress. I led my mother down a stone staircase, a shortcut to escape. As luck would have it, Leo was at the bottom, leaning against a wall with Marina. Either he'd just kissed her or was about to take the plunge. When she saw me, Marina edged away from him and crossed her arms in a display of hostility, presumably to let me know that she wasn't inviting his advances. I gave her a reassuring smile and tugged my mother past them without acknowledging Leo.

The rattle of the party gradually died out, until the clacking of the crickets was all we could hear. There were several taxis waiting along the gravel driveway (organized by me). As we neared one, my mother turned to me and said, 'If you want to get out of the flat, when you're back, you're welcome to stay with me.'

I looked at her, surprised. I hadn't told her what had happened with Clara the night before. Of course, she knew that there'd been tension, but not to the extent that it had reached.

'Thank you,' I said. I didn't, for a moment, consider her offer as something I'd take up, but I knew that she was only trying to be kind.

'Goodnight,' she said, kissing my cheek. She got into the taxi and it quickly disappeared from sight.

Walking back up towards the house, I considered going a different route so that I didn't have to run into Leo and Marina again, but then I thought, *Why should I?* As it turned out, it was only Leo, slumped against the stone wall with his head tipped back and his eyes closed, a Marlboro Red burning down between his fingers. At the sound of my heels on the hard ground, he opened his eyes. 'I've fucked up, haven't I?' he said.

Presuming that he was referring to Clara, I shrugged. The situation was so little about him by that point. If there was one thing I had to admit, it was that Clara had been right when

313

she'd said, *Unrequited love is really never about the other person. It's about yourself.* Being in love with Leo was just another easy way to avoid falling in love with anyone else. It was a way of making myself feel better for constantly returning for sex. An attempt to fill the empty space between us after all the incessant fucking. It was an illusion, not a truth. And I was done with it.

'Will you ever forgive me, darling?' he asked, as the music of the Cuban band wafted from above us.

'For which part?'

'You know what I mean.'

I considered for a moment. 'I'll forgive you, eventually, but it won't matter by then. We'll have been long over.'

'You know how much I adore you, don't you?' he said, seeming almost helpless in the claim.

I shook my head. 'No, actually, I don't. You say it, but you've never done anything to make me believe that it's true. In fact, you've done the opposite.'

'We're the same people, darling. We wanted the same thing from each other.'

'No, we didn't. We're not the same,' I said. Then, firmly, I added, 'At all.'

He sighed and took a puff of his cigarette. 'Are we going to be friends?'

'I really don't think that's necessary.'

I was done with the conversation. It wasn't worth it. Not with him.

I did not, however, feel ready to return to the throng of people above us. I turned away and walked back in the same direction I'd come from. My limbs felt heavy and fatigued as they grudgingly carried me down the path. I felt like I had small pieces of lead coursing through my veins and my poor lower back was burning with pain. I was wiped out. I had drained my batteries to their lowest point. I needed to be hooked up to an external force of energy and recharged. That's what you were meant to do with iPhones and laptops. Let them die and then start from the bottom up. Of course, I'd never had the foresight to do that with my devices, so they always dwindled prematurely. But when it came to myself, it seemed to be the only way I knew how to live.

This time, instead of heading to the driveway, I entered the walled garden, craving a moment of alone time. But just like the night before, I found a figure already there, sitting lonesome on the bench. This time it wasn't Ed. It was Ned. He had a cigarette in one hand and was manspreading in the most delicate way, if it was possible to delicately manspread.

Why oh why did I not want to dive into his arms and be swooped over for a Hollywood-style, end-of-movie kiss?

'You smoke an awful lot for a non-smoker,' I said, walking towards him. He didn't respond to my attempted wry humour but kept his eyes on me in a way that left me feeling unprotected. I sat down next to him. 'I'm sorry I behaved like I did, last night,' I said, truly despondent at the memory of my reaction to being told that someone so wonderful really liked me.

'Should we talk about it?' he asked, turning towards me.

'We should talk about it, but I'm sorry, I just can't right now. After I left you last night, I went to find White Trousers. Which was stupid, I know. You told me I shouldn't. I knew that I shouldn't. But, of course, I did it anyway.'

'Don't beat yourself up about it,' he said kindly, no suggestion of jealousy in his voice, which I found oddly disappointing.

'Well, I always do. But that's not the point. Basically, when

I got to his room, I found Clara there. With him.' I repeated, 'With him,' adding an unmistakably suggestive intonation. I watched Ned's eyebrows ascend into two perfect arches. Immediately, I became frantic with guilt. I always felt guilty about giving away too much about Clara, though it was not reciprocated. 'Please don't tell anyone,' I begged. 'I shouldn't be telling you, but I have to tell someone.'

'Your Leo?' he asked.

'He's not mine,' I said quickly. 'I don't even know if I have a right to be angry.'

'Of course you do.'

'I don't have the energy to be,' I said helplessly. 'I think I'm heartbroken, actually. Hard to tell. But I think I am.'

'Over what?'

'Losing the love of my life.'

We both knew that I didn't mean Leo.

'I know it must be very hard. But maybe you should look at it as a blessing in disguise,' he suggested breezily. I turned to look at him sharply. Where the hell was the blessing in this situation? He continued, 'Relationships end all the time. Once we get over the heartbreak, we accept that they weren't meant to be. Friendships are no different.'

I shook my head vigorously. 'Friendship is the most important thing in the whole world to me. It's all I have.'

You don't understand me at all.

'OK. But a friendship isn't a real friendship if it's imbalanced.'

I stood up in one fast motion and a debilitating pain shot through my spine. Grimacing with agony, I placed both hands on my lower back and squeezed my eyes shut. In that moment, I could have killed Ned for questioning the authenticity of my friendship with Clara. It was, I had always thought, the most real thing in my life. It was the deepest intimacy I'd ever experienced. If it wasn't real, did I really have the ability to be intimate with anyone, ever? If the deepest feeling of love I'd felt was based on a fake notion, then I was a fake. A disembodied human. A character in the piece of metafiction that was my life. Central theme: innate inability to connect. I was no better than *The Magus*.

'You should really see someone about your back,' said Ned, as I stood there wringing the pain out of my body. 'You're going to destroy it.'

'Yeah, thanks. I'm aware of that,' I said testily. 'I don't have the money to see some wizard.'

'You spend a hundred pounds a night on martinis. I've seen you do it. You could spend it on an osteopath instead. Or go to the NHS and wait for a physio appointment. It might not happen immediately, but it will happen eventually. It's better than not trying at all.'

'Any other pearls of wisdom for me?'

'Don't quit any more jobs that you're really good at, for little or no reason.'

'Love it. Keep them coming,' I said derisively. 'Stop trashing my body with copious amounts of alcohol? Is that on the list too?'

'If you say so.'

'Fantastic advice. What else?'

Ned remained infuriatingly calm through my mild hysteria. He continued, 'I'm not saying it has to be me, but maybe try not to push away everyone who makes an attempt to treat you the way you deserve to be treated.'

The pain that I'd felt in my throat when my mother had wanted me to be alright made a comeback. That time, it was a combination of feeling touched that he thought I deserved to be treated with love and distressed over the fact that I clearly didn't think so. All I could feebly respond with was, 'I've got divorced parents.'

'As do half the population, Jax,' he said softly. I knew that he meant it kindly, like an offering of hope, but right then, I took it to reveal his inability to understand me, at all, from the simplicity of his happy family.

'I'm going to say goodnight to my friends. And then I'm going to bed. Thank you for all your hard work.' With that, I walked away from him, out of the enclosure. On the other side of the wall, I gasped away a sob that was edging its way out. *Not now, little sob.*

I returned to the courtyard, twinkling with strings of tiny lightbulbs, under which a hundred bodies twirled about. Clara and Ed collaboratively sliced through four layers of berry-lined cake. His hand was on her waist, his fingers lightly curling around her hip bone. The guests clapped loudly. Clara laughed. She looked up at Ed, tilting her head back. He dipped to place a mindful kiss on her lips. *You do know it's not going to last, don't you?* I wondered if Bella's voice was tormenting Clara's mind at that moment, the way it was mine.

A hand clasped onto my wrist. 'I'm a free agent!' said Hazel, forcing my arm high above my head. She shook it out like a dirty dish towel and let out a loud, 'Wooo!' Then she added, 'Fabian's got magic mushroom drops. I'm gonna find him. I'll bring them back here.' And she was gone.

The thought of taking magic mushrooms with Hazel was both the last thing I wanted to do and a rabbit hole I was very tempted to jump into. I stood there, arms crossed, wondering whether I should wait for her return, or if she was returning at all. And then I saw Alice and Omni, sitting by the rust bowl firepit, waving me over to join. It felt as if the flames had jumped out of that pit and wrapped themselves around my heart. I walked over and sunk down next to them, in one of the low wooden armchairs.

'We want to make a toast,' said Omni, handing me a glass of champagne.

'To what?' I asked with the tiniest amount of cynicism.

'To the most meticulously planned and successfully executed wedding I've ever been to,' said Alice, lifting her own glass.

I smiled, reluctantly raising my glass to join. There was always that.

'To being single,' said Omni, completing the triage of flutes. She looked Alice in the eye and pointedly added, 'Welcome.'

'Thank you,' said Alice. 'To being fucked up.'

'To being fabulous,' I finished. The three glasses touched with a clink. And finally, we drank. I let out a huge sigh of relief, not because I'd needed a drink, but because I seemed to be returning to the room. 'Thank God we have each other.'

'Thank God, babe,' said Omni.

'Thank God,' Alice repeated.

We gazed into the fire for a few calm seconds, the heat warming our faces.

Then a familiar waiter appeared and crouched next to Omni. 'You look beautiful with so little sleep.'

'Used to it,' said Omni, throwing an ironic glance at us.

'When you go back to London?' he asked.

'Monday morning,' she said.

'Ah Monday. Maybe tomorrow we can have a dinner, or a drink, if you would prefer?'

Omni blinked down at him, bewildered. 'Are you asking me on a date, babe?'

'Yes. Like a date,' he said, so casual and confident about it. No bullshit.

Omni turned to us with a look that said, *Is he for real?* I shrugged and stuck both my thumbs in the air, a gesture that I'd never used before, unless you count emojis. Alice offered a nod of encouragement. Omni turned back to the crouching waiter and said, 'I'd like to go for dinner, please.'

I smiled, happy, but sad, but happy.

Perhaps if I'd entertained the idea of romance when I'd first met Ned, we would have got somewhere. It was true that there had been chemistry between us from the beginning. But my indifference had led me to set it aside, before having even dabbled with it. It was just like that photographer whom I'd had a laughy conversation with at that wedding ('Excuse the brevity and any errors. I'm on my period'). I'd drawn a line under that potential alliance before I'd even forayed into it, because he'd happened to leave a party early one night.

I had spent my twenties frantically looking away from attachment, so that I wouldn't be forced to engage with it. Oddly contrary behaviour for someone who hated being alone. But that was me: one big contrast.

That night, back in my *dammusa* – yet again, alone – I checked my phone for the first time in hours. An email appeared in my inbox that sent an unpleasant shooting sensation from my stomach to throat.

Shit, shit, shit.

It was from none other than Natasha, the features editor.

In all my replaying of the events of the night before, it

appeared that there was a patch that had been blanked from my memory, a patch about a certain 600 words that I'd haphazardly fired across the ocean.

Apprehensively, I opened the email.

> Ok um ... this was not what I was expecting
> at all. But weirdly I kinda love it! Needs a
> serious copyedit but we'll get onto that this
> end. Send me an invoice. Hope you're OK
> darling ??

Perhaps that email perfectly summed me up. Not what you'd expect me to be, weirdly loveable, but in need of some serious change. And she had a point. *Was I OK?* I knew that asking such sweeping questions of oneself in moments of micro-trauma never led to coherent answers, so I didn't dwell on it. Instead, I slept.

CHAPTER 20

The next morning, Clara did come to me. I was still in bed, eyes only half open and a gluey layer of sleep at the base of my throat, when her silhouette appeared in the doorway of my *dammusa*.

Her hair was half-up, half-down, and she was wearing one of the floating summer dresses that I'd packed for her at Ed's flat. She held a blue and white china cup at the centre of her chest like a geisha. 'Hungover?' she asked in a light, conversational manner.

I cleared my throat and pushed myself into a sitting position. 'Not any more than usual,' I said, still croaky with sleep. Clara stepped into the room and handed me the cup of coffee with outstretched arms, like I was an infectious patient she didn't want to get too close to. I knew that I was meant to find the gesture touching, but actually I felt more emotion for the coffee itself, which was somewhat surprising to me. *Thank you, darling coffee, thank you for being there for me.* To Clara, I just said, 'Thanks,' as I took the cup into my hands.

'Where's Omni?' she asked.

I glanced over at the single bed across the way from me, which had yet to be slept in. 'Don't know,' I said. I had a pretty good idea of where Omni was, but sharing that with Clara felt conspiratorial.

She sat down on the edge of my bed with her knees pressed together and both hands between her thighs. 'Thank you so much for everything,' she said, in the kind of voice that you'd use to thank a hotel manager for excellent service. 'It was my dream wedding.'

'I know it was.' Of course it had been her dream wedding. I had made sure of that. I had dived inside her and seen the world from her eyes in order to create something that I thought would make her so happy. Down to the minutest details, I had stopped at nothing to generate perfection. And what did I want for it, a fucking medal? I cleared some more sleep from my throat and said, 'Glad you had fun.' Then I took my first delicious sip of coffee.

Clara crossed one leg over the other and interlaced her fingers around her knee. She looked at the crease between the wall and the ceiling as she spoke. 'I know that my little revelation came as quite a shock.' She paused, waiting for me to say something, still focusing on that fascinating wall-ceiling point. I just sipped my coffee, grateful for its existence. Clara continued, 'I'd just really appreciate it if you didn't tell anyone.'

'What makes you think that I would?' I asked, my eyes fixed on her.

'I know you wouldn't do that,' she said emphatically, cleverly lathering butter all over me. 'But I'd also really appreciate it if you could please just not mention it to me ever again.'

I almost laughed – *and I thought I was avoidant!* – but thought better of it because there was still information that I wanted to draw out of her. 'Is it over?' I asked. 'Now that you're married?'

'Well, I don't know exactly. But Ed understands my need for . . .' she trailed off as she pondered the right word. Hastily, she said, 'We've come up with an arrangement.' It came out cold and disconnected. She must have known it did, because finally she looked at me with an expression that I interpreted as a plea for me to read between the lines.

'An arrangement?' I repeated, perplexed. *My arrangement?*

She sighed, disappointed at my failure to understand and comply. She had the appearance of someone who was about to make a confession. *No more confessions, please.* She went on slowly, 'Ed's not as straightforward as you might think. He has his own stuff to deal with. But we've made a lifestyle choice and have found a way to make it work. I think, anyway.'

Lifestyle choice? Cutting out dairy and switching to decaf were lifestyle choices. But accepting infidelity as a natural part of your brand-new marriage? Yes, there were some people for whom it apparently worked. But it seemed ludicrously un-Ed. I turned Clara's words over in my mind. *Ed's not as straightforward as you might think. He has his own stuff to deal with.*

'Sorry, Clara, you're going to have to elaborate,' I said with confusion. 'I'm struggling to make sense of everything.'

Her blue eyes went darting all over the room again as she sighed and said, 'Ed doesn't really like having sex. Not just with me. With anyone.'

'You've always known that,' I reminded her.

'Yes. I know. At the beginning I didn't think it would bother me because everything else about our relationship seemed so perfect. Then, after a while, it really did become a problem. I was so angry with him, all the time, but I couldn't explain why. It was miserable for both of us.'

'Why did you never tell me any of this?'

'I think I was probably embarrassed.'

'With me?'

'Yes, especially you, Jax,' she said. 'You would've told me

to leave the relationship. You wouldn't have believed that we could have loved each other without having a sex life. You still don't, clearly.'

'And when you started with Leo . . .'

'Things got better for Ed and I. Because I was less frustrated, maybe. I felt guilty, of course, but I think that might have even made me become a better girlfriend to him. I guess, because I was trying to make up for it.'

I squeezed my eyes shut and covered one with my palm. 'This just doesn't sound healthy, Clara.'

'Obviously it wasn't healthy, I was lying all the time,' she said. 'That's what made him so furious when he found out. He said that it wasn't the cheating itself that made him run away like that, it was the lying. And then I realized that I'd lied to him again when I said that I would end it. So, last night when we went to bed, I told him the truth. We talked things through. And he agreed that if it saves our marriage, by preventing me from getting all pent up with anger, then it's worth keeping things as they are. Because we do love each other and want to be together.'

'But Leo?' I asked incredulously. 'Is he really the most sensible choice for what's meant to be a rational arrangement?'

'Well, I'm never going to fall in love with him,' she said, almost laughing at the idea of it.

'Do you have sex with Ed, at all?' I asked, although I knew it was a private question.

For a few seconds she said nothing, and I got the sense that she was swallowing over a dry lump in her throat. Then she continued, in a tone that was littered with shame. 'We often try. Sometimes it works, other times it doesn't.' She gave me a small shrug and a sad smile. Instantly, I felt a pang of sympathy for her, for both of them. Clara must have recognized this. 'So, please, can we agree never to talk about this again?' she pressed, in a voice that was so sweet and so manipulative. 'Can you do that for me?'

I could agree never to mention the incident to her again. Once the revelations of the weekend started to fade into the background of our minds, we would go on as best friends. I would continue to be a feature of the Mortimer world, as and when it was convenient for her. I would pretend not to notice the thick smell of sexual chemistry – how had I not recognized it before? – when she and Leo were in the same room. I would go on giving her everything, and every part of me, as I always had.

A friendship isn't a real friendship if it's imbalanced.

Ned's words came to me instinctively, like little birds landing on my frontal lobe. What Clara was asking me to do was to take the last bit of authenticity out of our friendship. She was dumping an iron weight on the scale of our union and expecting me to work around it.

I shook my head. 'I can't promise that, Clara.' I kicked the thin bedsheet away from my legs and stood up.

And, for the first time in my life, I walked away from her.

I emerged into the sunshine and the rustle of trees blowing in the breeze with an unpleasant pain down the front of my body, knowing that in walking away, I was accepting that nothing would ever be the same again. But, despite the sensation, I did not feel like my world was falling apart. Instead, it felt like a small piece of that crystallized layer of shame that resided in my stomach had been chipped away. I felt spacious. It left room for a realization: I had always landed on my feet, and this time would be no different.

My friendship with Clara may have been the most intimate relationship in my life, but the safety of it had also been my resistance. I had resisted losing her, resisted moving on with my own life, resisted the idea of change. If I opened all of those doors, the possibilities could be endless. If I chose acceptance, everything could change. Like with a friend whom you'd suddenly remembered that you loved, having neglected them for other, more fun times, a friend whom you realized that you'd let down in a time of need, I was ready to become 100 per cent present with and nurturing of myself.

Because, surely, acceptance would lead to receptance. And I needed to allow myself to receive.

'What happens when you give a friend too much?'
by Jax Levy
3rd June 2019

Why is the measure of friendship how much one can give? I started this piece by conjecturing that we give everything to our female friends, because we want them to give it back to us. *Do unto other women as you would like them to do to you, because the men sure ain't going to.* But the truth is that if we give too much, we make it impossible for ourselves to receive anything back, from anyone.

To you, I gave it all. I stopped at nothing to make you happy because making you happy made me happy. Perhaps, indeed, I did it for myself and not you alone. I so wanted to create a perfect relationship, after we'd both been deprived of such a thing elsewhere in our lives. But now, I keep asking myself, over and over, *why did you not want the same?*

We so flippantly throw out those three words to our friends.

We say, 'I love you' the first time they make us laugh, at the end of a phone call, in an ad hoc text message or Instagram comment, when they are heartbroken, when they are behaving badly, or when they are being helpful. We don't hold back as we do with our romantic partners. We don't keep those words close to our hearts like a treasure to be granted only to those who are true to us.

Were you being flippant, all the times that you told me that you loved me? Did you say those three words only because you knew that they were the ones that I wanted – or needed – to hear?

Because I wasn't.

But perhaps it was because you saw my love for you, so weighted and real, that you didn't believe me when I said, 'I think I'm in love with him.' No wonder you tossed it aside, and told me to get over it, like it was a throwaway comment, an insecurity about an outfit choice that I wouldn't stop going on about. Why couldn't you just tell me? I gave you everything, and you gave me dishonesty. If I were able to rewrite the measure of friendship, it would be truth.

I wouldn't have minded. I wouldn't have hated you if you had turned around and said, 'You cannot love him, because he's mine. You don't know it, no one does, but at certain dark times I go to him for the same reasons that you do.'

I need you to know that I regret nothing. There was a time when you were there for me. When I needed to love someone to know that I could, you let me love you. You allowed me to fall in love with you, in a way that is reserved for friendship. It is a purer love than romantic love. You helped me grow. And most of the time, you were good to me. I promised myself that I'd be there to catch every tear that fell from your eyes. To break that promise breaks my heart. But now that I know that you have been building a wall between us, I can be the one to seal it, if that makes it easier.

When you give too much, you are left feeling empty. Not only empty but ruptured inside. I am howling with grief for what we've lost.

Yet, I love you and there is nothing I can do about it.

PART III

FEBRUARY 2020

CHAPTER 21

Being a 30-year-old woman is unexpectedly better than being a 29-year-old one because, in your twenties, you only have the narrow window of one decade to achieve everything in the world. After thirty, you finally have your whole life ahead of you.

In the run-up to the big birthday, I'd had a near mental breakdown and spontaneously cried almost every time I was on public transport. It was partly because I couldn't afford to throw myself a giant birthday party with an ironic vodka luge centrepiece, as I'd always thought that I would. And partly because I'd moved into a studio flat in Haggerston, and despite the fact that I was very happy there, I had a repetitive chorus in my head of, *I'm going to turn thirty alone in a studio flat that I don't even own.* I might as well have added, *and be found three weeks later half eaten by Alsatians* à la Bridget Jones to highlight what a cliché I'd become. Sure, I had a job as an editor for an online teen magazine thanks to a certain emotional outpour, which had broken – a small part of – the internet, and yes it gave me structure, an income and a team of fellow millennials to bounce ideas off, but a job didn't necessarily equal *foundations.* That was the root of my pre-thirtieth breakdown. *Where are my end-of-decade foundations?*

But then my birthday came and went and nothing catastrophic happened. I hadn't turned into a pumpkin. The noise

333

of an invisible egg timer did not start ticking at the back of my head. I still lived in a conundrum where I knew that casual sex made me feel empty but so did the absence of human touch, and the fact was that that was just something I had to deal with – like other people just have to deal with a weak bladder – until I found a way to have a meaningful intimate relationship with someone. The good news was that I felt I was making a slight bit of headway in that department because I'd once made love to myself while envisioning tender, attentive penetration with Ned, rather than animalistic, non-communitive sex with my circuit trainer. It was a real breakthrough in fantasy land. I didn't, however, make a habit of it for the simple reason that it really made me miss him. We hadn't seen each other since Pantelleria.

It had been almost eight months since Clara's wedding, but it could have been a lifetime. Britain had left the EU, some virus was swarming China, Prince Andrew was the country's number one moron and Omni was getting married.

That's right. The waiter of Pantelleria – whose name was really Piero – did more than just take her out for dinner. He convinced her to stay on the island for an extra week, then he followed her back to London. The impending nuptials she referred to as, 'My Big Fat Brexit Wedding,' since the rush was somewhat visa-related. But no one had raised an eyebrow at the decision. Not even me. If there was one thing in life that I was sure of, it was that Omni was In Love. The reason I was so sure was because nothing about her had changed. She still stayed out all night long when she wanted to, she still spoke about domestic coexistence with cynicism, she still wore the 'TIPS PLEASE' T-shirt to work at the pub. And also, Piero was uproariously funny. I was basically in love with him too.

Neither Omni nor Piero had proposed to the other. They had simply decided to get married after a rational discussion. *Decided*. Mutually. It was my favourite engagement story ever and I had retold it time and time again, like it was something revolutionary. To me, it was, given that it made marriage seem like less of a terrifying prospect. It took all of the dreaded imbalance out of a partnership and did away with the impossibly high bars that society had set for us. It might even be something I'd consider one day.

Omni didn't want a white dress, or a hen party, or a videographer, or forty different types of flowers. There was no six months of build up to one day that most people would be too drunk to remember. We didn't have to discuss wedmin every time we met for dinner. No one had to fork out a thousand pounds on flights, accommodation, gifts and outfits.

But, being Omni, she couldn't turn down a party when it was offered to her.

I received the first image of Omni as 'An Honest Woman' – her own words – when I was on the overground train to Willesden. It had been taken at the civic centre where said knot had been tied with no one but her parents to witness. Piero was in the foreground holding the camera above their heads. Behind him, Omni held two left fingers to her temple like a gun, her large red enamel engagement ring adding a pop of colour to their swarthy complexions. I sent a line of exploding head emojis, followed by a line of hearts. She returned with an image of the Mortimers' drawing room, bursting with daffodils and a buffet table similar to the one at Clara's pre-wedding party.

Bella was finally getting to host the wild wedding that she'd always wanted to.

Omni:
Literally have no idea what my aunt has
planned for today
She is so excited it's TM
Concerned she's ordered a stripper
or something

Me:
Lol. Wouldn't surprise me

Alice:
I'd be quite up for a stripper tbh

Omni:

Screen Time alerted me that I only had fifteen minutes left to
spend on WhatsApp that day. I quickly closed the app – and
our group that was still called 'No More Clara' – and returned
the phone to my pocket.

Alice picked me up at Willesden Junction in the convertible
Tesla that she'd bought herself with her Christmas bonus. She
sat at the wheel in cat-eye sunglasses and leather gloves, looking like a cross between a movie star and a psychopath. She
had cut her hair into an expensive bob when she first became
single, and every time I saw her, I had an urge to do the same
but was never brave enough when push came to shove at the
hairdresser's. I slid into the passenger seat beside her.

'Do I look like I'm going to a funeral?' she asked, glancing
down at her black dress.

'Sort of, yes.'

'Good. That's the idea.' She flipped the indicator and pulled away from the curve at a dizzying speed. 'Apparently you're more likely to secure a date at a funeral than a wedding.'

'You don't need any more dates!' I almost gasped. Less than a year single and Alice had already been on more dates than I'd been on in my whole life. But that was fine, because I had pretty much accepted that the dating scene just wasn't for me. Alice, on the other hand, seemed to find some joy in it.

'How are we feeling about today?' she asked. She had formed a habit of referring to me as 'us' or 'we' and I loved it.

'OK, I think,' I said, understanding that she was enquiring about my feelings on seeing Clara for the first time since her wedding. Omni and Alice had been trying to get us together for months, thinking that our falling out had been over nothing more than my lying to Clara about Ed. I had made it clear that I was completely open to it but wanted it to come from Clara. Unsurprisingly, she had avoided any social situation that I was involved in, which I understood and didn't hold against her. I knew Clara well enough to know that the idea of slight confrontation, or an uncomfortable interaction, would have sent her into an unbearable knot of social anxiety. But on this occasion, she couldn't avoid it.

We arrived at the house where a huge arch crafted out of spring-coloured balloons was floating above the crittall and wood gate, an uplifting contrast to the grey afternoon sky. The balloons didn't ring true to Bella's style, and immediately I wondered whose idea they had been. The gate buzzed open. Alice and I crossed the courtyard, taking the same steps that I had taken so many times before, but feeling so much less comfortable in each one. We crossed the threshold, into the house. The main room was erupting with colour, from the many daffodil arrangements to the stretched-out cloud of blue and white balloons that covered the entire ceiling, reminiscent of a summer sky. Below, a cluster of guests stood, with an air of awkwardness that I always felt was typical of the start of a day party. And beyond the guests was a long wooden canoe boat that had been repurposed to hold rows of multi-tonal cocktails, liquor bottles, niche tonics and wildflower arrangements. Behind the canoe, a bearded barman. The whole set-up was unmistakable.

Omni appeared from the scattering of people, who parted for her like the Red Sea. 'I've gone over to the dark side!' she said, spreading her arms wide. She was wearing a black bustier dress with a sheer tulle ballgown skirt and a matching veil covering her face.

'Happy matrimony!' I said brightly, lifting the veil to kiss her on the cheek. 'Are you in mourning?' I replaced the netting to its previous position, keeping one of my eyes on the canoe.

Faux dramatically, Omni replied, 'For my freedom!'

Across the room, the bearded barman handed a cocktail to a guest. I couldn't help but wonder whether Ned would appear at any moment. I'd been a keen follower of his business on Instagram and could tell that he was getting a lot of work, so there was every chance that he was no longer on site for all events. Sometimes, he appeared to have three jobs in one day.

'That service was intense,' said Omni, leaning on my shoulder. 'Never been more ready for a blowout.'

'I don't do those anymore,' I reminded her. I found that saying it out loud made it that much truer.

'Not even on my wedding day?' she whined. I didn't answer her because I was distracted by the garden door opening and closing. A figure slipped inside, carrying a bucket of ice. Ned was, in fact, on site for this one.

I pressed my lips right up to Omni's ear. 'Did you know he was going to be here?' I asked quietly. The canoe bar had been calculatingly left out of the photograph she'd sent earlier.

'Yup,' said Omni, as she and Alice exchanged a colluding glance.

'Why didn't you tell me?' I asked in a frantic whisper.

'Because you would've done something bizarre like turned up in a sombrero,' said Omni, flapping her hand about.

It was a fair point.

In the weeks that followed Clara's wedding, I'd kept myself very much to myself. I'd scheduled long stints of Alone Time, in which I'd lit scented candles to read self-care books and meditate in the bath and committed myself to a six-month goal of healing my back injury. I'd sent Ned a few friendly, professional messages, thanking him for all of his hard work at the wedding. He had replied with polite but sparing answers like, 'Sure thing,' or, 'You too.' Then, one day, when I was on my way to a gong bath, I'd spotted him. He was sitting outside a pub, half-opposite, half-beside a girl whom he very much appeared to be on a date with. She was not the Doc Marten-clad Vicky-pedia I'd pictured from his gender politics and feminist studies course. She had mousy hair, round spectacles and a kind smile. She looked shy and sensible. I darted across the road before he could see me, feeling inexplicably humiliated by the whole thing.

It was moments later, during the gong bath, that I had my own – very 2019 – Cher in *Clueless* moment. *Everything I think and everything I do is wrong. I was wrong about Harry. I was wrong about Leo. Now Ned hates me. It all boiled down to one inevitable conclusion: I was just totally clueless. What does Pub Girl want with Ned anyway? He's far too together to be emotionally intriguing. He's never known real-life pain. His pragmatism is demeaning. He's not even cute . . . in a conventional way. And he lives in a flat share. Couldn't take him anywhere. Wait a second, what am I stressing about? This is, like, Ned. Pub Girl looked too . . . unchallenging. She couldn't make him happy. He needs someone to shake him up a little. Someone he can take care of –* (problematic in 2020?) *– Then, suddenly . . . Oh my God! I love Ned.*

Maybe it wasn't quite that instant or that extreme. And also, he wasn't my stepbrother. If he was, I'd have a stable, loving stepfamily and possibly far fewer emotional issues. But you get what I mean. Since then, I'd thought about him frequently, in different contexts. When I imagined him naked or topless, I wanted to cuddle up to him and feel the warmth of his body. When I thought about bumping into him in a social context, I felt awkward and rejected, which didn't exactly make sense. Eventually, at Omni and Alice's insistence, I'd made contact by way of a text message, casually exclaiming that I missed him. It was the kind of message that you'd send to an old friend that you had gradually lost touch with. He responded with a smiley face emoji. Cryptic. Or not. I'd attempted to see him, but every time I suggested a plan, he'd come up with an excuse. In a characteristic jump to frenzied conclusion, I deduced that I had only ever been an unobtainable fantasy for Ned. When he sensed that the tables were turning, he had inevitably lost interest. Sure, that might have been out of character for him, but it was a pattern I was used to, and how else could I explain things to myself?

Seeing him stationed behind that canoe, I felt a warm surge of affectionate regret wash through my body. I watched from a distance as Moll approached him. He handed her a drink, looking her in the eyes with that sincere smile that I remembered so well.

'Go say hello, for God's sakes,' Alice said impatiently, flicking at my arm with the end of her long fingernails.

Gingerly, I headed for the canoe. Ned's brilliant grey eyes settled on me. God, I'd missed those eyes. I took a nervous inhale and smiled. 'I knew the balloons weren't Bella's idea,' I said.

He returned the smile and my heart liquefied inside my chest. He shrugged. 'She wanted it to look like a summer's day.'

'Shame about the weather,' I said. *Stupid joke.*

'How are you?' he asked, earnest, so earnest.

'I'm really, really well, thank you.' I said it slowly and proudly, emphasizing each word. For months, I'd been dying to tell Ned how well I was. Anything to prevent the version of me that he'd witnessed in Pantelleria becoming the lasting image in his mind.

'You look really well,' he said, placing his hands on the edge of the canoe and keeping his eyes firmly riveted on me.

'Thank you,' I said, doing all I could to stop myself from making a derisive joke. I'd been practising receiving compliments, rather than deflecting them, but it still didn't feel natural. I added, 'My back is better.'

'That's great!' said Ned, so enthusiastically that it made my liquid heart cramp up. 'How did that happen?'

'I stopped buying martinis and paid to see an osteopath who told me to go on an alkaline diet, give up yoga and high-intensity training, and only go to Pilates.'

'And you've stuck to that?' he asked with raised eyebrows.

'The diet lasted about a week. But I stuck to Pilates and it's really helped.' It really had helped. OK, I didn't get the buzz

341

of checking myself out in a sports bra while bursting with endorphins after a high-intensity workout or flirting with my circuit teacher, but perhaps that was for the best.

'I'm so pleased to hear that,' said Ned, so genuine in his pleasure. 'And congratulations on your new job.'

My organs gave an excited little jump up and down. I'd become an Instagram poster for the first time in my life, for the specific reason that I wanted Ned to know that I had a real job. 'Thanks,' I said, reaching for one of his avant-garde alcoholic creations. *My avant-garde mixologist.*

'Your articles are always so funny,' he said. Another leap of the organs, as I realized that he'd taken the bait. When my *Close Up* article had come out, an online teen magazine contacted me asking if I would start a 'Dear Jax' agony aunt column. Not only did I not trust myself to play therapist to younger me's, but I knew that it was a column that I didn't want to get stuck in – and I wasn't about to make that mistake again – so I turned it down. It then transpired that their culture editor was leaving. Would I like that job instead? Abso-fucking-lutely.

'I promise I won't quit it for little or no reason,' I said, taking a sip of the cocktail. Basil. Brown sugar. Vodka?

'Good,' he said, though he didn't show any recognition of remembering our conversation in the walled garden.

'Your cocktails are still the best in town,' I said, raising my glass up into the air.

Before he could answer, the heat of a body appeared next to me. A familiar smell. And then, 'Hi, Ned.' A honeyed voice. My heart started beating a fraction faster.

'Hi, Clara,' Ned responded, well mannered but not overly friendly.

It was unclear from the way that she turned to me so rapidly and said, 'Hi' in a high-pitched voice as to whether she had known that I was the one standing beside her. When she reached out to hook her arm around my neck, pulling me into a short, quick hug, it may have been because she was taken by surprise. But it only took a second in that hug for me to well up with emotion.

No one talks openly about the pain of losing girlfriends. There's a whole world of language for romantic break-ups. When you are heartbroken, it suddenly becomes acceptable to sit bleary-eyed at a dinner table, staring off into space. We spend weeknights on the sofas of the broken-hearted, eating ice cream, drinking wine and mopping up tears. We organize Girls' Nights Out to get them off of said sofas on the weekends. And eventually, we make it our mission to thrust them into the arms of someone else. None of that applies to those in the aftermath of broken friendships, even though the heartache is no less. That much I knew was true. My heart had been aching for Clara. I dreamt about her more nights than I didn't. Her phone number was still the only one that I knew off by heart. There were moments of my life when I automatically thought, *I must tell Clara about this.*

After our brief – and possibly accidental – hug, Clara seemed somewhat flustered. She gave Ned a tense smile, her two rows of teeth gnashing nervously against one another. 'Do you have anything non-alcoholic?' she asked. My eyes automatically went to her stomach.

'Grapefruit and thyme with a drop of CBD,' said Ned, handing her a glass, with that same winning smile. Then he moved to the other end of the canoe in a display of consideration for our privacy. There was so much more that I still wanted to tell him. That I'd become really good at the Japanese Art of Decluttering. That I sometimes spent Friday nights at home, alone, without panicking. That I had successfully completed dry January. But it wasn't the moment. That moment was for Clara.

She took a sip of the mocktail and turned towards me. 'I'm not pregnant,' she said, in answer to my gaze. 'I'm trying. But it's not that easy for me it seems.' She said it with a sense of guilty responsibility that broke my heart. *I'm trying*.

'It's not been that long,' I said gently, remembering what she'd told me about Ed the morning after her wedding, and simultaneously imagining a thermometer job every time she was ovulating.

'Eight months.'

'You'll get pregnant,' I assured her. I don't know how I really thought that I knew that, especially given her conjugal situation. But I was so sure of it.

She nodded tentatively. 'I don't know if cutting out alcohol helps or not, but it's worth a try,' she said, just as Ed appeared at her side. She raised the mocktail to his lips. 'Try this non-alcoholic cocktail,' she said pointedly.

Ed took a sip through the paper straw. 'Very nice,' he said before taking a swig of the beer in his hand. He turned to me and offered an awkward, 'Hello.'

'Hi, Ed, nice to see you,' I said, like he was an acquaintance whose existence I'd forgotten about.

'Nice to see you too,' he said. That was as far as our conversation stretched. Despite everything I knew about Ed, in reality I barely knew the man at all. Our history – if you could call it that – was a drop in the ocean compared to the years I'd spent with Clara. The memory of those few days leading up to their

344

wedding felt like something that had happened in someone else's life. It was a strange human trait to think about oneself with such a sense of distance. *Oh, that stupid person who did that thing all those years ago.* That's how I felt about my quest to find Ed.

I wanted to stay with Clara and talk, but there was a wall of awkwardness spiralling around the three of us and a red blotch had appeared on her neck. So, I moved away from the canoe and went to greet Bella, Derrick, Moll, Budi, Fabian, Theodora. They were all thrilled to see me, as I was them. But I felt no aching sense of nostalgia for my lost role in their family. Their lives had gone on as normal, and mine had too, albeit mine was a new normal.

The day progressed in sections. Lunch was served. Wine was poured. A band appeared. The winter sun went down. And the dancing began. Omni threw her bra into the crowd in place of a bouquet. She and Piero cut into a giant wheel of cheese. They both made speeches that were short and sweet.

Then Leo turned up, holding the hand of a petite redhead. Omni pulled me aside and said, 'Him, I did not invite,' which I assured her I already knew. He and I exchanged a hasty hello as we passed one another in the corridor. He introduced the redhead to me as his girlfriend. I smiled and felt nothing. Not even resentment.

At one point, I joined Omni in the bathroom, where she fuelled herself with chemical energy and began retouching her make-up in front of the mirror. She spoke to my reflection. 'I won't try to force you to take drugs. But if you do one thing for me on my wedding day, you will go and talk to that lovely man with his boat bar.'

'I'm scared,' I whined from where I was scrunched up in a ball on the loo seat.

'What are you scared of?' she asked, dabbing a fresh layer of red onto her lips.

'Awkwardness.'

'I felt so awkward with Piero at first.'

'Did you?' I asked, sceptical but curious.

'Yes! Are you joking? I bought a radio alarm clock so that we'd have someone else's voice to listen to when we woke up, in case there were any silences to fill.'

I tittered with laughter, remembering when she'd ordered the absurdly un-Omni digital clock radio from eBay. 'But you still stuck it out,' I mused.

'Well, to be fair, I didn't really have much choice since he'd flown over from Italy to stay with me. I just had to get on with it. And as we got to know each other better, the awkwardness went away. Then it felt as chilled as hanging out with you.'

'Interesting.'

I had always thought that if I didn't feel immediately comfortable in the company of someone I was flirting with, it meant that there was something wrong with me. But perhaps connection didn't happen instantly. Perhaps, just like it sometimes took time for an acquaintance to progress to the level of friend, it took time to feel natural interacting with a lover. I'd never stuck around for long enough to find out. As soon as the awkwardness hit, I shut myself off, assuming we had no connection, or even that I was incapable of forging one. I'd never considered the fact that everyone went through those moments of adolescent awkwardness, regardless of age. To me they seemed like a mountain that could not be surmounted, rather than just a bump in the road.

Nevertheless, I could do one thing for Omni on her wedding day.

When we left the bathroom and returned to the party, I approached Ned again, still diligently working behind the bar. 'How's the smoking going these days?' I asked. I hadn't smoked for months, but for a moment alone with him, I could sacrifice a couple thousand body cells.

He smiled, sweeping a lime wedge around the rim of a glass tenderly. 'Finally think I can call myself a non-smoker.' Disappointing. But so sensible. *So Ned.*

'Me too,' I agreed. There was a pause that followed. Then I spoke slowly, and a tad – you guessed it – awkwardly. 'I never thanked you properly for helping me out in my time of need. I can't believe how much I asked of you.'

'No thanks needed,' he said. 'I wouldn't have done it if I didn't want to.'

Before I had time to think about it, I asked, 'Would you like to go for a drink with me, one day?' as a combination of excitement and dread curdled within me.

'Of course,' he said pleasantly. 'I'm always up for a drink.'

I could have left it at that, but something in me knew that I owed it to myself to be clearer. 'Not just a drink,' I added. 'The drink is a metaphor really.'

He set down the lime and observed me through grey eyes. 'A metaphor for what?'

'For ... I really like you.' As the words came out of my mouth, I felt like a layer of skin was unravelling itself from my body, leaving nothing but a shell of vulnerability. I think I even closed my eyes for the few seconds that it took for the sentence to string together, despite the fact that I understood the importance of eye contact in these situations. *Baby steps.* It was the hardest thing I'd ever done. So much harder than telling Leo that I was in love with him, because this was actually true.

Ned – the world's number one eye contact expert – waited until he had my gaze locked in to say, 'I have to think about it, Jax,' as he twisted his face into an apology.

'No problem,' I said, so casually. My tone of voice was affected, but the surprising thing was that my skin was not – in fact – crawling with a shameful sense of rejection. I'd done what I needed to do. I could go on with my life knowing that I'd done what I could.

I sailed across the dancefloor, where bodies flung themselves carelessly at one another to the notes of Earth, Wind & Fire. Leo was there with his girlfriend. As I wove my way past them, he stepped into my path and clasped my shoulders. 'Darling,' he said, the husk of too many Marlboro Reds crawling from his throat. 'You look so great. This suit!' I gave a self-satisfied shrug. *I know.* Then Leo collapsed onto me, wrapping both of his gangly arms around my shoulders. 'Can we be friends?' he asked, yet again, clinging on for dear life.

'We can,' I said, setting him away from me. 'But I still don't think we need to be.'

His girlfriend appeared at his side. He squeezed both of my hands in his. 'I love this girl,' he told his girlfriend, referring to me. She offered me a cold smile. I could hardly blame her, so I left them to it. My memories of Leo weren't all bad. He had allowed me to play out my fantasies and chip away some of the shame that had, for so many years, encased them. I had accepted that that was the reason that he had come into my life, even if he had lingered for longer than necessary.

My interaction with Ned had left me feeling flushed. I needed air and a moment alone. With a cocktail in my hand, I slipped outside. I passed by all the smokers and headed across the courtyard, towards Derrick's shed. The far side of it was the only spot in the garden that could not be seen from any window of the house. When I slipped around, I found Clara sitting on the floor with her knees up, her head resting lightly on the wall of the shed. She had a glass in her hand. A cocktail identical to mine. Basil. Brown sugar. Vodka?

She looked up at me with a sheepish smile, like I'd just caught her in the act of misbehaviour. 'Ed's taking this clean-living thing very seriously. He wants a baby so badly,' she said, apologizing on his behalf. 'He's really making an effort,' she added pointedly, and I guessed she was talking about sex. Then she tapped the edge of the glass with her fingernail and took a sip. 'I just need one to take the edge off.'

'Well, your secret's safe with me,' I said, sitting down next to her.

'I know it is,' she said. I'd almost forgotten how sweet her voice was. In contented silence, we stared out at the oak tree ahead. I'd had my first kiss up that tree. Then, suddenly, impulsively, Clara said, 'I'm sorry, Jax.' I turned to look at her. She didn't look at me, but that was alright. I knew that she didn't need to look at me to mean what she was saying. Staring down into the multi-colour of the alcoholic drink in her hand, she continued, 'I'm sorry that I hurt you so badly. It was never intentional.'

'I know,' I said softly. 'I'm sorry that I interfered with your life.'

'You cared about me so much,' she said, so quietly that it was almost a whisper.

'I still do, you know?'

'I know.'

'Did you read my article?'

'I did.'

When it had been published, I'd felt sick with guilty nerves as I waited for an icy text message or email from Clara. But I received neither. She never mentioned it to me, or anyone, it seemed.

'Were you angry?' I asked curiously.

She shrugged. 'It was so vague that it sounded almost fictional. I don't think anyone would have thought you were talking about me.' I guessed that she had convinced herself that that was the case, in order to brush away the fear that anyone might have been speculating about her. She smiled, a small dimple appearing within her cheek, as she added, 'It was really beautifully written.'

'Thank you,' I said. 'Please don't stress about getting pregnant. It will happen.'

'OK.' She tipped her head sideways to rest on my shoulder. 'I believe you.'

It would take her a while because of the stress of wanting it so badly, but she would get pregnant and give birth to a healthy boy. I'd visit her and the new baby, because that's what you do when you've known someone your whole life. And I'd offer to sit with the child, in case Clara needed to get her nails done, or go to the supermarket, or to a yoga class, because I'd want to be helpful in some way. And she would, of course, decline my offer because I'd inevitably tip the child upside down and drop it on its head while she was gone. But still, I'd have offered. And when I lay in bed sweating with the fever of coronavirus, she would send me a care pack full of all the things that I loved, to keep my isolated spirit up. She would invite me to all of the milestone events in her life and I'd do the same. Sometimes I'd go, sometimes she'd come, but mostly, we wouldn't. And eventually, the contact between us would dwindle, gradually, naturally.

But still, the images that lined my brain like wallpaper would never peel away. The hours spent on top of that pink Wendy house, no one but the two of us, safe from the world. Whispered promises of a magical future life, between the sheets of her four-poster bed. My small arm squeezing around Clara's seven-year-old shoulders at the top of the stairs while her mother, naked, shouted at two blushing policemen. Our tiny bodies packed into one armchair while the smoke of adults wafted around us. Holding Clara's clammy hand as she lay in a hospital bed, after twelve Nurofen had been pumped from her stomach, while Fabian stood ashen-faced at the side of the room. Holding back her hair, the first time she ever got drunk. Walking into a restaurant on her eighteenth birthday when she leaned into me and whispered, 'I think I lost my virginity last night,' and I, with a panicked feeling that I was being left behind, excitably said, 'Wait! Tell me everything.' The first night we spent as grown-ups drinking red wine in her Canonbury flat. Sitting on the terrace of our hotel room in Pantelleria, disbelieving of the fact that we were old enough for one of us to be getting married. Clara, in her wedding dress, standing in the middle of the shell grotto, as I told her, 'You don't have to do this.' Holding a cup of coffee in my hands as I walked out of my *dammusa*, away from her.

Throughout all our years together, the world had felt like such a confusing place, because we knew so little about ourselves. Every year, we learnt a little more. I knew so much more about myself by the time she rested her head on my shoulder, sitting on the floor outside that shed. I knew that an uplifting film could reach down and pull me out of a slump. I knew that the days in which I felt exhilarated by something as simple as sunshine were a moment, not a state of being, so

I'd learnt to live fully in those moments. I knew that being alone did not equate to being lonely, nor did constant company bring inevitable happiness. I knew that there would always be times when I would marvel about the way I loved life so much that I didn't ever want to die, and times that I would cry into my shower towel. I knew that you didn't stop loving someone when you stopped seeing them.

And when Ned approached me on the dancefloor and said, 'The answer is yes. I would like to go for a drink,' I knew that it was a metaphor.

I knew that there was every chance that it would not work out how I wanted it to. And I knew that that wouldn't be his fault, or mine.

But I knew that I had to try my best.

I owed it to myself.

Acknowledgements

To the people who have made me a better writer and this a far more interesting novel than it was at first: Holly Faulks, my brilliant, supportive agent, and Bethan Jones, my dedicated, insightful editor. To Harriett Collins and all at Simon & Schuster, and those at Greene & Heaton, who continue to support my novels. I am forever grateful that a pipedream has become a career.

To Gabriella Wall, my dearest friend and dedicated manager, for always steering me in the right direction. And to Jason Richman, for helping to bring my work to life. For always championing my writing, Charles Finch and my Finch & Partners/Standalone Pictures family.

To my earliest readers, Xenobe Purvis and Claudia Costa, for enthusiasm as well as intimate and much-needed notes.

To my friends and family, who have been consistently there for me through this bizarre year: Amy Croxford, Amy Pelham, Barbara Ellison, Becky Levett, Beverley Abel, Carmel Ellison, Caspar Smyth, Eve McQuiston, Georgie Wolf, Hallie Bonnar, Lottie Neil, Lucy McGinn, Melita Gedye, Niamh Watmore, Oli Henry, Polly Lovelady, Polly West, Rifat Ozbek, Rochelle Katz, Ruby Boglione, Sophie Humphrey and Theo De Gunzburg. And Anna Bingemann, Annie Green, Gala Gordon and Gabriella Wall – now twice mentioned – for going above and beyond for me, always.

To my grandmother, June Zieve, whom I can only be relieved did not stay to see the latter part of 2020 unfold.

But mostly, to my parents, for living through this with me, minute by minute.

Did you love *Nothing I Wouldn't Do*?
Then don't miss

Scarlett Willems moves to London without a plan, but she manages to land a job at a modelling agency. Just when she feels like she's getting somewhere, her life begins to spiral out of control. But at least people know who she is. She is starting to become someone.

And surely it's better to be *someone* —
even if it's someone you hate?

Turn the page to enjoy an extract now ...

SIMON &
SCHUSTER

CHAPTER 1

Whenever the first of January came round, I had a habit of imagining myself a year on, as someone who had enigmatically outgrown the person I was in that moment. But year after year, it was like déjà vu – and it was starting to get old.

I had always thought of my life in Topsham as a sort of drawn-out prelude to the life I planned on eventually living. I'd expected that once I'd done all the things you're supposed to do – like finish school and university – I'd float naturally into a job for some London-based fashion designer, who would be blown away by a talent that even I'd been uncertain I possessed. I'd live in a flat with palm-printed wallpaper and a free-standing bath, wear embroidered kimonos and get a blue tick by my name on Instagram. I hadn't accounted for being sucked back into the arse-end-of-nowhere to pull pints and wait for a call from the recruiters who had sounded so eager when I was fresh out of the graduate oven back in June. And I certainly hadn't accounted for spending New Year's Day on yet another bathroom floor I didn't recognise, in England's tiniest town.

'You're not still looking for it, are you?' Billie called out from the other side of the door.

I cradled the toilet basin. 'Looking for what?' I said, moving my mouth as little as possible in case it put pressure on my

357

stomach, which was at that very moment threatening to expel the contents of the night before.

The door opened a crack and Billie looked down at me, her blood-red, boy-short hair standing up in all directions. 'Your G spot? Last night you were worried you didn't have one.'

It was then that I winced – not because of what she'd said, but because it reminded me that I'd sent an unsolicited selfie, at three in the morning, to Tim, the on-off fling who hadn't been ready for anything serious throughout the three years we were at university, whom I hadn't seen since graduating and whom I had been known – after a few drinks – to refer to as 'my first love'.

Please.

'Shit,' I muttered.

'Still missing then?' she said.

I wriggled my hand around the floor for my iPhone and braved a peek at the damage: an aerial shot of myself on the loo, captioned, 'Miss me?', as if murky urine framed by average thighs was a truly irresistible thing. Seeing it in the cold light of day, I had a vision of myself shrinking in size and morphing into the screaming face emoji.

I held the phone up to show Billie and moaned. 'This is a disaster!'

I never sent messages like that to Tim, or anyone I was seeing, in the daytime. I was very much Cool Girl in the day-time. That was my safe spot, even if it got me nowhere closer to the discovery of my G spot. That was what he'd always liked about me. No pressure, no strings. Nothing in it for me, basically.

Billie looked at the photo, shrugged, and said, 'At least your piss looks good,' because she knew it would make me laugh. She always knew how to make me laugh.

Billie and I met at school. She was in the year above me, where she had earned herself the uncreative nickname 'Dyke', owing to the fact that she was the only girl in her year who wasn't a walking blow job charity, and, to be fair, looked a lot like Ant or Dec. We came across each other on a tree-lined hill near school that was called 'the smoker's slope', and its function was self-explanatory. One day, when it was just the two of us, she said to me, 'Can I tell you something, as a friend? I don't think you know how to inhale a fag properly.' I looked at her, amazed that she'd taken notice of some girl in the year below. And it was true. I just took little bird-like sucks on the end of my Lucky Strikes, which was why my cigarettes took longer than everyone else's to burn down, though sometimes I'd blow into them to speed up the process. So Billie kindly taught me how it was done and we'd been best friends ever since. I'd been addicted to cigarettes ever since, too.

'Where are we?' I asked, unsticking my tongue from the roof of my mouth several times in a row.

She shook her head and gave me a look that said, 'You don't want to know.' Billie was my only fun friend and I was hers, so the people we ended up mingling with on nights out were usually unpalatable before the sixth tequila or when you were on their bathroom floor the next day, dying of alcohol poisoning.

'Can we Irish?' I asked hopefully, not in the mood to be polite to anyone.

Billie held her finger to her lips, reaching out with her other hand to haul me up off the ground. I caught a glimpse of myself in the mirror, looking like the grim reaper in a blonde wig – or, rather, an orange-tinged wig, thanks to the home-dye job. As I followed her out, I realized – or remembered – that we were on a boat. I had a fleeting vision of looking out the small window to find that we were halfway to France, but thankfully, or maybe disappointingly, we had not drifted from the sleepy quayside of the town that I'd spent my whole life waiting to leave.

Billie handed me my raincoat as she threw on the bomber jacket that I'd customized with patches and sequins for her when we were sixteen (I'd hardly seen her wear anything else since) and we made a beeline for the exit.

'Can I come back to yours?' I asked as we tumbled out onto the path and started walking.

'I love you, but I need a few more hours' kip before my shift,' she said. 'And you'll want to talk my ear off.'

I got it. She needed her space. Something that I found I had way too much of. Too much space was bad. Too much space led to boredom, and if you let boredom happen, it often mutated into something much gloomier.

'Can I come for a drink later, while you're working?' I asked.

'I'll kill you if you don't.'

With that we parted ways, and my mind began spinning with a faux-methodical reverie detailing exactly what I'd do from that moment on: walk briskly home, prepare a cheese and mayonnaise sandwich, boil the kettle, eat the sandwich while listening to some podcast that would likely instruct me how to be a better human, make coffee, run a bath, soak in said bath while drinking coffee, get into pyjamas, get into bed and take out my long-suffering sketchbook to draw for the rest of the day. I hoped that the familiarity of drawing would be comforting. More than that, I hoped that I'd feel resourceful by feeding the burgeoning fantasy of becoming a fashion designer, which was still loitering in the back of my mind, like something on a hypothetical to-do list.

When I reached the end of my road, I put the whole plan on pause and sat down on someone's doorstep to light a cigarette. My mother would probably be up and she didn't know that I was a smoker. You'd think as a fully-fledged adult, I'd be able to admit to it, take the disapproving headshake on the chin and move on with life. But, not so.

I took out my phone and opened the Notes application to do what you were meant to do at the start of the year, but what I probably should have done six months earlier.

1 January 2016, 9.02 a.m.

NY RESOLUTIONS
Delete Tim's number
Get job IN LONDON
Make money
Exercise 5 times a week
Have sex at least once a month
Find my G spot
Make more fun friends
Take a course in design
Give up carbs and sugar mon-fri
Rebrand personal style – less high st
Move out of home TO LONDON

'That's not how you chop onions,' said my mother. She took the knife away from me and started slicing them horizontally.

I sank down into one of the mint-green kitchen chairs and opened Instagram on my iPhone, resigned to the fact that I couldn't even chop an onion, let alone get a job, move to London or tick off anything else on the list of New Year's resolutions I'd only just made. I scrolled through the anecdotal squares as the smell of those onions filled the small kitchen, prickling my eyes. There was something so mindlessly captivating about the holidays of people I'd never met, the poached eggs drizzled with green sauce I'd never tasted, the £5 vouchers for a clothing brand I'd never heard of, the fitness videos and makeup tutorials that I always meant to emulate. I stopped on some supermodel I followed who had taken a mirror selfie in a fancy-looking room. She was wearing sunglasses and dangling a pair of high heels from her fingers. The shot was simply captioned, '@KurtGeiger 👠', tempting all of her impressionable followers onto the shoe brand's Instagram page. I clicked right through. Kurt Geiger's profile bio was a one-liner, promising anyone who clicked on the link to their shopping page a chance to feature on their Instagram. Again, through I went.

'What can you possibly still be looking at on that virulent device?' my mother's voice came cascading over my shoulder.

'I like these shoes,' I said, showing her a pair of metallic silver heels.

She glanced briefly then let out a small laugh that I would describe as a chortle. 'When would you wear those? You never go anywhere but the pub!'

'Where else am I supposed to go around here?' I muttered.

The doorbell rang before she could answer, though I'm not sure she had an answer to that question. Her friend Philip had arrived for dinner, like Friday-night clockwork. He was virtually her only friend and she was in love with him, although he was almost certainly gay. They were both lecturers at the University of Exeter, the reason I had been uprooted from an exciting South London life, at the age of four, and dumped into seaside monotony. My mother had taken the job when my father – 'a Dutch immigrant' as the locals now referred to him – left her for a buxom blonde. I'd always imagined she looked like Ursula Andress, but now I think about it, that is highly unlikely. It wasn't something my mother and I spoke about.

My mother and Philip were both reading some book about Russia's cultural elite, which sounded so depressing that I could have slit my wrists just listening to them unpack it over spaghetti bolognaise. The conversation then mutated into Brexit chat, as it always did, which seemed pointless given that we were all set on voting Remain, so what was there to really talk about?

And then Philip asked me the question that I so dreaded to hear, especially around my mother: 'So, Scarl, what are you doing with your life?'

I would've taken the Russian elite or Brexit over that conversation topic.

'I'm trying to find a job, but the recruiter says there's nothing at the moment,' I said, opening my mouth to allow a greedily large forkful of spaghetti to enter.

'The recruiter's been saying that for six months now,' said my mother, without looking at me, which was her way of saying, 'She's a lazy cow.'

'Can't be easy the way things are at the moment,' said Philip, no doubt hoping to open another riveting conversation about the state of our country.

'Yes, but we can't always rely on other people, like recruiters, to do everything for us, can we?' said my mother.

She liked to make comments like that when other people

were around, so that I was forced to curb my natural reaction. Instead of welling up with tears of frustration and storming out of the room, as I might have done in her company alone, I just muttered, 'When you live in Topsham you can.'

I couldn't bring myself to tell her that I'd sent off nearly a hundred job applications – to fashion houses, retailers, textile studios; to be a PA, to be a copywriter, to be a goddamn personal shopper; whatever came up on Indeed.co.uk when you typed in 'jobs in fashion London' – and had either been rejected or plain ghosted by every single one of them.

'She wants to work in fashion, you see,' said my mother, with a subtly mocking half-smile at Philip.

'Sounds ever so glamorous,' he said, brightly.

'Glamorous, maybe. Stable or lucrative, absolutely not,' she said, and that was settled.

After dinner, the two of them sat in the living room drinking Pinot Noir and jizzing over a Radio 4 podcast. When I popped my head in, Philip was sitting slim and dainty by the arm of the sofa and my mother was sitting unnecessarily close to him, twirling the ends of her long, silver-streaked hair around her fingers.

'I'm going to the pub,' I said, a sentence I knew she was bored of hearing.

'Are you working?' she asked.

'Nope.' (Couldn't even claim that excuse.) 'Just going to see Billie.'

She gave me something between a nod and an eye roll before holding up her hand dramatically, evidently anxious that she was missing some particularly arousing soundbite of condescending intellectual bullshit.

When I arrived at the pub, Billie was busy serving a couple

of battered kids who had come down to crawl the Topsham Ten, like the university students loved to do during term time. It had always baffled me – the idea of escaping the shackles of home and entering the freedom of uni life, and thinking the best you could do was a pub crawl in a town with a population of five thousand. But hey, each to their own.

While I waited, propped up at the bar, I re-read my New Year's resolutions, hoping they would seep into me by osmosis, and that a light bulb would miraculously appear above my head, or a rocket would force its way up my arse. Finally the kids staggered off, pints of dark lager in hand. It was the fifth pub on the trail and it was standard that they'd all be sick by the seventh, but who was I to judge, given my own track record with vomit?

Billie slid a vodka tonic over to me and tapped her long, acrylic nails against the bar top.

'No money,' I said, guiltily.

'What a surprise,' she said, and started rubbing a pint glass with a dirty tea towel.

'What am I gonna do?' I whined. She was better at coming up with solutions than I was.

'Just work more shifts here. It adds up,' she said.

'I need a proper job.'

'You mean a *Landan* job?' she said. She'd been teasing me about being London-beguiled ever since I'd gone to see the Alexander McQueen exhibition at the V&A museum the year before and had come back banging on about how the city had given me life.

'I don't know how I'm going to make it happen,' I said, and rested my head on the bar to show just how hard I was finding life.

'Why don't you shut up talking about it, pack your stuff up and just bloody go?' she said.

'Yeah, that's realistic,' I said, looking up.

'Why not? Just walk into one of these wank-arse fashion places you want to work for and tell them they'd be mad not to hire you. You've got nothing to lose.'

Nope, just my dignity, I thought, and returned my head to the sticky wooden bar top, where it belonged.

'You're so fucking hard to pity when you do nothing to fix your problems, Scizzle,' she said, which pissed me off, because I knew it was true. And also, 'Scizzle' was a nickname from school, and I was growing to hate what a stupid word it was.

Over the next few weeks, I continued sketching, scrolling, creating Pinterest boards and making lists of all my favourite designers and fashion icons in preparation for the job interview that I was becoming less and less confident was coming. I even started going on runs, adhering to at least one of my resolutions, in an attempt to prepare myself for the lifestyle that I still believed was ahead of me, though the route into it was nowhere in sight. I'd never been the sportiest of types, having opted for the smoker's slope or the art room rather than the lacrosse field at school, and was rather regretting those years as I rasped along the quay with a splitting pain from throat to abdomen.

It was towards the end of January, when I returned from one of my runs looking like a sweaty beetroot, that my mother announced, 'I've got you a job at the university.'

I reached over to pluck a digestive biscuit from the packet she was holding (runs meant that I could eat whatever I wanted, obviously) and asked, 'What kind of job?'

'Assisting one of the history professors with faculty research.'

'That sounds bleak,' I said, flatly, and bit into the biscuit, letting crumbs fall down my chin.

'It's not bleak, actually. It's very interesting,' she said defensively.

'I doubt *I* will find it interesting!' I retorted, amazed that she was still imposing her interests – which, clearly, were not mine – onto me. 'There's no way I'm doing that job.'

'Well what, may I ask, are you going to do instead?' she said.

'Not your problem!' I replied, though it probably was, given that I was living with her. 'Just leave me alone.'

Then she used her go-to weapon: 'God, you are so like your father.'

At one time, tears would have been my response to that remark, but I'd grown so used to hearing it that I simply snapped a sardonic 'Thanks!' back.

She carried on: 'You're never going to get a job sitting in the pub waiting for a recruiter to call. You have to be proactive, you have to—'

'I've applied for about a million jobs. No one fucking wants me!' It bubbled out of me unexpectedly, like a carbonated liquid that had been shaken too hard. Immediately, I felt embarrassed that I'd admitted to what I suspected she already thought: no one wanted me. Her cryptic silence prompted a creeping pain in the base of my throat, so I muttered, 'Just leave me alone,' and flounced away from her.

As I was slamming my bedroom door, I heard her call out my name, which I knew always reminded her of my father. He'd given me that name, after Scarlett O'Hara. I assumed it was because he was hoping I'd turn out to be a charming belle, but he'd not stuck around long enough to find out. There had been the odd visit in the early years after he left, but they had become more and more infrequent, until, finally, they were nothing but a memory. I didn't even know he'd married Ursula Andress until years after. I wondered if he'd be disappointed to see me now, the girl who was always 'too' something: too loud, too messy, too promiscuous, too bold.

The thought of his hypothetical disappointment made me angry. I was done. I was done being the 'too-something' girl with that very clever mother, who had somehow turned out to be so useless. *Somehow*. 'Somehow' meant that it was my fault. It didn't mean that my mother had been so engaged with her students and her writing that there had been nothing left for the child drowning in the room with her.

I heard Billie's voice in my head – *'Why don't you shut up talking about it, pack your stuff up and just bloody go?'* – and, without even thinking, I took out a suitcase and started packing.

If I wasn't in a bad enough mood already, the crinkled mound of clothes that were on offer to me really sent me raging. All of a sudden, I hated my Topshop jeans, my well-worn Dunlop trainers, the River Island boots that I'd begged my mother to buy me on a shopping trip to Exeter, and I particularly hated the collection of thrift-store dresses that she'd bought me over the years. But I packed them all anyway, because I had nothing else.

And then I saw a familiar bell-sleeve hauled up against the mound of disappointing garb. Momentarily forgetting about my packing stress, I pulled out Henrietta, the dress I'd crafted for my A Level final and named after my dead dog. As dresses went, it was pretty heinous, with its overly pointed collar, messy line of buttons and poor choice of Aztec fabric, but it still made me smile. I'll never forget the feeling of stepping back after the eight hours spent draping and stitching the patterns that my art teacher had helped me pre-prepare, and seeing the finished piece, which was offbeat compared to the country landscapes that the other students had gone for. My mother had barely acknowledged Henrietta, even on results day, when the only A grade on the page was for art, just as she'd never shown any interest in the paper dolls I'd spent all the hours of my childhood drawing, cutting and colouring whole wardrobes of outfits for.

I rolled Henrietta into a cylinder and stuffed her into the corner of my suitcase. Last, I added a collection of what I thought were my favourite books, because they'd been so heavily Instagrammed – Joan Didion, Zadie Smith, Jay McInerney – and my actual favourites – Caitlin Moran, Jilly Cooper, Tina Fey – and then I texted Billie to tell her I'd made a major life decision and that she was responsible for it.

When I went downstairs, my mother was sitting at her desk, marking essays. She was totally immersed, oblivious to the sound of my suitcase rolling over the wooden floors. Even when I planted myself right in front of her, she didn't lift her eyes from the paper. It was a familiar sight. In fact, this was exactly how my mother materialized in my head whenever I thought about her.

'I'm moving to London,' I said.

Her eyes flickered towards me for a millisecond, but she still didn't look directly at me. 'Don't be ridiculous.'

'Okay, bye, then,' I said in an infantile manner, and whirled away.

'Scarlett, you are *not* going to London,' she said imperiously.

'Yes, I am.'

She stood up and pressed her palms over her eyebrows, like I'd just given her a terrible migraine. 'I cannot afford to bankroll your zeitgeist millennial fantasy.'

'You don't have to bankroll it. I'll be bankrolling it!'

'Let's see how long you last in London before you're on the

phone, crying to me because you've hit the bottom of your overdraft and you're at some obscure train station or airport, completely alone, and I'll have no choice but to bail you out, or let you starve.'

To be fair, it sounded like a plausible scenario. Or, rather, something that had actually happened the last time I'd gone to London . . .

'Maybe I'll let you starve this time!' she added, and even in the dimness of the room, I could see that she was at the end of her tether.

'Great, I could do with the fucking weight loss!' I shouted angrily. I turned around and headed towards the door.

'Scarlett! Come back here!'

But I didn't. I slammed the front door like a teenager in a sulk and headed for the station.

Available to read now in paperback, eBook and eAudio.